AN AMERICAN KING

JOHN STONEHOUSE

Copyright © by John Stonehouse 2020
All rights reserved.

John Stonehouse has asserted his right under the Copyright, Designs and Patents Act 1988 to be identified as the author of this work.

All rights reserved. No part of this publication may be reproduced or transmitted in any form or by any means without permission of the author.

This book is a work of fiction. Names, characters, places and incidents are either a product of the author's imagination or are used fictitiously. Any resemblance to actual people, living or dead, events or locales, is entirely coincidental.

Cover Design by Books Covered
Interior Layout by Polgarus Studio

ISBN 13: 9798648560864

Chapter 1

Lake Fort Phantom Hill, Jones County, Texas. 2007

Quicksilver. Moonlight shining on the surface of a lake.

Red dirt country beyond a gravel lot—scrub and low-grown mesquite.

He sees nothing. Hears nothing. The broadhead arrow slicing through the night air is invisible. Silent. Its force exploding inside his chest incomprehensible. Beyond shock.

Last seconds.

Fleet cloud running across the moon.

Breath held, both hands clutching the carbon-wrapped, aluminum shaft protruding from his body.

Headlights moving on a stretch of county road.

Then a feeling like motion sickness. Blacking out. Pain.

As a second hunting arrow punctures clean through his side.

And only light comes.

A weightlessness.

Light floating through his brain.

Chapter 2

Abilene, Texas.

The sun is not long risen—the city of Abilene back-lit in shades of amber to the east of Winters Freeway. Deputy US Marshal John Whicher steers his Chevy Silverado along the bleached concrete two-lane. A flat sweep of West Texas beyond the windshield—stretching vast beneath a vault of sky.

Up already.

Up already, before the first call.

Six-thirty; light barely slanting through the blinds in the kitchen windows. Early dawn—the new place in Wylie unfamiliar still, the new home—ranch style, three-bed, with boxes from the move not yet unpacked.

Second ring.

Catching it on the second ring. Trying not to wake his sleeping wife and daughter. Answering a call from a sheriff's deputy, name of Mooney—Lyle Mooney—out of Jones, the neighboring county to the north.

The marshal eyes the road signs ahead, switches lanes on the freeway.

A couple of kids had reported finding a body at the city reservoir—Mooney was first officer on site; and didn't like it. He had a DPS state trooper protecting the scene, the two of them waiting on backup—the Coroner's Office, a CST, Abilene Police Department. And getting nervous.

"What do y'all have to be nervous about?"

"I think a federal presence could be warranted," Mooney told him. "I don't like the way this is. You'll see what I mean when you get up here."

Whicher rests an arm out the window of the Silverado, the still-cool breeze of an early June morning filling the cab. But heat is coming. Heat in the pale-hazed distant air—already, the sleeve of his crisp white shirt is warmed by the sun.

He feels the Ruger in the leather shoulder-holster as he straightens the neck-tie at his collar. The big revolver a back up for the service-issue Glock.

Settling his Resistol hat against the buffeting air rushing in from the open window, he pushes back in the driver's seat.

Eases down harder on the gas.

⋏

Lake Fort Phantom Hill.

Turning off of West Lake onto Farm Road 1082, Whicher steers along the two-lane across the top of a rolled-earth dam.

From the stone and gravel embankment, he looks out over the water at the northernmost tip of the lake. The surrounding land is scrub and rock and burnt dry grass and mesquite.

The lake water is low—a rocky shoreline exposed and stained.

Above the steel guardrail on the road, he sees the white hull of a fishing skiff, half out of the water, moored at a cement boat ramp.

Where the two-lane joins back with the curving headland, a Highway Patrol cruiser blocks the entrance to an empty dirt lot.

On the opposite side of the road are more law enforcement vehicles—plus a Ford E-Series van.

Whicher eases off the gas, lets the Silverado slow.

The DPS trooper is out of his car—watching from beneath the brim of his hat.

The marshal takes a badge-holder and ID from the charcoal jacket of his suit on the passenger seat. He brakes to a halt in line with the trooper. "Looking for a Deputy Lyle Mooney?"

The trooper checks his ID, points across the lot to a man and woman thirty yards back from the road. They're standing part-way down a bank, close to the edge of the lake. The man dressed in a short-sleeve tan shirt and Western hat, the woman wearing a white forensic zip-suit.

Beyond them is a black-clad, patrolman from the Abilene Police Department. With the street cop is a balding man in a wine-colored leisure shirt—cell phone pressed against his ear. Whicher recognizes Dave Spano, a detective from the city CID.

"You're the investigator?" The trooper says to Whicher.

The marshal reads the name on the man's badge; *Vance.* "Criminal investigator. Yes, I am."

"We're leaving the vehicles on over the road."

Whicher nods, drives his truck across to the other side of the baked asphalt highway.

He shuts off the motor, steps out. Reaches in for the suit jacket, slips it on, squares his hat, pulling down the wide, felt brim.

He eyes the long expanse of lake—the reservoir for the city of Abilene a dozen miles to the south. A body of water maybe four miles long.

"Jones County Sheriff were first here," the trooper says, pointing to the man in the tan uniform shirt. "Then me, about an hour back. Abilene police brought along a crime scene officer—she's somewhere back in the brush."

"Is the Coroner's Office here?"

"Yessir."

The marshal squints, recognizes the woman in the zip-suit; Celine Fernandez.

Stepping by the black and white DPS cruiser, he moves fast; six-one in his suit and hat, forty-three years old, tough, in shape.

An iron-hard track leads into brush and scrub where the deputy and Doctor Fernandez are standing.

The CID detective, Spano, starts to make his way over, phone still clamped against his ear.

Fernandez taps the deputy on the arm.

He turns, round-faced, with a dark mustache, a heavy

build, shirt tight at the gut.

"John Whicher," the marshal says. "USMS."

"Deputy Lyle Mooney."

Fernandez studies the marshal; eyes cool above an aquiline nose. She's slim, despite the loose-fitting zip-suit. Raven hair pulled back from her face.

Whicher raises the Resistol hat an inch. "Morning."

Detective Spano puts away the cell, stepping carefully through the scrub, grinning. "I'm glad they called you, not me. CST's taking photographs. I brought a couple patrol officers. One of them's out the other end of 1082 with the unit—to block off the road, keep folk away."

The marshal nods.

"We have a caucasian male," Deputy Mooney says, "down by the water. Doc's about to start the medical examination. We got the core area secured. Leastways, what we think is the core."

Whicher takes out a notepad and pen from the jacket of his suit.

Celine Fernandez points to a path marked with tape. "Let's keep disturbance to a minimum."

Whicher follows her to the foot of a burnt dry slope of salt cedar and juniper brush, the deputy and the detective line-astern behind.

In a patch of bare earth and ragweed, a man is laying face up to the sky.

He's dressed in chinos and a checkered shirt. His eyes are wide open.

Protruding from his body are three arrows—one in the

center of his chest, another in his right side, the third sticking from his upper right-arm.

Beyond the body of the man, a black woman in a green zip-suit is photographing the surrounding area. Whicher recognizes Gail Griffin, a former detective, now retired from Abilene PD.

The man on the ground has both hands wrapped around the arrow in the middle of his chest. His shirt is loose above his pants; ridden halfway up his torso, exposing a stretch of pale skin.

The marshal lets out a long, low whistle.

"Ain't that a doozy?" Detective Spano says.

"We got the call to the sheriff's office in Anson a little after six a.m.," Deputy Mooney says. "I was closest unit."

The marshal writes the time of the first call into his notepad.

"Lake Patrol cover till eight in the evenings," Mooney says. "After that, any call this area it's either us or Abilene PD."

"We spoke on the phone you said kids reported it?" Whicher says. "A couple kids?"

"That's right," Mooney answers. "Out of ACU."

"Abilene Christian University?"

"Yessir," Mooney says. "They were camping a ways back in the brush; night fishing, they said. They came in off of the lake, they were sleeping some, one of 'em gets up to take a piss just before first light. He said he saw the body, damn near messed himself…"

"Where they at now?"

"I took statements," Mooney says. "Neither one of 'em heard or saw a damn thing."

"You have their numbers?"

"I took their numbers, got 'em the hell out of here, before they screwed up the scene any more'n they already had." The deputy shakes his head. "This here's an open parking lot, it's public access. There's the boat ramp yonder." He angles his head toward the skiff. "There'd be a hundred different types of tire-print, shoe-print, any other kind of print…"

Whicher points at the feet of the man on the ground; splayed wide, the lower limbs unnaturally elongated. "Looks like he was dragged here, with the shirt, an' all. Way them legs are laying."

"Agreed," Doctor Fernandez says. "There's no chance he could have fallen like that."

The marshal studies the arrow shafts—camo-patterned, the vanes at the end a bright, neon orange. "Somebody shoots him in the parking lot? Then drags him on in here—in the brush?"

The crime scene officer, Gail Griffin, looks up from her camera. "We'll find signs if that's what happened."

"There any blood beneath him?"

"We're just starting to look," the doctor says.

The marshal breaks off looking at the man on the ground. "Alright. So, what do we know?"

The deputy shakes his head. "We don't know squat."

"ID?"

"No, sir, marshal."

"Anybody reported missing?"

The deputy lets out a tight breath.

Whicher glances up the slope at Trooper Vance by the black and white cruiser. "Highway Patrol hear anything?"

"They got nothing either," Mooney says. "I'll tell you, I got here, I took one look, I didn't like it one bit. I was here eight years gone, they had that woman had her skull bashed in? Y'all remember? Nobody was ever found for that. You ever see a man killed with a bow and arrow?"

"No," Spano answers. "Can't say that I have."

Kneeling by the corpse, Celine Fernandez turns to Gail Griffin; "Did you video the body in situ?"

"All done," Griffin answers. "Stills and moving image. You can go right ahead."

The doctor examines the arrow protruding from the center of the man's chest. "This one would almost certainly have killed him." She pulls a plastic tool box on the ground a little closer.

"I radioed dispatch in Anson," Mooney says, "told 'em right off we'd need somebody federal—you boys at USMS. Or FBI."

"I'm on call," Whicher says. "District-wide, anything like this comes in."

"Anything bad," Spano says.

"He don't belong here," the deputy says. "He looks like a farmer, way he's dressed an' all."

Whicher guesses the man to be late-thirties, to early-forties, his hair cut short, face tanned, weathered a nut brown, like his eyes. He's clean-shaven, carrying some weight. Wearing work boots, the dirt in the leather ingrained.

"Arrow in the right arm was probably subsequent to the one in the chest," Doctor Fernandez says. "He was grabbing hold of it," she mimes the action, 'it was sticking out of his chest—then that one hits him in the arm."

"So, no ID," Whicher says, "no vehicle, no idea who he is. No witnesses. And nobody's missing."

"Nobody in Jones County," Mooney says.

"We know the murder weapon," Spano says.

Mooney looks at him. "What good is that? Can't match a bow with any arrow."

Whicher cuts a look at Celine Fernandez.

"No rifling marks, certainly," the doctor says. "I'm not an archery expert. We'll find somebody that is." She places a gloved hand above the man's hip—positioning the scalpel. Makes a cut into the skin, no blood runs out.

Taking a probe from the box on the ground, she fits a thermometer, inserts it into the cut, pushing upward, toward the liver.

Whicher looks at Deputy Mooney. "There any kind of a time-frame going?"

"Them ACU kids reckoned to come by the lot here last night, around eight-thirty. They pitched a couple of tents over yonder—then left, just before dark. They said there was no-one here then."

"Just before dark," Whicher says. "That be what, around—nine-fifteen?"

"Around that."

"How come they all left?"

"They were picking up a couple of skiffs from over at the sail boat place," Mooney says. "They brought the boats into shore around three in the morning. To camp out, shoot the shit and whatever."

Whicher looks out over the water. "This sail boat place? Where's it at?"

"Over on the eastern shore," Celine Fernandez says. She lifts the dead man's legs, watches for any bend at the knee. Tries his feet, moving them from side to side at the ankle joint.

"So, some time after nine-fifteen last night?" Whicher says to Mooney. "And right around six o'clock this morning?"

"Yessir."

"That boat down there—that one of theirs?"

"They said not."

Whicher calls over to Gail Griffin. "Going to need the boat processing."

"Then we need more people out here," she answers.

Doctor Fernandez takes the thermometer from the dead man's body—she notes down the reading. Places her hands at either side of the man's neck, tries to move his head. "Rigor's setting in, it's still early. The extremities are still mobile." She eases the fabric of the man's shirt farther up his body. Dark red discoloration is on the skin where it's closest to the ground. She presses a gloved finger against it—it doesn't whiten. Bending in closer, she eases the man's side away from the dirt. "Okay, there's a lot of blood here…"

Whicher crouches low, sees the dark stain on the earth.

"Scratch marks, too," the doctor says, "consistent with being dragged. Post-mortem lividity indicates he's lain like this a while." Rolling the torso a little more, she stares at the back of the kidney area. "Goodness me."

A barbed arrowhead is sticking out of a tear in the man's side, blood pooled beneath it.

The marshal studies the three-bladed cutting tip, serrated steel edges meeting in a vicious point.

"That's a hunting arrow," Deputy Mooney says. "Broadhead. For bringing down big game."

"That's what it is?" the doctor says.

The marshal stares. "We looking for a hunter?"

Spano shoves his hands down into his pockets. "You're looking for a goddamn psychopath."

Gail Griffin moves in close, positions the camera, takes a series of shots.

"How about if the victim's from out of state?" Deputy Mooney says. "We may never know who he is."

Spano shrugs. "The most part, at the lake you're dealing with gangbangers and low-lifes peddling dope. Trouble out here doesn't look like this. It doesn't involve people who look like him."

"You imagine being out here last night?" Mooney says. "Have that happen to you?" He gives an involuntary shudder. "We may never know the victim, never know the killer. Like that woman eight years gone. It could be one of those cases. Where nobody knows a thing."

Whicher stands, pulls on the brim of the Resistol. Starts to turn for his truck.

"Somebody knows."

Chapter 3

Both doors are open on the Silverado, Whicher tosses his hat on the empty passenger seat.

He checks his watch.

Just gone oh-eight-hundred.

The roof and hood of the truck are starting to tick with heat.

He stares out through the windshield at a flattened sweep of battered scrub. Shifts his weight, takes out his cell, scrolls a list of stored numbers, presses on a key.

Whicher pictures his boss from the Abilene US Marshals office; Chief Deputy Marshal Evans. Neat, squat, with freckled skin, hair like rusted wire.

The ringer sounds over and over. Then picks up.

"Sir, this is Whicher. I'm sorry to bother y'all at home."

"That's all right," Evans says.

"I'm up at Lake Fort Phantom Hill. Responding to a call on a DB. North end of the lake. Out by the dam."

"Oh?"

"First responder was a deputy from the sheriff's office

out of Anson. He went out to take a look, called 'em straight back, told 'em he'd need some help."

"Why's that?"

"DB is a white male laying in the brush at the back of a dirt parking lot." Whicher sits forward in the driver's seat. "He has three arrows sticking out of him."

"Arrows?" Evans says.

"Yessir."

The chief marshal clears his throat. "Do we know who he is?"

"No, sir. There's no ID. The parking lot's hard by a two-lane road—we got no vehicle. Only thing we got here is a boat ramp. With a boat attached. We're pretty much in the middle of no place, I passed a wreckers yard on the way up, there's been barely a house since. A couple of kids from ACU found him, they were camping hereabouts. We got nobody reported missing. And the guy could be from almost anywhere. Interstate Twenty's around a fifteen-minute drive."

"You think the body could have been dumped?"

"Blood on the ground says he died here," Whicher says. "Looks like he was dragged—he's a ways back in the brush."

Evans is silent on the end of the line a moment.

"I thought to call it in," the marshal says. "Before this all gets going."

"A rural county sheriff's office would be stretched to cover it," Evans says. "I'm about to head in to the office, I'll need to run it by the chief of police and maybe the DA."

"Celine Fernandez is with the body," Whicher says. "And Dave Spano from the PD."

"Any of 'em have any ideas?"

The marshal scans the frontier land from the open window of the truck. Comancheria. Land of the Lords of the Plain. A gray hawk glides low, hunting snake, soundless, above the brush. "Folk out here seem a little—spooked…"

"Why's that?"

Whicher pulls himself upright against the steering wheel. "Hard to say."

He searches the air above the withered brush and buffalo grass—but the hawk is gone.

"There'd be no jurisdictional issues if we ran it," Evans says. "Stay out, stick with it."

"Alright, sir."

Evans clicks off the call.

Whicher catches his own reflection in the driver-mirror—wide-set eyes, hazel to green above a busted nose. He lets his gaze drift to the land beyond the windshield. Thinks of the stones of the ruined fort, just a couple of miles farther up the road. A place abandoned, burnt by its own. *Phantom Hill.* A mirage. Disappearing into thin air.

Leaving the truck, the marshal strides back toward the dirt lot.

Deputy Lyle Mooney spools a reel of black and yellow tape across its entrance.

"They block off the road down yonder?" Whicher says.

"PD have a unit at the turn from West Lake Road," Mooney says.

By the DPS cruiser, Dave Spano stands with the trooper and the Abilene beat cop, pulling at a button on the front of his wine-red shirt. "So, you doing this?"

Whicher steps around the tape. "Looks that way."

He crosses the lot—followed by Spano.

Reaches the brush slope, descends by the pre-determined access path.

The white skiff turns at the water's edge, sunlight on the lake splintering in a thousand shards.

Celine Fernandez has the victim's arms by his sides, now, bags over the hands—the bags fixed in place with tape at the wrists.

"You print the guy?" Whicher says.

She nods, not looking up. "I've called for an ambulance. There's no reason to keep him here, we're doing more harm than good. Gail's got everything we need."

The marshal turns to Dave Spano. "We need to get a line search running. You get more uniforms out here?"

"I can make a call." The detective takes out his cell, steps back along the pathway toward the lot.

The marshal turns to Celine Fernandez. "You find anything?"

"As a matter of fact," the doctor says, "I did." She points to the plastic tool box on the ground. "There was a wedding ring in his pants' pocket. Concealed, way down."

Whicher peers at the box, sees the ring inside a sealed, plastic evidence bag.

"It was stuck, right down in the seam," she says. "Snagged in a fold. Whoever killed him probably searched him, since there's no ID. They must have missed it."

The marshal picks it up, holds it out, turning the bag.

No inscription, no initials.

"It's just a plain gold band," Whicher says. "Why you think it's a wedding ring?"

"There's a pronounced mark on the skin," the doctor says, "third finger of his left hand. The ring would be the right size. I'll measure accurately, later."

On the scrub slope, Gail Griffin wags a pencil over her clipboard. "You get married a while back, marshal?"

Whicher looks at her. "Three years."

"Never thought you were the type."

The marshal leans his head on one side, stretches the collar of his shirt away from his neck. "You take a look at that boat, yet?"

"Real quick look," Griffin answers. "Mmm-hmm. Did you see what it has on the back of it already?"

Whicher eyes her.

"An outboard motor," she says.

"Folk usually leave a motor attached to a boat?"

She says, "Would you?"

He puts back the evidence bag containing the ring into the doctor's box. Descending the slope to the concrete ramp, he takes out his cell, opens up the camera, takes a series of shots of the boat—making sure to capture the letters and numbers painted on the bow. The skiff is maybe twenty feet in length. A fiber-glass hull, a couple of bench seats, the motor clamped at the back, on the transom. "Call whoever you need to call," he says to Griffin. "Get whoever you want out here."

He stares at the boat a moment, dull white against the bright water. Moves carefully back up the scrub slope, to Celine Fernandez. "We have any idea on a TOD?"

"Time of death will be sometime last night," she says. "Best guess—and it *is* just a guess, seven or eight hours…"

"Around midnight?"

"With the caveat," she inclines her head, "that summer temperatures can make any estimate difficult…you know all this."

"Where you fixing to move him?"

"Fort Worth," she says. "I'll do the autopsy at Tarrant ME."

The marshal leans right over the body with his cell phone, frames the man's face in the lens of the camera. Takes a picture, another. Checks both images.

"You're leading the investigation?" Fernandez says.

"Unless the city tells me no."

"You have my number if you need to call me?"

The marshal nods.

Detective Spano steps back along the tape-lined access path. "We got uniforms on the way."

"You get a search started for me?" Whicher says.

"Not a problem."

"I want to take a look around, check out the boat."

"There's a marina," Spano says, "as well as the sail boat place. On the east shore, a little way down the road."

"I'll call in."

Spano stares down at the body, grimaces. "Man, that's brutal, though." The detective squats. Leans in, studies the arrow shafts, the neon vanes. "You imagine? Checking out that way."

"Primal," Celine Fernandez says.

Whicher takes a last look at the dead man. At the stark, open eyes.

Fernandez scans the brush-choked land stretching out from the sides of the lake. "Like a visitation from another age out here," she says. "The way things must once have been."

"Seven hours," the marshal says. "Or eight…"

The doctor looks at him.

Whicher nods back. "No ghost."

Chapter 4

Windows open in the Silverado, wind singing in the power lines at the side of the road. Whicher takes 1082 across the top end of the lake, descending from the high-point of the dam, past the spillway, to where the land levels.

At the junction with East Lake, an Abilene patrol car is blocking the road.

Whicher holds up his badge—the driver waves him through.

The marshal steers around the patrol car, makes the turn on to a strip of cracked, gray, asphalt following the outline of the eastern shore.

Inland, bluffs are covered in scrub mesquite and prickly pear and juniper and Texas grama. Scattered cabins and trailers are the only signs of life.

The lake appears in glimpses beyond rocky inlets and stretches of burnt dry weed.

He sees the turn to a protruding headland—*Poverty Point*—follows the power lines a few hundred yards farther—spots the strip of road Spano told him to watch for;

a single lane disappearing through a grove of black willow.

He turns on to it, follows the road past more cabins and trailers, a few small houses. The surface pot-holed, badly broken up.

The road splits in a fork, he takes the one marked, *Arrow Point*.

A couple of pole lights mark the backs of shorefront properties, a line of timber-frame homes on fenced plots.

The expanse of the lake is visible, now, the road arriving at the outermost end of the headland.

Whicher brakes the Silverado to a stop in a gravel turn-around.

He shuts down the motor, climbs out into wind, into fine dust lifted by the tires of the truck.

Set back among the trees, expensive-looking homes are faced with stone, watered lawns lining their driveways. In front of him is a rick fence of weathered timber. A tube steel gate, locked with a chain.

Beyond the fence a score of sail boats sit on trailers, their sails furled, wind snapping the lines against their masts.

A clubhouse is down by the water—utility block at its rear.

The marshal steps up to the steel gate, climbs over.

Making his way around to the far-side of the clubhouse building he watches gulls float in the breeze.

A woman in jeans and a white T-shirt is dragging a high-pressure hose toward the upturned hulls of a group of small boats. Her fair hair is tied back, her arms tanned from the sun.

"Ma'am," he calls out.

She turns around, looks at him.

"US Marshals Service." He takes out his badge and ID. "Name's Whicher."

She sets down the hose.

"You work here?"

"A couple of mornings a week," she says.

"Hoping you might be able to help me out with something?" He takes out his cell phone, finds the photograph of the skiff.

Approaching, he holds out the phone to her.

She peers at it.

"You tell me anything about this boat? It come out of here?"

"It doesn't look like it," she says. "It doesn't have a sail." She frowns. "I could check the registration number with the club, they'll know if it has a mooring here."

"We found that boat this morning" he says. "The motor still attached."

"Has there been an accident?" She looks at him. "Is someone missing? Has somebody fallen in?"

"Not exactly." Whicher keeps his expression flat. "Ma'am, an electric motor, an outboard motor, that kind of thing an expensive item?"

"A trolling motor?" she says. "I guess."

"What kind of money?"

She shrugs. "Fifteen-hundred and up."

"Folk often leave a motor attached?"

The woman smoothes a strand of blonde hair at her

temple. "Well, they're easy to take off. I don't know why you'd leave it." Her eyes cut away, she looks out over the water.

Whicher follows her gaze to the far end, to the dam—a mile off to the north-west.

"Does this all have something to do with what's going on by the spillway?" she says. "Police are up there, nobody can get by."

"We're looking into a serious incident," Whicher says. "Ma'am, did y'all have a couple of kids from ACU out here last night? Students. Renting a bunch of fishing boats?"

"We did," she says. "I just got done cleaning them up."

She points to a couple of aluminum jon boats pulled from the water by a wooden dock.

"I cleaned the mud off of them, hosed out the insides," she says. "I was just about to start on some of the sailboats."

The marshal's cell phone starts to ring, he checks the screen. "Excuse me. I need to take this."

He steps away, holds the cell to his ear, hears the voice of his boss on the line, Marshal Evans.

"I just got done talking with the DA's office," Evans says.

Whicher descends a slope covered in reeds to stand near the dock at the water's edge.

"They're happy for you to lead the investigation."

"I left Celine Fernandez with the DB," Whicher says. "She's having it moved to Fort Worth."

"There anything more on an ID?"

"No, sir. Not yet."

"Fernandez will find something," Evans says. "She's got fingerprints to go at, dental-records, ante-mortem injuries. Or somebody might call it in, report the guy missing."

"Dave Spano's getting a line search running," Whicher says. "I'm looking to check out the boat, find out where it came from."

"Could you use a partner?"

"Say again?"

"A partner. If the victim's from out of state, there could be a lot of ground to cover. How about Ortega?"

"I don't know…" The marshal thinks of the recent recruit to USMS Northern District. "Sandro Ortega?"

"He's young," Evans says. "He could probably keep up. He could use the experience. We get a name on the DB, you'll need to find out what the hell he was doing there—an extra pair of legs could be a help."

Whicher doesn't respond.

"Call me if you get anything." The chief marshal clicks off the call.

Whicher puts away the cell, makes his way back up the bank. He turns to the woman. "Ma'am. You tell me your name?"

"Laura."

"You been out here all morning?"

She nods.

"What time you get in?"

"Around seven," she says.

"From?"

"I came out from Hawley."

The marshal thinks of it; a small town, a dozen miles west of the lake. "You see anything unusual? Anything different to what you'd normally see?"

"I had to come all the way around the south side of the lake," she says. "Instead of just going around the top. I never go that way, it took me twice as long."

"There's no other way around?"

She shakes her head.

The marshal stares at the hulls of the upturned jon boats. Beyond them, the water is reddish-colored close in to the shore. "Them kids bring the boats back clean? They mess 'em up? How were they?"

"They brought them back about the same way they went out," the woman says. "I just hosed the mud off of them."

Whicher thinks of potential evidence lost.

"If you want to know about that boat in the photograph," she says, "Lake Patrol might be able to help."

"I'll be sure to ask them."

The woman looks out across the water again, toward the dam. "Is everything alright up there?"

Whicher raises a finger to the brim of his hat. "Ma'am. You'll be hearing about it soon enough."

⭙

A single-track lane follows the inlets of the lake—through a land choked with sand sage and cactus and thornbrush. Properties are set at irregular intervals, clapboard houses beyond mesh-wire fences, deserted boat docks at the water's edge.

The marshal drives the Silverado back down onto the main road; East Lake. Past the locked entrance to an old power plant—steel transmission towers and lines still criss-crossing the disused site.

At either side of the two-lane, the ground is blackened from a recent burn. Metal fence posts stick out above the charred earth; Whicher thinks of arrows—stark, vertical, sticking out of the body of the dead man, his hands gripping the shaft embedded in his chest.

A thought sifts forward into the front of his mind; *the man came from the north—someplace to the north.*

If the victim came from somewhere south of the lake, why drive all the way around to the top?

If somebody arranged to meet with him, it would've been an obvious spot. *Turn off of West Lake, cross the dam, stop in the first parking place you see.*

But only if you were arriving from somewhere to the north.

Approaching the junction with a smaller road—Whicher hits the blinker, turns, steers along the backs of creek-side properties.

Ahead is a collection of metal warehouses. He sees a bait store, marine supply. Pulling into a V-shaped lot, he parks by a closed-up convenience store.

He shuts off the motor, climbs from the Silverado.

At the edge of the lake, a bearded man in coveralls is standing at a fuel dock—a woman with him, dressed in shorts and sneakers and a faded, green ball cap.

Boats are moored all the way along a small wooden jetty.

An open workshop is filled with outboard motors, drums of fuel and oil.

The man at the dock runs a hand over a gray-brown beard. He looks at the woman in the ball cap. Then back at Whicher.

"Something we can do for you?" the woman says.

"Marshals Service." Whicher shows the badge-holder and ID. He takes out the phone from the jacket of his suit. "Looking for the owner of a boat?"

The woman steps forward.

"This here yard belong to y'all?"

"Yes, sir," the man answers.

The marshal finds the photograph of the skiff on his cell. He holds it out.

The woman takes a battered eye-glass case from out of her shorts, slips on a pair of reading-glasses. She studies the picture.

The bearded man wipes his hands on his coveralls. "This all have something to do with what's going on up to the dam?"

The woman frowns, passes over the cell.

The man dips his head. "Looks kind of like Carl Avery's…"

"It can't be Carl's," the woman says. She gestures at the open door of the workshop.

"Ma'am?" Whicher says.

"We have his outboard in the shop," the woman answers.

"Mercury 40. Not starting real good." The man in the

coveralls looks closely at the photograph. "I seen that boat plenty of times, I'll say it's Carl's."

"It was up at the end of the dam this morning, first light," Whicher says. "That where he normally keep it?"

"No, sir."

"Does he keep it here?"

"No, sir, he don't. He keeps it right around on Cherokee, the next cove on down. He's got a place there. Say, is everything alright? Is Carl alright?"

Whicher takes out the notepad from his jacket, writes down the man's name. "Y'all tell me anything about the feller?"

The woman adjusts the bill on her ball cap. "He lives in Abilene. His place here is just a summer place."

"He's in business," the man in the coverall says.

"What kind of business?"

"Construction."

"Y'all have a number I could call him? An address?"

The woman gives a look.

"This here's in connection with a serious crime," the marshal says.

Her face blanches. "Alright," she says. "Well, give me a minute, I'll go see if I can find it."

"Is he out here now?" Whicher says to the man, "Mister Avery? Staying out here? Or back in the city?"

"Wouldn't rightly know."

Whicher scans a tin-roofed row of boat shelters. "You have this feller's outboard motor in your shop?"

"Yes, sir."

"The guy ever use an electric outboard?"

"A trolling motor? I never seen one on his boat."

The marshal stares out over the surface of the lake a moment, eyes unfocused. Then cuts a look at the boat yard owner. "Any idea how deep it is?"

"How's that?" the man says.

"The lake."

"Around sixty."

"Sixty feet?" The marshal thinks it over.

The woman in the ball cap walks back out of the workshop, holding a square of yellow paper.

Whicher sees a number written, an address beneath it. "Much obliged to you, ma'am."

"How come Carl's boat is on up there, anyhow?" she says.

The marshal takes the square of paper. "We don't know, yet," he says. "But I intend to find out."

The waterfront property is from the nineteen-forties—built on raised footings, its timbers weathered, a shaded porch stretching all the way across its front facade. Old palms and willows and cottonwoods dapple the grounds with shade. Whicher takes in the house from the driveway. Tries to pick up on any feeling—any kind of connection with the dead man at the end of the lake.

He climbs out of the Chevy, squares his hat.

The house looks closed-up—no vehicles in sight.

A fishing jetty is at the waterfront, there's a garden cabin, a wooden boathouse on pilings.

The marshal buttons the jacket of his suit, crosses the driveway, strides across a scorched lawn still strewn with leaves and strips of willow from the previous fall.

At the front of the house he climbs the porch steps, heat radiating from the board-clad sides.

He knocks at the door, listens for any sound.

The windows are unlit, closed, despite the heat of the summer morning.

He raps on the door again. "Anybody home?"

Somewhere out on the lake is the sound of a motor, a low drone on the breeze.

From the house, there's nothing.

He steps back, away from the door, walks along the length of the covered porch—the view of the water broken only by overhanging trees.

Listening for any sound from the house a moment longer, he gazes out toward the northern end of the lake—it's barely visible, the dam nothing more than a hazed line.

Climbing down the porch steps, he takes a pair of black, nitrile gloves from an inside pocket. Crosses the burnt grass slope—past the garden cabin, to the jetty. Staring at the plank-sided boathouse, he thinks of warrants, of search legality. He pulls on the gloves, tries a door inset at the back. It's not locked.

Checking around the door-frame, he sees no marks—nothing broken, no sign anybody's forced it.

A cylinder lock is beneath the handle, the bolt turned back in its housing, no sign of any damage to the strike plate or the box.

He pulls the door wide.

Inside, the space is lit by the opening to the water at the far end.

A garage-type retractable door is up overhead in its track.

The mooring place is empty. The marshal studies the mess of junk on the floor; old fishing gear, oil cans, a rusted anchor and chain. In one corner is a bent up frame, an aging Bimini top.

No cut ropes at the mooring posts, nothing broken, nothing obviously out of place.

He looks at the retractable door suspended above him, no damage he can see, the opening mechanism looks untouched.

He snaps off a series of shots on his cell, thinks of Gail Griffin—she'll need to come over. He'll have to call Evans, they'll need a judge, they'll need a warrant. He takes a last look around. Steps outside into bright sunlight.

A man in a blue cotton work shirt is hauling a bag of garbage to a dumpster on the neighboring property.

The man sees him, stops.

"US Marshal," Whicher calls out.

The man puts down the garbage bag. He's lean, tanned, his hair a downy-white.

Whicher guesses him to be around eighty.

"Mister Avery ain't home," the man says.

The marshal steps from the boathouse. "You know where he's at?"

The man steps into shade beneath a pecan tree.

"You know Mister Avery?"

"Hell yeah, I know him."

"You know where he lives?"

"The Hotel Wooten."

Whicher pictures the downtown hotel, an art-deco tower block, newly refurbished into modern apartments.

"Knew his father before him," the man says. "His grand daddy before that." He jabs a finger at the Avery house. "They had their place built in forty-two. About the same time my own pa was building ours. What's going on?"

The marshal walks to where the old man is standing. "Mister Avery keep a boat?"

"Everybody keeps a boat."

Whicher takes out the phone, brings up the photograph of the skiff. "That it?"

He holds it out.

The man pushes back his hair from a lined, high forehead. "It looks like Carl's, yeah."

"It's up at the top end of the lake right now."

"Where that bunch of police is at?"

"Mister Avery keep that boathouse of his locked?" Whicher says.

The old man looks at him, eyes hard. He folds his skinny arms over his work shirt. "Why don't you go ahead and ask him?"

Whicher studies the man's face; deeply tanned, the skin marked with sun spots, a faint grin playing at the edge of his mouth.

"What's going on up there? Did somebody die?" the old man says. "They never caught nobody for the one in forty-six."

The marshal pushes back the Resistol hat. "Before my time."

"There's been plenty others, since. In forty-six, a young woman was strangled. Had a boyfriend, just back from World War Two, he thought his girl had been cheatin' on him. She was meeting with him out at the lake one night, he told her he'd flash his headlights, so she'd know where he was parked. They reckon he strangled her, dumped her body out on the water. Nobody ever caught him. Folk say you can still see lights, some nights. Strange old lights. You never heard of her? The Lady of the Lake?"

Whicher shakes his head, runs a hand across his jaw.

"You not from around here?"

"The panhandle."

"Well," the old man says. "Lot of lost spirits, I guess. Lost souls. Here and on out to the fort. Always been that way. Indian country."

"That why Mister Avery don't spend a lot of time at his house?"

"That, and the rattlesnakes."

Whicher looks at the man, cracks a smile.

"According to Carl, it's all under-developed."

"Have you seen Mister Avery lately?"

The man puts a thumbnail to his chin. "Somebody was here on the weekend. Don't know who. He lets his buddies come stay."

The marshal makes a mental note of the detail.

"I'll tell you, though, it's getting worse around here for break-ins, folk stealing stuff, it's a gol darn disgrace. The guy that cuts Carl's grass told me somebody stole a leaf-blower out of the garden cabin just last week."

"Sir, you mind if I ask you something? Did you ever see a dead person before?"

The man unfolds his arms, tilts his head, scratches at his wrist. "I was in Korea. I seen folk killed."

"Like to show you another photograph, if it won't upset you any?"

The man's grin broadens.

Whicher calls up the image of the dead man on his cell—checks the shot is from the neck up only; showing the victim's face but nothing else.

He holds out the phone. "You know who this is?"

The man reaches out a hand.

"Go ahead." Whicher gives the cell to him.

The man takes it, holds it up close. "Nope."

"It's not Mister Avery?"

"No. No, it's not."

"You don't know him?"

"No, sir, I don't."

Chapter 5

Traffic in downtown Abilene is free-moving along the wide expanse of Cedar Street. Whicher sees the sixteen-story Hotel Wooten towering above all the other buildings.

Two blocks on, at the intersect with North Third, he swings the Silverado onto the cross-street, spots an empty parking bay, pulls over at the side of the old hotel.

Shutting off the motor, he studies the building's buff-colored facade in the midday sun—carved stone insets among the square and arched windows, a vertical cut-back at the fifth floor, brick and glass towering into the West Texas sky.

He steps from the Chevy, straightens his hat, buttons the suit jacket. Crosses the sidewalk to a set of wide doors, the letter *W* inscribed on the glass in gold.

Inside, half-panels of dark timber line a grand lobby—galleried, with plastered columns, plants in pots among the leather couches.

A woman is at a tall reception desk—the marshal makes his way over.

"Here to see a Mister Carl Avery." He takes out his badge. "United States Marshals Service."

"Oh." The woman arches an eyebrow. "Is he expecting you?"

"No, ma'am."

"Well, Mister Avery's suite is on the fifteenth floor." She looks at him. "But you need an access card…"

"It's in connection with a serious incident."

"I can give you a card," she says. "But did you want me to call up?"

She takes a plastic card from a drawer in the reception counter.

"You could do that."

The woman gives him the card, indicates the steel doors in a wall at one side of the lobby, across an intricate-patterned black and white tile floor. "The elevator's right over there. Floor Fifteen. Suite number one."

Whicher touches the brim of his hat to her. He crosses the lobby, steps inside the elevator, slides the access card into the reader.

Punching the button for floor fifteen, he waits for the doors to close, steps back.

The elevator starts to rise, he gazes at his reflection in the aged, sheet-copper lining.

At the fifteenth floor, he steps out into a carpeted corridor—bright windows lighting a small lobby, numbered doors leading off to separate suites.

He finds the door marked *1*—knocks.

After a moment, a lock clicks back, the door opens—a

heavy-set man in a cream suit stands in the frame.

His face is broad, his gray hair thinning, a salt and pepper mustache is above his full mouth.

"Mister Carl Avery?"

The man nods his head.

"Name's Whicher. With the US Marshals Service." He holds out his badge and ID.

Avery studies it.

"I come in? I need to speak with you, sir."

The man's hand remains on the jamb of the door. "Well, what about?"

"I step inside, sir?"

"I'm in the middle of a meeting, here, a business meeting," Avery says. "If you could have called ahead…"

"This won't take but a couple of minutes."

Avery makes a face. Steps aside.

The marshal follows him into a suite of expensively-appointed rooms—muted colors, glass and chrome.

At the window is a view right out over the city—to the vast expanse of land beyond; the Rolling Plains.

At either side of the window Hawaiian cane grows from a brace of burnished pots.

Two men are seated at a glass-topped table. The younger patrician-looking, with a head of dark-blond hair. His sea-green, silk shirt is open at the throat. Beside him, wearing a sport coat, is a powerfully-built man in his fifties. His hair is cropped. He's sporting a goatee beard, trimmed short. The table is strewn with papers and files and coffee cups and bottles of water.

"Gentlemen."

The three men in the apartment take the marshal's stock.

Whicher glances out of the window. "That's a long damn way you can see."

"Indeed," Avery replies.

"I need a moment of your time in private," Whicher says. "If you gentlemen wouldn't mind?"

The younger man rises first, pushes back his thick, blond hair. The older man stands, breathes from a flattened nose.

"Whyn't you grab something along the street," Avery says. "I'll come down just as soon as we're done. Pick a restaurant."

The older man collects a sheaf of papers from the table.

The two men step from the room and out of the suite—closing the door behind them.

"You see the lake from here?" the marshal says to Avery.

"Excuse me?"

"Lake Fort Phantom Hill."

Avery clears his throat. "Not well, no."

"Tallest building between Forth Worth and El Paso. Isn't that what they call it?"

"It was the tallest at the time they built it," Avery says.

"My office is right around the corner," Whicher says. "I look at this thing all the time."

Avery stuffs his hands into the pants pocket of his linen suit.

"You own a boat, sir?"

The man looks at him.

"Up on the lake?"

"Well, yes," Avery says. "As a matter of fact, I do."

"You know where it's at right now?"

"My boat? At my house."

"No, sir." Whicher looks the man in the eye.

"No?"

"No sir, it ain't."

"Well, where is it, then?"

"It's right up at the top end of the lake," Whicher says. "Up by the dam."

Avery frowns.

Whicher studies him. Takes out the notepad.

"It should be in my boathouse. I have a property on the lake."

"When's the last time you saw it?"

"When?" Avery takes his hands from his pockets, runs the flat of his finger over the neat-cut mustache. "I don't know. I guess a couple of weekends back…"

"You keep it locked? Your boathouse?"

"Yes, I do."

"You keep it locked."

"Look," Avery says, "what are you saying, has somebody stolen my boat?"

"I'm not saying anything, sir. I'm telling you it's out at the dam, right now."

"Well…" Avery says, "I'm afraid I have no idea what it's doing there."

"Somebody stole something from your property at the lake recently, according to your neighbor."

Avery looks confused.

"Did you report it?"

"You mean, the thing with the gardener?"

"Yessir."

"He said somebody took something from the cabin. I didn't get around to reporting it. Should I have?"

"You live here?" Whicher says. "In town? This apartment here?"

"Yes."

"How often you visit your place on the lake?"

"Well, whenever I like."

"You own a trolling motor?" Whicher says. "An electric outboard motor?"

"My boat has a gasoline powered motor. As a matter of fact, it's in for servicing…"

The marshal nods. "You don't own an electric motor?"

"No." Avery looks at him. "No, I don't."

"Could you have left the boathouse unlocked, you think?"

"Look, marshal—perhaps you'd mind telling me what this all is about?"

"Your neighbor says folk stay up there sometimes, friends, such like?"

"Excuse me?"

"When you're not using the place."

"What if they do?"

"Your boat was found this morning, Mister Avery. At the scene of a serious crime. You have any idea how it could've gotten there?"

"No," Avery answers. "I don't. A serious crime?"

"I'm here to ask that you not go anywhere near your boathouse until I let you know that it's alright to do so."

"Well, why not?"

"I need to search it, see if anybody broke-in. You can give me permission, or I can get a warrant. Your boat was found at the scene of a homicide. I need to know how it got there; you say you don't know."

Avery eyes him, his face still.

"Do I have your permission?"

The man gives a bare nod.

"You need to speak with me, I'm at the US Marshals Office, Northern Division. On Pine Street. Above the courthouse." He points out of the window. "Right there. Right along the block."

⁜

Back outside the Hotel Wooten, Whicher sits in the Silverado staring along the wide street at cars and trucks rolling up Cypress, toward the Paramount Theater and the downtown banks.

He grabs his cell, dials a number.

It answers on the second ring.

"Dave Spano…"

"You get that line search running?" Whicher says.

"We're on it now."

"Anybody find anything yet?"

"Trace evidence is going to be a goddamn nightmare," the detective says. "The wind's blowing in off of the lake, disturbing everything, there's trash all over. We've got latent impressions—but a public place like this…"

"What's Gail think, she seen anything?"

"She's working on the boat."

"I found the owner," the marshal says, "I just talked with him—some guy name of Avery, Carl Avery. Lives at the Wooten, here in town. He has a suite at the top."

"What's he have to say?"

"So far, not much."

Whicher starts up the motor in the Chevy, hits the A/C.

"You're downtown?" Spano says.

"Yeah."

"Talk with my old partner—Marlon Hutchins. Hutch? You know him? If you're downtown, you could go see him."

"Why'd I want to do that?"

"He was city police, he was a detective, he worked a couple of cases they had out here. Maybe he could give you something to think about, a couple angles."

The marshal watches traffic cruising by on the street. "Yeah, maybe."

"Two reporters showed up, already," Spano says. "We didn't tell them much, except that a body's been discovered. I didn't know what you'd want?"

"Keep it that way," Whicher says. "No details—especially the fact that it's a bow killing."

"Got it."

"If we need publicity—help finding out who the victim is, we'll let 'em know."

"Alright," Spano says. "Well, we'll finish the search, get everything photographed, we'll get anything bagged."

"Chain of custody starts now," Whicher says. "Anything you get, make certain we met the legal collection requirement."

"I know the drill. Are you coming back here?"

"Later," the marshal tells him. "I got to go talk to my boss."

※

Parking outside the Federal Courthouse building, Whicher shuts off the motor in the truck.

Above the Pine Street parking garage on the opposite side of the street, the Hotel Wooten towers, monolithic, above the city skyline.

The marshal steps out, locks the truck, eyes the courthouse—the same vintage as the Wooten, built from the same pale brick and stone.

Entering the building, he takes the stairs to the second floor.

At the end of a featureless, white corridor he reaches the USMS office.

He punches in a code. Opens up the security door.

Inside, the front office is deserted—a half-dozen desks and empty chairs and blank computer monitors.

The marshal sets down the Resistol on his desk.

Donna Garcia from civilian support sticks her head out of a side-office.

"Mornin'."

"Morning," she says. "Marshal Evans said to go right in, as soon as you got here."

He looks at her.

She only shrugs.

"Yes, ma'am." He crosses to a closed door marked, *Chief Deputy Marshal Warren Evans.*

He knocks.

"Come," a voice answers.

Whicher enters.

Evans is dressed in a suit, seated behind his desk.

Seated in front of him is the newly-appointed marshal—Alejandro Ortega.

He's dressed in a navy polo shirt and tan slacks.

He stands. He's mid-height, in his late-twenties. Athletic, good-looking, a head of thick, dark hair.

He offers his hand.

Whicher takes it.

The young man's grip is firm.

"Take a seat, John," Evans says.

The marshal pulls up a chair, Ortega settles himself back down.

The small room is lined with file cabinets. Light streams from the sole window.

"You find out anything on the boat?" the chief marshal says.

"Belongs to a feller name of Avery. Lives right along the block at the Hotel Wooten."

Evans clicks a pen. "The realty guy, the property developer?"

"Carl Avery," Whicher says. "That's what he is?"

Evans nods.

"He has a place up on the lake," Whicher says. "I've

asked permission to search for evidence of any break-in."

"You've already spoken with him?"

"Yes, sir. He says the boat's kept locked in a boathouse. Says he has no idea what it's doing up by the dam."

The senior marshal smooths his rust-colored hair.

"He was in the middle of some meeting," Whicher says. "Him and a couple of business partners. I'll say he was a little agitated."

"Avery's well known in commercial circles," Evans says. "He wouldn't want to be seen tied up with something like this."

"I took the names of the guys with him. Asked Avery for them."

"Why's that?"

"He lets folk use his property up at the lake—friends, acquaintances, and such. There may be evidence up there we'd need to rule out." The marshal takes out the notepad from his jacket, reads the names he's written. "A Riley McGuire and a Lance Tate." He looks at Evans.

The senior marshal shakes his head. "Don't know either of 'em." He puts his elbows on the desk. Leans forward. "I've been briefing Marshal Ortega. I'm pulling him from the general-duty roster, I want him assisting you."

Whicher cuts the younger man a look. "Ever work a murder case?"

"No," Ortega answers.

"Sandro's been assigned to court protection most of the two months he's been with us," Evans says. "Soon as you ID the victim, you're going to need to build up a picture of the guy's life, that can take manpower…"

Whicher nods. "Dave Spano says I should go talk with an old partner of his from the PD—Marlon Hutchins. He says the lake has history."

"You ever really work a case here in town?" Evans says.

"No, sir."

Evans turns to Ortega. "Northern District covers a hundred plus counties. The marshal here's usually working several counties away."

The young man nods.

"He's the best criminal investigator I've got," Evans says. "Nobody better to learn from."

"Good to know, sir," Ortega says.

Whicher shifts in his seat.

"Take Marshal Ortega up to the lake," Evans says. "Show him the site, walk him through it. The ME's office in Tarrant are slated for the autopsy today—according to the DA's office. They want to expedite fast. A non-ID victim makes people nervous."

"Alright," Whicher says. He turns to Ortega. "What car you driving?"

"Black, F250."

"Meet me around front of the courthouse, I'm in the Silverado."

Ortega stands.

"And get your gun from the safe."

⅄

Traffic is moving freely on Treadaway Boulevard, a four-lane highway heading north out of the city through the working part of town. Bordering the road are rental units and auto-yards, warehouse lots, a few brick stores. The marshal watches Alejandro Ortega's pickup in his rear-view; a two-year old black F250, short bed, newly-detailed, high-gloss shine on the hood.

The boulevard passes Cedar Hill Cemetery, sun high, now—bleaching out color from the sky.

Past the cemetery, tire shops and a boot store flank the highway. The few run-down houses have their windows caged with iron bars.

Whicher thinks of Carl Avery's place in the Cherokee neighborhood on the lake.

Why his boat?

Why Avery's?

All along the eastern shore boats were everywhere, he'd seen them from the road; tied to moorings and jetties.

He thinks of the lake itself; sixty feet deep. Not a bad place to dump a body. If you hauled it, the middle of the night, a boat that made no sound, a boat with an electric motor.

Ahead, the stop light at the intersection is on red.

The marshal slows.

The interop-channel of the radio flashes up inside the Silverado.

"All units—we have a robbery in progress—the corner of East North Tenth and Judge Ely Boulevard…"

Whicher glances at Ortega's truck in the rear-view mirror.

"Multiple shots fired," the dispatcher says, "suspects still at the scene—all available units please respond."

The marshal stops the truck, throws off the seat belt, jumps out—shouts to Ortega behind him; "*You hear that?*"

Ortega leans his head out the window. "*I heard.*"

"*That's a mile and a half from here…*"

"*Go, go—I'll follow…*"

The marshal gets back in behind the wheel, switches on the blue flashers mounted in the Silverado's front grille.

He pulls a U, runs the truck across the front of a Seven-Eleven.

Rejoining the highway, he mashes down on the throttle.

The Chevy accelerates, he checks for Ortega behind him—sees the blue lights popping.

Weaving in and out of cars and pickups on the highway, he drives the two blocks down to North Tenth—makes a left against the oncoming flow of vehicles.

Barreling up the four-lane, he crests a rise, descends into a residential area.

Through the truck's open window is the sound of tires squealing—a motor revving.

A silver Honda streaks out from a lane on the opposite side of the road.

The marshal sees two men inside the sedan—their faces covered with black masks, the man in the passenger seat holding an automatic rifle.

Whicher swerves, brakes—tries to block the path up the west-bound lanes.

The Honda steers around him, accelerates.

Whicher rips the Ruger from the shoulder-holster, skids

the truck to a stop.

He throws open the door, jumps out, thumbs back the hammer on the revolver.

Ortega tries to turn, to block the highway.

The Honda races toward him.

Whicher fires four rounds at the sedan.

It slows, swings around, its passenger door flies open— a burst from an AR-15 splits the air.

The Honda jinks sideways.

It speeds past the back of Ortega's truck.

Ortega scrambles out, whips the gun from his hip, opens up on the retreating car.

The sedan carves a way along the highway, traffic braking, peeling to left and right.

"Hold it," Whicher shouts to Ortega. *"Hold it. Hold your fire…"*

Chapter 6

The younger man lowers the Glock between his hands.

"You okay?" Whicher says.

Ortega nods.

"Let's go," the marshal says, "let's get after 'em…"

Whicher jumps back in behind the wheel of the Silverado—he cranks the steering around, checks the side-street, stamps on the gas.

Overtaking Ortega's black pickup, he can just see the Honda, almost gone from sight up the highway.

He grabs the radio from the dash-hook. "This is Whicher, USMS—responding to the robbery in progress—on North Tenth and Avenue F. I have a suspect vehicle—a silver Honda Accord, headed west on North Tenth. Suspects are armed and dangerous, be aware. Am in pursuit."

Whicher floors it out as the Honda cuts left into a side road.

He reaches the turn, steers across the highway, all four wheels on the Silverado in a slide.

He straightens up, guns it.

The road twists down into a subdivision—through rows of houses, grass lots, trees.

A left-right split is ahead, a fork in the road.

"Son of a bitch…"

He can't see the sedan.

He stops the truck, sees Ortega coming in behind him.

The marshal waves for him to pull alongside.

Ortega stops his truck by Whicher's open window.

"Go left," the marshal says, "I'll take the right…"

Ortega nods, accelerates away.

Whicher hits the throttle, steers down the right-hand fork of the road into a sinuous lane.

Ranch-style homes are packed at either side as the asphalt narrows. Now it's stopping—finishing in a wide circle. "God damn…"

He whips the truck around, drives back up to the fork—takes the left-hand lane to pursue Ortega.

He grabs the radio. "Dispatch…"

"Dispatch, go ahead."

"Suspect vehicle is now headed south…" he checks a street panel, "on Green Valley Drive."

"Copy that."

The road curves through a dense stand of trees, snakes to left and right, smaller residential streets appearing from both sides.

Sandro Ortega's black F250 sweeps around the turn—headed straight toward him.

Whicher brakes to a stop.

Ortega pulls alongside. "Dead-end…"

Whicher grimaces.

Ortega gestures at the adjoining streets. "They must've turned down one of those…"

"Dispatch," the marshal says into the transceiver, "this is Whicher—suspect Honda has broken visual contact—most likely headed south, onto Highway Eighty."

"Copy that," the dispatcher says. "Marshal, we have an armed suspect in the vicinity of the robbery. Suspect is on foot. Closest units proceed to East North Tenth—First Credit Premier bank, the corner with Judge Ely Boulevard…"

"Responding," Whicher answers. He looks at Ortega. "Just haul ass behind me."

He hangs up the radio, turns the Silverado around. Drives back up to the junction with the four-lane highway—an image of the passenger in the Honda burned into his mind. He'd been wearing something—*body armor*?

The marshal crests the rise in the road, accelerates down to a major intersection.

The bank building is just ahead—a shopping mall beyond it.

Law enforcement units are scattered to left and right, their doors open, light bars flashing.

A white, Brinks 500 armored car is outside the front of the bank.

Whicher pulls off the highway, stops alongside an Abilene PD unit.

Its driver, a sergeant, is out of the vehicle, radio in his hand.

"US Marshals Service," Whicher says.

The sergeant nods.

Two ambulances are on the other side of the Brinks car. Its back door is open, the rear lift-gate lowered to the ground.

Whicher reads the badge on the sergeant's shirt; *Rodriguez*. "Dispatch says you have a suspect in the vicinity?"

Rodriguez points up the boulevard. "A runner—he took off, north."

Ortega pulls up in his truck—he whips the door open.

"Y'all use some help?" Whicher says.

"You could take a sweep around," Rodriguez answers. "The more eyes looking, the better."

"We have a description?"

"Guy with an assault rifle," Rodriguez says, "wearing blue jeans, white sneakers, a grey top. Plus body armor, and a face mask."

"He went north?"

"Head up the boulevard," Rodriguez says. "The right-hand-side is fast food and the back of the mall, we have people in there—you could check the residential streets over to the left."

"I'll take the first one I come to," Whicher says to Ortega. "You take the next one after that."

"On it," the younger marshal says.

Whicher pulls past the armored car, sees brass on the lot—multiple empty shell cases.

He steers onto Judge Ely Boulevard.

Fifty yards up the road is a left, he makes the turn.

Cruising the residential road he eyes the one-floor

houses—shade trees, cars parked on the driveways. Adrenaline starting to sink out of him. The Ruger lying flat on the passenger seat.

Minutes pass.

One block, another.

A third.

He reaches a junction, makes a right, turns up onto the next street, to look for Ortega.

Knowing in his gut already.

It's too late.

The guy's already out, he's gone.

⊥

The black man squatting by the group of spent shell cases in the lot of the bank is Levi Underwood—Whicher recognizes the FBI agent from the Abilene field office.

The marshal climbs from the Silverado as Ortega pulls alongside.

Sergeant Rodriguez approaches.

Whicher shakes his head. "He's gone," he says.

The sergeant looks at him. "We still have people searching."

Ortega slides out of the pickup, clocks the brass shell casings on the ground.

"The guys in the Honda were on a planned route out," Whicher says. "They shook us loose real easy. Your runner would've had somebody waiting. Or maybe another car."

The FBI agent stands. "Says you." He looks at Whicher.

The marshal returns the man's stare.

"How come they didn't get any money?" Agent Underwood says. "If they had it all worked out?"

"What happened here?" Ortega says.

"We're still getting witness statements," Sergeant Rodriguez answers. "But the driver of the armored car says two men with assault rifles rushed the messenger as soon as he got out."

"Messenger?"

Levi Underwood takes a step closer. He smoothes the arm of his summer-weight suit. "The guy that handles the money," he says. "Armored car has a two-man crew—driver and the messenger. The delivery guy—he's the messenger."

"They carrying a lot?" Whicher says.

"Three ATM cassettes on the messenger's cart when he stepped out," Underwood says. "The messenger said two guys rushed him, one of them fired in the air, the other shot right at him."

Ortega whistles.

"He was wearing body armor, he took a couple in the chest, one in the arm. He managed to draw his weapon, return fire. Between him and the driver, they managed to run 'em off."

Ortega looks at the FBI man. "That sounds like a lot of rounds flying…"

"They responded with lethal force. The way they're trained. They're treating the messenger now, I don't think the injury's too bad."

"You working this?" Whicher says to Underwood.

"Violent Crimes Task Force is. I'm lead agent."

"We followed a silver Honda Accord on North Tenth. Two men inside it, wearing full-face masks, I think body armor. One of 'em had an AR 15. They opened up on us, didn't hit anything. We fired back. Chased 'em down into a residential road, Green Valley Drive."

"You get the tag?"

The marshal shakes his head.

"But you think they were on a pre-planned route out?"

"They knew where they were going. Y'all need statements from us?"

"Later," Underwood says. "A silver Honda Accord, you give us anything else?"

"They probably ditched it already." The marshal turns to Rodriguez. "I think your runner's gone. If y'all want us to stay, we'll stay. Otherwise, we have to move."

The FBI agent looks at him.

"Homicide, this morning. Up at the lake."

"No shit?" Underwood says. "There something in the air today?"

Whicher touches the brim of his hat. Turns to his truck. Stares at the Ruger on the passenger seat "I hope not."

᛭

Lake Fort Phantom Hill.

At the top end of the lake, black and yellow police tape flutters across the entrance to the dirt lot. Standing guard is a man by a Lake Patrol SUV—dressed in uniform shirt, fatigue pants, an olive ball cap.

A handful of cops and Dave Spano from the PD are still there.

Whicher steps out of the Silverado.

Ortega gets out of his F250—surveys the scene from across the road. He stretches out the muscles in his shoulders, straightens the pull-over polo shirt.

"Everything alright?" Whicher says.

Ortega looks at him.

"After the bank an' all?" Whicher says. "Getting shot at?"

The younger marshal gives a grin.

Whicher looks in his eyes.

"Sure," Ortega says.

He'd been solid; not too hot, not too pumped. The kind of guy Whicher liked as a young lieutenant leading the scout platoon back in Third Armored Cavalry. No big adrenaline rush, not too wired. "You did good," he says.

Ortega looks at him, puzzled.

Whicher points over the road. "You know Detective Spano?"

"I've seen him in court."

The marshal gestures for Ortega to follow him across the roadway.

The Lake Patrol officer approaches.

"USMS," the marshal says, "name's Whicher. I'm leading the investigation."

"Yes, sir, marshal. Officer Pickett."

Whicher eyes the skiff at the foot of the concrete boat ramp—riding the chop on the surface of the lake.

Detective Spano walks from the back of the lot—the uniform officers begin searching another section of marked out scrub.

"Y'all find anything?" the marshal says.

The detective makes a face.

Whicher sees Gail Griffin, standing with her back to him—sketching into an open notebook.

"Just trash, mainly," Spano say. "Cigarette butts, beer and soda cans. A few pieces of fabric, nothing that looks any good."

"This here's Marshal Ortega," Whicher says. "He'll be assisting on the investigation. I want to walk him through the site."

"Go ahead," Spano says.

"We caught the tail end of a robbery down in town, else we would've been here sooner…"

"At the bank?" the detective says.

"You hear about it?"

"On the radio in my car."

"On Judge Ely Boulevard," Whicher says. "We gave chase."

"Anybody get hurt?"

"I don't think." Whicher turns to Officer Pickett. "Lake Patrol?"

"Yessir."

"You tell me anything about the lake? What kind of trouble you get out here?"

"Fights, drunks," Pickett says, "problems with drugs, with deals going down. People come out, they get to foolin' around, drinking, smoking stuff. One thing can lead to another."

Whicher nods.

"We see sexual offenses; some prostitution. Anything serious we go ahead and call the police or the sheriff's department." Pickett looks at Dave Spano. "Other than that, I'd say stolen cars…"

"Cars?"

"People dump 'em in the lake. Every once in a while we have to drag 'em on out."

The marshal turns to Sandro Ortega. "Victim was discovered this morning at first light. A couple of kids out of ACU on a night fishing trip. They spotted a DB, called it in. It's looking like he was dragged from the lot to where he was found."

"No vehicle here?" Ortega says.

"Right. But that don't mean he didn't come in one." Whicher looks to Officer Pickett. "People dump cars? Could a vehicle be in the lake?"

The man tugs at the bill of his ball cap.

"If it was, how y'all going to know about it?"

"Sonar," Pickett says. "We got some pretty good sonar, a couple of the boats. People drive the cars off of ramps, mostly. They'll roll 'em off, there's some pretty deep water. Not here, but some of the other places the ramps are at."

"The water's shallow here?"

"It's shallow, then it drops away a bunch."

"Could we get a search running?"

Pickett nods. "I can make a couple of calls."

Ortega looks at the skiff at the water's edge. "How do we think the boat fits?"

Whicher steps past Detective Spano, motions for Ortega to follow down the tape-marked access-route. "We got to work on that. Victim had no ID. He was laying face up, three arrows sticking out of him." The marshal points to the spot where the body was found—dark stains are visible on the parched ground.

Gail Griffin approaches. "Dave said you found the owner of the boat?"

"I found him. He says he has no idea what his boat's doing here."

Griffin looks at the marshal, then at Ortega.

"We get any prints off of it?" Whicher says.

"We've got prints."

"This here's Marshal Ortega, he'll be assisting me."

She nods. "I want to get the boat towed into Abilene. We need it in workshop conditions to see exactly what it has on it."

"There anything here apart from the boat?"

The crime scene technician shakes her head. "The arrows, maybe," she says. "I'm guessing we could do something with them. There could be blood spatter in the lot, assuming he was attacked there. But it's probably all been walked on, it won't be well enough preserved."

"He was shot then dragged?" Ortega says.

Gail Griffin nods. "Doctor Fernandez might get lucky, she might find prints on the DB's skin."

"He was dragged by the ankles," Whicher says, "the way

he was laying. His hands were clutching hold of that arrow."

"No ID," Ortega says, "that means somebody removed it?"

"Doc Fernandez found a ring in his pocket," Whicher says. "There was nothing else."

Ortega bugs his eyes.

The marshal turns to Gail Griffin. "You get done here, I need you to take a look at a boathouse for me? At a property along the lake?"

She puts her head on one side.

"The owner's given permission."

"Looking for what?"

"Any sign of forced entry. Check for prints. I'll have Marshal Ortega meet you."

Dave Spano walks the narrow path toward them. "Talk to Hutch," he says.

Ortega looks at Whicher.

"Former detective," the marshal says.

"Buy him lunch," Spano says.

Gail Griffin raises an eyebrow. "Hutch could be a good call…"

"So far, that's it?" Ortega says. "We've got a body and a boat. That's all we have?"

Whicher turns on his heel. "It's not staying that way."

⁂

An hour later, in the old town north of Highway Eighty, Whicher sits in the family-run Mexican restaurant—eating flat beef enchiladas, rice and beans. Sandro Ortega leans back in his seat, sipping sweet tea, a plate of chiles rellenos in front of him.

Across the table, Marlon Hutchins watches both of them—his face fleshy, the little hair he still has left cropped close to the scalp.

His pale cotton shirt is open at the neck, over a heavy torso. He takes a pull at a Negra Modelo, relishing the cold, dark beer.

The marshal thinks of the few times he's seen the man in Abilene—a handful of occasions, only ever in court.

An elderly Hispanic man approaches the table—his thick, white hair, neatly-combed in place. "Gentlemen. Marlon. Is everything to your satisfaction?"

Whicher gives a smile, a nod.

"*Muy bien,*" Ortega answers.

"Fidel's been putting up with me for years," Hutchins says. "Him and his family."

"The pleasure is all ours."

Hutchins raises the bottle of beer as the old man moves to address another table.

"Appreciate you seeing us," the marshal says.

"I'm retired," Hutchins says. "Coming on two years. My time's my own."

"How you like it?" Ortega says.

"I can sink a few of these of an afternoon, nobody gives a damn." Hutchins picks at a plate of brisket tacos and refried beans. "Cops keep getting younger. It feels like. Criminals, too. Comes a point you get tired of keeping up."

The younger marshal grins.

"You look pretty new yourself?"

"I'm out here six months," Ortega says. "Before that, I was with San Angelo PD."

"Second job already?" Hutchins says. "You look too young."

"I'm twenty-eight."

"What brings you to Abilene?"

"Family," Ortega says. "My wife has family. She wanted our kids to see their grandparents, their cousins, their uncles, aunts."

Whicher gives the younger marshal a side-ways glance.

"Where you at?" Hutchins says. "What part of town?"

"Elmwood."

"Out near Dyess? The Air Force base?"

"Closer in. East of the Freeway. San Jose Drive."

"Kids grow up fast on a cop. They in school?"

"My eldest, Alicia, she's starting first grade. My little one, Amelia, is only three."

Whicher thinks of his own daughter, Lori—three years old—the same age as Ortega's youngest.

Hutchins keeps his voice low. "So, what can I do for you fellers?"

"Dave Spano tell you anything about this?" Whicher says.

"DB at the lake. He said you had about zip."

Whicher nods, cuts into the flat-stacked enchiladas. "Victim was killed overnight—we have no ID, no place to start. You tell us anything about the lake area in general?"

Hutchins sips on his dark beer. "You're not from around here?"

"The panhandle," Whicher says. "Briscoe county."

The former detective thinks it over a moment. "At night, the lake is kind of a marginal place. Close to the city, but outside. Kind of wild, kind of remote."

"People go out there with trouble in mind?"

"Over the years there's been some serious crime," Hutchins says. "Homicides, assaults, rapes."

"Lake Patrol told us problems with narcotics," Whicher says. "Stolen cars."

"A hitchhiker was beaten to death," Hutchins says, "they got three people for that. The remains of a woman were found about eight years back, the south end of the lake. Blow to the head. Skeletal remains only."

"You work that one?"

"Nope."

Whicher sips on a glass of ice water. Studies the picture on the menu card—a matador and a bull, the matador drawn up, flamboyant; the animal bloodied—banderillas piercing its neck and shoulders. "Ever see a man shot to death with a bow and arrow?"

The ex-detective looks into the marshal's face.

"If you had," Whicher says, "you'd remember."

Hutchins takes a forkful of the tacos on his plate.

"So, it's kind of bad-ass?" Ortega says. "The place, in general?"

"Folk go out," Hutchins says, "they think they're far from civilization. Far from the rules."

"You ever come across a guy name of, Avery?" Whicher says. "Carl Avery?"

"The property guy?"

"Ever have dealings?"

The former detective shakes his head. "Listen, you find somebody out there, you got to ask yourself, what were they doing? He was alive when he went there, the vic? He died up there?"

Whicher nods.

"I'd be looking at drugs. Or something sexual. Or a fight."

"Why go out there to get in a fight?" Ortega says.

"Maybe he didn't have a choice." Hutchins takes a slug at the Negra Modelo.

Whicher studies the former detective, overweight, louche, out of touch.

He lets his eyes slide off of the man, feels a black mood descending.

Drugs or a sexual connection.

Prostitution.

If there was any evidence for that, Celine Fernandez would find it. Nothing about the scene felt that way.

The body was stripped of ID, but not abused. No sign of a struggle. The presence of the boat somehow at odds—like something planned, but wrong at the same time.

Across the table, Hutchins takes the beer bottle from his mouth. "You don't go there at night."

The marshal gives him a questioning look. "People go…"

"You're not hearing me," the retired detective says. "You go there, to the lake, you got a pretty damn specific reason."

"We can't investigate the reason," Whicher says. "If we don't know who the man is."

"Talk with Narcotics and Vice, maybe. At APD. Find out if any of them knew him."

The marshal shrugs.

"Or the DEA," Hutchins says.

"Victim didn't look like any drug dealer."

"Then talk to Vice."

"The guy was shot to death with a hunting bow."

"Have you thought about that angle?"

"The hunting community?"

The former detective sets down the bottle. "You could see if anybody involved in bow hunting had gotten into any kind of trouble?"

The marshal blows out his cheeks.

"It's a strange one," Hutchins says, "I have to admit."

"Killing a man with a bow would take some cold, hard planning," Whicher says.

"Right," Ortega looks at him. "We're not talking about a heat of the moment kind of thing."

"It was pre-meditated," the marshal says. "Pretty much an execution."

"How about if it's some nut?" Hutchins says. "You know? Some freak? Somebody killing just to kill."

The marshal eyes him.

"Bad enough nobody was ever caught for that woman eight years gone."

Whicher grunts. "This guy's not getting away."

Hutchins looks at him. "You're right, I've never seen a

man killed with a hunting bow. But I've seen trouble out there. Plenty of it. And I still say this—that place at night is a place apart. You go out there—you got to have a reason."

Chapter 7

In the Marshals Office at the Federal Courthouse building, Whicher surveys the case notes of serious crime investigations from all law enforcement divisions—everything he can find from Lake Fort Phantom Hill and the surrounding locale.

A man shot to death by his own brother, another killed on County Road 503. Off of West Lake, a woman stabbed to death in a wooded area, a suspicious drowning. Added to that, a list of aggravated assaults, rapes, sexual offenses, biker shootings. Drugs. Thefts, break-ins. Vehicle crime.

At a corner table, Sandro Ortega flicks through a series of files on a computer screen.

Whicher stares at the edge of his desk. Tries to think of any kind of pattern, connections, potential strands.

The idea of the victim being from somewhere to the north nags at him.

The main door to the office opens.

Donna Garcia from civilian support enters from the outside corridor.

Clutched at her chest is a paper grocery bag.

She calls over to Ortega; "You want me to put this in the kitchen for you?"

The younger marshal looks up.

"I can put it in the refrigerator?"

"If you don't mind," he answers.

Garcia carries the bag across the open office-space.

"Thank you…"

The woman gives Ortega a motherly smile, disappears into an adjoining kitchen.

Whicher looks at him.

"Gallon of milk, a dozen eggs," Ortega says. "For pancakes. For the girls."

Whicher stares at the younger man for a moment.

"I told my wife I'd bring home something…"

"This afternoon you need to be over to Carl Avery's place," the marshal says. "To meet with Gail Griffin."

"Not a problem," Ortega answers. He gestures at the computer screen. "I looked Avery up. His main company is a construction business, Summerwood Realty and Construction. He's building houses, here in Abilene."

"There any record of him being in trouble?"

"None that I've found."

"They worth a lot of money? The company?"

"I didn't check finances yet. But they're building property all over the city."

Whicher's phone rings. He looks at it, lifts the receiver off the cradle.

"Marshal?"

Whicher recognizes Levi Underwood, from Abilene FBI. "I do something for you?"

"You give any statement yet?" Underwood says. "On this morning?"

"Not yet." The marshal sits back in his seat.

"I wanted to check on a couple of things."

"Go ahead."

"That car you tried to chase down—you said two people were inside it? A driver and a shooter. You couldn't see anything of their faces?"

"Both wearing masks," Whicher says. "The shooter was wearing body armor, I think. The driver, I didn't really see."

"Sounds like they were dressed the same as the runner," Underwood says.

"That's a bunch of serious people you got there," Whicher says. "You better watch your ass. Y'all find that Honda?"

"We found it. At the end of Cal Young Park, south of Eighty."

"Stolen?"

"Yeah, it was stolen—about a week back, outside of Anson," Underwood says. "You said you thought they took you down a pre-planned route, getting out of there?"

"They knew where they were going."

"Tell me about the part where they shot you up? You returned fire?"

"In self-defense. There'll be a report."

The FBI man falls silent a moment. "I'm investigating two other incidents similar to this—on armored cars. One over at Sweetwater, the other back in Cisco. Sweetwater was around six months ago, Cisco was before that. They got a ton of money."

"Cisco I think I heard about," Whicher says.

"Both towns are off Interstate Twenty—forty miles either side of Abilene. These robberies are getting more violent, the guy this morning, the messenger with the money? He's lucky he didn't end up killed. They were trying to shoot him down, his armor saved him, but it could've worked out a whole other way. He's pretty shook up. I sure as hell need to find these guys."

"Anything we can do to help, you let me know?"

"We're on it," Underwood says. "But thanks, all the same. And send me your statement, you and your partner."

"I'll do that."

Underwood clicks out the call.

"FBI found the car," Whicher says to Ortega, "the Honda. They're saying the robbery looks like it could be part of a series. Did you make out a firearm-discharge report?"

"Not yet."

"Let me see it, before you give it in to Evans."

Ortega looks at him.

"It needs to be right, is all." Whicher checks his watch. "I need to head over to Oak Street, to see Celine Fernandez." He closes down the files on his computer. "Plus I need to speak to the kids that found the body this morning."

"You want me to do that?"

"As soon as Gail Griffin calls, I need you to head on up

to Carl Avery's property. It's off of East Lake, the Cherokee neighborhood, I'll leave the number of the house. Meet her out there, go on through the boathouse, see what you can find."

"Is Avery a suspect?" Ortega says.

The marshal stands, slips the suit jacket from the back of his seat. He grabs the keys to the Silverado. "I don't know what the hell he is. But so far, he's the only damn name we got."

⁂

Whicher parks his truck in front of the two-car-garage on the driveway of the house in Wylie, alongside a three-year old Chevy Impala in gun-metal gray.

He stares through the truck's windshield, past his wife's car at the new house—the family home. Two thousand square feet, three bed, two bath. Faced with brick and timber. Bay windows looking out over a burnt dry lawn. Live oak shading a third-of-an-acre plot.

He lifts a grocery store bag off the passenger seat, steps from the truck.

At the front door, he opens up, enters the house.

Moving through the living room to the kitchen, he sets the grocery bag on a granite countertop. Through the window he can see into the yard in back—his wife Leanne, his daughter, Lori. Leanne in shorts, and a green and white sun top, her chestnut hair loose. Graceful, handsome. The look of a forties actress; sitting beneath the shade of a patio by the in-ground pool.

His daughter, Lori, is holding a plastic unicorn and a yellow, foam dog.

He opens up the kitchen door, steps out into dappled light from the canopy of a live oak.

Leanne hears him, she looks up. Her mouth full, jaw strong, brow dark above the wide-set blue eyes.

He takes off his hat.

Lori turns around. Dressed in butterfly wings and a ballerina costume.

Leanne stares. "I didn't hear you leave this morning."

Lori drops the unicorn, runs across the grass as Whicher bends low.

He lets his daughter pull the Resistol hat from his hand. She puts it on.

"Paddle…" She points the foam dog at the swimming pool.

"I told her she can't," Leanne says. "It's too hot."

Lori tugs at his arm.

"Listen to your Momma. It's too hot."

She spins, turns her butterfly wings on him, runs back to the shade of the patio, the marshal's hat falling from her head onto the grass.

Whicher picks it up, brushes down the nap in the felt.

Leanne stands, steps from the patio.

Lori stoops to a collection of toys on an upturned laundry basket.

"I guess I had to leave early," Whicher says. "A call came in…"

His wife kisses him on the mouth. She scans his face.

"DB," he says, beneath his breath. "Out at Lake Fort Phantom Hill. Kind of grisly."

Leanne folds her arms across her sun top. "You going to be working late?"

The marshal thinks of Celine Fernandez—already gone before he'd gotten to the Coroner's Office; headed for the ME in Fort Worth. Three hours for the autopsy, a two-and-a-half-hour ride back. He could try to meet her when she got back into Abilene, get whatever she had by then. "I don't know yet," he says. "I brought something…"

Her eyes come back onto his.

"I stopped at a store on the way back. Bought milk and eggs."

She makes a question with her face.

"For pancakes."

His wife puts her head on one side.

He looks at Lori. "She likes pancakes."

"Yes, she does." Leanne smiles. "Do you want something to drink? You want to go on inside?" She calls across the yard, "Lori, come on over here, sweetheart."

Whicher crosses to the shaded patio, reaches out an arm.

Lori grabs it—he swings her up.

"Why are dogs yellow?" she says.

"They're not. Not all of them."

"I want a red one."

He carries his daughter into the kitchen.

"You want to eat?" Leanne says. "You want coffee?"

Whicher sets Lori down, she spins, runs out of the room, down the corridor toward her bedroom.

"I can't stay," Whicher says. "A bunch of things are going on. Somebody tried to rob an armored car."

"There was a news report, lunchtime," Leanne says, "on TV."

"We caught the tail end of that. Gave chase. To a car fleeing the scene."

"We?"

"New guy I'm working with. Ortega. Alejandro Ortega."

Leanne pours water into a coffee machine. "They said a man was shot during the robbery?"

He watches her standing; face turned away. The only sound in the room is the hum of chilled air pumping from a vent in the wall. "Everybody's alright."

She gives a small nod.

"I've been asked to work the DB," he says.

"With this new guy?"

"Right."

"What's he like?"

"Ortega? He's okay."

Leanne looks at him, frowns. "That's it?"

"He's young, twenties, only been here a couple months. He lives over in Elmwood."

"Married?"

"Yeah. He has a couple of young kids."

"A partner," she says. "You alright with that?"

Whicher grunts. "Why wouldn't I be?"

She gives him a flat look, brushes a strand of chestnut hair from her face.

"Listen," the marshal says, "you have any idea where my

old work clothes are at? Boots and jeans, and such, for yard work?"

"The guest room," she says. "One of the boxes we still haven't unpacked."

"You know which one?"

"You'll have to look. How come Abilene police aren't handling the DB?"

He meets his wife's eyes a moment. "It could be complicated. It's kind of strange…"

Lori runs back into the kitchen. "Where's yo-yo?"

The marshal looks at her.

"The dog," Leanne says. "You left him outside."

Lori grabs at the kitchen door, pulls it open, scurries across the yard.

"You think we should re-decorate the guest room," Leanne says, "before we get it all set up."

"If that's what you want."

"We could clear it, we could get somebody in." Leanne takes a china mug from a cupboard. "Why do you need your old clothes?"

"Could be a late one, I might be getting dirty."

"Why's that?"

"Up there at Fort Phantom Hill," Whicher says. "We may have to drag the lake."

Chapter 8

Pulling into the driveway of Carl Avery's property, Whicher sees Sandro Ortega's black F250, an E-Series van parked beside it. Beyond the house, in the shade of an overhanging willow, Gail Griffin stands with Ortega by the jetty at the waterfront.

The marshal steps down from the Silverado, crosses the scorched grass to stand in the shade.

"Nobody broke in," Gail Griffin says.

"Y'all sure on that?"

Ortega shrugs. "There's no sign."

Gail Griffin looks toward the boathouse. "Door wasn't forced," she says, "either it was open, or somebody had a key."

"How about the waterside door," Whicher says, "the pull-up door for the boat?"

"Undamaged," Griffin answers. "Unmarked. It must have been unlocked."

"The neighbor came by," Ortega says, "he told us Avery leaves that door open."

"You think it's worth lifting prints?" Whicher says to Griffin.

The crime scene technician spreads her hands. "Nobody broke in. The owner leaves the door open, according to the neighbor. He lets his buddies use the place to fish, he lets them use the boat. They're lawfully visiting."

Whicher pulls at the collar of his shirt.

Two sites; both open-access, no way to isolate a thing.

Anything they did find would be barely admissible as evidence.

Was that a choice?

"Has to be somebody local," Whicher says. "Somebody who knew they could get in." He stares through the overhanging threads of willow to the lake beyond. "That location—all the way up there by the dam; that's a strange place for anybody to meet. Y'all want to go out there at night?" He looks at Ortega and Griffin in turn.

"Maybe he didn't know what it was like?" the younger marshal says.

"Right. If he didn't know the area."

"So, how would he find it?" Griffin says.

"First place you can park once you cross the dam. If you come in from the north."

"So, local killer, non-local victim?"

"Nobody's reported missing," Whicher says.

The scene technician looks at him. "That could give you one hell of a problem. You need an ID, marshal."

Whicher rubs a hand across his jaw. "I'll head down to see Celine Fernandez just as soon as she's back from Fort Worth."

Ortega moves beneath the trees, looking at the boathouse by the waterside.

The marshal looks toward the main house—standing empty, sun lighting up the porch along its front. "Meet me up at the dam tonight," he says to Ortega. "Say around nine?"

The young man nods.

"I want to check it out after dark," Whicher says. "You want to take off till then, head home, it's alright with me." He turns to Gail Griffin. "Somebody put a motor on that boat, a silent motor. Avery claims he don't have one. You get the boat towed back into Abilene?"

"It's there now," Griffin says.

"Find something on it for me."

She shoots an eyebrow. "A lot of people could've used that boat."

He sets his hat, bunches his shoulders. "Then I'll talk to 'em all."

⋏

Officer Pickett's Lake Patrol SUV is still blocking the dirt lot by the dam. Across the road from it is a Jones County Sheriff's unit. Whicher stops his truck beside it. Spots Deputy Lyle Mooney on the scrub-filled slope—the first man to respond to the scene.

Dave Spano and the Abilene police team are gone.

Whicher checks his watch; past five o'clock, the afternoon heat still building.

Deputy Mooney walks from the scrub slope toward the parking lot.

Officer Pickett talks into a two-way radio.

Farther down the shore, a Lake Patrol boat moves slowly in the water.

Whicher leaves his truck, crosses the road, steps over the black and yellow police tape.

He takes a few strides down toward the water, studies the Lake Patrol boat—aluminum hulled, two crew aboard it, in an open wheelhouse. It's starting a turn—coming about; the vessel maybe thirty feet in length—dragging a line in the water.

Deputy Mooney nods a greeting. "They're going over some of the possible spots for vehicles."

Officer Pickett clicks off the call on his radio. "So far, there's nothing," he says.

"What's that line they're dragging?"

"Side-scan sonar."

"How deep's it need to be," Whicher says, "to conceal an automobile?"

"We found one in twelve feet of water," Pickett says. "It depends if it's muddied up, or it's clear. If it's muddy, you'd be on top of it, you wouldn't see a thing."

"There's places y'all find 'em?"

"East boat ramp," Pickett says, "that's a good one."

"That's folk that know the area," Deputy Mooney says, "the lake an' all."

The marshal watches the sonar boat now fully turned—the bow pointing toward them, heading back in their direction. "Y'all find vehicles pretty regular?"

Pickett nods. "We're running to five or six a year."

"Whoever did this," Mooney says, "if they ain't local, they wouldn't know the spots."

"Killer could be local," Whicher says, "even if the victim ain't."

"Most times," Officer Pickett says, "we run a search, it's 'cause somebody spotted something—guys fishing, or whatever. We know where we're looking, we're not just trawlin'."

The marshal watches a cattle egret stalk the water line beyond a bank of salt cedar.

"That's a big ol' lake," Deputy Mooney says.

Whicher turns to Officer Pickett. "You keep that sonar running?"

"Long as we got light," the man answers, "we'll keep her running."

⁂

Oak Street, Abilene

Evening sun is streaming through the windows at the Coroner's Office in downtown Oak Street. Celine Fernandez arranges notes and papers on an inlaid rosewood desk. Whicher takes in the framed picture on the wall above the medical certificates; a family gathering, the doctor among a half-dozen brothers, sisters and cousins, the women poised, in expensive-looking dresses, the men lean, in dress shirts and suits.

The doctor's brief case is open, overflowing with documents. She touches a strand of long dark hair at her temple. "Arrow injuries…"

Whicher places his Resistol hat on one knee.

Doctor Fernandez glances at the marshal from across her desk. "We have barely any literature on this," she says. "It's not a common class of wound in forensic pathology."

"Nobody I've spoken to has ever seen it," Whicher says.

"Injuries and cause of death are obvious," she says, "particularly if the arrows are still in place. But localizing the shooter relative to the victim…" She stops. "I talked with a couple of colleagues, one of them recommended an archery expert—a man named Anderson—a bow hunter."

"Right now," the marshal says, "all I'm looking for is the victim's name."

"I know that."

"You get any fingerprint results?"

"They came back from IAFIS. I'm afraid he's not in the system."

"No record?"

"No."

"So, never been in the military," Whicher says, "or law enforcement. Never been in legal trouble, never been bonded. You find prints from anybody else?"

"On the victim, no."

The marshal shifts in his seat, sits forward. "How about ante-mortem conditions? Injuries, dental work? The guy's clothes?"

"There are things we can follow up on, certainly," Fernandez says. "But all of that will take time. We have the arrows. Easton arrows, with broadhead hunting tips—I have the make and model. The fact they didn't pass through the body may be significant, also."

The marshal looks at her. "How's that?"

"A broadhead is capable of passing right the way through—according to this Anderson. Even a large animal, an elk, or a moose."

Whicher studies her.

"They're designed to leave a good blood trail," she says. She shrugs.

"How close would the shooter have to be to make the shot?"

"Sub-twenty meters would be common, apparently. Over thirty-five meters is rare." She picks out a separate wad of notes, skim-reads a page quickly.

"So, the shooter," Whicher says, "is standing that kind of range from the victim? In the dark, he wouldn't see anything, hear anything?" The marshal lets his gaze rest on the carpeted floor of the office. "How's the shooter see his victim?"

She leans her head on one side. "That's for you, marshal, not for me."

"You think it could have been from the boat?"

"I asked Anderson the same thing," she says. "He thought it was highly unlikely. He said if you were in a boat your body-position would be bent, you'd get a less-than-full draw—which would mean a poor release. To hit a target three times in quick succession, from a boat rocking in the water…"

"So, somewhere on that headland?" Whicher says. "Somewhere back in the scrub?"

"Or on the other side of the road?" the doctor says. "There are a lot of variables, depending on the type of bow used, its construction, the skill of the shooter, their strength."

"Can we place where the victim was standing?"

Fernandez shakes her head. "We know he was dragged to the spot where we found him, evidence is consistent for that. We can't say where he was initially shot—most likely that dirt lot, but everything's too disrupted—we'll never pick out the exact place."

"How come there's no blood—if he was shot there?"

The doctor leans back at her desk. "The arrows stayed in him, there's just one exit-lesion in the skin at the back of the torso. The shirt he was wearing caught any blood initially. I'd say loss of consciousness and death occurred very rapidly, the heart wouldn't have been pumping. There was blood on the ground where he was lying. Any trail left behind when he was dragged would be minimal, it's almost certainly been disrupted."

Whicher turns the hat on his knee, thinks of boots on the ground before he'd even gotten there. "There any way to link an arrow with a specific bow?"

"None that we're aware of," the doctor says. "The arrowheads, we could try to trace. Try to trace the shafts to a point of sale."

"The arrows are clean, no prints?"

"Nothing," Fernandez says. "We have hardly any literature that relates to bows—most of the documented injuries are either from people falling out of hides in trees, or from cross-bow bolts. We have one suicide."

The marshal looks at her.

"A suicide, I know. Somebody used their foot to draw back the bowstring, shot himself in the gut."

Whicher takes the Resistol from his knee, flicks the hat band with a thumbnail.

"Considering what an effective killing-method it is," Fernandez says, "you'd think we'd see it more often."

"You can pick up a gun about anywhere," Whicher says. "It don't take squat to point and shoot."

"We'll find out who this is," Fernandez says, "we'll get an ID, but it could take time. In the morning I'll check with the hospitals, and the dentists. Start checking on the clothes, the footwear, some of the other things we have."

The marshal stands. "Whoever did this," he says, "they're already disappearing. They're in the wind."

⼈

Lake Fort Phantom Hill

The last of the light is fading, wind chopping at the water under a moonless sky. Off the headland, past the sail boat yard, the Lake Patrol vessel searches in the distance, its forward light projecting into oncoming night.

No light shows at the far, northern end of the lake. Nothing among the mesquite and scrub.

A mile away, on the West Lake Road, a truck rumbles along a rural highway.

The dirt lot is still closed, taped off, the entrance blocked by the Lake Patrol SUV.

Whicher sits in the Silverado across the deserted two-lane road. Windows rolled, the scent of the lake coming into the cab, the smell of night, of baked earth, of scorched-dry grass.

Across the road Officer Pickett watches the search boat from the concrete ramp.

Whicher checks his notes from earlier in the day.

Two telephone numbers are written at the top of a page; numbers given to him by Deputy Mooney. A Lucas Kennedy. And a Stacey Wise—the numbers for the kids from ACU.

The first name on the list is Lucas Kennedy—the marshal enters the number on his cell.

He pushes back in the driver's seat as it rings. Waits for it to pick up.

"Hello?" A young man's voice.

"Evening. Is this Mister Lucas Kennedy?"

"Yes, it is. Who is this?"

"Name's Whicher, I'm with the US Marshals Service."

The line goes quiet.

"You reported finding a body this morning at Lake Fort Phantom Hill. I'm leading the homicide inquiry. Like to talk to you about it?"

"I already talked with a deputy…"

"I know that, sir. I need to meet with you anyway. Tomorrow morning?"

"I have a class at ten," Kennedy says.

"I can come out."

"And chapel at eleven."

"Say, eight-thirty?"

"Well, alright. But I spoke with a deputy this morning, I told him everything I could."

"You were fishing overnight?"

"We were fishing, we camped out after we got through. We found the body in the morning."

"I just need to speak with you, sir, go over it for myself."

"There's not much more I could tell you."

"Eight-thirty on campus. I have a Stacey Wise on my list," Whicher says. "Like him to be there. Will you see him?"

"Stace? Yeah. Yes, I'll see him."

"Can you ask him to be there? Or I can call him?"

"I'll ask him," the young man says. "I'll see him later, anyway."

"Where do you want to meet?"

"Oh. Well, how about the amphitheater?" Kennedy says. "It's close to the main entrance, it's easy to find. You'll see the Tower of Light, a big tower right by the amphitheater."

"Tower of Light," Whicher says.

"It's right behind the Biblical Studies building."

"Eight-thirty. I'll be there."

The marshal clicks off the call.

He checks his watch, nearly nine—Ortega ought to be there soon.

He thinks of him—jumping from the F250, leveling his gun.

The silver Honda bursting out from a side road. Masked men, an AR-15. Automatic rifle fire, the whip of fear.

He stares out at the approach of night.

Back in Wylie, Lori would be asleep, Leanne somewhere in the house. The new place meant to be a fresh start. Not quite home yet—the place still un-molded, unshaped by their lives.

He'd need to be there.

He searches the darkening scrub, thinks of Marlon Hutchins in the restaurant—he knew the place for what it was. Out beyond the lights of town—Abilene nothing but a glow in the distance, miles to the south.

From the direction of the spillway, a vehicle is approaching along the road from the east.

Whicher opens the door of the Silverado, pushes himself out of the seat.

He stands at the side of the road as the vehicle approaches—Sandro Ortega's black F250 truck.

The younger marshal steers onto the hard ground to park. He shuts off the motor, snaps off the headlamps. Climbs out. Turns to stare at the search boat's distant light flickering on the surface of the water. "Did they find anything?"

"Not yet." Whicher gestures for the younger marshal to follow him.

Crossing the road, he holds down the black and yellow police tape with his boot.

Ortega steps over it.

The two men cross the lot, descend the slope toward the boat ramp.

Officer Pickett turns at their approach. "They're about to pull it," he says. "It's too dark. They'll start up again in the morning."

"What's happening with the site overnight?" Whicher says.

"Abilene PD are sending up a car," Pickett says. "They'll stand guard."

A breeze is picking up across the water. A solitary vehicle moving in the distance, disappearing among the bluffs.

No craft are on the lake, no navigation lights.

"You think that boat that was here could've found its way in the dark?" Whicher says to Pickett.

"With no lights?" the man says.

The marshal thinks of the World War Two murder—the boyfriend flashing the headlamps on his car to show his girl where he was. He scans the narrow two-lane highway from the West Lake Road along the earth dam—he can barely see it.

To the north, the road disappears into undulating scrub.

The victim could have been waiting on someone. Waiting on a car to arrive?

If he was, he'd be watching the road. The arrows had been in his front—he'd been facing his assailant.

"You want to head on out," Whicher says to Officer Picket, "we'll wait behind for the PD."

"Alright. Then, I guess I'll say goodnight."

Sandro Ortega shoves his hands into the pockets of his chinos.

Officer Pickett walks back up the lot.

He steps over the police tape, climbs into his SUV. Fires up the motor, pulls around on the deserted road, headed east.

Whicher stares into the mass of darkness above the black water. "Sure feels different," he says. "Now that it's night."

The light on the search boat turns toward the shore.

The old Comanche land is silent, abandoned. Whicher sweeps the distant shore line; barely a light winks from any property. "Do me a favor?" he says. "Take a walk on out in the scrub."

"What for?"

"I want to see if I can still see you."

Ortega shrugs. "How far you want me to go?"

The marshal thinks of the archery expert, his estimate of a killing range. "Twenty yards."

"Which way?"

Whicher indicates a spot beyond the dirt lot, in line with the concrete ramp.

Ortega walks back into the scrub, stride elongated, counting out steps along the way.

Turning back to the boat ramp, Whicher eyes the water, then the road.

He turns around again.

Ortega's barely visible; nothing more than an outline.

The marshal scans the sky; not quite full dark, but getting close. "Move back another ten yards."

He turns away and then around once more.

Vague shapes on the headland mark the places where the scrub is grown high. He can barely make out Ortega. "You want to get behind some of that brush, the mesquite or whatever it is?"

"Get concealed?" Ortega says.

"Try it."

The younger marshal moves sideways, stoops behind a thicket of vegetation.

He's gone from sight.

"Alright," Whicher calls out. "Alright, you want to come on back?"

"An hour from now," Ortega says, "it'll be black as pitch out here."

Whicher nods. "Lonely place," he says. "To go to meet your maker."

Chapter 9

Out on West Lake a set of lights is moving in the night air; headlamps. The marshal tracks them over the scrub til they slow, turning onto the rural two-lane half a mile away.

He steps from his truck, sets his hat as the vehicle comes closer.

In the lake, its lights flicker—splintering, strobing against the footings of the steel guard rail on the dam.

He can hear it now, the sound of the motor—an Abilene Police car—light bar set across its roof.

It slows as it approaches.

He can make it out—a Ford Crown Vic.

As it stops, he reads the letters on the door—*Sheriff's Office*—it's not the Abilene PD.

The driver steps out.

Deputy Lyle Mooney.

Ortega opens the door to his truck.

Mooney looks at the pair of them. "Officer Pickett said y'all were still out here."

Whicher steps forward. "What's going on?"

"I just took a call from a buddy of mine—at the county jail." The deputy's round face is lit up in the car's hi-beams. "He says an inmate there just told him he knows who did this…"

"Come again?" Whicher crosses the asphalt two-lane, Ortega following.

"A guy in the jail," Mooney says. "A guy picked up for auto-theft, a couple days back. Says he knows who did it."

Whicher tips back his hat. "You serious?"

"The feller that called from the jail is a former deputy at the sheriff's office," Mooney says.

The marshal shakes his head.

"Name of Clarence Klein. He talks a lot with the inmates."

"Most guys in a jailhouse are full of shit," Whicher says.

"He might know something," Ortega says.

The marshal looks at him. "He was picked up for auto-theft a couple days back?"

"One Anthony Hernandez," Mooney says.

"Two days ago the victim was still alive, this guy was already in jail," Whicher says.

Deputy Mooney turns in the glow of the Crown Vic's headlamps. "You don't even want to talk with him?"

"PD are sending up a car to guard the site. Soon as they're here we're headed for home," Whicher says. "The guy was in the jail when it happened. Anything he has to say is hearsay. We'd need a lawyer—this time of night you think we're going to get one? I'll talk to him in the morning."

"Heck, you're lead investigator," Mooney answers. "I

thought you'd want to know." He puts a hand on the driver door, eases it wide. "Y'all do what you want to do. I'm going to see him tonight."

⋏

Thirty miles.

Thirty miles of flat highway through a blackened land, nothing moving. The tail lights of Mooney's cruiser dull red up ahead.

Coming into the outskirts of Anson, now, the Jones County seat.

Past the Baptist church, shotgun shacks, a few rough-looking trailers.

Mooney leads the column of three, Whicher and Ortega in line behind him.

The deputy slows at a stop light—makes a right by a Subway, heads downtown onto Commercial.

Whicher follows along the arrow-straight road toward the lit-up County Courthouse, Sandro Ortega in the F250 behind.

They pass the Anson Auditorium, rows of sidewalk stores.

From the town's old square, the road passes behind the courthouse, past the ornate facade of a disused opera house.

The sheriff's office is on a side street—a jailhouse built beside it, a nineteen-forties concrete block.

The marshal sees flashing lights out in front of it; emergency vehicle lights—an ambulance drawn in at the curb.

Mooney accelerates into the street, he pulls over.

Whicher eyes the ambulance—its back doors wide open.

He brakes into a slot beside Mooney's car.

The deputy is out of his vehicle, running.

Whicher shuts off the motor, jumps out.

Ortega pulls in at the far side of the ambulance.

Mooney's already at the door to the sheriff's office—tapping in a number on a keypad in the wall.

Ortega runs around the back of the ambulance. "What's going on?"

Mooney pushes open the door to the office, holds it wide, "C'mon, let's move, let's go…"

Whicher follows the deputy inside, Ortega right behind him.

Mooney takes a key from his duty belt, hurries through a wood-veneered reception. At the end of a small corridor, he unlocks a heavy door—exposing the steel bars of a secure gate.

He works the locking mechanism, slides the gate back on greased runners.

A bright-lit corridor extends behind it, plate-steel cell doors lining either side.

An open area is ahead, a communal space—a small room off-set from it, a TV room.

Two EMTs are kneeling over a man on the floor in prison whites; a CO beside them.

The corrections officer looks up.

"Clarence?" Mooney says.

The man on the floor is face up, bloodied, one of the

EMTs giving emergency CPR.

"Somebody shanked him," the CO named Clarence says.

The second EMT stands. "We need to move him—get him to the hospital. He's lost consciousness."

"It's the feller I told you about…"

The EMT runs back down the corridor. "We need to move him—now…"

Chapter 10

Lyle Mooney drives the sheriff's cruiser light bar popping—leading the ambulance north out of the town.

The few cars and trucks on Commercial Avenue pull to one side out of the way.

Whicher rides in back of the cruiser with Sandro Ortega—the corrections officer, Clarence Klein, up in the front.

"What happened?" the marshal says.

The CO turns in his seat. "A bunch of 'em were watching TV. We got the B-Roster in their cells for the night, A-Roster, we were locking 'em down next. I was with one of the other officers. It went a little quiet, there was some kind of a ruckus, one of the inmates comes running out the TV room, this guy Hernandez has gotten himself stabbed."

"You know who did it?"

"No, sir."

"How about the guy that ran from the room?"

"The boy that ran is an alimony de-fault," the CO says. "Ain't him shanked the feller. He damn near fainted, I thought he was going to puke."

Mooney slows, pulls the cruiser off of the main drag. He drives beneath a line of street lamps to a clutch of one-floor buildings—A/C units on their roofs, a load-in area lit up in sodium light.

Peeling to one side, he lets the ambulance go on in front.

The ambulance stops, the back door snaps open, the driver runs around.

The EMT in back holds a saline bag in the air.

A doctor and two nurses are out of the hospital building, moving fast.

"Hernandez is still a prisoner of the county," Mooney says, "we best go in."

The doctor and the nurses and the EMTs wheel the gurney from the back of the ambulance.

"They messed him up," Klein says. "They messed him up pretty bad."

The marshal catches the CO's eye. "You and me need to talk."

⊥

Nobody is in the waiting room, all the lights are turned low. A center table is covered with aging magazines, a dozen plastic chairs line the walls.

Whicher checks his watch—coming on ten-thirty.

Deputy Mooney settles on a seat in the middle of a row.

Clarence Klein sits down beside him—to watch the corridor.

Ortega crosses the room to an automated drinks

machine in the corner. "Anybody use something?"

Whicher nods. "Coffee, no cream, no sugar."

Mooney and Klein shake their heads.

"What do y'all know about this guy, Hernandez?" Whicher says.

"What I read on the charge sheet," Klein answers. "And what he done told me himself. He was arrested outside of Hawley."

Whicher thinks of the small incorporated community outside of Abilene.

"He says he's out of Dallas, with no fixed address. Somebody reported him acting suspicious, casing a couple of homes."

"Out in Hawley?" Whicher says.

"Yessir. Arresting officer ran the license plate on the car he was driving—turns out the vehicle was stolen. There were items in the trunk he couldn't account for. Power tools, garden equipment—the kind of thing you'd get from breaking into yards or garages."

Sandro Ortega returns from the drinks machine, two plastic cups in his hand.

Whicher takes one.

"He had a couple of battery chargers," Klein says, "and an outboard motor."

"Say again?"

"A trolling motor."

The marshal looks at Ortega.

"It's all in the county evidence room," the corrections officer says.

"He tell you where he get any of that?"

"He said he broke in a couple of the yards over at the lake. A bunch of them properties ain't occupied but half the time."

"That guy with the boat?" Deputy Mooney says.

Whicher nods. "Carl Avery. His place is down on Cherokee, a neighbor reckoned somebody broke in. What'd Hernandez have to say about the homicide?"

"It's been on TV," Klein says, "they've all seen it."

"He give you any name? Any actual name?"

"No, sir," Klein stares at the floor between his feet. "But he said he knew who did it—some guy hanging out in Abilene."

"Hanging out?"

The jailer nods. "He said the guy was from out of town, like himself. Said he could identify him if he saw him again, or saw a picture of him. He reckoned he met the feller in a bar in Abilene."

The marshal takes a sip at his cup of coffee. "Hernandez met him in a bar?"

"Well, yessir," Klein says. "He said it was kind of a biker bar. I reckon he might've been trying to sell some of them stolen items…"

Whicher thinks about it.

"He said the guy told him he was a bow-hunter, a survivalist or some such. He was talking about the lake, said he'd been out at the lake."

"How come this Hernandez guy told you all this?" Ortega asks the jailer. "He looking to cut a plea, get a lighter sentence?"

"I'd guess."

"You think he might've sold him anything?" Whicher says. "Could he have sold this guy a trolling motor?"

"You'd have to ask him." Klein's shoulders sag. "If the son-of-a-bitch don't croak."

Sandro Ortega takes a pull at his cup of coffee.

The CO takes a long breath, exhales. "He said this feller reckoned to be fixin' on doing some shooting. Kind of braggin' on it, Hernandez said. He thought it was just a bunch of bull, but when he asked him what he was going to be shooting at, the man said, 'live target.' Something about the way the feller said it gave Hernandez the creeps, he said."

Whicher stares out into the long, dark corridor.

Turns the phrase over in his mind.

Live target.

⋏

At ten minutes to midnight a doctor in a white coat enters the room. He's pale skinned, sandy haired, his features neat, his face composed.

The marshal rises from his seat, takes off the Resistol.

Ortega and Mooney and Klein look up from the row of chairs.

"I'm afraid it's bad news." The doctor turns a pen between slim fingers.

Sandro Ortega gets to his feet.

"He'd suffered multiple stab wounds to the upper thorax," the doctor says. "Penetration to the left ventricle of the heart, and both lungs. He was haemorrhaging internally before he got here. We couldn't save him."

"Did he say anything?" Ortega says.

"He was out when he got here." The doctor spreads his hands. "He never regained consciousness. We did everything we could."

The corrections officer, Klein, stretches the skin over his cheekbones. "There was no sign of any trouble. Not a thing, there was nothing…"

⁂

Winged insects buzz the lights in the load-in area, the night air on the street warm after the air-conditioned chill of the hospital. A faint hum is on the breeze from the center of the town of Anson half a mile distant.

Whicher scans the street, hears a motor, looks for Mooney bringing around the Crown Vic.

"What happens now?" Ortega says.

The marshal eyes him, thinks of himself at the same age; not long back from the First Persian Gulf War. "Tomorrow morning I'll need to brief Chief Marshal Evans. We'll need to start early." He stares out into the street at a line of palms moving in the rising wind. A small-time thief could explain Avery's boat, the trolling motor—if Hernandez had fenced it out, if he'd told somebody where they could get a skiff from an unlocked boathouse. "I got a bad feeling about all this…"

"Because of what happened?" Ortega looks back toward the hospital building. "Him dying in there?"

Whicher stands, arms folded, the Ruger heavy in the

shoulder-holster. "Jailhouse testimony," he says. "Court don't like it, nine times out of ten it's inadmissible. But this Hernandez feller opens his mouth to a CO—next thing you know he's in the hospital—and the next thing they're laying him out dead."

Ortega thinks about it.

"Somebody got wind he was talking," Whicher says. "There's power in this."

He lets his gaze run out beyond the few properties at the edge of the town—into dark prairie, no lights showing, not a living soul out there. A feeling in him; inside, an unquiet feeling.

On a day of dying.

An unknown man shot to death with arrows, a jailhouse inmate stabbed to death. No names, except for Hernandez, a small-time thief. And Avery, a business man in a high tower.

A homicide investigation.

Maybe more than that.

No way to say where things could be going.

He turns to Ortega, sees the question in the young man's face.

"You believe Hernandez was telling the truth?" Ortega says.

"I believe it," Whicher says. "I believe it now."

Chapter 11

The body beside him is warm in the dim light of the bedroom. Reaching out a hand, he switches off the insistent alarm on his phone.

Whicher puts down the cell on the nightstand. Lets himself lie flat against the mattress a moment longer.

Beside him, Leanne turns, her eyes still shut, a small frown across her brow.

She reaches out a warm hand, touches the cool skin of his shoulder.

He watches her in the half-light, in the quiet of dawn—drapes closed across the window, stillness in the room, no sound from the house.

Nothing is moving outside on the street. Lori still asleep in her room.

He thinks of the day ahead of him. Of the jail and the hospital the night before.

In the light at the edge of the window he sees a man struck down by arrows, a lake, a boat. A masked man firing from a silver sedan. A jail, a dead thief.

Things in the dawn, rising.

Thinking of all of those things—in the growing light at the wall.

⅄

Lori sits on the tile-floor in the kitchen, looking up at her mother, her chestnut hair mussed from sleep.

The marshal sits at the kitchen table, shirt freshly-ironed, his suit jacket hung from the back of a chair.

Leanne pulls a bathrobe about her, leans against the countertop. "What do you want to eat for breakfast, Lori?"

"Pancakes."

Leanne looks at her daughter, and then at Whicher. "We made a lot of mixture."

The marshal considers for a moment. He nods. "Why wouldn't you?"

Lori claps her hands together.

Whicher fixes a neck-tie in place.

"You want some?" Leanne says.

"If you have enough."

Leanne takes a metal clip from the pocket of her robe, puts up her hair, arranges it in place.

She walks to the refrigerator, takes out a covered bowl from a shelf. "Amanda's coming over later."

"Amanda?" Whicher says. "Grace's daughter?"

Leanne shakes her head. "That's Mandy. Amanda's Sue and Rick's—from next door."

Sue and Rick.

The neighbors.

In three months he's seen them twice. Grace, Leanne's friend, the minister's daughter, he hasn't seen at all. "Y'all going out?" he says. "Or you having them over?"

"Swim," Lori says, "swim…"

"Maybe," Leanne tells her daughter.

Whicher looks out into the yard.

"This morning, maybe," Leanne says. "If it's not too hot."

"You want me to take the cover off the pool?" Whicher says.

"I can do it."

Lori claps her hands, rocking back against a cupboard in her sleep-suit.

"So long as you eat your breakfast," Leanne says. "And brush your teeth."

The girl stands, springing up, turning a circle in bare feet. Then runs by Whicher.

"Where you goin'?" he says.

"Teeth…"

"Let her," Leanne says. "At least it gets done."

The marshal watches his wife pour pancake mixture from the bowl into a skillet on the stove.

"Will you be out all day?" she says.

"Could be."

She sets down the bowl.

"Last night, we had a call," he says. "About an inmate at the jail up in Anson."

"That's why you were so late?"

"A guy that reckoned to know something about…" The

marshal lets the sentence trail off.

Leanne glances over her shoulder. "About—the thing at the lake?"

Whicher nods. "We went over to see him. There was some kind of a fight before we got out there."

"You take your new guy?"

"Ortega, yeah." Whicher lowers his voice. "This guy ended up in the hospital—he was stabbed. He died last night."

She turns her face away.

He stares at the soft, tanned skin on the back of his wife's neck.

"Don't say that." She flips the pancake in the skillet. "This thing'll go on and on…"

Whicher lets his breath out slow.

Lori runs back from the bathroom, skips by the kitchen table, the marshal reaches out an arm, sweeps her up.

Leanne serves the pancake. "Let daddy have the first one." She sets down maple syrup on the table, plus a fork along with the plate.

Whicher unscrews the top from the bottle of syrup, pours some out, cuts a forkful of the pancake. Gives it to his daughter.

Leanne pours more mixture from the bowl. "So, how is he, your new guy? You keep him out all night, too?"

"Think I should've sent him on home?"

"His wife's going to love you." Leanne takes a carton of milk from the refrigerator, finds a glass for Lori. "You can't get to all of it, you know? Not all of it, not every time."

The marshal eats the food on his plate, mopping syrup, saying nothing.

"You don't have to fix it." She turns around, looks at him. "Remember that. You don't have to fix it all."

♏

Whicher drives the Buffalo Gap Road, window down, low sun across the parched grass—shadows stretching long from advertising hoardings at the sides of the road. Traffic is light on the four-lane highway, what little there is headed uptown through the mix of homes and plazas and churches and rick-fenced pasture.

Approaching the clover-leaf at the freeway, he passes the mall of Abilene, the parking lots still empty.

He thinks of Hernandez—of his story about a bow-hunter—a man he met in a bar.

How much could he have gotten from the TV?

Whicher follows the road onto Sayles Boulevard, block after block of neat ranch homes, new condominiums. Passing the McMurray University campus, he thinks of ACU—of Lucas Kennedy and Stacey Wise. Eight-thirty. Carl Avery will be next on the list, he'll have to call, arrange a meeting with the man.

He drives on till the uptown sprawl spreads to meet him—a world of pawn shops and pay-day loans and used car lots.

Making a right on South First, he joins the busy road.

Across the burnt-dry grass of the median, the towering Hotel Wooten stands in the distance, pale brick etched against a cobalt sky.

♏

Sweeping down the spur for Abilene Christian University, Whicher eyes the faculty buildings set among a manicured landscape. Glass and brick and stone at the end of a looping driveway—already he can see the Tower of Light—distinct above every other building.

He steers toward it, finds a parking lot, chooses a spot in the shade of a planted row of trees.

Shutting off the motor in the truck, he steps out, the day already shaping hot.

A brick walk-way leads out of the lot, he passes along the tall sides of an amphitheater, turns past the end of a descending wall.

The foot of the Tower of Light is directly in front of him, set in front of the amphitheater itself.

Rows of steps are pale gold in the early sunlight, the tower casting shadow over a campus restaurant and store.

Two young men sit on the steps, both in shirtsleeves and slacks.

They stand quickly, one of them, blond, taller, with a look of the mid-west. The second young man is short, dark, athletic.

Whicher takes out his badge and ID.

"Lucas Kennedy," the blond young man says.

The shorter man nods. "Stacey Wise."

The marshal scans the deserted plaza. Climbs the steps to where the young men are standing.

He pulls the brim of his hat down against the glare from the stone. "We talk here?"

Kennedy answers. "If it's alright with you."

The three of them sit.

The marshal takes out his note pad and a pen, looks around the amphitheater, at the plaza, the tower, the green canopy of trees beyond. Order. Structure. A projected sense of peace. "What y'all studying?"

Wise answers; "Business administration."

"I am, too," Kennedy says.

"Yesterday morning, y'all reported finding the body of a man up at Lake Fort Phantom Hill?"

"We spoke to a deputy," Lucas Kennedy says.

"Deputy Lyle Mooney."

"We told him we didn't really see a thing."

"We'd been out fishing," Wise says.

"Night fishing," Kennedy says. "We rented a couple of jon boats from the sail boat club. We pitched a couple of tents up by the spillway."

"Tell me what happened overnight?" Whicher says.

"Well, we just went fishing," Kennedy says.

"Close to the dam?"

Stacey Wise runs a hand through his ink-dark hair. "We fished all over. We went down along the eastern shore at first, and then out into the center."

"Once it was dark," Kennedy says, "it was hard to tell a thing. We hardly knew where we were."

"You see or hear anything unusual?" Whicher says.

Kennedy shakes his head.

"Think about it for me."

Wise leans forward. "That's just it. We've thought about it, both of us. We've gone over and over it. We can't think of a thing."

"I feel pretty terrible," Kennedy says. "I mean for that poor man."

"What time y'all finish up?"

"Around two in the morning," Wise says.

"And then you camped out on the north shore?"

"We used the GPS on my phone," Kennedy says. "Otherwise I don't think we'd have found the tents, there's not much light. We found the dam, the road runs right along the top of it, we knew the tents were on shore along from there."

"How about vehicles?" Whicher says, "y'all see many of them?"

Wise shrugs. "No. There was the odd car, not that many."

"Did you see the boat? That white fishing skiff? The one that was moored there in the morning?"

Kennedy and Wise both look at him.

"I don't remember," Wise says.

"We used a flashlight to find the campsite," Kennedy says. "I don't remember seeing it, but we weren't looking for it."

Wise spreads the palms of his hands. "Everywhere we went, there were boats. It's a lake, there's mooring spots all over."

The marshal nods.

"We found the tents, we got ashore," Kennedy says. "Then sacked out." The young man stifles a shudder.

"It was you that found him?"

"Yes," Kennedy answers. "Just as day was breaking. I left

the tent to take a leak, I walked back a little in the brush, I saw him. I went back and got Stacey. We were pretty freaked out, I mean it was just yards from where we were sleeping…"

"Did you touch the boat, the skiff?"

"No," Kennedy says, "neither of us touched the boat. I grabbed my cell, called 9-1-1, they put me though to the sheriff's office. Ten minutes later the deputy was there."

"You walk around near the victim?"

"Just a little," Wise says. "We didn't think about it…"

"Let me ask you something; you see anybody flashing the lights on their car last night—anything like that?"

Both young men think it over.

"Or did you hear anything strange?"

Kennedy looks at him. "What kind of thing?"

"We're looking for a vehicle," Whicher says, "we think it may have been dumped in the lake."

"There was nothing like that," Wise says. "We anchored in a couple of different spots, drifted around a lot. It's gets so dark, you hardly know where you are half the time. I mean we were just having some fun, we weren't taking anything too seriously…"

Whicher taps on the notepad. "Did y'all have dealings with any reporters, afterwards? With TV people? Or with the press?"

"No, sir," Kennedy says.

"I'd appreciate you not mention details, if anybody asks. The fact of arrows being involved, in particular. That kind of thing getting out can hamper an investigation."

Both the young men nod.

"How about friends here, fellow students? Y'all speak with any of them?"

"To be honest," Wise says, "a lot of them know already. It's a community, word gets around."

"We talked to a couple of friends," Kennedy says. "They probably talked about it in turn."

The marshal scowls. "How many students you have here?"

"About five thousand." Kennedy pushes up his shirt sleeves. "I'm sorry. We should have thought."

Wise looks at Kennedy, then at the marshal. "As a matter of fact, we think somebody might have been looking for us here last night. Campus police told us they stopped somebody in a pickup truck. They asked him what he wanted, the driver said he was a friend of mine. They told him they didn't give out details of where people lived. The guy left."

Whicher writes on the notepad. "I'll talk to them."

"Maybe it was a reporter?" Kennedy says.

The marshal raises up, puts the notepad in the pocket of his suit. "I may need to talk with y'all again. I'll stop by the campus police on my way out. Where they at?"

"The back of the university," Kennedy says. "Right along from the museum, opposite the theatre."

Whicher takes out two business cards. "Anybody else comes looking for you—y'all be sure and let me know."

⅄

Off of 16th, the campus police department is on a tree-lined street—the first unit in a store-front row—low-key, bordered by a florist, a salon and beauty parlor.

The marshal parks the Silverado in an empty bay alongside a white, law enforcement SUV.

He climbs out, crosses the sidewalk as a bell tolls across campus in the Tower of Light.

Entering the small office, he finds a uniformed sergeant seated behind a desk.

The sergeant's thick-set, in his late-fifties—the name tag on his shirt reads; *Estrada.*

The marshal shows his badge and ID. "John Whicher," he says. "Running the homicide investigation on the body discovered up at Lake Fort Phantom Hill."

Estrada nods.

The marshal guesses him to be a former cop with the city PD. "The body was found by a couple of students here at the university? They say you fellers had somebody on campus asking after them last night?"

"We did?" the sergeant says.

"You weren't here?"

"No, marshal. I can check for you. See who was?"

"Like to talk to them. You stop a lot of people? Here on the campus?"

The sergeant shakes his head. "If we stop people, mostly we're just looking to see if they need help."

"You get much trouble?"

"Not so much," Estrada says. "But people come on campus that shouldn't be here. There'll be thefts now and then, maybe a fight."

"If somebody was asking after these two students…"

"We'd be wary of that—depending on the situation."

"You guys have surveillance?"

"A few cameras. Not so many."

"The guy asking about these two students was driving a pickup truck. You think there's a chance it'd be on CCTV?"

"We could take a look," the sergeant says.

"I'll need to speak with the officer that stopped the guy. Can you have him call me?"

"Not a problem, marshal." Estrada looks at him. "Why the interest?"

"Might have been a reporter," Whicher says. "I don't want details of the case getting out."

"I was here till ten," Estrada says, "it must've happened after that."

"After ten?"

"Little late for a reporter," the sergeant says.

Whicher hands the man a business card, an uneasy feeling in his stomach. "Be sure to have your man call."

Chapter 12

The front office at USMS in downtown Abilene is empty—all the desks un-manned except for Sandro Ortega's.

"Mornin'," Whicher says.

The younger marshal is dressed in a dark blue suit and shined shoes in place of the polo shirt and slacks.

He looks up from a printed report. Grins.

"You make a start on something?" Whicher says.

Ortega nods. "I was looking at the record on Anthony Hernandez. The man did plenty of time in jail, there's a long list of convictions. Everything from theft, breaking and entering, fencing stolen property..."

Whicher jabs a thumb toward Evans's door—it's open, the chief marshal staring at a computer screen on his desk.

The younger marshal pushes back his chair, stands.

Both men cross the room.

Evans sees them, waves them in, points at two chairs in front of his desk. "I hear you have Lake Patrol dragging the lake?"

"Looking for cars," Whicher says, sitting. "If we could

find a vehicle for the victim, we might get a start on an ID."

Ortega takes the second seat.

Whicher takes off his Resistol, crosses one leg over the other, sets the hat on his knee.

"Have you spoken with Celine Fernandez?" Evans says.

"Last night," Whicher answers. "Right after she got back in from Fort Worth."

Evans makes a question with his face.

"There's no ID," Whicher says.

"Nothing at all?"

"Not yet. But the doc's been in touch with an archery expert. They think the person shooting the bow would have to have been close, not more than twenty or thirty yards away. And likely not on the boat."

Evans threads his fingers together, sits back. "Gail Griffin's processing the boat?"

"We'll chase that, today." Whicher pins the senior marshal with a look. "Sir, something happened last night. When we were out at the lake. Deputy Mooney from Jones County Sheriff showed up. He said he had a new line of enquiry—a guy at the jail in Anson."

"The county jail?"

"Yes, sir. A guy name of Hernandez, Anthony Hernandez—a guy that reckoned to know something about who did this. We went on up, but by the time we got out there, some kind of a fight broke out, this guy Hernandez had gotten stabbed. We got him across to the hospital in Anson. But he died a couple hours later."

A frown crosses the chief marshal's brow.

"Never regained consciousness," Whicher says.

"Well, what do we know about him?"

"He was picked up for auto-theft and possession of stolen property," Whicher says. "A couple days back, in Hawley. He'd been breaking and entering into properties around there, and around the lake. Stealing power tools, and such. He had a trolling motor in his car when they arrested him."

"He was an habitual offender," Ortega says, "I've been checking on his record."

Whicher goes on; "According to a corrections officer at the jail, this guy Hernandez reckoned he met a feller in a bar in Abilene, a bow-hunter. It's possible he might've fenced him a trolling motor. I hate to build a case that has anything at all to with jailbirds…"

Evans nods.

"But the fact he ended up dead?"

The chief marshal thinks about it, says nothing.

"How would he know it was a bow killing?" Ortega says. "Was that made public?"

Whicher shakes his head. "I left word with Dave Spano for it not to be revealed. But I went out to ACU this morning to interview the two kids that found the body. They may have talked about what they saw, they may have given some of the details away."

"They have anything that could help?" Ortega says.

"Not much. One thing, maybe—police there stopped a guy on campus claiming to be looking for them last night. Guy in a truck. We'll need to follow that up. Maybe somebody thinks they saw more than they did."

The chief marshal blows out his cheeks. "Chase Gail Griffin about the boat, maybe we could rule out Avery?"

Whicher looks at Ortega. "Ask her to send over details on the trolling motor. We need to find out where it came from, where it was stolen, and when. Else it's one ugly-as-hell loose end."

The younger marshal nods.

"And take a look at the record on Carl Avery," Whicher says. "I'm headed out to see him, when I get done we can head up to the lake, see if Lake Patrol got the search started again."

"I don't like this thing with Hernandez," Evans says, "I don't like him getting killed."

"Maybe he opened his mouth all the damn time," Whicher says. "Maybe he couldn't keep his ass out of trouble."

"I don't like it," Evans says again.

Whicher stands, fits his hat.

"I don't like it," the chief marshal says, "and neither do you."

⸎

Thirty minutes later, north-east of the city off of State Highway 351, Whicher surveys the line of parked cars and trucks in front of Carl Avery's office. Along with the regular sedans and pickups is a steel-gray Hummer and a black, Mercedes SL 500.

In the adjacent lot is a depot with metal siding. Cabin-like site offices, a construction yard. The depot's doors are open, back-hoes and a bulldozer parked inside.

At the depot is a man in a sport coat—powerfully built, with a goatee beard—one of the two attending the meeting with Carl Avery in the Hotel Wooten; Riley McGuire. He's standing talking with a construction worker, a guy in a T-shirt, hair like a surfer, tattooed arms.

Both men notice the marshal.

The man with the surfer's hair says something to McGuire, McGuire doesn't respond.

Whicher turns to the offices of Summerwood Realty and Construction—pushes open the plate glass door.

Inside, the air in the lobby is chilled, the walls hung with original art. Texas landscapes, oil on canvas.

A blonde female in a business suit glances at him from behind a slim monitor on her desk.

"Ma'am." The marshal takes out his badge and ID. "Here to see Mister Carl Avery."

The woman takes in the badge, studies the marshal's face a moment.

"Name's Whicher."

She picks up a phone, keys a number. "Won't you take a seat?"

Whicher checks his watch, gone ten o'clock already. He steps toward a leather couch, studies a piece of art hung on one of the walls.

"Mister Avery, sir," the woman speaks into the phone. "There's a gentleman to see you in reception. A Marshal Whicher…"

The painting on the wall depicts a body of water framed by trees. A name-plate set beneath it reads—*Lake Fort Phantom Hill.*

The thick-set figure of Carl Avery appears at the reception counter. He's dressed in a dark suit, his thinning, gray hair combed back. "Marshal?"

"Mister Avery."

"Are you going to be making a habit of this?"

"I appreciate your seeing me, sir."

"I have to leave in fifteen minutes. If you'd let me know in advance, I could have made more time…"

"Law enforcement, that's not always possible," Whicher says.

Avery presses his full mouth shut.

The woman on reception turns to her computer screen, lets her eyes go blank.

"Well, could we walk and talk?" Avery says.

The marshal nods.

Avery gestures with a hand, steps across reception, pushes open the glass door.

Whicher walks with him along the side of the office.

"So, what can I do for you?"

"It's about your boathouse, at your property on the lake, sir."

"Of course, of course."

"I had a crime scene technician take a look at it yesterday. There's no sign anybody forced their way into there, no damage to anything, no evidence anybody broke in."

Crossing over into the construction yard lot, Avery stops

by a line of chained cement mixers. "Is that good or bad?"

"I need to know how your skiff got from the boathouse up to the end of the lake."

"I'd like to know that, too."

"A neighbor of yours reckons the door is sometimes left open. That be correct?"

Avery shrugs. "Sometimes guests don't close it. They forget. I guess I don't worry too much about security, I've never really had any problems."

"The boat will be examined," Whicher says. "But I'd like to know who used it, we'll need to rule folk out."

"Good Lord. A lot of people will have used it. I'd have to look at my diary, I couldn't tell you offhand."

"Anyone you had up there," Whicher says, "anybody you let stay. Your boat was found at the scene of a homicide, I need to know how it was involved."

"Can I call you on it?" Avery swallows. "The truth is, there are various sets of keys to the house, I'm not even sure where they all are."

The marshal eyes him.

"Look, it's years since I've lived at the place, I guess it was never much to my liking. It's hot in summer, it's pretty basic—I prefer the city. I like my modern conveniences."

The door to one of the cabin-offices opens, a young man emerges—the younger of the two men from the meeting at the Hotel Wooten. His dark-blond hair is pushed back, his shirt open at the throat.

"I've gotten to treating the place more like a summer shack," Avery says, "I'm pretty lax about who stays there.

It's a horrible thought, though. To think the boat was taken, maybe used someway in this…incident."

The blond man descends a set of timber steps from the office.

"Lance Tate," Avery says, "you've met already."

Whicher nods. "You have a lot of people working here, Mister Avery?"

"For the company? I guess around a hundred or so."

"Doing what?"

"Building houses. We're working on creating several new subdivisions out here along the beltway."

Tate shoves his hands into the back pockets of a pair of pressed jeans. "Residential development is under-represented this side of the city."

"You own a lot of land?" Whicher says to Avery. "To build all of those houses?"

"Not as much as we'd like," the young man says. "We're always looking to buy, if you've got anything for sale?"

Avery shifts his weight, looks uncomfortable.

From the far side of the depot, a dark green, four-door pickup emerges—the man with the surfer's hair at the wheel.

Riley McGuire is beside him in the passenger seat.

McGuire throws a look in their direction.

The pickup pulls out of the yard, out onto the street.

"Did you have any other questions?" Avery says. "I have to brief Mister Tate on a couple of points before I leave this morning."

"No, sir," Whicher says. "Not at this time,"

"I'll check my diary. I'll try to find out where all the keys are."

Whicher hands the man a card, cuts a look at Lance Tate. "I'm interested knowing who used Mister Avery's place up on the lake. Anyone who stayed there lately. Or used the boat."

"I did," Tate says.

The marshal looks at him.

"A couple of weekends back."

"You used the house," Whicher says, "or the boat?"

"I used them both."

Avery clears his throat. "Lance? Do you have one of the sets of keys?"

"Sure." The young man makes a face. "Actually, no. No, I don't. I gave my set to Riley. He was going out to barbecue or something."

Whicher lets his gaze rest on the young man.

"He had a buddy coming in from out of town. He asked me was I planning on being there, I told him no."

"When exactly was this?"

"Last weekend."

Whicher looks back to Avery. "You didn't know?"

Avery blanches. "I know this must seem odd."

"I'll need the man's number," Whicher says. "I'll need to talk to Mister McGuire."

⚜

Heading west on 351, past new built condominiums, the marshal reaches to the dash-mount, presses a key on his phone. Bare fields are leveled for construction—in the distance, the outline of a brand new Walmart Center.

The ringing sound is loud in the cab despite the rolled windows, despite the noise of the road.

The call answers; "Chief Marshal Evans."

"Sir, it's Whicher, I'm over around Buck Creek. I was just with Carl Avery at his offices—at Summerwood Realty."

"How'd you make out?"

"A lot of people have been using that place of his on the lake, it's going to make it damn hard isolating evidence."

"Wait and see what Gail Griffin finds on the boat."

"I'll likely head over and see her this morning," Whicher says. "I'll check in with Lake Patrol next."

"Ortega left," Evans says. "He's headed up there."

A signal cuts in behind the call to Evans. "Sir, I got somebody trying to call me—campus police were going to get back to me, I may need to take this…"

"Go ahead," the chief marshal says.

Whicher clicks to end the call to Evans, then connect the new one.

The line is dead.

He presses the key for the last caller—a name comes up; D. Spano.

Detective Spano from Abilene PD.

Whicher presses to redial.

The call picks up.

"Marshal?"

"You just tried to call me?"

"Yeah." Spano's voice is animated.

"What's going on?"

"We think we might know who the guy is…" Spano says.

"Come again?"

"The DB at the lake—we think we might know, we think we've got the man's name."

Chapter 13

Whicher steers the truck into a gravel run-off at the side of the highway, dust billowing into the open window as he brakes the truck to a halt.

An eighteen-wheeler blows past, blasts out a stab on its air horn.

The marshal picks the notepad from the passenger seat, grabs a pen.

"Hoffman," Detective Spano says, "Elijah Hoffman."

"That's the name?"

"Highway patrol found a vehicle abandoned—just outside of Shreveport."

"Shreveport, Louisiana?"

"A little place outside of there," Spano says, "Greenwood, it's called. The vehicle was outside of a trailer park—the shoulder of the highway in a restricted zone."

"What vehicle?"

"A three-year-old GMC Sierra pickup. The motor was still warm under the hood," Spano says. "The trooper didn't think it could've been there long. It was causing a hazard to other road users—the owner didn't return, the trooper had it towed away. It's registered at an address thirty miles north of Lake Fort Phantom Hill. There's a compound bow on the back seat. With a set of broadhead arrows. Louisiana Patrol called Texas DPS. Texas DPS know about the bow killing, they called down to Abilene PD."

"When was this?"

"The call just came in," Spano says, "I've been trying to track you down. The truck's from just outside of Stamford."

Whicher pushes back in the driver seat, stares through the windshield, thinks of the place—a highway town to the north of Anson at the edge of Jones County.

"Nobody can raise this guy," Spano says, "I called Stamford police, they're sending out a unit, they're going out to the house, it's some kind of a farm."

"Elijah Hoffman?"

"Right."

"You get me the address?"

"Sure…"

The marshal pushes the shifter into drive. "I'm moving, I'm on my way…"

⋏

Ortega is already at the lake site, briefed over the phone, his black F250 parked by a Lake Patrol SUV.

The marshal pulls in fast, leaves the motor running.

Ortega jogs up the dirt lot in his dark blue suit.

Behind him, Whicher sees the search boat dragging the sonar line at the far end of the dam.

Ortega calls out; "You want to stand the boat down?"

"Let 'em run," Whicher answers, "till we're sure."

Ortega reaches his F250, takes out his keys.

"Leave it," Whicher says. "Get in here, you can ride with me."

⚔

Barns and a collection of outbuildings make up the farm—the house itself is offset to one side, fields of low cotton surround it, stretching out to all sides.

Whicher peels from a grit track, runs the Silverado into a hard dirt yard.

A black, police department SUV is already parked up.

No other vehicles visible.

A uniformed police officer steps from the SUV.

The marshal parks in front of an empty barn, shuts off the motor, cracks the door—no sound, no dogs, no animals.

He eyes the farm buildings—red clapboard sides, tin roofs painted white.

Ortega unhooks his seatbelt.

Whicher and the younger marshal step out.

The yard is empty.

No stock, no farm machinery.

The uniformed cop starts toward the Silverado. "Officer Irwin," he says.

"United States Marshals Whicher and Ortega."

The cop nods, hooks a thumb into his duty belt.

Whicher takes in the house; single-story, half faced with stone, half weatherboarding, a steep-pitched roof. He scans the porch, the sash windows.

Irwin eyes him.

"There anybody home?"

"Nobody answering," the officer says.

"You know this guy?" Ortega asks.

"Not really," Irwin says. "Hoffman's a cotton farmer. I think recently divorced."

"Kids, family?"

"None that I know of."

"Where's the wife at?" Whicher says.

Officer Irwin spreads his palms.

"This guy known to y'all—in law enforcement?"

"No, sir, marshal."

"You know him well enough to recognize him?"

"I see him getting gas," Irwin says. "Around town, at the store."

Whicher takes the cell from out of his jacket, lights it up—calls up the photograph of the victim from the lake. "Know him by sight?"

Irwin shifts his weight.

Whicher holds out the phone.

Irwin takes it—studies the photograph of the victim's face. He nods.

"Yeah?" Whicher says.

"I'll say that's Hoffman."

The marshal takes back the cell. "Good enough."

"Are we going in?" Ortega says. "We need a warrant?"

"Homicide investigation, we can go in," Whicher says.

"I tried the front door," Irwin says, "it was locked. I was waiting on y'all arriving before I did anything else. There's a window open around in back."

"Show me."

Irwin leads the way around the side of the house. "Folk out here don't always get to locking up. Farmers an' all, they're in and out all day…" At the back of the house Irwin points toward another door. "Might want to try that."

Whicher takes a pair of black, nitrile gloves from his suit jacket, pulls them on. He steps to the door, tries the handle.

The door opens.

"*US Marshals*," he calls out.

No answer comes back.

"*Anybody home?*"

Stepping inside, into a mud room, he finds a light switch, flips on a fluorescent tube.

No sound is coming from the house.

The marshal moves on into the kitchen, Ortega and Officer Irwin following behind.

"Don't touch nothing," Whicher says, beneath his breath.

The countertops are filled with cans and empty bottles and dishes—the smell of garbage coming from the kitchen trash.

Whicher moves on through an arch—into a living area.

Sagging couches and farmhouse furniture fill the room. On one wall is a giant-screen TV.

Framed photographs line the far wall. A man in a vacation shirt smiles out from one of them—palm fronds behind him, a bruised sunset smearing the sky, a woman at his side.

"That's Hoffman," Irwin says.

Nobody is in the house.

Nobody is on the farm, nobody in any of the outbuildings.

A sallow-skinned man named Wilbert Jarvis, the local chief of police, now stands by a Chrysler Sebring—talking into a two-way radio.

Waiting on Gail Griffin to arrive, Whicher eyes a Ram pickup pulling into the yard. It's battered, covered in dried-on dirt. Heavy-duty tires on its rusted rims.

The driver of the pickup is a woman, wearing a John Deere cap.

The local chief of police clicks out the call on his radio. "Mary-Jo Rucker," he says to the marshal. "Nearest neighbor."

The woman shuts off the motor, peers at the house through the open window of the truck.

She squints at Chief Jarvis, at Whicher and Ortega both in suits.

Officer Irwin, standing alongside the police SUV nods to her.

Pushing open the door, she steps out, heavy-set, around fifty.

Her face is broad, with an outdoor complexion, hair put up beneath the John Deere cap.

She's wearing jeans and a flannel shirt rolled to her elbows. She's smiling, but a hard look is behind her eyes.

Chief Jarvis steps toward her. "Mary-Jo."

"Don't tell me he killed her?" The woman called Mary-Jo swings the door of the truck closed. "Or did she kill him?"

"These here gentlemen are two marshals up from Abilene."

"I saw y'all go by. I was out in one of the fields. I figured something must be going on."

The police chief eyes her. "Elijah was found yesterday at Lake Fort Phantom Hill."

She looks him up and down. "What do you mean found?"

"His body was found, ma'am," Whicher says. "Yesterday morning."

Mary-Jo Rucker stands slack-faced, her mouth part open. She looks around the yard, looks at Officer Irwin.

"We're investigating his death," the marshal says.

"Good God Almighty," the woman says. "Is Jean here?"

"Mrs Hoffman?"

"Is she here?" Rucker turns to Chief Jarvis. "Is she here? Does she know?"

"Nobody's here," Whicher says.

Mary-Jo looks from Whicher to Ortega, then back again. She tips back the John Deere hat.

"How well do you know these folk, ma'am?" Ortega says.

She shoves her hands onto her hips.

"Can you tell us anything about them?"

"She told me she was about ready to leave out. Jean. She told me that, weeks gone…"

"She's not here?" Whicher says. "Not living here?"

"I mean, they were fighting an' all, I knew things had gotten pretty bad…" Mary-Jo stops mid-sentence, shakes her head.

"Are you in touch with her?" Whicher says.

"With Jean? We're neighbors, is all. I'll see 'em time to time, we're not real close."

"You saw us coming by?" Ortega says.

"I was working one of my fields, the irrigation feed at the north reach." She looks at Chief Jarvis.

"You see people coming here?" Ortega says. "People coming and going?"

"Not unless I'm at the top end of my property. My place is miles from here."

Whicher scans the flat fields, the growing cotton. "You have any way of contacting Mrs Hoffman?"

Rucker nods her head at the farmhouse. "I want to speak to Jean, I'll call her up out here."

The marshal turns to the chief of police.

Jarvis shakes his head. "We don't have anything"

Whicher takes off his Resistol hat, runs a hand through his hair. "You tell me anything about the kind of problems they'd been having?"

Mary-Jo breaks out a pack of cigarettes from the pocket of her flannel shirt. Her eyes narrow as she lights up the smoke.

"Any idea why Mister Hoffman might have gone down to Lake Fort Phantom Hill the night before last?"

"That's what he did?"

Whicher studies on her.

She leans against the side of the Ram pickup, takes a pull on the cigarette.

"There be another woman involved?" the marshal says.

"I wouldn't think."

"You have any idea?"

A pained look crosses Mary-Jo's face. "I'd say money."

"Money? They having financial problems?"

"Who ain't?" She flicks the ash on her cigarette. "Most of the land here is leased out. Leased to private contractors."

The marshal looks around the yard. "That why there's nothing here, no gear?"

"It's sold, already," Mary-Jo says. "Some of the growing land, too. That all is part of the problem; selling everything, getting other folk to raise a crop…"

"Lot of farmers lease out," Chief Jarvis says.

"Wilbert. He was selling anything that wasn't nailed down."

⅄

The white, E-Series van passes a barn at the edge of the property. It rolls into view along the fence-line of the grit road.

Pulling into the farmyard it brakes to a halt alongside Whicher's Silverado.

Chief Jarvis and Officer Irwin stand with Mary-Jo Rucker beside her pickup truck.

The driver shuts down the motor in the van, steps out.

"This is Gail Griffin," the marshal says to the chief. "She's a crime scene officer, former detective at APD, she'll be in charge of the house, of the scene here."

Chief Jarvis and Officer Irwin nod.

Griffin opens up the side door of the van. "Where do you want me to start?"

"Wherever you like," Whicher answers.

"Did you call Celine Fernandez?"

"I'll call her."

"Dave Spano says they've got the vehicle?"

Whicher turns to Mary-Jo Rucker; "You know what vehicle Mister Hoffman drives?"

"Sierra pickup," the woman answers.

Whicher nods. Approaches the van with Ortega.

"Boat's not looking great," Griffin says. "There's prints. A lot of prints." She lowers her voice. "But nothing specific to the DB."

"I want to see the truck," the marshal says. "See the place they found it, in Louisiana."

"You're going out there?"

"It's going to take you a while to process anything here."

"We could have the truck shipped down," Ortega says.

"It was found by some trailer park, outside of Shreveport," Whicher says. "I want to see the locale. Somebody might've seen who left it."

"You want me to process the truck, too?" Gail Griffin says.

"I'll have 'em put it on a loader, have it brought back down, just as soon as we're done." Whicher looks at the house, and then at Griffin. "I don't think anything happened in there, but we need to check."

She makes a clucking sound with her tongue. "You know, you never can tell."

She takes down a zip suit from a hook in the truck, starts to take out her gear.

Whicher turns to Mary-Jo Rucker. "The Hoffmans know anybody back in Louisiana?"

The woman pushes off the side of her pickup. "Not that I know."

"Who'd be the best person to talk to about them? They have family around here? Who are their friends?"

"No family, that I know. But we're not real close. She has a couple of sisters."

"How about you chief?"

Jarvis shrugs. "I didn't know them. I could find out who did."

"You think this here's been going on a long time?" Whicher says to the woman. "The problems they had?"

She nods her head. "Years."

"Mister Hoffman have problems with anyone in particular? Could he have owed somebody money?"

"I can't speak to that," she answers. "But it'd be a miracle if he didn't."

⼈

In the diner in the town of Stamford, Whicher finishes up a steak sandwich, Sandro Ortega seated opposite him in a booth, a radio playing behind the counter, sun streaking the glass-front stores across the street.

A handful of truckers and farmers are the only other customers in the place.

Ortega works his way through a plate of chili and beans and corn tortillas.

The marshal watches the few passing cars and trucks.

Calls to Chief Marshal Evans and the Coroner's Officer are both done—the Lake Patrol boat taken off of the search.

"You think anything could've happened back there," Ortega says, "at the house?"

"I think Hoffman died at the lake. Doc Fernandez thinks the same. Judging by the house, I'd say he'd been living alone a while."

The younger marshal nods. "It explains why nobody reported him missing."

Whicher sits back heavy, rests his weight against the back of the booth. "Gail can check out the house, I want to see Hoffman's vehicle. Whoever had it probably killed him."

"That's at least a five-hour drive," Ortega says.

"You'll get used to it."

"What if they were just passing through, en route to someplace else? What if there's no connection with the place?"

"Then why stop?"

The younger marshal stays his fork in mid air, thinking on it. "I don't know."

"Sit on your ass scarfing that chili all day, you ain't going to know."

Ortega cracks a grin, raises the fork to his mouth.

"We'll pick up your truck from the lake," Whicher says, "leave it here at the police department. You might as well ride along with me, save on the gas."

Across the street, a couple stroll along the sidewalk, dressed in jeans and T-shirts, the muscled arm of the man draped around the woman's slim shoulders.

Whicher thinks of an afternoon with Leanne at a Western Art show outside of Stamford; the Texas Cowboy Reunion grounds. Four years gone, was it? Crowds of people milling about a rodeo ring, music playing, people dancing. The second time he'd taken her out. Trying to figure out what he was doing asking her, why she even agreed to go. "I want to know where the wife is at…"

Ortega glances out at the couple in the street. "You want to be the one to tell her?"

CHAPTER 14

Shreveport, Louisiana.

On the outskirts of the city of Shreveport, off the cloverleaf for the interstate and the Inner Loop Expressway, steel fencing surrounds the impound yard—rows of junkers and abandoned automobiles set in malformed lines in the early evening sun.

A Louisiana State Patrol sergeant named Rousseau leads Whicher and Ortega to a three-year-old, red GMC Sierra pickup.

Whicher takes a walk around it—legs stiff from the long ride east on I-20.

The pickup's the extended cab model—nothing in the bed, the vehicle in good condition, new-looking tires.

No marks, no scrapes. Nothing that sticks out, nothing that catches the eye.

The marshal cuts a look at Rousseau; a hefty black guy with a laid-back air. "It was towed away on a parking violation?"

"Trooper decided it was an unsafe location," Rousseau says. "A restricted zone. Blocking off the sight-line to a highway."

"This is yesterday morning?" Whicher says.

"Yes, sir. The vehicle was unlocked, the trooper attending said he waited twenty minutes, nobody came on back. He called the pound, had 'em send out the tow-truck."

"To Greenwood?"

"Greenwood, right."

The marshal pulls on a pair of nitrile gloves. Bending toward the driver window, he peers in. A bow is inside, a compound hunting bow across the back seats. Arrows with it, camo arrows with bright orange vanes.

"It's not locked," Rousseau says.

Whicher looks at him. "Who's been in there?"

"Trooper attending the scene, Trooper Frazier," the sergeant says. "Him and the tow truck guy, I guess."

The marshal opens up the driver's door.

Ortega puts on a pair of gloves, opens the passenger-side door.

Inside is a faint smell of cigarettes.

Nothing is in the front of the cab, nothing on the seats, no obvious sign of anything wrong. No blood, no fresh transfer from the ground.

Whicher squats.

In the footwell, beneath the driver's seat is a folding knife. Hashed metal side-grips, the finish a dull black. "Knife on the floor," he says to Ortega.

The younger marshal leans into the cab to where he can see it.

"Frazier said there was a knife," Rousseau says.

"What do you think?" Whicher says. "Three-inch blade? Bushcraft knife?"

"Are we going to open it?" Ortega says.

"Leave it for Gail." Whicher gestures toward the rear of the cab. "Kind of goes along with the bow, the arrows an' all."

He stands, opens up the rear door. Stares at the compound bow on the seat.

The grip and the limbs are painted a camo pattern—multiple cables, cams and pulleys are threaded between them. The arrows are fitted with triple-blade broadheads.

Same arrows, the same heads.

Ortega opens up the rear door on the passenger side. Glances at Whicher over the roof of the cab, a smile, now, at his mouth. "There have to be prints…"

Whicher turns to Sergeant Rousseau. "We'll take this."

"You want to take possession?"

"We got a murder weapon right here, the truck belongs to the victim. Marshals Service will pick up the tab."

"You want it, you got it."

"Can you show us out to Greenwood, where this all was found?"

Rousseau nods. "I'll call Trooper Frazier, have him meet us there."

⁂

The air is pumped with heat, the sky filled with fattened, white cloud. Leaves of live oak and cottonwood and hickory hang limp from the branches of the roadside woods. Up ahead, the town of Greenwood shows a handful of aging buildings; stores and businesses and houses set along the highway among the overhang of trees.

The trailer park at the side of the road is cluttered—old cars and battered trucks among the single and double-wide units.

Whicher follows Sergeant Rousseau's cruiser through a gateway into the gravel turnaround at the entrance to the site.

A second cruiser is already parked—its driver, a thin-limbed officer, standing in the shade of a bald cypress tree.

Alongside the trooper is a woman in a denim skirt and a cotton top, her graying hair cut short.

The marshal slows, parks at the side of a deserted-looking site-office, a trailer unit up on cinder blocks.

Ortega gazes out through the passenger window.

"What do you think?" Whicher says. "Why leave the truck at the side of the road, here?"

The younger marshal doesn't reply.

Sergeant Rousseau steps from his cruiser, approaches the trooper waiting with the woman.

Whicher cuts the motor on the Chevy. Steps out into sweltering heat.

A group of women sit out on plastic garden chairs, watching. Drinking from soda cans and bottles of beer.

Ortega follows the marshal across a gravel lot.

"This is Trooper Frazier," Sergeant Rousseau says.

The trooper touches a finger to the brim of his Campaign

hat. "This lady is a resident here—she says she saw the driver of the truck."

Whicher looks from the trooper to the woman. "Ma'am? You think you saw him?"

"According to the lady," Trooper Frazier says, "the driver called on somebody with a trailer here."

The woman looks at Whicher. She looks across at the group of seated women. "I was sitting out, I saw the officer here come in." She gestures at Trooper Frazier. "I was here yesterday, when they towed the truck. It was parked right on over there…" She points at a spot on the highway, by the trailer park entrance. "The driver came on in, he got to looking around some. He headed up toward the row in back."

"Can you describe him, ma'am?" Ortega says.

"White guy in a leather vest. Jeans. Kind of slick. He had his hair all pushed back, black hair, like a greaser." She runs a hand through her own hair, mimicking the look. "Kind of full of himself," she says. "Bare arms, a lot of muscles."

"What kind of age?" Whicher says.

"Around thirty."

The marshal studies her. "Anything else?"

"He was kind of good-looking."

"You see where he went?"

Officer Frazier cuts in; "He called on a young woman here, named Candy Brolin…"

"I talked to Candy's neighbor," the woman says. "She saw the guy back there with her."

"This lady here now?" Whicher says.

"I just got here," Frazier says. "I was waiting on you all to arrive."

"What time was this yesterday?" Ortega says.

"Around ten," the woman answers.

Frazier nods. "I called the pound for the truck at ten-twenty-five."

Sergeant Rousseau addresses the woman. "Ma'am? You want to show us this lady's trailer?"

The woman leads the way past the un-manned site office—along a track of dirt and sand and fallen pine needles.

She slows at a numbered mailbox in front of a double-wide trailer.

"This it?" Sergeant Rousseau says.

The woman nods. Takes a pace to the side.

Whicher takes out his marshals badge and ID—steps forward, knocks on the door.

Three trailers along the row, a couple sit out in folding chairs, a woman in a straw sun hat, a man in a New Orleans Saints jersey of white and gold, a German Shepherd laying at his feet.

A passing kid on a cycle stops, puts a foot on the ground to stare at the group of four men.

The door to the trailer opens—a young woman with bleach-blonde hair looks out. Last night's make-up is smudged around her eyes.

She's wearing track pants, a crop top, a lit cigarette trails from her hand.

Whicher holds out his badge.

The young woman's face is blank.

"Candy Brolin?"

She nods.

"US Marshals Service, ma'am."

The young woman named Candy takes a drag on the cigarette—blows smoke out the side of her mouth.

"You have a man call in here yesterday morning? A man wearing a leather vest and jeans?"

She doesn't answer. A thought passes behind her eyes.

"Ma'am?"

"Yeah. I guess."

"Could you tell me his name?"

"I don't know," Candy says, "I don't know him. He was looking for Grady."

"You don't know him?"

"Grady who?" Ortega says.

She looks from one to another of the men at her door—two in uniform, two dressed in suits. "Grady," she says. She folds her arms. "A friend of mine."

"What kind of a friend?" Whicher says.

She picks at a strap on her crop top. "Boyfriend."

"Ma'am," Ortega says. "Did this man tell you his name?"

The young woman looks off at the neighboring couple now talking with the woman in the denim skirt. "What's going on?"

"This here's a serious matter," Whicher says. "Did the man tell you his name?"

"Ray," she says.

The marshal looks at her.

"Just Ray?" Ortega says.

"He said his name was Ray, he wanted Grady, is all. I told him Grady wasn't here."

"Grady?" Ortega repeats.

"Grady Pearce."

Whicher takes out his notepad, writes down the name. He looks at Sergeant Rousseau and Trooper Frazier, wondering if either know him.

Both the officers shrug.

"You ever see this man before?" Ortega says.

Candy takes a hit on the cigarette. "No. And if Grady did something, it's on him, it all don't have a thing to do with me…"

Whicher looks at her. "What'd he say to you, this man?"

She stares back, resentment in her eyes now, replacing the alarm. "He was looking for Grady, said he was a buddy an' all. I told him Grady wasn't here." She takes another drag on the cigarette. Her face hardens. "This place is my place. I thought maybe Grady owed him money. He said he was driving back from Texas, stopping by. He said he was headed down to Cajun country."

Ortega looks at her. "He tell you where?"

She pushes up her chest. "No."

"He tell you anything else?"

"He said, I ever felt like visiting, he could show me a real good time."

The marshal studies on her. "How long was he here?"

"I don't know."

"Ten minutes? Twenty?"

"I guess," she says. "Something like that."

"Looking for a friend of yours? Grady Pearce?"

"I ain't seen Grady in a week."

"Have you talked to him?" Whicher says.

She shakes her head.

"This boyfriend have an address?" Ortega says.

"He's out in Shreveport," she says.

Sergeant Rousseau speaks, "Where in Shreveport?"

"Off of I-20. By the oil refinery."

"Calumet?" Rousseau says.

"Right. Up from there. On Desoto."

"That's Exit 14," Trooper Frazier says. "Queensborough,"

"He got a house," Rousseau says, "this boy? An apartment?"

"He's got a house he rents."

"What's he do?" Whicher says.

"He works the door, a couple clubs."

"He have a car?"

She looks at him. "Yeah."

"What kind?"

"I don't know."

"You know the plate?"

She bugs hers eyes. "It's blue. It's kind of fancy."

"I'll need the house number," the marshal says. "And his phone. I'll need to call him."

Her eyes slide away, then come back.

"I'm running a serious crime investigation, ma'am. This man that was here yesterday—he turned up in a truck belonging to the victim of a homicide."

"You know your boyfriend's date of birth?" Sergeant Rousseau says. "We're going to need that, too."

⚔

Back at the entrance to the trailer park in the Silverado, Sergeant Rousseau sits in his cruiser with Trooper Frazier, running Pearce's details through the terminal in Rousseau's car.

Whicher tries the cell phone number for Grady Pearce. It rings briefly—clicks through to voicemail.

"Yo, this is Grady…leave a message."

The voice southern, brusque.

The marshal stares out of the open door of the truck at Sandro Ortega standing beneath a live oak at the edge of the gravel turnaround—a man is approaching—the man in the Saints jersey; Candy Brolin's near neighbor.

Whicher clicks out the call to Pearce, climbs from his truck.

"Candy wouldn't hurt nobody," the man in the Saints jersey calls over. "She ain't a bad person."

"You know her?" Whicher says.

"She's been out here two years. She came out after Katrina, she was living back in New Orleans. She lost her place, her job, her car, about everything—ended up here. She works in Greenwood, over at the mini-mart. She don't run with the right folk, is all."

"What kind of folk?" Ortega says to the man.

"That boyfriend of hers, I know he's done some jail time. He runs with the wrong-ass crowd."

Whicher eyes the man. "You know what he was in jail for?"

"Handling stolen property, fighting—he's a big ol' guy, you don't want to mess."

"Have you seen Mister Pearce here, lately?" Ortega says.

"No, sir."

"The feller that called on Ms. Brolin yesterday?" Whicher says. "How about him, have you seen him before?"

"No, sir. Never have."

"Would you recognize him," Ortega says, "if you saw him again?"

"I guess so. I guess I would."

"He speak to you?" Whicher says.

"He never said nothing to me, he was talking with Candy, is all. Outside her trailer."

"Did he go on in?"

"No, sir. He never went in."

Across the lot, Sergeant Rousseau is out of the cruiser.

"Take the gentleman's details," Whicher says to Ortega, "we'll need a witness statement."

"It's him you need to be talking with," the man says, "Grady Pearce. He drives a Plymouth Road Runner. Kind of chopped, kind of cut down low..."

"I'll be sure to do that." The marshal tips his hat. Crosses the lot to Rousseau and Officer Frazier.

"We ran Pearce's name," the sergeant says, "we got his address on Desoto, a driver's license picture, take a look..."

Whicher leans into the air conditioned cruiser. On a swivel mount between the front seats is a laptop computer terminal—the screen showing a heavy-looking caucasian male. Cropped hair, square face, tattoos on his neck. His eyes are deep set, his face lined. "Reckon we'll take a ride on into Shreveport. See if we can't find the feller. He's not answering his phone."

"That address," Rousseau says, "in Queensborough, some of that area can be pretty rough. Pass the airport, it's a couple of more miles. Get off at 14, you'll see the oil refinery. Head down on Midway a couple of blocks, make a left, you'll find it. You need back up? You want us to ride along?"

Whicher shakes his head. "I don't want the guy to see us coming."

Chapter 15

Shreveport, La.

Magnolia and pine and live oak line the crumbling residential street. Whicher cruises the block, window down, scanning the small wooden houses on grass plots.

Smokestacks of the oil refinery belch out a smell of sulphur into the humid air.

On a corner plot is a tan, painted clapboard house—a blue Plymouth Road Runner parked in back on a double strip of cement.

The marshal stops in the shade of a tall oak at the curb before an intersection.

Ortega sits forward in the passenger seat.

Whicher rolls the window closed, shuts off the motor, pops the door.

At the rear of the house, trees shade the yard, the perimeter fence is falling down.

Both men step out.

"Head around back," Whicher says, "in case he runs."

Ortega looks at him. "Why would he run?"

"If his girlfriend called."

The younger marshal nods, unfastens the top button of his shirt, loosens the neck-tie at his collar.

He crosses over the street, tracks down the side of an uncut grass verge.

Whicher moves along a weed-strewn path beneath the trees.

He checks up and down the street—three blocks up is the interstate—down at the other end, the buildings of the oil refinery.

He eyes the house, eyes the Road Runner sitting in the yard. Taps the bulge of the Ruger in the shoulder-holster. Thinks of the image in the driver's license picture—the face of Grady Pearce.

Reaching the front door of the house, he stops.

No noise is coming from inside, no TV—no sound, no voices.

He raps on the door, listens.

"*US Marshal,*" he calls out.

The house is silent, no lights showing, no windows are open.

He knocks again, hard. "*US Marshals, anybody home?*"

He tries the door. It's locked.

Stepping away, he crosses the yard to where he can see down the side of the house.

The only sound is traffic rumbling on the interstate.

In back, Sandro Ortega is standing, waiting.

"Anything?" Whicher says.

The younger marshal shakes his head.

"Guess the man ain't home."

Ortega nods at the Plymouth. "Car's here."

Whicher takes out his phone, tries the number for Pearce again.

It clicks straight to voicemail. He puts away the phone, stares at the house.

"What do you want to do?" Ortega says.

The marshal pulls down the brim of the Resistol. "Grady Pearce is the best lead we got. This guy Hoffman was killed, some feller shows up next morning in Louisiana driving the man's truck? Asking for Pearce?" He motions for Ortega to follow him back along the side of the house.

Ortega jogs ahead to the front door, hammers on it.

"Long ways from here to that cotton farm," Whicher says, "Hoffman's farm."

The younger marshal peers in at the front window. "You think of any connection?" He shouts out; "*Anybody home?*"

Across the street a black woman is at the edge of a yard. She twists a dish rag between her hands, a frown on her face.

"US Marshals Service, ma'am." Whicher takes out his badge.

"Y'all looking for him, you?"

"Grady Pearce," Whicher says. "You know him, have you seen him?"

Ortega steps away from the front door.

"He was here this morning."

"You saw him this morning?" Whicher says.

The woman nods.

"You know where he might be?"

"What he do?"

"We need to talk to him."

"His car's still here, ma'am," Ortega says. "Does he have another car?"

"He'll get a ride some days," she says.

"You know where?"

"He works a job at the casino. Over the river. In Bossier City."

"The casino?" Whicher says. "You know what it's called?"

She shrugs, shakes her head. "It's over the river, my husband tol' me."

"Do you know Mister Pearce?"

"He ain't lived here but six months. Why would I know him? He ain't hardly here." The woman turns her back, walks away, lets the dish rag hang loose.

⋏

A five mile trip across the city of Shreveport—three phone calls along the way. Evening light is starting to fall along the riverside hotels and casinos across the Red River Bridge in Bossier City.

Whicher pulls the Silverado into an employee-only lot.

A big-wheeled riverboat is just visible at the end of a hotel jetty.

At the edge of the lot is a single-story office with smoked glass windows. A black man dressed in slacks and a zip-front navy jacket emerges from it.

The marshal climbs from the truck, shows his badge and ID.

"Chester Thompson," the man says, "I head up security here. You spoke to my assistant on the phone?"

"Yes, sir. Regarding an employee of yours, a Grady Pearce?"

"His shift ended," Thompson says, "he's not here. Is there some kind of problem?"

Ortega steps from the passenger side of the truck. "We just need to speak to him."

"You mind if I ask what for?"

Whicher takes in the multi-floored concrete parking garages, the facades of hotels against the city skyline. "I'm running a homicide investigation, sir. Mister Pearce may have encountered a suspect I'm trying to locate."

Thompson looks into the marshal's face.

"What's Mister Pearce do here?" Ortega asks.

"General security on the parking lots," Thompson says. "Monitoring cameras, making regular tours. He works the doors for us some nights. Look, if he's in some kind of trouble, I'd need to know—that could be a problem for us. He's only part-time, he's only been with us a few months."

Whicher looks at the man.

"He's on parole," Thompson says. "We work with the parole board here in the city. Try to place some of their people. But any problems, I'm obliged to report it."

"You know why he's on parole?"

"He got a year's sentence. Third-degree assault."

"At this point we just want to talk with him," Whicher

says. "When y'all expect him in again?"

"Tomorrow," Thompson says. "He works several other jobs."

"You know where?"

The man shakes his head. "I can give you his address?"

"We have an address over the river," Whicher says. "Over in Shreveport."

"We send his paycheck to an address in Greenwood," Thompson says, surprise showing in his face. "Every couple of weeks. So far as I know..."

⋏

The fried chicken restaurant is busy with folks in ball caps and shorts and T-shirts and ripped jeans. Whicher sits with Ortega along a wall at the back, elbows of their suits on the vinyl-topped table, trays before them, filled with chicken strips, crinkle fries and sides.

The marshal watches the street, almost dark now—passing cars and trucks only visible by their lights.

Ortega eats. Chugs on a cup of crushed ice and lemonade.

"Ten o'clock yesterday morning," Whicher says to him. "The time this guy in the leather vest showed up in Greenwood?"

The younger marshal nods.

"Doc Fernandez thinks TOD on Hoffman was around midnight. It's a five or six hour ride out here. So the guy must've set out no later than four in the morning, to be here in Hoffman's truck."

"If he killed Hoffman around midnight," Ortega says, "why wait four hours?"

Whicher dips a chicken strip into hot sauce, loads up a forkful of slaw. "Maybe he didn't wait. Maybe he lit out, maybe he stopped someplace else before he arrived."

"How about this Grady Pearce?" Ortega says. "Why you think he tells folk he lives in Greenwood?"

"Hard to say."

The younger marshal checks his watch. "I ought to call Sofia…"

"Your wife?"

Ortega nods.

Whicher thinks of Leanne at the house in Wylie. "Call her after we get done here. We can stop in Queensborough again, check Pearce's house."

The younger marshal bites into a piece of Texas toast, the butter and garlic liquid on his hands. "You think he could be back there?"

"If he ain't, we'll swing by the trailer park in Greenwood. If no-one's there, we'll head for home, I'll have the Shreveport Marshals office try to find him."

"You think Candy Brolin could've told Pearce we're looking for him?"

The marshal scowls, eats the food.

"That bother you?" Ortega says. "You think he could run?"

Whicher watches headlights moving on the street beyond the restaurant window. "If he's accessory to murder," he says, "he'll run."

Chapter 16

Midway Avenue in Queensborough is full dark, now—an edge in the city air with the onset of night.

Whicher makes a left, away from the lights of the refinery, into dark blocks of tumble-down houses, derelict lots and trees.

Groups of young black men watch from the stoops of shacks as the Silverado rolls by.

The few street lamps throw scattered shadows on empty sidewalks and yards.

Turning onto Desoto, overhanging trees mask the view of the houses. At Pearce's place, the Road Runner is still parked out in back.

Whicher steers along the narrowing street.

No lights show in the house.

He pulls in at the curb, takes the notepad from his jacket—writes a couple of lines, writes his cell phone number, rips out the page. "If he ain't home I'll put this under the door."

Ortega looks at him.

"Word to call me."

The marshal shuts off the motor, steps from the truck into the deserted street.

The smell of the refinery hits him, music is playing somewhere down on the block.

He crosses the front yard of Pearce's house—at the door, he folds the note, stops.

Light is coming from around a gap in a roll-down blind on the window.

Whicher moves to it, puts his eye to the pane of glass.

A light is on—but he can't see inside the room.

He turns back toward the Silverado—Ortega's already out of the truck.

The younger marshal clips along the street, comes up into the yard.

"Light on in there," the marshal says.

"You want me to watch around back?"

Nothing is coming from the house, there's just a rumble from the interstate.

"Maybe he just left a light on," Whicher says. "But go ahead."

Ortega hustles to the side of the house.

Whicher raps the dirty white paint of the door.

"*US Marshals…*" He steps away.

A car is rolling down the street—a rusted, eighties model Dodge Charger.

Three young black men inside, staring straight out.

Ortega makes a sudden move, shouts; "*US Marshals Service—stop…*" He runs for the back of the property.

Whicher sprints after him along the side of the house.

A man is disappearing into grass and weeds in an adjacent lot.

Ortega runs after him.

The marshal doubles along the road to the corner with the next street—sees the man bust out of the lot, recognizes Grady Pearce from his driver's license photo.

Ortega pushes through the overgrown vegetation further down the street.

Pearce stares, holds his arms out by his sides.

The Dodge Charger turns into the roadway, cruising, now; looking for trouble.

Whicher cuts a look in the direction of the car, sees the faces of the three men, lets the suit jacket fall open, exposing the holstered Glock at his hip.

The men in the car stare back, dead-eyed.

The sedan moves away slowly up the street.

"Friends of yours?" Ortega says to Pearce.

The man doesn't reply.

Whicher walks forward, his face shaded from a streetlamp by the brim of his hat. "US Marshals Service." He holds out his badge. "You and me need to talk Mister Pearce."

"What for?"

"About yesterday."

"What about it?"

"Somebody came looking for you at your girlfriend's place."

Sandro Ortega moves within a few feet of the big man.

"I wasn't there," Pearce says.

"You're on parole," the marshal says. "You get in any kind of trouble, your ass is headed back in the can."

Pearce stares at him. "I didn't do a damn thing."

The marshal looks toward the house. "Just need to talk to you."

The man bunches his fists.

"You want to let us step inside? Or we can haul your ass downtown," Whicher says, "find a police cell, call a lawyer. Call your parole officer…"

"Son of a bitch…" Pearce stomps by the marshal without a word, moving up toward the house.

Ortega looks at Whicher, the marshal gestures to follow.

At the back of the house, Pearce kicks open the door.

A dim rectangle of light shows a filthy kitchen.

"Think it's okay," Ortega says, "to go in there? You don't want to take him downtown?"

"I need him talking. He gets a lawyer, he don't say squat."

At the back door the two men hesitate, glance around the squalid interior.

Whicher's hand drifts toward the Glock, he unfastens the retaining strap, "Just in case I got this wrong…"

"You want to shut the goddamn door?" Pearce calls out. He stands at the entrance to a room at the end of the hall.

Ortega pushes the kitchen door closed.

Whicher follows Pearce into a living room filled with thrift store furniture, an old TV, a low table stacked with empty soda cans.

Pearce rubs a hand over his arm, shakes his head at the

room. "Straight-time," he says. "This all is what you get."

"That why you give out your address as Greenwood?" Whicher says.

"It's so people can't find me. People I can't be around."

"Like the man asking for you yesterday?"

"Like that son of a bitch," Pearce says, "yeah."

Ortega, blocks the doorway to the room. "What's his name?"

Whicher takes out the notepad.

Pearce glares at the threadbare carpet. "Ray Dubois. Whatever he did, it don't have a damn thing to do with me. He turned up looking for me, is all."

"What was he doing out at your girlfriend's place?" Ortega says.

"I told him that's where I lived. I knew him a few years back. Then he was in jail the same time I was. I ain't seen him since I got out." Pearce blows out his cheeks, looks from one marshal to the other. His shoulders slump. "Candy said this guy came by looking for me, she gave him my number. She don't want me telling folk I live there, she told me to take care of my own shit…"

"This guy called you?" Whicher says.

"He told me he needed a ride. He just said to burn rubber." Pearce sits down on a battered leatherette couch. He stares at the wall. "Somebody asks, you got to help a brother. All I did was drive on over there. He said he was in a spot, he needed a ride…"

"He tell you why?" The marshal studies him.

"He was driving back from Texas, headed east, he said.

Driving all night, coming into Shreveport, he wanted to see me."

"You didn't know he'd be coming?" Ortega says.

"Swear to God. I wouldn't have seen him, the man's a whack-job."

Whicher taps a pen on the notepad.

"One of them prepper types," Pearce says.

"A prepper?"

"Lives-off-of-the land, into all that shit. Into preparing—for when it all breaks down. End of the world, all the lights go out."

The marshal nods.

"He left his truck outside the trailer park, said he didn't want nobody seeing him. The time he found Candy's trailer, got to speaking with her an' all, he said he went on back to his truck, this highway cop's parked at the side of the road looking at it. He couldn't go back with the cop there, he said. He wouldn't tell me why."

"Then what?" Ortega says.

"I guess I gave him a ride."

"Where to?"

"Lake Charles."

Whicher says, "That's a long damn way from here."

"Three hours. I dropped him short. Some place called Moss Bluff."

"What's the guy's full name?" Whicher says.

"Just Ray, Ray Dubois. A lot of folk call him Cajun Ray."

"Why's that?"

Pearce sniffs, runs his arm beneath his nose. "The hell would I know?"

"Why was he inside?"

"Larceny. He got less than a year."

Whicher looks at him.

"All I know is what I told you." Pearce runs the flats of his hands against his temples. "I knew him years back. Alright? The guy's a goddamn freak. He was caught up in Rita, two years gone, Hurricane Rita, nearly drowned, he said. He was living out one of the bayous…"

"Which one?"

"Snake. Something like that…"

"Snake?"

Pearce shrugs.

"He like to hunt?" Whicher says. "Fish? Live off the land?"

The man nods.

"He know how to use a bow?"

"All of that crap he knows, that's what he does."

"And you took him to where he lives?"

"Near there," Pearce says. "He had me stop before we got real close. Said he'd call one of his prepper-ass buddies to come get him—a bunch of 'em live out on the bayou, back in the woods."

"Why come looking for you in the first place?" Whicher says. "How come he stopped in Greenwood?"

Pearce glares at him.

"We'll take this downtown, you hold out on me…"

"I know people." Pearce corrects himself; "*Used* to know people."

"What's that mean?"

The big man shakes his head. "He was looking for somebody to take the truck—get rid of it."

"You fence automobiles?"

"I know people that buy 'em, sell 'em. I don't do that shit no more."

"He came by wanting you to take the truck?"

"I guess."

"And he needed a ride?"

"The goddamn cops showed up…"

"So you gave him a ride out to Lake Charles?"

"All I did."

"I want the exact place you left him," Whicher says. "And everything you got on Ray Dubois."

⋏

Back outside in Pearce's front yard, Whicher stands in the dark with Ortega.

"Call your wife."

Ortega looks at him. "Sofia?"

"Tell her you won't be back tonight."

The younger marshal gives a slight nod, keeps his face neutral.

"We need to head south. See if we can pick up the trail on this guy, Dubois."

Ortega takes out the phone from the pocket of his dark blue suit.

"Blame it on me," Whicher says.

The younger marshal flashes him a grin.

Whicher walks to the Silverado, opens up, climbs inside.

He takes out his phone, presses on a key to dial. Stares out of the windshield along the deserted street.

The call answers.

"Leanne?"

"Where are you?"

"Out in Shreveport," he says, "Louisiana. Somebody found the DB's vehicle, a truck, way out here."

He hears his wife's short breath at the end of the line.

"In Louisiana?" she says.

"Victim's a cotton farmer."

"You know already?"

"Out of Stamford," Whicher says. "I went out to his place. He's divorced, no kids. No sign of the wife. His truck was found just outside of Shreveport. Murder weapon in the back."

"Really?"

"I'm having the truck shipped back from the impound yard here."

"You're moving pretty fast."

"So far," Whicher says. "We need to head down into southern Louisiana, I'm with Ortega, we've got a lead. We have a suspect, now, a name."

"You're not coming home?"

"We'll get a couple rooms." The marshal pulls himself upright on the steering wheel. "How's Lori?"

"She's alright."

He hears the note in his wife's voice. "Is everything okay?"

She says, "I guess."

"She go swimming?"

"Lori? For a while," Leanne says. "Before it got too hot."

"She gets that from you; swimming. I never had a pool."

"Huh. You had a horse."

Whicher nods to himself. "Think she'd like that?"

"She's only three."

The marshal watches shadows beyond a street lamp along the block. "Guess you're right. So, you okay?"

"We're okay."

"Listen, I'll call in the morning. We're headed down to Lake Charles tonight. I'll check in with local law enforcement, the parish sheriff there. Run this guy through the system."

"Alright."

"We have a guy we know was in the victim's truck. We need to run him down, longer he's loose, the more likely he is to stay that way."

"Just come back in one piece…"

The marshal finishes up the call.

He takes a last look at Grady Pearce's house on Desoto. Pushes open the door of the truck.

"C'mon," he calls to Ortega.

The younger marshal waves a hand back.

"Let's move out. Let's roll."

CHAPTER 17

Jefferson Davis Parish, Louisiana.

Four hours later at a window seat in the riverside restaurant, Whicher scans the low, thick woods bordering the highway east of Moss Bluff. Just a mile or so into bayou country, the Louisiana land is dark, remote, a pole lamp throwing weak light on the Silverado down the road outside of an old motel.

On the restaurant table are dishes of crawfish and gumbo and cornbread and maque choux.

A band plays on a makeshift riser, couples starting to fill up a small dance floor.

Three hours south of Shreveport on I-49 and then the highway west of Natchitoches. Three hours on top of the drive out from Texas. Enough road for one day.

The marshal sips a cold beer, listens to the music, the drawled Cajun words of the band's singer.

Elijah Hoffman's GMC Sierra would be back in Texas for Gail Griffin to process in the morning. She'd check for fingerprints, for DNA, she could check out the knife they found in the footwell.

Ray Dubois had served time in jail, there'd be a record; prints. She'd find something of the man if he'd been in it.

Ortega takes a forkful of boiled crawfish, raises his glass of beer—clinks it against the side of Whicher's glass.

The marshal looks at him.

"Day two," Ortega says.

"And?"

"We have an ID on an unknown homicide victim. Plus a prime suspect. Plus the murder weapon. Plus the likely locale of the offender."

The marshal breaks off a piece of cornbread, dips it into the maque choux. "Maybe."

"Why come here unless you think we can find him?"

"I aim to find him."

Ortega takes a pull at the glass of beer.

"If the guy's into preparedness," Whicher says, "he might've upped and run. That's part of the deal, ain't it? If the shit hits the fan?"

The younger marshal thinks it over.

"He screwed up, he knows that," Whicher says. "Cops towing away Hoffman's truck. If he's got some place he was planning on going, he might've gone already, we might have a hard time finding it."

"How about Pearce?" Ortega says. "You believe him? You believe what he said?"

Whicher picks up a spoon, takes one of two bowls of gumbo. "Dubois turned up at his girlfriend's place, we got witnesses to that. We know Pearce gives out his address as Greenwood. If he'd wanted to see Dubois, why meet there, like that?"

Ortega nods.

Out on the dance floor, couples spin and turn, the band move from one number to another, barely pausing, calling out just the name of the song.

"How's your wife liking it?" Whicher says. "Two days in and you've hardly seen her."

"It's not so different from San Angelo PD," Ortega says. "I worked swing-shift, the graveyard shift…"

"How about your girls?" Whicher says, "your daughters?"

"Six-year-old can give me a hard time. The three-year-old not so much."

Whicher takes some sweet potato and okra.

"Alicia and Amelia," Ortega says.

"Six years old, she understand what you do?"

"She knows I'm some kind of cop." Ortega takes another forkful of boiled crawfish, shrugs. "How about you? You have a daughter?"

"Lori," Whicher says. He sips on his beer. "She's just three."

"You talk to her? When you're not coming home, times like this?"

"Northern district of the marshals office covers half the state," Whicher says. "Lot of times you end up on the road, hundreds of miles from home, you might be anyplace. She's usually asleep. This case with Hoffman is the first I've worked around Abilene."

"We're five hundred miles away on a bayou in Louisiana," Ortega says.

"I noticed that." Whicher nods. "Just so long as you know what you're getting into."

"I hear you."

"We'll talk with local LE in the morning, they ought to have an eye on the back woods, folk living out here."

"If we find him, do we arrest him?"

"If his prints are in Hoffman's truck."

A waitress approaches a nearby table with an order of cocktails and beers, stage lights above the band illuminating her flame-red hair.

She sets down the glasses from her tray, Whicher signals to her.

She crosses to the table. "I get you gentlemen somethin'?"

"You want another one?" Whicher says to Ortega.

"If you do."

"Two more beers."

"Comin' right up."

"Ma'am, I ask you something?"

She looks at him.

"You know of a bayou around here name of—'snake'?"

"Bayou Serpent?" she says.

"Serpent?"

"Right on up the river."

"Is it close to here?"

"It's not real far."

"You know it, are you local?" Whicher glances over at Ortega.

The waitress gives a look. "Why you want to know?"

"Thinking of doing a little fishing."

She brushes a strand of red hair behind her ear. "You can fish right off of the end of the pier, honey. Right here."

"You know a feller named Ray Dubois?" Whicher says. "Supposed to live around there someplace..."

The waitress looks toward the back of the room, to the bar counter. "There's some camps out there, a couple of places, not so many folk living there. Let me get you those drinks."

She steps away across the room, past the dance floor, toward the bar in back.

A group of men seated on stools watch her. They eye the marshal and Ortega in turn. They're dressed in band T-s and camo pants, ripped shirts and jeans, their hair all styles—long and matted, half-shaved, clumped into spikes.

"Bayou Serpent?" Ortega says.

"Sounds like it could be the place," Whicher answers.

"You think she knows Dubois?"

The marshal shrugs.

Ortega looks down at the jacket of the suit he's wearing. "I guess we look a little out of place..."

The waitress brings back two glasses of beer.

"Ma'am?" Whicher says. "If a feller was looking to do a little bow-hunting, you know anyplace he could do that?"

She sets down the drinks.

"Or anybody that could take him out, show him around?"

She gestures at the men seated at the bar in back. "You

want to head into the swamp there's some boys back there you could try."

She moves away, to another table of diners.

On stage, the band switches tempo again—to a tune in waltz-time, the accordion player stepping forward under the lights.

"What do you think Elijah Hoffman has to do with any of this?" Ortega says.

"We'll dig into Hoffman's background," Whicher answers. "Find out what was going on in his life."

"You think Dubois is our killer?"

"How else would he have the truck?"

"How about if he was just the driver?"

"With the bow and the arrows in back?" Whicher watches the couples dancing, swaying. Across the room, the waitress talks to one of the men seated at the bar.

Three of them rise, troop out through a door to the side.

"I went to see Carl Avery this morning," the marshal says.

Ortega slides the other bowl of gumbo across the table.

"Turns out the last person to use Avery's place on the lake was a guy named Riley McGuire. He was there the weekend just gone. He had keys, a set of keys, Avery has a few of 'em, he gives 'em out to anyone who wants to go out and stay. McGuire was there at Summerwood this morning, he works for Avery. He didn't look real pleased to see me."

Ortega thinks about it.

"Somebody took that boat up there to where they found

Hoffman," Whicher says. "And somebody must have made sure it could be taken."

⚔

Midnight is fast approaching on the short length of road back toward the old motel.

The band plays on at the riverside restaurant. Whicher and Ortega walk the deserted two-lane in the dark.

Music drifts on the still air beneath the trees. Ahead, at a rural intersection, a scattering of cars and pickups are parked—some by the motel, a few at an aging commercial strip; a forties building with a covered walkway, beneath its shade an ice-cream parlor, a bait shop and outdoor supply.

A group of four men are in one of the lots—drinking from cans of beer, talking, smoking, leaning on two battered pickup trucks.

"What time you think folk turn in around here?" Ortega says.

Whicher looks at him.

"Maybe I'll put in for a transfer."

"To Louisiana?" Whicher says.

"Could do worse."

The marshal thinks of late-night bar-trawls—years gone, now, overseas in the army.

He pulls out two sets of keys from his jacket, tosses one to Ortega. "You want to go open up your room, I'll move the truck around."

Leaving the ribbon of road, the marshal crosses a gravel lot.

Ortega continues toward the front of the motel.

Whicher opens up the Silverado, climbs inside.

Sitting up behind the wheel, he looks out over the hood of the truck.

The men drinking at the pickups have moved—they're walking toward Ortega.

They're dressed in jeans and work shirts and boots, their arms held out at their sides.

The marshal climbs back out of the truck.

One of the men steps to Ortega, the other three fan out.

Whicher curses beneath his breath, swings the truck door shut.

The man at the front of the group is strong-looking—big, sporting an unkept beard. Beneath his ball cap, long dark hair is spilling out. Two of the others are wiry—one of them shaven-headed, in a check-shirt—the other in a tank top and fishing hat.

A fourth man is dressed in a denim shirt, his hair a mess of spikes, a small plait at the side of his face—Whicher recognizes him from the bar.

The bearded man juts his chin, says something to Ortega.

The younger marshal stands his ground, feet apart.

Whicher calls over; "*What's going on?*"

All four of the men turn toward him—Whicher notices the guy from the bar say something to the bearded man out front.

The marshal closes down the space in the lot, feels a lick of adrenaline.

The bearded man stares. "Where you think you're going?"

"Y'all back the hell up," Whicher says.

The spike-haired guy from the bar takes a step to the side.

Ortega glances at Whicher.

"I don't like suited pricks," the bearded man says.

"We're going to our rooms," the marshal says. "Head on back to your trucks."

"I said; I don't like suited pricks—like the two of you."

Whicher eyes the guy from the bar. "What's going on?"

The man doesn't answer.

"You call your buddies 'cause we ask about the fishing?"

"You or anybody else," the bearded man says, "come out here, you'll get the same thing."

"The hell're you talking about?"

"Oil man. Right?"

Whicher shakes his head.

The bald guy in the check shirt cuts in; "They all look the way you do."

Ortega takes a pace forward.

The bearded man starts to square up. "You getting in my face, beaner boy?"

The younger marshal stares at him, eyes flat.

"What's the matter? You done lost your leaf-blower?"

"Get the hell out of his way," Whicher says.

The bearded man lunges—Ortega weaves, hits him with a straight right.

Whicher grabs the bald guy by his shirt, pulls him sideways, drives a fist into his jaw.

The man in the fishing hat swings an arm—the marshal

hits him hard in the gut—dropping him to his knees.

Ortega catches the bearded man with an uppercut, kicks out as the man with spiked hair comes at him. He grabs his arm, pulls him forward, sweeps a foot out, taking the man's legs.

Whicher smashes a fist into the bearded man's torso, piling into the short rib.

The bald man hits him in the side of the head, the marshal drives him back with a flurry of blows—till he trips, falls hard.

Ortega has the spike-haired man's arm up his back—he reaches for the pouch fixed to his belt.

The bearded man and the bald guy and the man in the fishing hat gape at the silvered handcuffs Ortega pulls out.

Whicher looks at the younger marshal, shakes his head; *no*.

Two cars leaving the restaurant have slowed on the road—to watch the fight.

The bearded man dry-retches, the guy in the fishing hat is doubled up, hands at his knees.

The bald man sits in the gravel lot.

Whicher straightens, waves the two cars past.

⋏

Twenty minutes later, adrenaline sinking out of him, both hands starting to hurt.

The lights are low in Ortega's room as Whicher crosses to the window—he pulls back the blind from the glass.

The Silverado is outside.

Across the gravel lot, both the pickup trucks are gone.

On the cell phone in Whicher's jacket are two photographs—the license plates of both vehicles.

The marshal lets go the blind, steps away from the window.

"Think they'll be coming back?" Ortega says.

Whicher shakes his head. "Still want to put in for a transfer?"

Ortega laughs. "I'll think about it. I'll let you know." He glances across the room toward the window. "We could have told them we were law officers…"

"Could have," Whicher says.

"Yesterday I get in a shoot-out—today, it's a fight in a parking lot."

"You want to go on back to court protection?"

The younger marshal looks at him.

Whicher only grunts.

"If it was me," Ortega says, "I would've arrested them, though."

The marshal takes his Resistol from a hook on the door.

"Was it the 'beaner' thing?" Ortega says.

The marshal studies the far wall. "They pissed me off, is all."

"What happens if they come back?"

Whicher takes out the keys to his room next door. "We'll talk to local LE in the morning. Meantime, lock up and be happy."

"Alright." Ortega dips his head.

"And sleep with your gun on the nightstand."

Chapter 18

A pale sun breaks from white cloud as a tall, black deputy in sports sunglasses steps from the parish sheriff's Ford Taurus. He's wearing an olive uniform, ball cap, fatigue pants, hi-top boots. He stares across the lot at the front of the motel.

Whicher finishes a cup of coffee, steps out from the threshold of the room.

"You the marshal?"

"Name's Whicher."

"Lemar Broussard. Jeff Davis Parish Sheriff. Watch commander said you called this morning?"

"Appreciate you coming out."

The door to Ortega's room opens, the younger marshal steps outside.

"My partner," Whicher says, "Marshal Ortega."

Broussard nods. "You're out from Texas? Looking for local assistance?"

"I buy you a cup of coffee?"

The deputy shakes his head. "I'm all good."

"We're looking for a suspect," Ortega says. "Somebody we think could be in the area."

Broussard takes a step closer. "You come in last night?"

Whicher nods. "We're working a homicide—back in Abilene. We had a lead out of Shreveport. Information a suspect could be in this area."

Broussard takes the pair of them in. "Y'all wouldn't be the fellers got into a fight hereabouts last night?"

Whicher eyes the man. "Somebody make a complaint?"

The deputy turns the dark shades in his direction. "Not yet, they didn't."

"Word gets around fast," Ortega says.

"You better believe." Deputy Broussard's face is set hard. "We got enough lawlessness already. Don't need any more shipping in."

Whicher angles his head a fraction.

"Tell me about your suspect?" Broussard says.

"The man we're looking for is a prepper. Into preparedness, in case of…societal breakdown."

The deputy nods.

"Y'all have some folk like that around here?"

"We got a bunch," Broussard says, "since Rita blew in two years gone. Some of that 'societal breakdown' stuff make a little more sense, you see a thing like that."

"Maybe you heard of this guy we're looking for?" Ortega says.

Broussard takes off his sunglasses, folds them, puts them in a pocket of his shirt.

"Dubois," Whicher says. "Ray Dubois."

The deputy thinks about.

"Cajun Ray,' Ortega says.

"He's done jail time for larceny," Whicher adds.

The edges of Broussard's mouth turn down. "I'd have to make a call, ask around. That all you wanted?"

"Tell the truth," the marshal says, "we wanted to go take a look-see up to Bayou Serpent."

"That where you figure this guy is at?"

"We could use someone who knows their way around."

Ortega says, "Could you take us out?"

Broussard looks from one to the other of them. He moves toward the Ford Taurus. "I need to make a couple calls."

Whicher looks at him.

"Y'all want to go see a bunch of swamp Cajuns? We'll be needing a boat."

⚓

An hour later, the brown water of the Calcasieu River parts in front of the bow of the sheriff's department vessel. Whicher tips the brim of the Resistol against the shimmer of sun, sweat already running down the side of his face.

Duck weed stretches out in patches from the banks at either side of the river—pieces of driftwood float among the overhanging bald cypress.

At the wheel of the steel-hulled boat, Deputy Lemar Broussard follows the curves of the wide channel. Cottonwood and cypress and tupelo choke the back wood land.

Along the banks, wooden houses sit on top of pilings—festooned with rope and rag, old nets and buoys and tangles of fishing gear.

Small boats are moored at sagging jetties. Above it all, the forest rises from all sides.

Ortega sits forward in the prow of the boat, scanning the shacks and houses, the jacket of his suit blowing open in the breeze. "People live out here all of the time?"

Broussard answers above the sound of the outboard motor. "Some. There's power lines running through the back woods to a few of 'em. You got power, you can run a pump, get ground water, you ain't got to pull from the river. You can hook up your refrigerator, you got your lights." He points to a metal box and fan-housing on the side of one the shacks. "Even A/C."

"There many like that?" Whicher says.

"Hell, no. Mostly, you'll get a few built together—little camps. Somebody builds one, somebody else builds another. Most of them are just the same way they were thirty or forty years gone. Off the grid, off the map, even."

"What happens if the river rises?" Ortega says.

"Then they get the hell out."

On the near bank is a two-story wooden home—a tin-roofed gallery extending over the deck at the water line.

"This the only way to get to these places?" Whicher says. "By boat?"

"Out here, it's the only way," Broussard says.

The younger marshal scans the two-tiered wooden property. "Pretty wild-looking."

Broussard flashes a gold-tooth grin. "Fine-ass place for a bunch of thieves and cut-throats."

"What kind of trouble you get?" Whicher says.

The deputy eases back on the throttle, slowing the boat as the channel starts to narrow. "Crime here is mainly inland, urban. Folk see a bunch of rice and crawfish farms and swamps. But I-10 brings a lot of drug traffic, we got us a thriving trade in crack. You get that, you'll get a bunch of other things right along with it, y'all know that. Addicts. Crime. Prostitution."

"That kind of thing make it all the way out here?"

"Some of it, yeah, since Rita. A lot of things are messed up. We get people ripping houses. There's derelict homes, abandoned places all over. A property gets left empty, you'll get folk moving in, squatters, they ain't up to no good."

Ahead, around a curve in the river, a clearing shows at the bank—wooden jetties, one after the other, shacks and tumble-down houses just out of the water. At the moorings, pirogues and flat boats of every kind.

The marshal scans the woods along the riverbank, dense, primal. He thinks of Hoffman, laying in the dirt at the side of a Texas lake—arrow shafts sticking out of him, eyes still open.

"Last night," Broussard says.

Whicher eyes the deputy.

"That ruckus y'all got into? You want to tell me what that was all about?"

"Somebody didn't like the look of us," the marshal says.

"They know you all were law enforcement?" The deputy cuts the power to the motor, lets the boat drift—gliding it toward the line of jetties under its own way.

Whicher set his hat back an inch.

"How come you didn't bust their asses?"

"I'm not sure what the hell it was even about," the marshal says.

Broussard stares straight ahead, concentrating on steering the boat. "We've had incidents," he says, "lately. Over oil and gas. Oil companies putting in pipes, now they want to run more and more. A bunch of folk living out here don't want that."

"What's any of that have to do with us?" Ortega says.

"Maybe it don't. But the way y'all look, the way you're dressed…" The deputy eases back some throttle to help with steering. "Some of the factions around here ain't above assaulting company men."

"Assaulting oil company people?"

"See, they'll come around offering money, making promises," Broussard says. "They're looking to get people off of the land, buy 'em out."

"Any of them prepper-types have land out here?" Whicher says.

"Most of 'em, they move around, they got houseboats, kind of floating shacks."

"They can do that. Go where they like?"

"You want 'em out, you got to go fetch 'em out. They'll camp on land belongs to absentee-owners. Lot of the swampers don't like it, more oil, more gas, more pipes.

There's always a few bustin' for a fight. You know? They're fired up. They're drawing lines."

⁂

Twenty yards from the river is a dirt clearing—a woman walking among crab traps and ropes and rusted oil drums. Her face is weathered, skin burnt brown from the sun. Her hair is piled in a red neckerchief. She wears a canvas work shirt, shorts, a pair of jump boots.

Whicher scans the clearing—discarded fishing gear among the trees, a pile of old tires stacked at the side of a clapboard shelter.

Deputy Broussard approaches the woman.

She looks at him, glances at Whicher—tall in the Resistol, Ortega in his dark blue suit.

Broussard takes off his sunglasses, fits them on the top of the ball cap. "Velma?"

"Lemar," she says. "What's goin' on?"

"Need a minute of your time. This here's a couple of US Marshals." Broussard turns to Whicher and Ortega. "Gentlemen; Velma Cormier."

The woman wipes her hands on the sides of her shorts.

"Miss Cormier fishes the bayou, here and on down the river."

"Ma'am," Whicher says.

She looks at him, none too friendly.

"She knows about everybody," Broussard says.

The marshal nods.

"They need to ask you a couple questions, Velma."

"It's in relation to a serious matter, ma'am," Whicher says, "a homicide inquiry."

Velma Cormier looks to Deputy Broussard. "Somebody get their ass killed?"

"Not here," Ortega says.

"Out in Texas," Broussard puts in.

"We have somebody we want to speak with," Whicher says. "A person of interest."

Velma Cormier squints at Broussard. She takes a pouch of rolling tobacco from a pocket in her shirt.

"They're looking for one of the folk up on the bayou," Broussard says. "The folk getting ready for the end-of-the-world?"

The woman named Velma Cormier slips a pack of cigarette papers from out of the pouch. She takes a pinch of loose tobacco, a paper, rolls a cigarette—runs her tongue along the gummed edge.

"Ma'am?" Ortega says. "Do you know any of the people from the prepper community?"

"The guy we're looking for goes by the name of Ray Dubois," Whicher says.

She says nothing, fishes out a lighter, sparks it up.

"You know him, Velma?" Broussard says.

She holds the cigarette to the flame. "People come and go out of here all the time." She takes a drag, blows it out, searches the marshal's face. "There's one of 'em up river goes by the name of Cajun Ray."

Whicher looks at her.

"I don't know him. I've seen him around a couple times.

Him and a bunch of others."

"You know where he's at?"

"Up river," the woman says. "You'd have to go look up beyond the point." She turns to Broussard. "Up to Blackman Bayou."

"You've seen him?" Whicher says.

"I fish where the water's salt, but I'll head up river, time to time. I see those people up there." She takes another drag on the cigarette. "They'll camp wherever they've a mind."

Broussard turns to Whicher. "Pretty wild up there, that's the back country."

The woman blows out a stream of smoke.

"They like to hunt?" Whicher says. "These folk. With bows, arrows, and such?"

"They run around hunting," she says. "Fishing, trapping, getting drunk all day. You ask me, it don't amount to much."

"We'd have to think about how to go in there," Deputy Broussard says.

The woman shakes her head. "They'd hear you coming a mile away."

"We got marine patrol, some K-9," the deputy says. "We could get 'em. But not today."

"Last I seen of any of that crew," the woman says, "they were up by old man Garnier's place. You know it?"

Broussard shakes his head.

"A couple of miles up river. I could smell their cooking fires—smoke was coming out of the forest. They were up one of those old drainage canals, on the north bank. You find Garnier's place, you'll see a jetty, a shack behind it. The old man painted it green; to hide it from the IRS, he says. You go by there, you look real hard, you'll see an entrance to another waterway—that's the old canal."

"We get up it?" Broussard says.

"Your boat got a flat bottom?"

The deputy nods.

"You could try. If you can't go up, you could take a look on foot. I know they been out there, they leave their garbage everywhere they go." She cuts a look at Whicher, at Ortega—turns back to her crab traps. "I don't know, Lemar, okay? All I know is, last I seen of those people, that's where they were…"

⼈

Among the lush foliage on the bank of the bayou, the jetty and the green shack are visible beneath a canopy of trees.

Whicher eyes the shadow-streaked world just beyond the water's edge.

At the shack there's no sign of life, no-one around—no boat.

"Got to be the place," Broussard says.

The marshal nods. "We could tie up, maybe? Take a look around?"

The deputy brings the boat in slow, lessening the noise of the motor.

At the jetty, Ortega reaches out, catches hold of a mooring post.

Whicher climbs from the boat out onto rough plank boards.

Ortega hands him the bow rope, the marshal runs it

through an iron ring, secures it.

Broussard shuts off the outboard motor.

The only sound is the boat rocking, water lapping against the pilings—a faint hum of insects. Birds calling in the trees.

Ortega steps out.

Broussard follows him up onto the jetty.

Stepping to a screen door at the shack, the deputy peers in, raps against the board sides. "Anybody home?" he calls out. "Mister Garnier?"

"No boat," Whicher says. "I guess nobody's here."

Ortega steps to the end of the jetty, leans out to look into the trees. "We could head up the channel Miss Cormier talked about?"

"That's swamp country back there," Broussard says. "You fellers ain't exactly dressed for no tour."

Whicher peers into the dense back woods, sunlight knifing down among the black willow and water elm and reed.

"Can we walk in there?" Ortega says.

"Some of that ground," Broussard says, "not a bunch."

"Let's take a look anyhow," Whicher says.

Broussard steps back onboard the boat, Ortega follows.

The marshal unties the bow rope, pulls it free from the ring.

He lowers himself into the vessel.

Broussard starts the motor, steers out into the river.

A group of pelicans lift out from the trees.

An overhanging willow obscures the outlet where the drainage canal empties into the bayou—its man-made edges just visible. Broussard steers toward it, keeping the motor revs low. From a toolbox on the deck, he breaks out a honed machete—passes it forward to Ortega in the prow. Nudging the boat up toward the channel entrance, the deputy slows.

The younger marshal takes a swipe at the overhang of the tree.

Whicher scans the swamp woodland, feels an oppressive pulse of heat.

Broussard works the boat up the drainage canal. He gestures with his head—farther up the channel, the waterside vegetation has been cut back.

Whicher nods. "Somebody's been up here."

Forty yards in, the channel is narrowing.

Broussard shuts off the throttle. "I don't think we can get through that." He cuts the motor.

Ortega holds out the machete, points at something at the side of the canal. Duck boards are strung along the ground between marsh fern and clumps of cordgrass.

The boat drifts to a stop.

Whicher grabs hold of the protruding root on a cypress tree.

Ortega steps out, ties the bow rope onto a thin-grown water tupelo.

Whicher climbs out.

Stretching back into the woods is a duck board pathway—just wide enough for one person to pass at a time.

"Welcome to swamp country," Broussard says. "Stay on the boards if you don't want to sink."

For ten minutes, Ortega leads the way—Whicher scanning the trees and wetlands, a primordial world of shadow and light.

The forest is water elm and swamp oak and black willow and bald cypress. Spanish Moss drapes down from branches, trumpet vine and muscadine scaling trunks and limbs.

Insects and birds are everywhere, the heat, the humidity stifling.

Ortega carries the machete at his side; swinging now and then at an overhanging vine or branch.

Raised up in some of the mature trees are makeshift platforms—hunting platforms for firing down onto prey.

Light is streaming from a clearing where the boards lead, the forest dense at either side, brackish water on the surface of the ground.

A sound is in the air suddenly—a high keening.

Ortega stops.

The keening sounds again—shrill, arcing through the saturated air.

Whicher feels a sixth sense—a sensation from his days in the military.

Someone is close.

Ortega runs a hand across the sweat at his brow.

Someone is watching.

Broussard stares out into the forest.

The marshal scans the trees, hand close to the Glock. He eyes the hunting platforms, thinking like the army scout he once was. "Somebody knows we're here."

A dull rip sounds from somewhere, a rip followed by a mechanical clank.

A motor bursts into life—an outboard motor.

Whicher moves past Ortega, taking point.

He runs along the wooden walkway.

Sunlight streams though the trees.

Approaching the clearing, he sees a hole dug in the soil at one side—it's filled with plastic bottles and bags.

The marshal steps from the duck boards—the earth underfoot wet, just firm enough to walk on. The place is deserted. He motions for Ortega to follow, leads him through to the clearing's far side.

Another waterway leads off into another part of the woods—a narrow creek, its waters churned.

The sound of an outboard motor echoes along the channel—Whicher scans the thirty yards he can see until the creek takes a blind turn into the woods.

"They're gone," Ortega says.

The marshal nods. Turns around.

At the side of the clearing, Deputy Broussard stands by the hole in the ground, eying the part buried garbage. "Dump site," he says. "Got a bunch of shake and bakes here, one-pot meth labs."

"They're cooking methamphetamine?"

"Somebody is."

The marshal walks to the hollowed-out pit, studies the plastic soda bottles thrown into the hole, a granular substance in the bottom of them.

He stares back along the duck board pathway toward the drainage canal. "We'd have to haul ass back to the river to catch them."

"By the time we do that they could be anywhere," Ortega says.

Broussard nods. "We're going to have to come back."

Whicher scowls, takes off the Resistol.

"Can't do it, brother," the deputy says. "We can go after them. But not today."

⋏

An hour later at the motel, Deputy Broussard pulls the Ford Taurus into the lot by Whicher's Silverado.

The marshal checks his watch; not yet one.

He climbs out of the Taurus, Ortega follows.

Motel reception looks deserted. Whicher tries the door—it's locked.

He steps away, scans the small row of motel rooms. "There another motel someplace around here?"

Broussard gets down from his vehicle.

"If this guy Dubois knows law enforcement are coming after him, he could take off," Whicher says to the deputy. "He could go underground. I don't want to wait."

"We don't know he was in there."

The marshal finds the keys to his truck, opens it. He takes off his suit jacket, eases the Ruger in the shoulder holster away from his shirt. "How big of an area is it?"

"It's not the size, man," Broussard says, "it's the access. It's a swamp, it's too damn easy to hide."

"You get your meth-cookers," Whicher says, "we find our guy, Dubois."

The deputy trains the black sports shades onto him. He

shakes his head. "I'll call up headquarters…"

Getting back in behind the wheel of the Taurus, Broussard grabs the radio transceiver.

The lot is baking in the midday sun, heat radiating from the asphalt. Whicher waves Ortega into shade beneath a live oak. "Back there, in the swamp," he says, "I think he was in there."

"What's that on?"

Whicher rubs a hand across his jaw. "Intuition. Gut."

"We could find out what's known about him?" Ortega says. "Check federal records? Maybe call the Marshals Service in Lake Charles?"

"You want to head on back to Texas, get home?"

Ortega looks surprised; offended. "I'm here just as long as you want."

"A homicide case, time's important." Whicher softens, acknowledging the rebuke. "You get a lead, you need to run it down. Longer it goes, the harder it is finding suspects, gathering evidence, getting a conviction."

Inside the Ford Taurus, Broussard speaks into the transceiver.

Whicher takes out his phone, checks the screen, sees a missed call.

Deputy Mooney.

"You have something?" Ortega says.

"Must've been while we were in the boat, there was no network." The marshal presses to return the call.

Inside the Taurus, Broussard replaces the transceiver.

At the end of the phone line, Deputy Lyle Mooney

answers. "Marshal? I've been trying to get a hold of you."

"What's going on?"

"We've found Mrs Hoffman."

"You found her?" Whicher says. "Is she alright?"

"She's coming out to the farm, she's been staying with a sister, up to Dallas. I spoke with her over the phone. She's coming out to Stamford, I thought you'd want to be there."

"I'm in Louisiana."

"Gail Griffin said you were over to Shreveport."

"That was yesterday. We're down on the bayou, now."

"Well, what do you want to do?" Mooney says.

Whicher looks at Broussard, out of his vehicle now, approaching across the lot. "Can you hold?" The marshal covers the cell with his hand.

"Can't do it," Broussard says. "Sheriff says he'll need time to draw up a search and arrest team."

Whicher speaks into the cell again. "What time y'all expecting Mrs Hoffman?"

"Sometime this evening."

"We'll be there. I'll call from the road. Don't talk with her till we get there. She might be a suspect."

"You think she should have a lawyer?"

"If she asks for one, you let me know."

Chapter 19

Eight hours driving west back to Texas—time enough to think on Cajun Ray Dubois.

Time to brief Chief Marshal Evans, to call Leanne. Time for Ortega to call his own wife.

Two stops for food and gas, plus a third at the Stamford police department in Jones County—to pick up Ortega's truck.

The longest call to Gail Griffin—to let her know about Ray Dubois.

A prime suspect.

And the victim's GMC Sierra now in Abilene.

Solid progress.

Steering the Silverado along the dirt road to the Hoffman farm, the sun is setting amber over the fields. Through the open driver window, the air is filled with the smell of earth, of dry dust, of the low-grown cotton.

Whicher looks up into his rear-view.

Behind him, Sandro Ortega follows in his F250.

The barns and the farmyard are as empty, as abandoned-looking as before.

A Jones County Sheriff's truck is in front of the house, alongside an older model blue Camry.

Whicher parks in line with the two vehicles, shuts off the motor.

Sandro Ortega pulls in by his side in the truck.

The door to the house opens.

Deputy Lyle Mooney stands hat in his hand, smoothing down his dark mustache. He turns his round face to Whicher in the Silverado. Steps from the door into the yard.

Sandro Ortega climbs out of his truck. "Is she in there?"

Mooney nods.

Whicher steps out, swings the door shut. "She have somebody with her?"

"The sister offered to bring her back from Dallas," the deputy answers. "She turned her down, drove on out herself. She says she don't want anyone."

"How is she?" Ortega says.

"Shocked. I guess pretty shocked."

"She tell you anything?" Whicher says.

Mooney stares out across the yard into a field of cotton, keeps his voice low. "She says they've been separated, living apart the last couple months."

The marshal eyes him.

"I can't figure any of this," the deputy says. "How's a farming family mixed up with a bow-killer back in Louisiana?"

Whicher steps across the yard to Mooney at the threshold of the house. "What's happening on Hernandez? The killing at the jail?"

Mooney looks at him. "Sheriff's running an investigation."

"The COs have any idea what happened?"

"Who's going to talk?" Ortega says. "The last would-be informer was stabbed to death."

Whicher takes off his Resistol, buttons the jacket of his suit.

"They say you're a good investigator, marshal," Mooney says. "I sure hope, for her sake, that's true."

The deputy leads both men into the house, down a hall into the kitchen in back.

A lean woman is seated at the table—flaxen haired, good-looking, with fine, high cheekbones. She's wearing a running top, jeans and sneakers, her body inert, her face slack.

"Mrs Hoffman," Deputy Mooney says. "These here are US marshals. This is the gentleman in charge of the case."

The woman rotates her head a few inches. Her pale blue eyes are like glass.

"I'm sorry for your loss, ma'am," Whicher says.

She blinks once.

"We need to ask you some questions at this time."

No response.

"If you wanted somebody with you, we can come back?"

"No," she says, her voice flat. "You're here, now."

The marshal nods. "This here's Marshal Ortega."

Jean Hoffman glances at the younger marshal. Lifts her hands from the table, clasps them together. Then stands, the chair rasping across the floor.

"Ma'am?"

"Could we do this outside? If we've got to talk could we at least get some air?"

⁂

The sun is sinking low across the flat lands west of the Hoffman property—stretching shadows from power lines along the hard dirt road, lighting up the planted fields, streaking the bare earth in tones of red.

Jean Hoffman leads Whicher and Ortega through the deserted farmyard.

She stops behind one of the machinery barns at an abandoned garden plot.

"I miss this." She looks at the ridges of turned earth, the thin-grown weeds. "But not much else."

"Deputy Mooney says you've been living back in Dallas?" Whicher says.

She stares at the fallow garden.

"With a sister?" he says. "You've been separated for some time?"

"Three months," the woman says.

Whicher looks at her. "When was the last time you saw your husband, ma'am?"

Jean Hoffman swallows, walks on a little. Puts a hand to the corner of her eye. "About ten days ago," she says. "I told him I wanted a divorce."

She stops again, turns to face the house and the farm buildings.

"You have any idea why your husband might have been killed, ma'am?"

"Elijah?" She holds her arms at the elbows. "It would have been over money…"

The marshal glances at Ortega.

"What makes you say that, ma'am?" the younger marshal says.

"Because he's…" she stops herself. Her eyes shine. She sways on her feet. "Because he *was*…an inveterate gambler."

Whicher studies her in the evening sunlight; arms tight about herself, stillness to her body.

"They say all cotton farmers are." She looks at him. "Did you know that? They say you might as well go to a river boat and blow all your money in there."

"The cotton business?" Whicher says.

"It's hard to grow." She shakes her head. "You never know what a season will bring. If the weather will be right, if the boll weevils will infest your crop, you don't know what you'll harvest, what the markets will do…"

The marshal looks out at the worked fields beyond a withered row of fence posts.

"Somebody else grows it all, now," she says.

"Ma'am, your husband was a gambler? A habitual gambler?"

She nods. "He took to just doing that."

"And the farm, ma'am?" Ortega says. "Was it in financial difficulty?"

"We were looking to sell. It was the only way."

"There were debts?" Ortega says. "Money outstanding?"

"There still *is*…"

Whicher looks at her. "Do you know much about your

husband's debts? Who your husband owed money to?"

Jean Hoffman steps to a row of wooden stakes in the ground. Dead tomato plants and beans are still tied-in to them. She starts to pull them up, along with handfuls of weeds. "Some, I know."

"Only some?"

"We stopped talking about it. We ended up fighting all the time." She throws the dead plants and weeds into a pile by an old chicken house.

"If we need to take a look at your financial records?" Whicher says.

She shrugs. Pushes up the sleeves on her running top, pulls more dead plants from the ground. "You can check at the bank. You can check whatever you want."

Whicher turns his gaze east, beyond a brace of white-roofed barns. "Did your husband travel to Louisiana? To gamble?"

"Oh, yes."

He looks at her. "You know he did?"

"It's an illness? You know? A full-blown addiction? With him, it was."

The marshal takes a pace along the side of the old fence row.

"You don't have the look of a gambler," she says. "Maybe I'm wrong."

"Mrs Hoffman," Ortega says, "do you know any of the details about your husband's gambling? Places he liked to gamble? Any of the people he gambled with?"

"I was sick of it," she shakes her head, "so sick of it."

"It could help."

"I didn't want to know, I just wanted it to end."

Whicher glances at Ortega, notes the look passing across the younger marshal's face.

Jean Hoffman bends to the hard ground again, pulls out more stalks of long grass and weed. "You think it was somebody from that world?"

Neither man answers.

She hurls a handful of vegetation onto the pile. "He wasn't a bad person. He wasn't mean, or violent. He never hit me, never cheated on me…"

"But you fought?" Ortega says.

"He wasn't cut out for this." She straightens.

The younger marshal frowns.

"He was a weak person."

"Not cut out to be a farmer?" Ortega says. "Or to grow cotton?"

"For hard work." She looks over at Whicher. "He wasn't a resilient man."

In front of the farmhouse Deputy Lyle Mooney stands, hands in his pockets, looking out along the empty dirt road.

Jean Hoffman's gaze rests on him a moment. "The sheriff's department say Eli was shot with a bow and arrow." Her face is stricken, suddenly, her body crumpling inward on itself.

Whicher nods.

"Do you know why?"

The marshal shakes his head.

"Do you have *any*thing to go on?"

Whicher takes a step toward her. "Ma'am do you know a man by the name of Ray Dubois? Cajun Ray?"

Her eyes are quick, searching the ground in front of her. "I don't know," she says. "I don't know, I don't think. These last months, we've been living apart, living separate lives. If it was someone he met since then…"

"Did you ever travel to Louisiana, Mrs Hoffman?" Ortega says.

Confusion is in her face now. "No. No, I didn't. Is this man Dubois a suspect?"

Whicher ignores the question. "How about a man named Carl Avery?"

She puts a hand to her cheekbone. "Yes," she says. She nods.

"You know Carl Avery?"

"I think my husband did," she says. "I'm pretty sure I've heard the name…"

⚜

Lights still show in the windows at the house in Wylie.

The marshal snaps out the truck's headlamps. The clock on the dash of the Silverado is coming up on ten.

At the window to the living room, a figure appears pulling back the blind.

Leanne raises a hand from behind the glass.

Whicher climbs down from the truck, runs a knuckle over the stubble at his chin.

The front door opens.

He takes off the Resistol.

She steps out. "Back from the bayou…"

"Back from Stamford."

She walks to him, puts her arms around him, kisses him.

Breaking off, he searches her face a moment. He follows her into the house, through the living room, into the bright-lit kitchen.

He puts his hat on the table, unclips the Glock from his belt, unclips the extra magazines of ammunition.

In the hallway, at the side of the living room, Lori is standing looking at her mother and father. She's dressed in a yellow sleep suit, her auburn hair ruffled, her face lined from her pillow.

Whicher puts the semi-automatic pistol and the ammunition on a shelf above the counter.

His daughter walks forward, reaches up with both hands.

Whicher takes her beneath her arms, hoists her to him. Breathes her scent as she leans in, feels the heat of her small body.

Carrying her to a seat at the kitchen table, he lowers himself as she pulls at his neck-tie. He sits her on his knee. "It's good to see you, sweetheart." He takes off the tie, gives it to her.

She plays with the strip of fabric.

"You want something to eat?" Leanne says. "There's brisket tacos and fried okra left over from dinner?"

"Whatever you got."

Leanne takes out dishes from the refrigerator, places them on the countertop. "How about something to drink?"

"I'm good," Whicher says.

Lori tosses the neck-tie onto the table. She leans against her father's shirt, puts a hand to the Ruger revolver in the shoulder-holster.

The marshal moves her hand away, leans forward, slips off the rig.

"Daddy chases bad men."

Whicher holds out the gun and holster to his wife. "No bad men come around here."

Leanne carries the rig to an armoire, she hangs it inside.

Lori makes the shape of a pistol with her hand.

"What have you been doing?" the marshal says. "Since I've been gone? Momma said you went swimming?"

His daughter bounces, claps her hands. "Jumping in…"

"You been jumping in the water?"

Leanne puts together a plate of food, puts it into the microwave oven. "She's getting good, she likes it."

"What else?"

"You helped me today?" Leanne says.

Lori looks up at her mother.

"What did we do?"

Whicher wraps his arm around his daughter.

"We baked cookies."

Lori nods, smiles. Then yawns. Looks blank across the kitchen.

"Why don't you take her on back to bed?"

The marshal gathers her up.

Lori puts her face into her father's shoulder.

He carries her from the kitchen, through the living room, down the hall to her bedroom. Low light shows from an animal-shaped lamp in the wall outlet, a faint orange glow.

Leaning down to the bed with her, she clings on.

"Come on, let's get you in here," he breathes, "I'll stay, it's alright."

She unclasps her hands from around his neck, slides onto the bed.

He slips the pillow beneath her head, pulls up the coverlet.

Sitting on the floor by her, he draws up his knees.

Her eyes grow heavy.

He strokes her hair, listens to the silence in the room, the sound of her breathing. Watches his daughter, still, now, sinking into sleep. For a few minutes, sitting in the half-dark, no other thought in his mind.

Leanne appears in the doorway. She waves him away.

Whicher follows his wife back through the house into the kitchen.

On the table is the plate of tacos and cornmeal fried okra. He takes his neck-tie from the table. Straightens it out, hangs it on the back of a chair. "She okay?"

Leanne nods.

The marshal takes up a knife and fork.

"She must have heard you. She's been missing you. We both have."

"We got a little deep in the weeds," Whicher says. He eats, hungrily. "We couldn't get back."

"She notices more," Leanne says. "Now that she's growing up. She notices if you're not here."

"You think it's alright—to tell her I chase bad people?"

Leanne looks at him. "What should I tell her?"

"I mean, you think it's okay?"

"She's always asking where you are, why you're not here."

"You don't think it might scare her?" He cuts into the tacos.

Leanne says, "I can't protect her from your life."

Whicher catches the reflection of the room in the glass-panelled door to the back yard. A man stiff-backed at a kitchen table—a woman at arms-length at the countertop.

"She needs to know what's so important to keep you away all of the time," Leanne says.

The marshal nods. "We spoke to the widow tonight."

His wife's face softens. "How was that? How was she?"

Whicher searches for the right word a moment. "Numb," he finally says.

"Did she have somebody?"

"She was alone," he says. "She drove herself back from her sister's place in Dallas."

Leanne exhales—a long, drawn-out breath. "Poor woman."

The marshal says nothing, takes another forkful of the food.

Leanne looks at him intently. "What's that on your face?"

He puts a hand up to his cheek.

"You have a cut," she says, "a graze, or something." She steps to him, leans in close.

"I was with Ortega. Last night. Some moron got in his face."

"You got in a fight?"

Whicher shifts in his seat. "Wasn't much of a fight."

"You weren't going to mention it?" Leanne steps back, looks at him a long moment. "You think he's having the same conversation right now? With his own wife?"

"He was a cop before this." Whicher tries a smile. "He's been in law enforcement, I'd guess she's used to it."

"He switched jobs?" Leanne says.

"So he said."

"It doesn't have to be forever?"

He looks at her.

"This life," she says. She starts to clear the serving dishes from the countertop. "People retrain, don't they?"

The marshal watches her moving, doesn't answer. "She told us something tonight, the widow."

"Oh?"

"Could be something useful."

"She have any idea why her husband would be murdered by a man from Louisiana?"

"More to it than that," Whicher says.

Leanne turns around looks at him. "You don't think your answer's out there? Out in Louisiana?"

"A piece of it is," he says. "The rest is close to home. It's close, it's right here."

Chapter 20

The sun is barely up over Jake Roberts Freeway as Dwayne Cameron pulls into the gas station off of Loop Road 322.

He steers his Nissan Sentra off the asphalt lane onto a bleached and oil-stained concrete forecourt. No other cars are at any of the pumps, the store unit in back is unlit—not yet open.

Cameron shuts down the motor, leans back in his seat. In no particular rush. Already thinking on the working day ahead—an out-run to Albany and Breckinridge to the north east—sixty miles, two drops, four pick-ups.

Then down to Cisco, another drop, and then on to Baird along I-20. Back in Abilene, a final pick-up before he can call it a day. He rubs a hand across his shirt—the breakfast biscuits heavy in his gut; just as well to have eaten.

He steps out of the car, checks his pants pockets, they're empty.

Reaching back in across the front seat, he grabs his billfold. As a white, Mazda sedan rolls to a stop on the wide lane opposite.

Dwayne Cameron takes out his credit card—takes a moment to stare into the rising sun beyond the pillars of the freeway. The elevated road just a dark slash. Scorched earth banks of the lane drenched with a wash of pink and gold.

Hot one.

Going to be another hot one.

He slides his credit card into the reader on the pump, taps in the number, waits for the machine to slide the card back out.

Fumbling it back into his billfold, he unhooks the gas pump—twists off the filler cap, sticks the nozzle into the car.

Only then looking out across the lane at the white sedan with its window down.

Stationary, maybe thirty yards off. The driver inside in a ball cap and aviator shades—twisting behind the wheel, lifting something off of the passenger seat.

Cameron rubs his nose, glances back at the meter running on the pump. Tank it, what the heck.

Something about the white sedan registers. He thinks about it. About the man inside behind the wheel.

Dwayne Cameron looks back across the deserted lane at the car.

Unmoving.

Empty scrub lots surrounding it.

No reason for it to stop there.

No buildings, no houses, not a thing.

Something is pointing out of the vehicle's open window. Thin. A piece of metal, a tube.

And only then does the cortex in his brain receive the signal—like a shocking bolt.

As the fire-flash in the muzzle connects—with the white hot rip of pain in his center.

To only light.

Chapter 21

Steering through the commute traffic, police units are visible a quarter-mile away from the elevated road. Whicher studies them in the early morning sun—light bars flashing and popping; a lot of units.

He slows, takes an off ramp, running down to a four-way lane.

Turning sharp north, he drives the truck beneath the concrete bridge carrying Jake Roberts Freeway.

Emerging from the bridge's shadow, he sees a gas station opposite a scrub-filled lot.

It's closed-off, police vehicles surrounding it. They're blocking off the gas station and the loop road along the freeway's side.

Two panel vans are parked with the police units. Local TV channels. Whicher eyes the vans, thinks of driving by, not stopping.

Among the gas pumps is a tall black figure in a suit—Levi Underwood from the Violent Crimes Task Force at FBI.

The marshal signals, steers the truck into an entrance way on the concrete apron.

A uniformed cop steps toward him.

Whicher takes out the badge-holder.

The officer sees it, waves him through.

The marshal parks at the rear of the lot at the side of a store.

Stepping out, he scans the forecourt—four gas pumps, a Nissan sedan beside one of them, broken glass and bullet holes in the vehicle, impacting from the side nearest the lane.

Two crime scene techs are kneeling, working around the car.

Levi Underwood talking into a cell phone, TV crews milling by the sides of their vans.

Whicher buttons the jacket of his suit, steps slowly toward the vehicle at the pump.

Underwood spots him, holds out a hand.

The marshal stops. Blood is on the concrete around the area at the back of the Nissan.

The FBI man finishes the call, fixes the marshal with a look.

"More work for the Task Force?" Whicher says.

"Like we need more."

"What happened?"

"Some guy was gunned down this morning," Underwood says, "a little after six. Looks like an automatic weapon, maybe fully-automatic." He points toward the scrub-filled lot opposite. "From the impact of the rounds in the vehicle, it looks like the shooter must've been somewhere out over the road there."

"Y'all have slugs?"

"We got slugs."

"How about brass?"

"Nope. No shell casings," the FBI agent says. "We'll run a thorough search. But if it was from a vehicle the brass might've ejected inside it."

Whicher sees no businesses or buildings close by. "Think you'll get a ballistics profile?"

"Should be," Underwood says.

"Any witnesses?"

"Not a one."

The marshal scans the underside of the gas station roof—the steel supports, the canopy. He turns, looks back toward the one-floor store. "I see three cameras."

"There's a fourth around back, we'll check them all," Underwood says.

"You get my statement? Ortega's?"

"I got 'em." Underwood cuts him a look. "There shouldn't be a problem, you were acting in self defense."

The marshal nods. "How come the press are hanging out?"

"They got a scent, you know?"

"A scent?"

"The smell of blood. The victim here this morning," Underwood says. "One Dwayne Cameron. He was on his way in to work. Two days back, we get an aggravated robbery attempt at the bank over on Judge Ely? Now this."

Whicher fixes the FBI man with a look.

"He's a driver," Underwood says, "sometime messenger. He spent his working life around money—inside of armored cars."

⁂

Pine Street is still quiet outside the Federal Courthouse building as Whicher pulls the Silverado in at the curb. He locks the truck, glances at the Hotel Wooten above the parking garage on the opposite side of the street.

Entering the courthouse building, he takes the stairs up to the corridor—heads down to the USMS office. He opens the door with the code, finds two marshals already arrived—George Shea and Iago Perez, both of them dressed in suits for court duty—Shea, heavy with sand colored hair, Perez, short with a neat, black mustache.

A TV is on in the corner of the room, the volume low.

Perez looks at Whicher. "You come in up 322 from Wylie?"

The marshal nods.

"Up the freeway, hombre? You see that drive-by?"

"I stopped at it," Whicher says, "FBI are there."

George Shea points toward the TV. "Reporters, too."

Whicher looks at him. "Lot of shots were fired."

From the civilian support room, Donna Garcia enters—a paper slip held in one hand. "You have a message from Gail Griffin," she says to Whicher. "A result back from AFIS. She said to call."

"Alright," the marshals says, "thanks."

Shea continues; "They say the shooting could be linked

with that armored car thing? On Judge Ely?"

"Could be." Whicher checks his watch. "Is Evans in?"

Perez nods.

Whicher picks up the phone from his desk, dials a number.

Gail Griffin answers on the third ring.

"John Whicher. You had a message for me about an AFIS result?"

"Marshal, yes. We've got confirmed fingerprints for your suspect."

"For Dubois?"

"Some good clean prints," Griffin says.

"That's fast."

"We knew the prints we were looking for," she says. "They match the record on file."

"You have prints on the bow? Or any of the arrows?"

"On the wheel of the truck," Griffin says. "And on that hunting knife. And on the door handle."

"But not the weapon?"

"We can test for DNA, but it'll take time, we may not get anything we can use."

"But we can put Dubois in the truck?"

"A hundred per cent. He was in there."

"You find any evidence of Dubois inside the farm house, Hoffman's house?"

"None," the scene tech officer says.

"Alright. You working on the truck still?"

"I'm on it now."

"Anything comes up…"

"I'll let you know, don't worry."

The marshal finishes the call, takes off the Resistol, crosses the room, knocks at Chief Marshal Evans's door.

"Yeah," Evans answers. "Come on in…"

Whicher enters the office.

The chief marshal is seated at his desk, small frame hunched in front of his computer monitor. "Louisiana State Patrol sent pictures yesterday, I was just taking a look." He turns the monitor for Whicher to see—it shows a GMC pickup in a dusty compound.

"Hoffman's truck," Whicher says.

"Three-year-old GMC Sierra." Evans clicks onto another image—the compound bow on the back seat of the cab, the set of broadhead arrows on camo shafts.

"Gail Griffin has fingerprints inside of the truck, belonging to the guy we went looking for yesterday."

"Dubois?" Evans says.

"Ray Dubois."

"What's it going to take to find this guy?"

"We'll need the parish sheriff's office in Louisiana."

Evans sits back in his seat.

"It's swamp and bayou, we'd need to know our way around," Whicher says. "We'd need boats, dogs, maybe. What little we know of Dubois, he's some kind of survivalist. If he decides to bug out, we might have one hell of a time trying to run him down."

"How about the Marshals Office out there?"

"Parish sheriff likely know the ground best."

"You want me to call?"

"Yes, sir. I'd think."

Chief Marshal Evans clicks a pen, makes a note on the pad on his desk.

"Last night, I interviewed the victim's widow," Whicher says, "Jean Hoffman."

"How was that?" Evans looks at him.

"She seemed shocked, confused."

The chief marshal nods.

'One thing—she thinks her husband did know Carl Avery."

"How so?"

"I'll need to talk with her again," Whicher says, "maybe on the record. But they were in trouble, the farm's in hock, Hoffman was a gambler, according to her."

Evans pulls at a strand of rust colored hair behind his ear.

"I'll need to speak with Carl Avery again," Whicher says. "Find out how he knew the victim."

"What's happening with the kids that found the body, the kids out at ACU? Campus police were going to call you?"

"I'll chase that today, I'll go on over."

"That jail house murder is keeping me awake," Evans says. "Hernandez? The auto thief?"

Whicher considers it. "Sheriff's department investigation is already running."

"Well," Evans says, "I have a meeting with the Chief of Police. The city's briefing the press this morning."

Whicher looks at his boss across the desk.

"You know there was a fatal shooting already today?" Evans says.

"At a gas station, I came by it," Whicher says.

"The Chief of Police will be responding to questions on it. Somebody from the Bureau will be there. I'll be responding to developments on the homicide at the lake."

"You can tell them enquiries are proceeding," Whicher says.

"I could tell them you have a suspect. A spate of violence like this, the city wants to show law enforcement has a firm grip."

"I don't want my guy knowing we're coming after him."

"It's looking pretty damn lawless," Evans says, "the last couple of days."

"It's not staying that way."

⋏

Whicher drives the short distance across town in the Silverado. Scrolling the contact list on his phone he finds the number for campus police at ACU.

He presses to send the call, switches over to hands-free.

A voice answers. "Sergeant Estrada speaking."

"US Marshals Service. Name's Whicher, we spoke yesterday. I'm leading the investigation into the homicide up at Lake Fort Phantom Hill."

"Marshal, yes—did my colleague call you?"

"I don't think. I was out most of the day, out of state…"

"We've been checking CCTV footage," the sergeant says, "I don't think we picked up your truck. But the officer that spoke to the driver is on shift now, he could tell you more about it than me."

"I'll call by," Whicher says. "I'm just a few minutes away." He clicks out the call.

At the junction with North 16th, he waits in the turn lane.

Above the trees he can see the campus buildings, the pale, stone edifice of the Tower of Light.

Scrolling the list of phone contacts again, Whicher finds Ortega's number—he presses to make the call.

The younger marshal answers.

"It's Whicher, where you at?"

"I'm headed over to Pine Street."

"I spoke with Chief Marshal Evans this morning," Whicher says, "we're going to try to lean on the parish sheriff out in Bayou Serpent, see if we can get 'em to help us out finding Ray Dubois. Take a look at the record on him—see if there's anything we can use for extra leverage."

"Beyond being a primary suspect in a murder case?"

"If there's anything else outstanding, we could use it," Whicher says. "We need to find this guy fast. I'm calling in to ACU campus police, then I'll head up to see Carl Avery again. I want to ask him about Elijah Hoffman—find out how come the two of 'em knew each other."

"Let me know what happens?"

"I'll see you back at the office…"

Pulling in off the street into Campus Court, Whicher drives the half-block over to the University Police department.

He parks in an empty bay by a pair of white SUVs. Steps out, crosses to the glass front unit.

The police sergeant from the day before sees him—he steps to the door, pushes it open.

"Mornin'," Whicher says.

"Marshal." Sergeant Estrada waves him into the small office.

A second officer is inside—a younger man, square-faced, wearing steel-rimmed glasses.

"This is Officer Cole," Estrada says. "It was him stopped the man driving the pickup."

Whicher nods a greeting. "You know what this is about?"

"Yes, sir, marshal."

Whicher addresses Estrada; "You got nothing on camera, so far as you know?"

"Most of the surveillance cameras are over on the east side of the campus," Officer Cole says. "The risk of break-in is higher."

"Where'd you stop this feller?"

"He was over on the north side, behind the coliseum, in one of the lots." Officer Cole pushes the glasses up the bridge of his nose. "I can tell you what vehicle he was in, marshal."

"Go ahead," Whicher takes out his notebook and pen.

"Dodge Ram, four-door quad cab."

"A Ram pickup?"

"Dark green in color."

"You get any of the plate?"

"Marshal, I didn't," Cole says. "Tell the truth, if I took the number of every vehicle I see around here I wouldn't have any time to do my job."

"How about the driver, what'd he look like?"

"White guy, I'd say around thirty. He was wearing a ball cap, shades. Dressed in a gray T-shirt." Cole taps the upper arm of his shirt. "He had a bunch of tattoos."

Whicher makes another note.

"He said he was from the sail boat club—over at Lake Fort Phantom Hill. Said somebody left a set of car keys up there, they were wondering if it was one the kids from here, one of the boys that reported the body."

"That's what the man said?"

"Yes, sir."

"And you told him you didn't give out address details?"

"We don't give out anything like that, where people live, where they're staying and such."

"Then what?"

Officer Cole shrugs. "The guy just kind of left. I didn't think much of it. I guess later I thought to mention it to the kids."

"If y'all see this guy again, take his license plate number, call me?"

"We'll do that, marshal," the sergeant says.

"And if you find the pickup on one of your surveillance cameras…"

Estrada nods, "You'll be first to know."

Chapter 22

Parked beneath a Mexican white oak in a corner of the lot at Summerwood Realty, Whicher scans the metal-sided depot and site offices in the adjacent construction yard. The depot's doors are closed, just a few cars and pickups scattered along the length of one side.

He closes up his truck, starts to walk toward it. Thinks of Riley McGuire—the last person to use the lake house and the boat.

At a cabin-office he climbs the short flight of timber steps to the door. He puts a hand to the wire grille covering a near window.

He tries the door, it's locked.

Pressing on the buzzer, he turns around to look across into the Summerwood lot.

A noise sounds from behind him, the door opens.

The blond-haired construction worker steps out; the man with the surfer's hair.

"Looking for Mister McGuire, Riley McGuire?" Whicher says.

The blond man looks at him

"With the US Marshals Service. Is he here?"

"No."

"You know where he's at?"

The man looks out across the roadway—west toward the city. "He's out on a site."

"You know where?"

The blond man's eyes cut in the direction of the Summerwood lot.

Turning, the marshal sees a black, Mercedes SL500 coupe steering in.

Behind the wheel is Carl Avery.

Whicher descends the wooden steps as the Mercedes parks.

Avery lets the motor rumble beneath the hood a few moments before he shuts it off. He steps out, his face flushed. "I can only give you a few minutes, marshal, I'm afraid."

"I tried to call your secretary…"

"I have a full schedule, I'm sorry, I have a company to run." Avery calls across the lot to the blond man; "Frank, is Riley back in there?"

"No, sir, he already left."

"Are you headed out on site? Can you have him call me?"

"Yes, sir. Not a problem."

Avery waves the man away, reaches into the Mercedes—takes out a black, leather attache case. He speaks over his shoulder. "If we go into the office, I'm supposed to go straight into a meeting with my architect. Could we talk out here?"

"Wherever you want," the marshal says.

Avery indicates a bench beneath a cedar elm at the side of a strip of irrigated grass. "What did you want to see me about?"

"Do you know a man named Hoffman? Elijah Hoffman?"

Carl Avery stands by the bench a moment. He runs a hand through his head of graying hair. "Can you give me a little more to go on?"

"His wife said the two of you were acquainted."

"Oh?"

"It's this man Hoffman's death I'm investigating."

Avery looks at the marshal, eyes uncertain. He sits.

Whicher sits down alongside him.

"I meet a lot of people in business, marshal."

"Cotton farmer," Whicher says. "A cotton farmer out of Stamford."

"In Jones County?"

"Right," the marshal says.

Avery leans back against the bench. "He was looking to sell some land, as I recall. We were interested in buying it."

"A farm?" Whicher says.

"A couple of years back, this was, at least," Avery says. "We were thinking of putting wind turbines on the land we need power. The new properties we're building need power. If we can help produce it, we want to do that. As I recall, the land was pretty much due north of some of the sites we're developing. It would've been an easy run via the existing network."

"Y'all wanted his land for a wind farm?"

"We didn't get it," Avery says. "It was in negotiation a long while. I think it just sort of died out. I'd pretty much forgotten about it, to tell the truth."

"You didn't know Hoffman well?"

"Not at all."

"Did he ever stay out at your property on the lake?"

"What? Why would he?"

Whicher lets his gaze run out over the construction yard lot.

"I suppose I met him a handful of times at most," Carl Avery says.

"How about Mister McGuire?" The marshal says. "Would he have known him?"

"Riley's something of a right-hand man to me." Avery frowns. "He's involved in all aspects of the company."

"So, he would've known him?"

"Yes, he would."

"Is Mister McGuire involved in acquisitions—land purchases and the like?"

"Certainly, he is."

"I'll need to speak with him," Whicher says. "So far as we know, he was the last person to use that property of yours on the lake, that be right?"

"Well, what's that supposed to mean?"

"It's a point of fact," the marshal says, "that's all."

Avery glances at him.

"Where could I find Mister McGuire?"

"He's over in the Sears Park Area," Avery says. "Supervising a new site we're just opening up."

"Sears Park?"

"We have some new condominiums, some prestige individual properties we're building. Just off of the Old Anson Road, Vogel Avenue. Listen, I don't know why you'd need to see him, I can vouch for him personally, he's worked for me for years."

Whicher doesn't respond.

"It's a terrible thing that's happened with this man," Avery says. "But I can assure you it has nothing to do with me or with anyone working for my company. I have no idea why my boat was found near the scene of this man's murder, but it must have been taken, stolen. I can see now that I should've been more careful. I should've kept the place locked and secured. I can assure you I intend to do that from now on. But if you're going to want to speak with me everyday, or talk with people on my staff, I think perhaps it might be better to shift things to a more formal setting."

"You want a lawyer present?" Whicher says.

Carl Avery spreads his palms on his lap. "I feel that I'm being scrutinized and I don't understand why. I can understand your initial interest, with the boat, of course…"

From the far side of the adjacent yard lot, behind the depot, a pickup truck rolls into view.

A dark green pickup.

It's a four-door cab—the same as the description of the vehicle on campus.

Behind the wheel is the blond-haired man.

Whicher points, "The guy in the truck, there? What's his name?"

"Frank?" Avery says. "Frank Nelson. One of our construction foremen."

Whicher pictures him two days back, talking with Riley McGuire—wearing a T-shirt, his arms scrolled with tattoos.

He watches the pickup pull out from the yard toward a feeder road for the highway.

Ram four-door quad cab.

Whicher writes down the plate.

⋏

Back across town in the courthouse building on Pine, the cup of coffee on the desk grows cold.

Whicher reads the Record of Arrest and Prosecution on Frank Nelson—current construction foreman at the Summerwood Realty Corporation, a former member of the Bandidos motorcycle club. Two prosecutions for assault and battery are on his file—the first, five years back, a Class-C misdemeanor resulting in a fine. The second, three years gone, a Class-B resulting in six months in the county jail. A further charge but no conviction for an assault defined as threatening behavior and intimidation. DMV record shows Nelson as the owner of the Ram pickup—it's not a company vehicle.

The door to the office opens.

Sandro Ortega steps in.

He's carrying a plastic document wallet. Wearing the same dark blue suit as the day before, sporting a fresh shirt and neck-tie.

He holds out the wallet. "I was up the street. At the bureau."

"How's that?"

"FBI office. Checking on the Triple-I."

"We can't get that here?" Whicher says.

"We can. Their version is more up-to-date." The younger marshal flashes a smile. "Back in San Angelo, at the PD, that's what we'd do."

Ortega sits at a corner of the empty desk by Whicher's. He opens up the plastic wallet, takes out a printed sheet. "Interstate-Identification-Index says Raymond Landry Dubois received a year's custodial sentence for larceny. He stole a boat."

Whicher swivels in his seat. "Dubois stole a *boat?*"

"That's what it says on the record. This was two years back, 2005. I did a little digging, turns out it was during Hurricane Rita. He stole a boat either during or in the immediate aftermath of the storm. According to him, it was a means of survival—the owner didn't see it that way."

"Grady Pearce told us Dubois was caught up in Rita," Whicher says.

The younger marshal nods.

"Anything else?"

"Since release, Dubois has been in a couple of bar fights local to Bayou Serpent. Nothing resulting in any charge."

"Not much of a rap sheet."

"Maybe he never really did anything," Ortega says. "Till now."

Whicher grunts.

"No?"

"Maybe he ain't big on getting caught," the marshal says.

Ortega slips the sheet of paper back into the plastic wallet, puts the wallet on Whicher's desk.

Marshals George Shea and Iago Perez enter from the main corridor.

"Court's in recess," Perez says.

Shea pushes back the cuff on his suit jacket. "Anybody want to go get lunch?"

Perez looks at Whicher.

"Work to do."

Shea runs a hand over his shirt, across his gut. "Hey, so do we."

The small, neat Perez glances at Ortega. "You want to go get lunch, mano? Lookin' sharp, by the way."

The younger marshal glances at Whicher.

Whicher shakes his head. "Later."

"We have to be back in court in less than one hour," Shea says. "No offense."

Perez winks. "Adios."

The door closes itself behind the pair of them.

Whicher rests his gaze on the document wallet, thinks of Dubois, the report about the boat.

"How'd it go with the campus police," Ortega says, "at ACU?"

The marshal gestures at the open file on his computer monitor. "Looks like the guy they spoke to could've been one Franklin Nelson; a construction foreman for Summerwood Realty."

"Hey, no shit?"

"The man's a former biker, he's been in jail for battery.

There's a charge of threatening behavior and intimidation on his record."

Ortega stands, peers at the computer screen. "We know it was him?"

"Campus police are checking their surveillance footage, to see if they have him, or have his truck."

"Should we speak to him?"

"He fits the description," Whicher says. "We'll bring him in, but not yet. We need to check with Gail Griffin, see if Nelson's prints are on the boat or anywhere in Hoffman's truck."

"Did you call her?"

"I only just found out. We need to know where that trolling motor came from, too, maybe Nelson's prints could be on it?"

At the far side of the room, the door to Chief Marshal Evans's office opens. He calls over; "Got a minute?"

Whicher stands, crosses the office.

"I just gone done talking with the Jeff Davis Parish sheriff's office," Evans says. "They can put the two of you into the bayou tonight."

"Tonight?"

"Sheriff's office say the best time to look for any of the backwoods folk is around dusk."

Whicher looks at him. "Why's that?"

"They're done moving for the day, they're back in camp. It's too tough moving around in the dark, the sheriff's office say. We could get you on a flight out of Abilene to Lake Charles. There's a stopover at Dallas Fort Worth—flying out just before three o' clock. Get you there around six."

"They have people available?" Whicher says.

"They're putting together some kind of a team for a search. You want me to confirm you can be there?"

"Yes, sir," Whicher says.

"There enough evidence to bring Dubois back if you find him?"

"I can put him in a stolen car belonging to a murder victim."

"You'd arrest him?"

"We have witnesses in Louisiana to say he was driving that thing."

"Alright." The chief marshal nods to himself, his eyes come back on Whicher. "Did you talk to Carl Avery?"

"Avery's company were trying to buy the farm property from Hoffman."

Ortega cuts in; "That's how Hoffman knew him?"

"According to Avery."

Evans runs a finger around the collar of his shirt. "You think this realty corporation has something to do with all of this?"

"The person searching for the two ACU kids could've been a Summerwood Realty employee, name of Frank Nelson."

Evans lets the thought sit. "I need to call the sheriff, tell him yes." He steps back into his office, pulls the door.

Ortega takes off his suit jacket, smoothes his short, dark hair.

"We need to do this," Whicher says.

"Not a problem."

"We need to pick up Dubois, take him off the board." He looks at the younger marshal. "If we don't, he'll be gone. Sheriff's office probably want an excuse to go in there—they got a bunch of meth cookers and God-knows-what-all out in the woods."

"We take any equipment?" Ortega says.

"I'll put in a message on the system," Whicher says, "let the airport know we'll be flying armed. We'll flight-case a couple of extras in the hold. Assault rifle, maybe. Shotgun…"

"Put me down for an AR-15."

Whicher nods. "We'll need body armor, too, I don't want to stop an arrow any more than I want to stop a round. You'll need fatigues, we can't dress like this. You want to head back home, get yourself something?"

"Alright. How about you?"

"I got some old clothes and boots in the back of the truck, I was going to use 'em for dragging the lake. I'll break out an 870 from the gun room."

"Shotgun," Ortega says, "not a bad choice."

Whicher nods.

"And the flight is at three?"

"What the man said."

Ortega looks at him. "How'd it go with Carl Avery?"

Whicher chews on his lip. "There's some kind of connection between all of this and his company," he says. "This guy Frank Nelson went looking for two potential witnesses to the murder. Riley McGuire was the last to use the house and maybe the boat on the lake. I want to head over to see him before we leave. He's on a construction site near Sears Park."

"Want me to ride along?"

The marshal shakes his head. "Go home, get whatever you need. If you have time before we leave, check for more background on Frank Nelson. And call Gail Griffin for me."

"Got it."

"We find this Ray Dubois, we bring him in, we're going to break the back of this. We could break it tonight."

Chapter 23

A choking cloud of dust swirls around the back-hoes and bulldozers leveling the parched red dirt off of Vogel on the Sears Park site. Whicher leaves the Silverado on a patch of scrub grass outside a mesh-wire perimeter fence. He walks the thirty yards across the denuded earth toward a group of men in bump caps in the shade of a construction site office.

A second group, Hispanic, are clearing dirt and stones from a trench behind a crawler tractor with a ripper.

Already, the marshal can see Riley McGuire; dressed in jeans and a sport coat, a white, full-brim hard hat on his head, mirrored sunglasses hiding his eyes. Tate is there also, Lance Tate, talking with a construction surveyor.

McGuire stares in Whicher's direction as he enters the site. Then turns toward a man driving one of the bulldozers thirty yards off, the man wearing a dirt-smeared T-shirt, his arms tanned, tattooed.

The marshal stops, waits a few yards from the site office—waits for McGuire to separate himself from the group and walk over.

A few of the men watch, only barely interested, Whicher just another man in a suit, his hat pitched forward against the glare of high sun.

"Marshal," McGuire says. "Mister Avery called me this morning. Told me you might come around looking for me."

Whicher eyes him.

"He told me that if you did, I should call one of the company attorneys. Have somebody present."

The marshal scans the site, squinting as a cloud of dust drifts from the blade of one of the bulldozers.

"Mister Avery thinks you have some kind of a fixation. With him, with this business. He's concerned about potential damage to the company reputation."

"You want to talk somewhere private, I can take you down to the US Marshals office?"

McGuire pumps his bull-neck.

Whicher stares into the man's mirrored shades. "I'm pursuing a line of enquiry related to a homicide investigation."

"You really need to speak with me?"

The marshal takes out the notebook from his suit, takes out a pen.

Across the site, the driver of the bulldozer idles the throttle—his gaze cuts across to McGuire and Whicher.

The marshal sees the bulldozer driver is Frank Nelson.

"Carl's boat was found close to the scene of this murder," McGuire says. "I can understand that, understand your interest. But the boat was obviously taken, stolen by somebody."

Whicher watches the Hispanic men at the newly-broken ground, pausing to wipe sweat from their eyes as the ripper works its way another few yards.

"You ought to be looking for whoever took the boat," McGuire says.

"We're looking."

"What did you want to talk to me about?"

The marshal turns to McGuire again, stares directly at him. "Last person to use Mister Avery's house on the lake was you. By all accounts. You have a set of keys? You were at the house at the weekend?"

"The hell does that have to do with anything?"

"Your fingerprints are going to be all over the property. We have to be able to account for that."

A muscle works in McGuire's jaw, he scratches at the goatee beard.

"You were there. Did you use the boat?"

"I've been there a bunch of times."

"I need to know about it, if I'm going to rule anybody out."

"I've been out there a lot of times, so have plenty of other folk."

"It's you I'm asking."

"Alright," McGuire says. "Alright. So, I was there."

"Anybody with you?"

"A buddy of mine, out of Dallas."

"Name?"

"Johnny Rawlson."

"How come y'all were staying up on the lake?"

"We were fishing," McGuire says. "Kicking back, you know, for the weekend? Getting out of town, away from the city."

"Rawlson." Whicher writes down the name.

"He doesn't have a damn thing to do with this either."

"Y'all use the boat?"

"It has no motor. The motor's in the shop for servicing."

"So, you didn't use it?"

"We didn't, no."

"Where y'all fish?"

"Right off of the jetty. With a cold-box of beers."

"The boat house, was it closed up?"

McGuire looks at him.

"Was it closed? When you left the property?"

"No. Well, hell I don't know."

The marshal taps the pen against the note pad.

"We didn't use the damn boat," McGuire says, "Carl already told me it was out of action."

"He told you that?"

"Yes, he did. We fished off of the jetty, mostly. We tried a couple of times from the end of the boat house. Just to try another spot."

"Why didn't you close the door to the boathouse when you left?"

"It was open when we got there, most of the time that's just how it is." McGuire shrugs. "I guess we've all been a little lax. Carl leaving it that way, the rest of us doing the same."

Whicher studies the man, pictures Avery's place, the wooden boathouse, the door up on overhead runners.

McGuire could have left it open, facilitated the boat being taken. So could Avery. "You stay up there all weekend?"

"We stayed Friday night, all of Saturday. Johnny went on back to Dallas Sunday afternoon."

"Just the two of you?"

"Right."

"Nobody else."

"Nope."

"This guy, Rawlson?"

"He's a buddy of mine, he works in the oil business."

"I'll need to speak with him," Whicher says.

"So, speak with him."

"Does the name Hoffman mean anything to you?"

McGuire frowns, shakes his head.

"Elijah Hoffman? Mister Avery's acquainted with him. I imagine you would be too."

McGuire puts a hand to the brim of his hard hat.

"Hoffman's the owner of a cotton farm outside of Anson," Whicher says.

McGuire finally nods.

"Mister Avery told me y'all were trying to buy land from him. The corporation was. For a wind farm. That something you were involved in?"

"So what if it was?"

"Elijah Hoffman is the man we found murdered up at the dam."

McGuire angles his body a fraction away from the dust blowing across the construction site. His body is taught, his face guarded.

High up on the bulldozer Frank Nelson still watches.

"Were you party to the negotiations with Hoffman?"

McGuire barely nods.

"We're going to need to talk about that," Whicher says.

"It was a simple land sale."

"We can talk here," Whicher says. "Or we can do it across town at the USMS office."

McGuire breaks off from looking across the site at Frank Nelson. He turns the mirrored shades onto Whicher. "Across town then," he says. "We set a time, we set a date. If this is going to drag on and on, if you're going to read something into everything I've done, everything I say, I'll want my lawyer present."

"That's your right, sir."

"None of us had a damn thing to with this, marshal. I barely knew him."

Whicher puts away the notepad. "A man was shot to death with a hunting bow…" He turns to leave. "And you knew him."

🙶

The view south beyond the end of the runway is a heat haze of flat scrub and ranch land, ochre and green stretching to a blue-gray faded distance. From the departure gate at Abilene regional airport, Whicher studies the view from the plate-glass windows—the edge of the city a scattered roof line to the west, sun pinning everything, hammering the Texas land.

A twin-engined, fifty-seat ERJ jet is at the stand for boarding; the flight to Dallas Fort Worth.

Whicher sips on a cup of coffee, a canvas bag at his feet. Inside is a pair of jeans and an old pair of army boots, a gray T-shirt, a tan cotton jacket.

Checked and signed in to the aircraft's hold is a locked flight case containing Kevlar ballistic vests, an AR-15 plus magazines and a Remington 870, along with double-ought rounds.

The marshal watches a small propellor plane taxi onto the runway, ready for take off. He slips out his phone, keys the number for home—lets his gaze run out in the direction of Wylie, ten miles over to the southwest.

The call answers.

"Leanne?"

At the end of the line is the sound of someone breathing.

He hears his wife's voice in the background. "Lori, say hello…"

"Hello." His daughter speaks uncertainly.

Whicher leans back in his seat.

"Hello?"

"Hey, sweetheart."

More silence. Then Leanne; "We saw it was you, she wanted to answer. And then she didn't."

"She sounds funny."

"She sounds cute," his wife says. "Where are you? Is everything okay?"

"At the airport." Whicher leans forward. "I'm flying out to Lake Charles. With Ortega. That's why I'm calling. The parish sheriff's office are putting together a search team. We're going to try to bring out our homicide suspect."

"Right now?"

"Tonight."

Leanne is quiet on the end of the line.

"We have a flight to Dallas, then a connection out to Lake Charles. We're going in—if we can find him, we'll bring him on back to Abilene."

"You'll be gone all night?"

"Yeah. I guess."

"You think you'll find him? You think there could be any trouble?"

The marshal pictures Bayou Serpent, the swamp, the backwood land off of the river. He thinks of the fast-abandoned forest clearing, the meth-cooker's lair. The flight case in the aircraft's hold. "No."

"No?"

"Sheriff's office know what they're doing."

He hears his wife exhale into the end of the phone.

"We're just there to pick him up, we'll make the arrest, and come on back."

At the entrance to the gate, Sandro Ortega is walking in—eating a burrito from the airport concession. He's dressed in cargo pants, a black polo shirt, a sports bag slung over his shoulder.

"Call me," Leanne says, "let me know what's happening."

"I will."

"And be careful."

"I know. I will."

Ortega raises a hand, waves the burrito.

"Kiss Lori, for me," Whicher says.

"Alright. But call me later."

"I got to go, Ortega's here."

The younger marshal crosses the gate area, swings the bag off his shoulder, sits down in the next seat but one.

Whicher puts away the phone, checks his watch. "You get back home? You get everything you need?"

"All good." Ortega nods.

"I checked the hardware in, cleared it with the airport."

"You're still wearing your suit?"

Whicher indicates the bag at his feet. "I brought a change of clothes."

"What is it," Ortega says. "Another suit?"

Whicher cuts a look at the younger marshal.

Ortega cracks a smile, takes a bite of the burrito. Winks. "Just kidding."

"You see your wife?" Whicher says.

"I saw her."

"You tell her you won't be back tonight?"

"Mm-hmm."

"How she like you working a homicide investigation?"

"Hey. It was her idea to come to Abilene."

"To see more of the family?" Whicher says. "How's that working out?"

Ortega chews on the burrito, nods, conceding the point.

Whicher looks out of the window at the sleek fuselage of the jet on the stand. "Riley McGuire's asking to be interviewed with a lawyer present."

Ortega finishes the mouthful of burrito. "You saw him?"

"I caught up with him at their construction site. I don't

think he put three arrows into Elijah Hoffman," Whicher says. "But maybe he made sure the boat was accessible. Made sure somebody could get it."

"Somebody like Ray Dubois?"

"McGuire said he was there on a fishing weekend—with a buddy out of Dallas. I asked him about the boat, did he use it, he told me no. I asked him about the boathouse, about the door, he said he knew it wasn't closed."

"Alright," Ortega says.

"At least one other person was involved with this," Whicher says. "If Dubois fired the shots, he wasn't firing from any boat—Doc Fernandez's expert testified to that."

Ortega nods.

"Maybe somebody else was there to take the body, dump it out in the middle of the lake."

"Dubois took off in Hoffman's truck," Ortega says, "we know that. But, you think McGuire?"

Whicher doesn't answer.

"How about this 'fishing buddy'?"

"Guy named Johnny Rawlson, out of Dallas. We'll need to get him checked out."

"I got another theory."

Whicher looks at the younger marshal.

"Gail Griffin says there's no trace of Elijah Hoffman on the boat. I called her before I left, when I got back in to Pine Street. She's trying to get a lead on the trolling motor, find out where it came from. I asked her to check for Frank Nelson's prints."

"She find them?"

"Multiple prints, she said, but none of them are too clear."

"We need to check Riley McGuire, and this other guy, Rawlson, see if either one of 'em have ever been printed." Whicher looks at Ortega. "What's the theory?"

"I've been looking deeper into the records for background on Frank Nelson—those threats, intimidation charges? The complainant was a landowner."

Whicher shifts in his seat.

"A guy being harassed by bikers," Ortega says. "Guys riding in on his property, threatening him and his family."

"Do the records say why?"

"Complainant said the bikers started coming around about the time he was approached by a company looking to buy the land. He hadn't been thinking of selling, but he started getting a whole bunch of trouble—people riding around, partying out there. When he tried to get them to leave, they turned nasty. It went on for months, he said. In the end he took up the offer to sell."

A public address system chimes into life in the airport— a female voice announcing the flight to Dallas ready for boarding.

"You know who bought the land?" Whicher says.

"It was bought by a holding company," Ortega says, "named Contaldo."

"We know anything about them?" Whicher asks.

Ortega shakes his head. "We can find out."

CHAPTER 24

Bayou Serpent, Louisiana.

The sun is starting to set behind the Louisiana forest. In front of the empty fire station building, a group of sheriff's trucks are parked off the two-lane road on a concrete square.

Boats are hitched to the backs of three of the trucks, a half-dozen deputies assembled. K-9 handlers attend to three alert-looking German Shepherds.

Whicher, in jeans and boots, stands with Ortega—both men wearing Kevlar *US Marshals* vests.

Ortega's armed with the AR-15 as well as the Glock at his side.

Whicher sports the Remington 870 shotgun, along with a Glock, the Ruger locked inside of the flight case.

The tall, black deputy, Lemar Broussard stands with the parish sheriff, Darius Baldwin. Whicher studies him; a tough-looking fifty-year-old with thinning blond hair.

The ride out from the airport at Lake Charles had been fast enough with Broussard at the wheel. Just enough time to listen to the deputy's briefing.

Broussard now indicates something to the sheriff on an enlarged map. The sheriff steps forward, clears his throat to address the assembled group.

"Alright—I'll keep this brief. We need to move out while we still have light. We have information tonight in regard to two individuals suspected of production and supply of a Schedule II controlled substance. Also, we have intel concerning a man wanted for questioning on a felony vehicle theft—and potential involvement in a homicide." Sheriff Baldwin turns in the direction of Whicher and Ortega. "Two US Marshals out of Texas are along with us this evening, they'll be accompanied by Deputy Broussard."

Whicher nods as the group of sheriff's deputies glance over.

Sheriff Baldwin continues. "The search area consists of a group of shacks forming a camp up beyond Point Couteau on the northern bank of the river." The sheriff holds up his map. "Y'all have a copy of this, you know what you'll be doing. But I want to say the men we're looking for are armed and dangerous—I want everybody aware of that. We have reason to believe the suspects will be in the area targeted by our search tonight. We'll put into the river here, move upstream. We'll keep noise to a minimum, there's a high risk of flight into the backwoods and cane breaks and fields beyond. Let's be mindful not to alert anybody of our approach. We'll keep the dogs back, bring them in if people start to run."

Broussard raises a hand.

"Lemar? You want to say something?"

The deputy steps forward. "Most you were here when Rita hit, the place was messed up, water up over the houses, everything gone to hell. These people were here then, they about lost everything. But they made it out. They self-identify with a survivalist lifestyle. So they're ready for when the shit hits the fan. That makes 'em more likely to run, more likely to give trouble."

"I'll add this," the sheriff says. "I've been wanting to get in, flush a few of them out of here. Finding a dump site, plus there being a homicide suspect among 'em, means we can go in pretty hard."

From his fatigue shirt, Broussard takes out a sheet of Xeroxed paper printed with the mugshots and names of the various suspects. "You've all been issued with these," he says. "Any of these individuals you can detain."

The sheriff nods. "Anyone failing to comply with a request from any officer can also be detained. We'll bring 'em in and let 'em go if we can't charge them. Better that than not bring 'em in at all."

Broussard looks at Whicher and Ortega. "Does the marshals service want to say a word?"

Whicher steps forward to the head of the group, looks among the faces. "You folk know these woods an' all. You know the kind of people we're looking for. I'll say the murder suspect on this list, Raymond Landry Dubois, is thought to have shot and killed a man with a hunting bow out in Texas. So keep in mind the sound of gunfire may not be the only alert that you're in danger. Some of these folk won't necessarily use a gun. I don't know about all of 'em up there, up river in the woods. But this one, Dubois, y'all need to be careful. Everybody needs to have each other's back."

⚔

The heat trapped in the swamp is stifling, sweat runs in Whicher's hair, down the back of his cotton T-shirt beneath the Kevlar ballistic vest. His hands are sticky against the steel of the barrel and the butt of the shotgun. The sun is gone completely, now. In the gloom of dusk, branches of bald cypress hang skeins of Spanish moss over the brown waters of the river.

Deputy Broussard steers the flat-bottomed boat along the serpentine channel—outboard motor running low, two sheriff's boats line-astern behind them, the dog-handlers and the German Shepherds in the rearmost craft, a specialized marine unit launch.

Ortega scans the overgrown bank, AR-15 over his shoulder on a two-point sling, the muzzle of the rifle pointed down.

Ahead in the channel is a split—a fork where a smaller waterway branches left, toward the northernmost bank of the river. Duck weed and hyacinth float on the surface, masking its course.

Broussard steers to port, taking the aluminum-hulled boat toward the mouth of the smaller channel. He turns around to the boats behind, signals to them with his hand.

Whicher watches the two boats to the rear take the

lead—to steer ahead into the gloom on the central course of the river; Broussard's briefing en route from the airport had been clear—their role would be tactical, a back-stop for anybody breaking out behind the line of sheriff's men. The two boats now taking point would be the main force, headed for the front door.

The deputy cuts the outboard motor, lets the vessel drift on its own wake.

Ortega turns, looks at him.

Broussard takes a paddle from the bottom of the hull.

"Think they'll be there?" Ortega says.

"Our source does."

Whicher eyes the deputy.

"Velma Cormier," Broussard says, beneath his breath.

Whicher nods. "You call her?"

"She called me." Broussard spears the paddle into the water, pushing the boat on. "She got to thinking it over. A bunch of meth-cookers running around out here is bad enough. A suspected murderer running around with 'em? I think she decided enough was enough."

"She likely to catch any blowback?"

The deputy shakes his head. "She don't scare easy. Rita didn't get her, these sons-of-bitches won't."

Whicher stares into the gathering darkness in the trees at the water's edge. The weight of the Remington between his hands, an image of Cajun Ray Dubois in his mind's eye. He thinks of Elijah Hoffman—laying face up in the dirt at Lake Fort Phantom Hill. Three arrows sticking out of his body, eyes wide open to the sky.

Deputy Broussard shifts the paddle from one side of the boat to the other.

The stream stops only a few yards farther ahead.

Whicher peers into the half-light in the backwoods.

Ortega readies himself to jump from the prow onto a bank shadowed with rampant willow.

Broussard silently propels the boat forward through the muddied stream.

The marshal studies the northern side of the channel. Through the trees he can see a field of cane, sugar cane, ten feet high.

Broussard bends his back, pushes the boat up onto the bank.

Ortega jumps out, stoops beneath the overhang of branches. He holds the flat-bottomed vessel as Whicher and Broussard step out.

The deputy grabs hold of the prow, drags the boat clear of the water.

Within the growth of trees, Whicher feels the trapped heat pulsing.

He stares into the woods' interior—between tupelo and cypress and oak and willow.

Deputy Broussard adjusts the straps on his bullet-proof vest. He checks the semi-automatic pistol at his hip. Clipped to his shirt is a two-way radio. He steps away from the bank of the stream, parts a string of air vines hanging from the canopy overhead. "We can track in a little way here," he says. "Then we're going to need to fan out."

Whicher gestures at Ortega, signaling for him to follow

behind Broussard, the marshal taking up position last in the line, shotgun pointed at the forest floor.

Pushing into dense undergrowth, the ground is waterlogged. The sound of lubbers and cicadas and winged insects all around.

Broussard raises a hand. Stops, turns around. "The headland is up ahead," he says, beneath his breath. "Point Couteau and the camp. You guys want to push out on the flanks, we'll hold a secondary line along here."

"How far you want us out?" Whicher says.

"About a hundred yards either way, if you can get that far."

"I'll take the right," Whicher says.

Ortega nods. "I got the left."

"I'm on radio with the search team," Broussard says. "I'll shout up if I hear they got 'em taped, or if something happens. This is going to be real quick, they'll hit the camp it's going to be over."

Whicher swings the shotgun out in front of himself, starts to make his way between the cypress and gum and live oak and knee-high bush palmetto.

Sweat is running freely on him now, the T-shirt clinging, denim jeans dragging at his legs. Ground-water is over his boots, his feet are soaked. He feels his skin prickling against the suffocating wall of heat.

Pacing off the yardage, he moves low, the 870 Remington balanced between both hands.

He steps into a small clearing—a few stumps where trees have been cut and taken out. Aligning himself with the direction of the river camp he lets his breathing settle, listens to the sound of the swamp and the forest. The silhouette of a heron appears overhead in the sky and then is gone.

He scans the clearing, adjusting to the light, to the sound and the air around him. Memories of night ops. overseas in the back of his mind, old memories triggered, heart rate quickening, mind alert.

He checks his watch. He can barely see its face.

Squatting, he listens, adjusts his grip on the shotgun.

Anybody trying to run from the back of the camp, officers would already be in place; waiting, that was the plan.

Whicher settles, eyes sweeping back and forth across the small clearing. First sign of anybody would be noise, not visual.

He pictures Deputy Broussard and Ortega—as the dark descends. The night woods a living mass, sound and scent and crawling heat.

A flat report breaks the momentary stillness.

Distant. Deflected, by the trees.

Another.

Small-arms.

Followed by a burst—automatic rifle fire.

The marshal raises up from the squat position—mouth open, straining to pick out anything in the near dark.

The sound of shouting comes through the trees—voices, multiple voices—he can't place where.

They're muffled, somewhere out in front, not close.

He listens for anything from Broussard, anything from his left.

A rattle of gun fire breaks out again—short bursts, single shots. More shouts.

It's from far-off to the left of his position—where Ortega is stationed.

Whicher strains his eyes to see through the trees at the edge of the clearing.

No lights, no muzzle flash.

No sign of anything moving.

More voices are calling out.

All of it, far left of his position.

"*Broussard?*" Whicher shouts.

No answer comes back.

"*Broussard, you need to move left.*"

Whicher fixes on a bearing through the trees, pushes into the undergrowth. Moves as fast as he can through the tangled vegetation.

More shots.

He spots Broussard, fifty yards from him.

The deputy has a hand to the ear-piece on his radio. He sees him.

Whicher moves close. "What the hell's going on?"

"Somebody started shooting," Broussard says, "they held back, now they think some of them have run."

Through the dark woods is the sound of barking.

"They put the dogs in?"

Broussard nods.

Whicher points into the trees. "Close up with Ortega. I'll cover the position here. They'll likely come up that side, they'll bug out straight in the woods."

Deputy Broussard takes out the semi-automatic pistol, finds a flashlight, moves into the trees.

"Call out if you get anything on radio…" The marshal watches till he can't see the deputy. Turns to face in the direction of the camp.

Dogs are barking, people shouting. He wipes sweat from his eyes, dries a wet hand against the leg of his jeans.

Suddenly there's something.

He hears it. Feels it.

Somehow knows it.

He puts the butt of the shotgun to his shoulder—swings the barrel. Steadies his breathing, eyes darting to left and right.

Something is pushing through the forest.

"Broussard?" Whicher calls out.

For a moment, there's nothing—and then it's there again, something moving forward, at speed.

"*US Marshal,*" Whicher shouts.

A shape is running through the woods—a dark shape—thirty, forty yards off.

"Hold it. Stay where you are…"

The figure is gone. He can't fire, he can't make it out.

Whicher turns, runs back in the direction of the waterway behind them—fending off vines and branches.

The boat is behind—it's behind on the bank of the stream.

The sound of dogs is louder now, more voices, distant shouts in the air.

In the trees there's just a phantom to follow—the

marshal thinks of cutting straight to the bank of the stream.

He pushes on, tries to shield himself from the overhang of vegetation.

Light is seeping in, he can sense he's nearing the water's edge.

Where the tupelo and oak start to thin, he makes a lunge for the bank—emerging from the tree line, the water up over his boots.

Upstream, he can see the boat, still there—nobody near it.

Beyond, for a split second, he sees the outline of a man.

A figure leaps across the stream at its far end, where it stops among the trees. His feet land in the water, he scrambles up through the willow and oak.

Whicher sprints along the bank side, to the place where the man went over.

Shotgun above his head, he jumps, hits the water, grabs a hold of a willow branch, pulls himself up.

A wall of cane is before him, the edge of a field, the cane dense, full-grown, a year-old crop.

He pushes in, nostrils filled with the smell of dust and vegetation and cane trash and damp earth.

Somewhere, the fleeing man has gone in.

Whicher forces his way through; just enough space among the cane stems and debris to move.

Years of army service and law enforcement tell him the man won't yet have gotten far.

Forty yards into the field there's just the open sky above his head, cane high in all directions, trapped heat.

He stops. Listens—tries to pick out the sound of any movement.

A crackling sound reaches him from somewhere.

A smell catches in the air; bitter—acrid in the back of his throat.

Smoke.

And then a flare of light leaps up into the sky.

Orange light.

Flame orange.

A burst and then a falling shower of burning ash.

He feels his heart come into his mouth. *The field of cane is on fire.*

For a split second he stares back at the growing flames, the fire blooming out, spreading sideways—flame licking into the sky, becoming a ragged wall.

Whipping around he can just make out a line, a trench, between two planted rows.

He smashes forward, fighting back a rising panic, dead stems and brittle leaves wrapping around exposed skin.

A roaring noise of burning is building. He steals a glance back over his shoulder, sees the spreading sea of white and red and orange fire.

Animal fear grips him. Black smoke roils.

Scrambling along the dip of the trench, his heart beats like a trip-hammer. Strips of cane and leaf cut at him, tangling around his feet. No going back. No going sideways. Yard on yard, second after second he smashes forward, half-blind.

Adrenaline coursing, smoke blowing, the sound of the

fire now a roar. His lungs burn, the muscles in his legs start to scream.

And then the cane is thinning—he's at an edge—he drives forward, crashes into clear air.

Onto a verge at the side of a narrow road, a forest beyond it.

A pickup truck is stopped in the middle of the roadway, headlamps blazing.

Two men are by it, staring at the field on fire.

Another man is at its rear, lit red in the tail lights.

Whicher swings up the shotgun, levels it from his shoulder.

All three men stare.

"US Marshal. Get your hands in the air."

The two men by the pickup raise their arms slowly.

The man at the back of the truck is in a leather vest, his arms bare—black hair pushed back from his face.

Whicher steps wide, draws a line on the man lit red. "Raymond Landry Dubois…"

"What the hell's going on? What is this?" the man says.

The marshal holds the 870 hard on him. "I'm arresting you on suspicion of the murder of Elijah Hoffman. In Jones County, Texas."

Chapter 25

Whicher sits on the cluttered jetty of a stilt-house, shacks and docks on pilings at either side. The old fishing camp is built from rough-sawn plank boards—the tin roofs of the shacks warped, streaked with rust.

Old tires and rope and drums of fuel and oil are everywhere. Clothes and backpacks and food and sleeping mats.

The fire in the field of cane is almost out, units from the down river fire station still fighting it.

The marshal runs his gaze over the piles of general garbage on the dock—in amongst it, melted pots and pans, plastic tubes, bottles of paint thinner and cold medicines. Drain cleaner and antifreeze. A crank-cooker's kit.

Cajun Ray Dubois sits handcuffed in the sheriff's office main boat, Ortega alongside of him, four other men in handcuffs—two each on the other two boats.

The men are dressed in combat pants, boots, ripped shirts and Ts, their hair long and matted, tattoos covering their dirt-ingrained skin.

Whicher watches the sheriff's deputies conduct a search of the shacks and the main house with flashlights and two of the dogs.

Sheriff Baldwin and Deputy Broussard interview a female, in her twenties—skinny, her jeans and top dirty—she wrings her hands in front of them, jabbers.

Broussard writes something onto a notepad. Leads her, zip-tied, to the edge of the jetty, toward the main boat.

Whicher eyes Sheriff Baldwin.

The sheriff takes off his hat, steps over.

The marshal nods. "Y'all get what you came for?"

The sheriff gestures at the pile of methamphetamine detritus on the dock.

"You're charging everybody?"

"They shoot at my officers, they're headed for the jail and then a prison yard after that."

"Anybody get hurt?"

Sheriff Baldwin shakes his head. "We came around the bend in the river, set to mosey up easy. One of these sons-of-bitches pulls out a piece and starts firing."

"I heard it," Whicher says. "I heard it back in the woods."

"We had to go on by, we couldn't put in downstream. By the time we got onto land they were running."

"You know who did the shooting?"

Baldwin points at one of the men in the boats. "That son of a bitch right there. He threw the gun out into the bayou, we'll get it though, I'll send a goddamn diver down."

The marshal studies the man on the boat, his jaw set as

he stares glass-eyed into the moss-strewn branches of bald cypress on the banks. "You think any of them managed to get away?"

"I don't think," Baldwin says. He looks at Whicher. "You believe that son of a bitch, Dubois? Setting light to a field?"

"I believe it. I'd like to know how he did it."

"One of my officers saw him grab a bottle of gel fire-starter, when he ran. Like, a 32 ounce bottle. To set the field alight. What kind of a crazy sumbitch is that?"

The marshal doesn't answer, he thinks of Hoffman shot dead like an animal at the lake.

Baldwin shakes his head, replaces his hat.

Whicher stands, picks up the Kevlar vest from the jetty. Swings up the 870 Remington. "I don't know," he says. "But I aim to find out."

Chapter 26

Ten miles outside of Abilene, a low sun hangs over the French Robertson Correctional Facility on the flat prairie land to the north-east of the city.

Whicher escorts Dubois along a prison walkway, weary from the five a.m. flight out of Lake Charles. Ortega brings up the rear.

Block work walls extend up both sides of the outdoor walkway, a dozen-feet high.

So far, there's been little enough from their prisoner; Dubois sitting near-silent, handcuffed between them on both of the flights.

At Fort Worth, the change at least gave time to scan Dubois' file from Lemar Broussard. The notes from the sheriff's office record the boat theft during Hurricane Rita—a spell in Angola awaiting trial, sentence served out in Dixon, north Louisiana. Since release, he's been pulled in twice by the sheriff's office—once for drunkenness and affray, a second time for public disturbance—a fight, no charges, none pending.

There's no list of prior delinquency or criminal behavior. The report only goes back five years, Dubois is not a native of the parish.

At the end of the prison compound walkway, Whicher presses on a buzzer by a security door.

Mechanical latches draw back, the door opens. A corrections officer awaits—Carlos DiMaria, Whicher recognizes the head of the property department.

The marshal pushes Dubois forward. "I have a suspect to book in till I can get him into court today, get him arraigned."

The corrections officer nods.

Whicher glances at Dubois in the morning sunlight—shy of six feet, his black hair slicked back, face chiseled, cut with spite. The body odor is pronounced, the man's jeans and boots filthy from the Louisiana swamp. "Raymond Landry Dubois."

"What's the charge?" DiMaria says.

"Handling a stolen vehicle."

"And destruction of property," Ortega adds. "Arson."

DiMaria looks at the younger marshal.

"He set fire to a field," Whicher says.

"Really?" DiMaria writes onto a form attached to a clip board.

"You can put him in with the general population," Whicher says, "if you're tight for room."

Dubois turns on him. "The hell're you talking about?"

Whicher sees the bullying self-regard of a small-time thief, or a wife-beater.

"He was in Angola," the marshal says, "the big house. Man ought to know the routine."

"I get a cell to myself," Dubois says. "I ain't convicted of any crime."

"You'll go where I tell you to go," Officer DiMaria puts in.

Dubois flexes his muscled arms against the handcuffs. "I want to talk to a lawyer."

"We fly five hundred miles," Whicher looks at Ortega. "The guy don't say squat."

"Now he wants to talk?" the younger marshal says.

"You get a phone call," Officer DiMaria says, "just as soon as I'm done processing you."

"Assuming you don't piss the man off," Whicher says.

Dubois stares ahead into the near-distance.

The CO steps back from the doorway, motions for them to enter.

Whicher pushes Dubois inside. "You a motorcycle man?" he says.

"The hell do you care?"

"Got the look of a biker. Lot of bikers on a prison yard. Ever run with that crowd?"

"I got nothing to say to you."

Officer DiMaria leads the way into a sparse, unfurnished room. On a central counter, boxes and plastic bags are laid out, along with a pile of forms.

"You know a man name of Nelson, Frank Nelson?" Whicher says. "He's a biker. A construction foreman. Here in Abilene."

"I told you," Dubois says, "I want representation. I want a lawyer."

"You'll be assigned one," the CO says.

"That truck you were driving," Whicher says, "out in Greenwood? The one you left at the trailer park?"

"I live on the water, man, I don't drive no truck."

"We found your hunting bow and your arrows inside it," Ortega says.

"I don't know what the hell you're even talking about."

Officer DiMaria reaches beneath the counter, pulls out a plastic tray of laundered prison whites.

"Your prints are all over the vehicle," Whicher says.

Ortega looks at Dubois. "We have witness statements to testify you were driving it."

Whicher turns to Officer DiMaria. "There some single-occupancy cells in the transient block, that right? For people awaiting trial?"

The CO eyes him.

"Away from the animals," Ortega says.

Dubois juts his chin. "You got no right bringing me here."

"If you cooperate," Whicher says, "maybe the officer could find one for you."

"I didn't do a goddamn thing…"

"You speak to a lawyer, be sure and tell him we're holding direct evidence," Whicher says. "We've got you in a car belonging to a homicide victim."

Ortega takes a half step toward Dubois. "The sheriff of Jeff Davis parish wants to charge you with attempted murder of a peace officer."

"You tell him he can stick it where the sun don't shine," Dubois answers. "I ain't afraid of this bullshit. Drop me in the jungle, this one or any other, I'll be just fine."

"I hope you're right, mano," Ortega says.

Officer DiMaria looks at Whicher. "If you're done, you can hand your prisoner over to me, I'll take it from here."

"Before I come back you think about something for me," Whicher says to Dubois. "I want to know how come you knew Elijah Hoffman?"

Dubois' expression is ugly. "I never even heard of him."

"You shot him to death up at Lake Fort Phantom Hill."

"Yeah?" The man's eyes shine.

"If you didn't know him," Whicher says, "I guess you must've been with somebody that did."

"Screw you."

The marshal motions to Ortega. He steps away to leave. "I could be interested, understand? Go on and think about that for me."

⋏

Back in Wylie, the Impala is gone from the driveway, the house deserted. Breakfast dishes are still on the countertop, a skillet on the range, mixing bowl in the sink.

Pancakes again.

Whicher smiles to himself, makes a mental note to thank Ortega.

He showers, changes into a charcoal suit. Dumps last night's clothes in the laundry basket, thinks of throwing out the pair of army boots.

He changes his mind, puts them out in the yard, he can clean them up sometime. He stands a moment in the dappled-shade—fallen leaves are on the pool cover, he ought to sweep them up. There's a rail on the fence to fix, where Lori tried to climb it, two weeks back.

He stares at her toys in a pile beneath the shaded porch. The absence of his wife and daughter strange in the stillness of the home.

Stepping back into the kitchen, he makes coffee, eats granola, buttons his shirt, fixes a dark blue neck-tie in place. He slips the tan leather shoulder-holster over the shirt, fastens it in place.

The phone on the kitchen table starts to ring, he picks it up, sees the number—Chief Marshal Evans. He presses the key to answer.

"Sandro Ortega just told me you nearly got yourself set on fire last night?"

"Ortega was going home to catch some rest…"

"Well, he's here," the chief marshal says. "And he says the pair of you arrested Dubois? You want to charge him with murder?"

"We don't have enough for that," the marshal says. "I want to talk to the DA's office, we can charge him with possession of Hoffman's truck. Gail Griffin says his prints are in the vehicle. If that's not enough, he set fire to the field I was chasing him through last night, the parish sheriff's office thinks it ought to go as attempted murder."

"Are you kidding?"

"Nope."

"Well, what do you intend to do?"

"Rattle Dubois," Whicher says. "Or rattle his lawyer's ass when he gets one. Hit him with it. If the prosecutor sets out the possible charges, the judge ought to set any bail condition high."

"You're going to lean on Dubois?"

"I sure as hell am."

"He have a lawyer?"

"I'm guessing he'll go with the public defender."

"Ortega said you're going for an arraignment later today."

"Initial arraignment. I'll talk with the DA, see what they want to do."

Evans is silent a moment. "You don't think it's too early? You don't want the man to walk."

⼈

Traffic is light on South 1st, the windows rolled on the Silverado. Whicher drives the four-lane across town, past the banks and body shops, the pawn stores and pay-day loans.

The phone on the dash-mount lights up—Whicher sees a number he doesn't recognize.

He keys the phone onto speaker.

"Marshal? Levi Underwood."

Whicher pictures the FBI agent from the Violent Crimes Task Force.

"Following up about the attempted armed robbery of the armored car? On Judge Ely?"

"Right," Whicher says. "Go ahead."

"I spoke with people here about the firearms-discharge reports. Review team don't think there'll be any problem. You pass that on to your partner?"

"I sure will."

"I thought you'd want to know."

Whicher checks the rear-view, nods to himself.

"How you making out on the homicide case?" Underwood says.

"We arrested somebody last night."

The FBI agent whistles into the phone.

The stop light ahead changes from green to red.

Whicher lets the Chevy slow, pulls up at the intersection alongside an Exxon tanker truck. "What's happening with that gas station shooting?"

"We're working on it," Underwood says. "One thing— there was something hinky about the guy that was shot— Dwayne Cameron. According to the armored car company."

"Why's that?"

"They already suspected an employee might be providing assistance on the robberies. They had a number of people in mind, he was one of them."

"That so?"

"Too much went right during the robberies," Underwood says. "In terms of timing, in terms of how to take the cars down. They think somebody must've been providing details about the drops, about the kind of money on board."

"The shot guy was an inside man?"

The stop light turns to green, Whicher slides his foot off the brake, hits the gas.

"We've got bullets at the scene resembling some of the lead from the armored car raid on Judge Ely," Underwood says.

"No shit?"

"Not conclusive. But it could have been an AR-15, the same AR-15. Which could make it an execution."

"For what?" the marshal says.

"For the raid going south? Or just to shut the guy down, finito. I talked with the guy's widow, there were some things going on in the man's life, things that might've made him vulnerable. The guy had a gambling problem…"

Whicher pushes back in the driver's seat. Accelerates onto the road ahead of him, lets the air race in from the open window. Thinks of Hoffman. Money problems, gambling. An execution-style killing.

"I might need to talk with you some more on that…"

"Oh?" Underwood says.

"It's maybe nothing."

Whicher lets his mind hunt, his thoughts range.

The FBI man is silent. He comes back on the line. "You don't sound like it's nothing…"

Chapter 27

In the marshals office on Pine Street, Gail Griffin is the first call on the list. She can make an eleven o'clock meeting; Whicher calls the DA next—the prosecuting attorney's office can see the pair of them in the federal building at eleven-thirty.

Ortega's seated at a desk in the far corner—checking for more background on Riley McGuire, and Frank Nelson—keyed-up, riding a wave of nervous energy, a second wind.

Whicher thinks of the little he still knows of Elijah Hoffman. The DA's office will look for evidentiary weak points before recommending a charge. He clicks open a desktop computer, runs a search on the man's name.

There's barely a mention, aside from reports in the last week, since Hoffman's discovery at Lake Fort Phantom Hill.

Working another angle, he types the farm address into a search engine.

Several listings come up from the website of an Abilene realty agency.

Whicher clicks onto the detail page of one of them.

Multiple photographs show the Hoffman farm—the house and outbuildings and barns, there's a map, a description of the land.

The property is marked; *Sale Recently Completed.*

The marshal searches for an on-screen telephone number. He picks up the phone from the desk, dials.

A receptionist routes him through to an office manager—a man with the name of Garth Sharpe.

"I'm calling from the US Marshals Service," Whicher says, "here in town, in Abilene. About a listing on your website. A cotton farm out in Stamford, in Jones County?"

"Marshal, yes."

"It's listed as a recent sale?"

"Yes, sir."

"Your office handled it?"

"Yes, sir. How can I help?"

"Mister Sharpe, were you aware the owner of the property was recently found deceased out at Lake Fort Phantom Hill? It's been on the local TV networks, I guess the radio…"

"To be honest," Sharpe cuts in, "we'd been wondering if somebody from law enforcement was going to call."

The marshal cradles the phone in his neck, searches for a pen. "I'm leading the investigation into Mister Hoffman's death."

"I see."

"I'm going to need to ask you some questions about the sale of the property."

"Yes, of course," Sharpe says. "Anything we can do.

What would you like to know?"

"Who purchased it? How recent was the sale?"

"The purchaser was BluClear Energy. They're a power company, they install wind and solar."

Whicher thinks of Carl Avery; he talked about wind power. He writes down the name of the company.

"The sale was agreed about six weeks back," Sharpe says.

"The deal is done, the property's sold?"

"Both parties ratified the contract. There was no financing contingent on the deal. So, it was a cash sale, basically. Closing attorneys have carried out the title search, so far as I know. The binder is complete, I think, all of the legal documents are in place."

"So, they're the owners?"

"They are, marshal."

"How come Hoffman hasn't moved out? All of his belongings are still right there?"

"I'm not sure of all of the particulars," Sharpe says. "They may have agreed an extension to vacate."

"How much the place go for?"

"They got the full asking price."

"Which was?"

"For the house, the barns and everything else, plus all of the land, it came in at one-point-three million. It's a pretty substantial property, there's a good amount of productive land."

"One-point-three million dollars?"

"Yes, sir, marshal. There was plenty of interest in it, too."

"BluClear Energy, that a local business?"

"They're based back in Dallas, I believe."

The marshal thinks about it. "You said it was a cash sale? Where will the money be at, now?"

"You'd have to speak with the acting attorneys."

"Would it be in Hoffman's bank?"

"I couldn't tell you that. I simply don't know."

"Can you give me the name of the attorney?"

"One moment, marshal, I'll see if I can find it from the file."

Two more quick phone calls, one to the office of the closing attorney representing Hoffman in the sale—the next to the manager of the bank the money was wired to.

The full amount from the sale is sitting in a checking account in the names of Elijah and Jean Hoffman.

Whicher stands, checks his watch. Runs a hand over his jaw.

He walks across the office to Ortega, taps him once on the shoulder.

Ortega turns around.

"News."

Whicher squares his hat.

The younger marshal looks up, blank.

"Jean Hoffman has one-point-three-million dollars sitting in a checking account, here in Abilene."

Ortega's eyes widen.

"The farm out there is sold."

The younger marshal sits back in his chair. "She mention that?"

Whicher shakes his head.

"Jean Hoffman is the sole beneficiary?"

"We head out now, we could stop in at the Hoffman farm—before we pick up Dubois for the arraignment hearing." Whicher takes the truck keys from his pants pocket.

"You think Jean Hoffman could've been a part of this?"

"Let's move." The marshal flips the truck keys in his hand. "Let's go, let's hit the road."

Stamford, Tx.

North of the Jones County seat, Whicher steers the Silverado along the dirt road—the outbuildings of the Hoffman farm just visible; an outpost in a sea of cotton, a land of heat haze and desiccating wind.

Ortega sits alongside him in the shotgun seat. "You don't think it'd be a good idea to call ahead?"

The marshal stares out through the dust-streaked windshield. "If she's out here, I don't want her forewarned—I don't want her prepared."

"How about if she's not here?"

Whicher angles his head toward the rear of the cab. "Then we head on over to French Robertson. Pick up Dubois. There's a D-ring in back on the floor, a length of chain in the toolbox, we can hook him up."

Ortega cuts a sideways look over his shoulder.

"Tell me what you have on Frank Nelson?" Whicher says.

The younger marshal's face is guarded. "I called a couple of street cops on the PD. This morning."

"People you know?"

"Friends of friends," Ortega says. "Of my wife's family."

"So, what do you hear?"

"Word-of-mouth," Ortega says, "nothing official. But the biker link is pretty deep. That history of intimidation…"

"Including harassing landowners," Whicher says.

"I think Frank Nelson knows plenty of small time crooks, maybe even some jail birds."

Whicher glances at the younger man, sees a side he hasn't seen before; uncertainty, doubt.

Ortega looks off out of the window of the truck.

"This stage of an investigation," the marshal says, "sometimes you have to follow gut."

Ortega picks at a hangnail on his thumb. "The guy that was shanked in the county jail, Hernandez? I can't help thinking Nelson could've had something to do with that. He would've known how to put the word out, pull some strings."

Whicher nods.

"I don't have evidence."

Whicher lets the truck slow passing the first of the farm's outbuildings. "Hernandez got his ass killed over something."

"Riley McGuire's no angel, either," Ortega says. "People have a habit of dying around the man."

"They do what?"

"I need to check it out a little more. But a guy was killed on a construction site, one of McGuire's sites. A guy that fell off the side of a building. No criminal charges," Ortega says, "it went down as an accident. But the guy's family tried to bring a civil case. There'd been a dispute between them. Long-standing. Over money. This was back in Dallas."

"He's out of Dallas?"

"According to the record."

"What else you hear?

"McGuire's first wife died," Ortega says.

Whicher slows the truck to a stop in the farmyard.

"The man backed his car over her; on the driveway of his house."

The marshal shuts off the engine. "Serious?"

"Four years back," Ortega says. "A night in December. She'd been out to some party. Drinking heavily. Post-mortem report recorded the presence of marijuana and cocaine. According to the Coroner's report, McGuire was backing out of his drive, setting out to look for her, he said he was worried, he didn't know where she was. A friend dropped her off already, down the street. He said she fell, he hit her. Called an ambulance. Tried to save her. But it was no good."

Whicher studies the younger man's face.

"There'd been fights, according to the family, a lot of things going on."

The marshal lets his hands slide around the edges of the wheel. "The company that just bought this place is out of Dallas…" He stares out at the empty yard, at the facade of the house. "McGuire was staying with a fishing buddy out of Dallas; out at Carl Avery's place. We need to check that out."

Ortega nods.

Whicher pops the door of the truck, pushes it wide.

Both men step out.

The yard is deserted, no vehicles.

Whicher steps to the front door, tries the bell. "Jean Hoffman was staying with a sister in Dallas…"

"You really think she might have something to do with this?"

No sound comes from the house, no lights show in any of the windows.

"One-point-three-million says she might have." Whicher wraps the door handle with the edge of his jacket—he tries the door, it's locked.

He scans the surrounding land—the farm, the neighboring fields. A heavy air of isolation hangs over it all; phone poles and power lines the only feature tracing roads to unknown places. "A woman living in a place like this…"

Ortega shrugs.

Whicher leads the younger marshal around the side of the house.

Looking into the kitchen window, he sees no lights, no sign of anyone home.

Skirting the outbuildings, he stands, finally, by the overgrown vegetable garden, by a pile of pulled-up weeds.

"What's the connection?" Ortega says. "Between any of them—between her and Cajun Ray Dubois. McGuire, Avery, Frank Nelson."

Whicher leads the way back to the truck.

With no answer.

A mile along the dirt road headed back toward the highway, a Ram pickup with heavy-duty tires is parked at the edge of a field. Alongside the truck is the pump-housing to a pipe feeding water to a center-pivot irrigation system. A Hispanic man works the blue-painted shut-off wheel on a section of the pipeline, a woman in jeans by his side.

Whicher slows. "Ain't that the neighbor?"

The woman turns at the approach of the truck.

Whicher brakes the Silverado to stop in a cloud of thin, red dust.

He shuts off the motor, steps out.

The Hispanic worker eyes him.

"Marshal," Mary-Jo Rucker says.

"Ma'am."

"The damn water pressure's too low," the woman says.

Whicher looks along the span of galvanized pipes and trusses supported above the green crop.

"Felipe's about to take a look at the pump. The soil's so dry, I need to do something."

"We were out at the Hoffman place," Whicher says. "She's not there. Y'all know where she's at?"

The woman's gaze drifts away. The Hispanic man's face is stone.

Ortega climbs from the Silverado, leans his arms on the roof of the cab.

"I went over the night before last." Mary-Jo shakes her head. "She said she couldn't stay here. That she didn't want to no more."

The younger marshal looks at her. "She say anything else?"

Whicher thinks of the sale, the property sale. The power company, the new owners.

"She says she just can't bring herself to be here…" Mary-Jo gives a small shudder. "It was pretty awful. Poor Jean. She's just in shock. She's not really there. She said she'd go on back to Dallas, to be with her sister, stay with her, least, for now."

"You know when she left?" Ortega says. "Did you see her leave?"

The man named Felipe mutters a word to Mary-Jo in Spanish. "*Ayer…*"

"Yesterday?" Ortega says.

Whicher looks at the man. "What about yesterday?"

"Oh," Mary-Jo says. "Yes. A truck came by. We were out checking on the field, over at the tower, yonder." She indicates the pivot point at the center of the span of pipes. "A man came by driving a truck. Couldn't tell you much about it, just that we noticed it."

Whicher looks at her. At the man, Felipe.

The Hispanic pulls at the sleeve of his work shirt, says nothing.

"Nobody much comes past here," Mary-Jo says. "If somebody does, you'll notice it."

The marshal glances at Ortega, then back at Mary-Jo. "What kind of truck?"

"Marshal, I don't know."

"How about the color?"

"It was sort of dark."

Ortega looks at the man Felipe. "How about you, hermano?"

The Hispanic shakes his head.

"There was a blond man at the wheel," Mary-Jo says.

Whicher eyes her. "Blond man?"

"That's all I could tell you."

Chapter 28

The Ad Seg wing at French Robertson is scrubbed and bleached; white-painted walls, polished concrete underfoot, two featureless floors interspaced with plate-steel doors.

Whicher follows a heavily-built, black corrections officer, Ortega at his side.

Through slit-windows in the cell doors are glimpses of the occupants—some moving, others motionless within a solitary world.

The CO slows, stops outside of a door at the end of the wing. "I'll go in first," he says. He works the locking mechanism, swings the door open. Calls out, "Officer entering."

He steps inside.

Whicher waits at the threshold of the small cell.

Dubois stands in its center, dressed in prison whites, loose cotton pants and a pull-over shirt. In the corner is a stainless-steel combination toilet bowl and sink. Along one wall is a metal cot, a seat and table top bolted into the wall.

The corrections officer motions the marshal forward.

Ortega follows in behind.

"Got your own room?" Whicher says.

"In Ad Seg?" Dubois replies. "Solitary. Locked up twenty-three hours a day?"

"You want to go into gen pop, it can be arranged," the corrections officer says.

Dubois opens his mouth to say something. Decides against it.

"We're here to move you," Whicher says. "Take you on down to Abilene. You'll go before the court this afternoon. Then we'll bring you back here."

"How about if I make bail?" Dubois says.

Whicher looks at him. "A murder charge? That's automatically denied."

Dubois flares his nostrils, looks from Whicher to Ortega and back again.

"I told you to think it over," the marshal says. "'Less you had something better to do. Put your hands together out in front of you." Whicher takes a pair of cuffs from a pouch on his belt.

Dubois grits his teeth, puts his hands together at the wrists.

"You got some decisions you need to make here, life-changing decisions." Whicher snaps on the cuffs, directs a question at the CO; "His personal belongings? You get everything logged?"

"Who signed him in?"

"DiMaria, Officer DiMaria. This morning, early."

"He'll be off-shift now, but everything should be in order."

"We good to go?"

"All good, marshal."

Ortega takes hold of Dubois by the arm. "Alright, Cochise, let's go, let's take a walk."

Whicher steps from the cell into the corridor, ushers out Ortega and Dubois.

The corrections officer closes the door, locks it.

"You know the evidence against you?" Whicher says.

Dubois shakes his head. "I don't even have to talk to you."

The CO steps around all three of the men—leads the way back down along the wing.

"I've got a crime scene technician working that Sierra pickup you stole from Elijah Hoffman," Whicher says. "Retired detective, she is, real sharp-eyes."

The CO approaches a motorized gate made from floor-to-ceiling steel bars. He keys a code into the gate, it starts to clank back on greased runners.

"We drive your ass down to Abilene," Whicher says. "Then I'm meeting with the DA." He turns, looks Dubois in the face.

The man stares back, blank.

"Why you steal that boat? From Carl Avery's place on the lake?"

"I don't know what you're talking about."

"You got a prior for that," Ortega says. "You make a habit of stealing people's boats?"

"That shit was in Rita," Dubois says, "the middle of a goddamn Hurricane. You ever find yourself in the path of a category five? I was just trying to stay alive."

The sliding gate clicks fully open—the corrections officer presses on an intercom box. "Officer coming through with one prisoner and two Deputy US Marshals."

"Rules don't apply," Dubois says, "a thing like that."

"Rule of law applies," Whicher says.

Dubois makes a face, cracks out an ugly laugh.

The CO makes a gesture to step through the gate.

Ortega pushes Dubois forward.

"You know what prima facie evidence is?" Whicher says.

"I don't know what the hell you're talking about."

Whicher steps into the next corridor. "Evidence sufficient to establish a fact. Or raise a presumption. I'm going on into the DA's office—I'll tell them where I think the evidence points. You speak to your lawyer, he's going to tell you to think about that."

"So, get me a goddamn lawyer, cowboy."

Whicher eyes Dubois, not breaking stride.

"Your best bet," Ortega says, "is you need to work with us here, mano."

The corrections officer points to a reinforced plate-steel door in the wall. "We can head on out over here."

⚔

Twenty minutes later, the lot in front of the Law Enforcement Center on Pecan is flooded with mid-morning sunlight. The Silverado parked in a bay by a row of Texas live oak, motor ticking heat beneath the hood.

Whicher leads Dubois and Ortega in to the LE Center

through smoked glass doors at the front of the building.

A black-clad Abilene Police sergeant is at the front desk. He clocks the man in prison whites, two suited men either side of him.

Whicher approaches the desk. "I have a meeting at the DA's office in fifteen. I need a holding cell I can leave a prisoner?"

"Not a problem," the sergeant says. "What's the charge?"

"Felony possession of a stolen automobile. But the man's a principal suspect in a homicide."

The sergeant opens up a drawer, takes out a custody form. He picks up a phone, calls for an officer to come to the front desk.

Ortega pushes Dubois forward. "You'll stay here till your arraignment."

Dubois cocks his head, shrugs his shoulders.

"I don't think you acted alone," the marshal says. "But if you're going to play dumb…"

"The hell you mean by that?"

"State of Texas carries the death penalty, same as they do in Louisiana."

A young APD officer approaches from a side door.

"You're nailed on for the murder of Elijah Hoffman," Whicher says. "Supposing you could beat that, the sheriff of Jeff Davis is ready to charge you with attempted murder of a federal officer."

Ortega takes hold of Dubois' arms—lifts them up and out.

The APD officer places a second set of cuffs above

Whicher's, snaps them closed.

Whicher takes out a key, unlocks his own set, retrieves them. "You ain't walking, no way, no how. You're some kind of a survival freak, you best start thinking on how you're going to live through this."

The young officer leads Dubois away.

"We just need you to fill out the paperwork," the sergeant says.

Whicher nods, turns to Ortega. "I'll talk with the DA. Meantime, head on over to Summerwood, introduce yourself to Carl Avery. We need a statement from him—a list of people that used his property on the lake in the last month. If he hands you off to a lawyer, get the lawyer's details, we can call them. Anyone else you see there, talk to 'em, let 'em know we're around. If Riley McGuire's there, rattle him a little. Ask him about his fishing weekend—Rawlson, his buddy out of Dallas. We need to trace the friend."

Ortega grins.

"You get done with that, take off," Whicher says. "It's been a long one already, go on home."

⁂

Inside the Federal building on Oak Street, the office of the District Attorney is quiet but for the faint hum of air conditioning blowing from the vents in the walls. Whicher studies the veteran prosecutor seated behind a black veneered desk—Richard Hampton, sharp-suited, patrician, his gray brown hair parted neatly to the side.

Hampton's face is slack in concentration—he studies a slim file of case notes on USMS headed paper.

It's not the first case Whicher's presented; he knows enough to be wary of the man. Hampton's careful, thorough, not known for making mistakes. The marshal's own reputation sits uneasily between them—Whicher known to spar, to challenge brass, to dig in his heels. Not known for backing off.

Gail Griffin sits in an office chair, suited, one leg crossed over the other.

The attorney skim-reads a passage, cross-referencing a section in the marshal's report with the evidence summary prepared by Griffin.

Adjusting the heavy framed eye-glasses, he makes a series of notes.

Finally, he lays the open file on the desk in front of him.

"Dubois?" Hampton says. "Where is he now?"

Whicher gives a flat look. "In a holding cell at the LEC."

The attorney studies the photograph attached to the topmost sheet. "Raymond Landry Dubois. Do you really think you've got your man, marshal?"

"We got one of 'em."

"For the capital murder of Elijah Hoffman?"

"He's given no account of anything—no reason why his fingerprints are in Hoffman's truck."

Hampton raises an eyebrow. Leans his head on one side.

"Witnesses in Greenwood, Louisiana, are willing to testify they saw Dubois driving the vehicle."

"This is at the trailer park site?"

Whicher nods.

The prosecutor turns to Gail Griffin. "You're happy with the fingerprint evidence?"

"A hundred percent."

"The bow," Hampton says, "this compound hunting bow?"

"He's denying it's his," Whicher says. "But we know Dubois is a bow hunter." The marshal thinks of Grady Pearce back in Shreveport. "I can get sworn statements."

Hampton turns to Gail Griffin. "It says in your report Celine Fernandez spoke with an archery expert—and there's no current way to match arrows with bows?"

Griffin rotates a ball-point pen between her fingers. "Dubois had Hoffman's truck three hundred miles away the morning after the man was murdered. He had a hunting bow in the back seat."

"It doesn't mean this bow was the murder weapon," the attorney says, "it doesn't prove that."

Whicher tips back the Resistol an inch.

Hampton picks at the cuff of his pressed white shirt.

"We got a bunch of photographs any jury would find compelling," the marshal says. "Elijah Hoffman with three arrows in him."

"The public defender," Hampton says, "will raise the question of whether someone other than Dubois fired the shots."

"He was driving a dead man's car with a hunting bow in back?"

"Dubois served time for theft of a boat," Gail Griffin

says, "during Hurricane Rita. A boat was stolen for use in this, it's another link."

"What evidence do you have of its use?" Hampton says.

The crime scene officer frowns. "It was right by the body at the scene."

"That lake is sixty feet deep," Whicher says. "Dubois could have been fixing to dump the corpse, get rid of it."

"Then why didn't he?"

"We don't know," the marshal says. "I think the scene might have been disturbed."

"In what way?"

"We know a couple kids were fishing out there. Maybe they turned up before there was a chance to dispose of the body."

Hampton laces his fingers together. "The crime scene report doesn't include material evidence related to the boat."

"We're still working on it," Gail Griffin says. "It had a trolling motor onboard, we're trying to trace where it came from. We believe it was stolen."

A look of discomfort spreads across Hampton's neat-groomed features. "This is the potential link to Hernandez?" he says. "The car thief stabbed to death in the Jones County jail?"

"Yes, it is," Whicher says.

"The investigation on Hernandez appears to be going nowhere, so far," Hampton says.

"You know as well as I do, nobody in the jail house is about to talk."

"Well then, tell me about Dubois," Hampton says, "you

went out to Louisiana and arrested him?"

"Part of a joint operation with the sheriff of Jeff Davis County," Whicher says. "The sheriff's office was looking for meth-cookers, known associates of Dubois."

"You don't think it might have been too early?"

"Given the flight risk, no."

"At which point," Hampton peers over the top of his eye glasses, "a field of cane was set alight, with you in it?"

"Dubois set it on fire," Whicher says. "The man's a survivalist, I think he prepared a fall back position. They had plenty of gasoline for their outboard motors, one of the sheriff's people saw Dubois running with a bottle of fire-starter. I think he torched the field to stop anybody coming after him."

"If this goes before a Grand Jury," Hampton says, "at least nine of the jurors will have to agree the evidence presented is sufficient to return an indictment."

"If you don't think we have enough," Whicher says, "then charge him with what we do have—possession of a stolen vehicle, attempting to fence it, assisting in the production of controlled substances…"

"That would be for the prosecutor in Louisiana."

"At least get it onto the sheet."

Hampton sits forward, presses his mouth closed.

"The parish sheriff's office think Dubois ought be charged with attempted murder…"

"You really think he was trying to kill you?"

"Cane fire burns plenty hot."

Hampton glances at the report on the desk. "Tell me

what's the connection with Elijah Hoffman? What's the motive for Dubois?"

"The son of a bitch ain't talking, we got no way to know that, so far. I don't have evidence against anyone else—I have ideas. I sure as hell don't think Dubois acted alone. This here is prima facie evidence, the way I see it."

The prosecutor raises an eyebrow, sits forward slightly, leaning into the desk. "Tell me what you want out of this, marshal?"

"I want him locked up while I put this all together."

"There's no way Dubois isn't in this," Gail Griffin says.

Hampton looks at the marshal a long moment. "You're saying you think you could get him to talk?"

Whicher nods.

Hampton looks to Gail Griffin.

The crime scene technician returns his stare.

"He's given no explanation for any of this," Whicher says.

Hampton lets out a breath, sits back in his seat. "I'll put it before the court this afternoon. I can't make any promises as to what the outcome will be."

"If we let him out, he vanishes."

"Come, come," the prosecutor says. "Can anybody really vanish, marshal?" He squares the papers on his desk.

"This boy could."

⁂

In the driveway at the front of the house in Wylie, Whicher parks alongside the gun-metal Chevy Impala. He shuts down the motor in the truck, runs a hand across his face. Glances into the rear-view, sees tiredness in his eyes, in the slack sheen on his skin.

He takes off the Resistol, dumps it onto the passenger seat.

The front door opens, Leanne steps out.

Lori runs out from behind her mother.

The marshal climbs from the cab.

"It's four o'clock in the afternoon," Leanne says.

"Don't look so surprised."

"Is it a good thing you're home early? Or a bad thing?"

Whicher reaches down to pick up his daughter. "Hey, sweetheart."

Leanne puts her head on one side.

The marshal leans his daughter in to his chest. "We arrested somebody."

"Arrested," Lori says.

"Not daddy," Leanne says. "Daddy arrested someone else."

Lori makes a face.

"We're waiting on the court—but I don't think they'll be making bail."

"We?"

"Me and Ortega."

She nods. "Did you send him home, too?"

"Yes, ma'am."

"Why don't you invite him over?"

Whicher looks at her.

"Invite his wife, invite his girls. I'd like to meet them."

"I sent him home to get some rest. He's been out on the job all night."

"Later, then," Leanne says. "Tonight."

Whicher steps to his wife, slips an arm around her waist. Pulls her to him.

"You never introduce us to anyone you work with. It wouldn't hurt to let people get to know you. Let them get a little closer."

"Alright, I'll call him."

Leanne's eyes widen.

"I'll do it. I'll call. I'll see if he's free."

Chapter 29

The sun is down behind the neighborhood houses, Whicher turning beef rib and German sausage over a smoking bed of oak and pecan in the brick and stone barbecue hearth. Dressed in shirtsleeves, jeans and boots, the better for three straight hours of sleep, the bottle of Lone Star in his hand marbles with condensation against the evening heat.

At a table in the yard, Sandro Ortega sips an ice cold bottle of beer in a T-shirt and shorts. Setting it down on the table, he fixes water wings on his youngest daughter Amelia's arms. The eldest, Alicia, dangles her feet at the edge of the pool.

Lori sits grinning at the top of the chromium-plated steps.

Ortega turns Amelia loose, she runs to the pool to join the other two girls. Three years old, the same age as Lori. Taller, darker. Alicia, six, turns around to catch her father's eye.

The younger marshal glances in Whicher's direction.

"They can go ahead and get in," the marshal says.

Lori grabs one of her toy foam dogs, tosses it into the pool—Amelia squeals, claps her hands.

Alicia flicks back her long dark hair, composed as she slips into the water.

Whicher takes a slug of ice-cold beer.

Leanne emerges from the kitchen, wearing cotton pants, a sleeveless top, a tray with sides of okra and cherry peppers and dill pickles cradled in her arms.

Ortega makes a space on the table, moving aside dishes of potato salad and pinto beans and pickled jalapenos and sliced bread.

Sofia Ortega steps from the kitchen, brandishing two bottles; a chilled white wine, and a red from the Hill Country.

Leanne sets down the tray of sides.

Sofia places the wine beside cartons of juice for the girls, and an unopened bottle of Big Red.

The girls start to splash in the water.

Sofia smiles—striking in a green patterned floral summer dress. "Thank you," she says, "for letting them swim. We don't have a pool."

"Neither did we," Leanne says, "before we came here."

"It's a lovely house. How long have you had it?"

"About three months."

Alicia swims slowly. Burnished in the glare of light from the water's surface.

Leanne turns to Ortega. "You've only recently moved to Abilene?"

"About six months," Ortega says. "Before that we were

down in San Angelo. Sofia is from here."

"We wanted the girls to see more of the family," she says.

Leanne looks at Whicher. "Now you're working a case like this."

"We're used to it," Sofia says. "It was the same in the police department. The girls know their father works long hours. But they know he comes back."

Whicher thinks of the phone call from Evans—it had come while he'd been asleep. Leanne had taken it, unwilling to wake him, Evans relaying the news Dubois would remain in custody on felony possession of a stolen automobile.

Leanne pours a glass of white wine for Sofia Ortega, pours one for herself.

Lori climbs the pool steps, scampers around to the side, leaps back into the water, turning in the air.

Amelia shrieks, delighted, pulls herself out. Then jumps straight into the still-rippling water.

Alicia completes a careful length of the pool, concentrating—raising her gaze to catch the eye of her father.

"Good, honey," he tells her, "real good. You want to show me another?"

Sofia Ortega takes a step toward the barbecue, breathes the scent of the cooking meat. "It smells delicious. You cook it the way they do out west. Very simple. Smoke and heat. Is that where you're from?"

"Briscoe County," Whicher answers.

"Oh?"

"The Panhandle. Up by the Caprock Canyons."

"I've heard of them," she says. "I've never been out there."

"They got the state bison herd, a lot of badlands. Hills."

"They have nice pools?"

"Not where I grew up."

She nods. "And where was that?"

"Little farm," he says. "Pretty remote. Little place outside of Quitaque."

"A farm? With lots of brothers, sisters?"

"No," he says. "There was only me."

Leanne says, "Always the loner."

"What brought you here to Abilene?"

The marshal takes a step away from the heat of the barbecue, pulls on the bottle of cold beer. "I joined the army. Moved around a bunch. I got done with that, I joined the Marshals Service. They started me out in Laredo. Then I got a job with Northern District, ended up out here."

"The army," Sofia Ortega says. "Not the police?"

"No, ma'am. I served in an armored regiment. Here. Overseas. I lead the scout platoon. Always trying to track folk down…"

"Now you work as an investigator? Sandro hopes to do the same one day."

"It means a bunch of travel," Whicher says. "We're not tied to any county or state. Northern District runs from back east in Dallas, up to Amarillo—down through San Angelo where y'all were at."

"Sandro likes it," Sofia says.

Ortega frowns, takes a sip on his beer.

Leanne pulls out a hardwood chair from the table, sits down opposite the young marshal. "How long were you with the police department in San Angelo?"

"Five years."

"You were always going to be a cop?"

"My old man was a cop."

"How come you left?" Whicher asks him.

Ortega shrugs, smiles.

"You could've come work for the PD in Abilene," Leanne says.

"True," Ortega says. "But you don't have to be the same thing the whole of your life, you know? You don't have to do the same thing."

Whicher notices Leanne look over in his direction.

In the water, the two youngest girls throw the foam dog back and forth, trying to catch the spinning toy.

Alicia, at the edge of the pool, drapes her sun-brown arms over the sides.

Leanne raises up from the table. "I better go find us some plates."

"Let me help," Sofia says.

"Keep an eye on the girls," Leanne says.

Ortega gets up from the table. To Alicia; "Can you do two lengths one right after the other?"

His daughter sweeps her hair back from her face, dips low in the water, pushes off.

In the gold hue of evening light, the air is still deadened with the day's heat. Whicher thinks of the farm up at Stamford, of Jean Hoffman—of the blond man seen driving there. He turns to Ortega. "You think the guy the Hoffman's neighbor saw driving out to the farm was Frank Nelson?"

The younger marshal looks at him. "Do you?"

Whicher turns the meat on the grill. "Could Nelson have known Jean Hoffman?"

Ortega thinks it over, takes a sip on his bottle of beer.

"Anything else we can find on him, we need to find it," Whicher says.

"Just as soon as we get back in the office, I'll get on it."

"How you make out over at Summerwood? You talk with Carl Avery?"

"He wasn't there." Ortega watches his eldest daughter swim. "I left a message for him. Told him we'd need a statement."

"How about Riley McGuire? Frank Nelson?"

"Both out on one of the construction sites. I spoke with another guy, Lance Tate."

The marshal nods.

"He said Nelson's a good worker. He wasn't aware of any connection to any motorcycle gang. I'll get back on it tomorrow, see what else I can find. But there's a pattern, already. A pattern of intimidation."

"By Frank Nelson and McGuire?"

"People that have stood in the way," Ortega says. "In business. In realty. In buying and selling. In construction."

"You said two deaths were linked to McGuire. How about that?"

"Still working on it."

Alicia touches the end of the swimming pool with her

fingertips, turns to go back.

"Maybe we should pull Frank Nelson in," Whicher says, "lean on him. We're pretty sure he went out looking for those two kids from ACU; maybe he was looking to threaten them, too."

"Tomorrow, boss," Ortega says.

Whicher cuts the younger man a look. He takes a pull on the long-neck bottle of beer. "Right," he says. "Guess it gets to be a habit. Talking shop."

Ortega's eyes are on his daughter. "Five minutes ago it seems like Alicia was three—the age Amelia is now. Don't let it pass you by, my old man told me."

Whicher turns to watch the girls in the pool.

"He worked a lot of nights," the younger marshal says. "He told me that. Right after Amelia was born."

"He making up for it, now?"

"He was sick by then." Ortega's voice is quiet. "He would have," he says. "He only had a few months left."

Whicher glances at the younger man. Watches his own daughter. Thinks of time he's already missed.

"It's a ride down the river," Ortega says. "No stopping. No going back. Maybe that's why we wanted a fresh start…"

Sofia Ortega emerges from the kitchen, a short stack of china plates in the crook of her arm.

Alicia reaches the far end of the pool.

"You did it, sweetheart. Bravo."

Breathless, she holds her arm aloft in triumph.

The younger marshal clinks his bottle of beer against Whicher's. "If we close this case out soon, don't send me back to court duty."

Whicher looks at him.

"I like tracking down bad hombres."

In the doorway to the kitchen Leanne appears, wiping her hands on a dish rag. "Telephone," she says, a frown on her face. "Levi Underwood? Calling from the FBI. He's asking to speak to you."

⚔

Two hours later, street lamps are lit along Treadaway Boulevard as Whicher takes a turn off the highway, steering onto North 13th.

He passes dark warehouses, a boarded out grocery store. Stone awake now, after sleeping in the afternoon. Thoughts running, unable to switch them off.

Cruising slow in the truck, he looks for the turn onto Mesquite Street. The meal over, Ortega and his family gone home—Lori asleep in bed, Leanne resigned to him going out again.

Whicher sees the street sign, the outline of the city lumber yard. A couple of young men are on the sidewalk in hoodies and shorts. There's little traffic, the side street is dark.

He signals, turns in.

The roadway ahead is unlit—it's flanked with derelict lots of shinnery oak and scrub grass and garbage blown in on the wind. The few houses are run-down looking, bars across their windows and doors.

Parked at one side of the street is a dark blue Ford Crown Vic.

The marshal pulls in at the curb ten yards back from it.

Shutting off the motor, he steps out, takes a glance up and down the length of the street.

No-one in is in view—the neighborhood is deserted.

Whicher walks along the roadway to the Crown Vic.

Its driver window is open—behind the wheel is Levi Underwood.

The FBI agent motions for him to get in.

Whicher opens up the sedan, climbs inside, pulls the door.

"You could've come see me in the morning," Underwood says.

"I slept this afternoon," Whicher says. "I'm out of whack. I'm not about to get any sleep."

"Not feeling the pressure?"

The marshal looks at him.

"That young tyro you're working with; Ortega."

"I'll be up half the night anyway," Whicher says.

Underwood nods, grins. "He seems pretty keen."

Whicher stares through the windshield of the Crown Vic. "You fixing to be out here all night?"

"It's a DEA operation," Underwood says. He points along the darkened street. "Next block over, they're staking out an address, waiting on the occupant of a property to make an appearance."

"Drug bust?"

The FBI agent nods.

"What's your interest?"

"Guy's a biker," Underwood says, "into all kinds of

criminal activity. I think he could be involved with this string of armored car robberies."

The marshal looks at him. "How so?"

"We've had sightings of bikers around the locales where armored cars have been attacked," Underwood says. "Witnesses reported seeing them. Guys on motorcycles, beforehand, at the scene."

The marshal thinks about it.

"We think they could have been acting as lookouts. A camera picked up a license plate on one of them, we think this is the guy." Underwood angles his head toward the windshield and the street.

"DEA are going to bust him?" Whicher says.

"They start talking to him, I'll start talking to him. We'll see what he's willing to give up."

The marshal thinks of the armored car on Judge Ely. The silver Honda, the gunman opening fire.

Agent Underwood reaches into the rear of the Crown Vic—lifts a briefcase off the back seat. "I spoke to your boy Ortega when he was by the office, yesterday. He told me one of the people in your homicide investigation is a biker named Frank Nelson? Ortega was looking for out of state information on him."

"He's a person of interest."

"Frank Nelson is an associate of some of the people I've been looking at," Underwood says. "Some of the bikers we've got under investigation."

"You think he might be one of your lookouts?"

The FBI agent spreads his hands.

The marshal studies the man's face a moment. "Does Frank Nelson know this guy the DEA are waiting on?"

"I think he does."

"What's his name?"

"Terrell Cribb."

Whicher says the name over in his head; he's never heard it before. "If the DEA bring him in, will they charge him?"

"If he's holding controlled substances."

"Wouldn't mind interviewing the guy myself."

"You'd have to wait in line." Underwood opens the briefcase, takes out a document wallet. "Anyhow," he says, "Terrell Cribb ain't the biggest of my problems—he's just leverage, a way in, if I can get him to talk. My biggest problem is the guy that was shot dead at that gas station; Dwayne Cameron. So far we have no witnesses, nothing on any of the cameras, there's damn little to go on—except he drove armored cars and his employers were starting to ask themselves questions about him."

"About whether he might have been an inside man?"

"He was gunned down, nothing stolen. Somebody just offed the guy. You remember I interviewed the wife?"

Whicher nods.

"She said they had money problems, Cameron was a gambling addict?"

"If you kill a man that owes you," Whicher says, "how you going to see that money again?"

Underwood shrugs. "Sometimes it's to remind others. You know? Don't mess with us. Here's the last guy that did…"

Whicher gazes out of the Crown Vic at a house on the street, dim light at the window. He pictures Grady Pearce's house by the refinery in Shreveport. Pearce worked security at a Casino.

Underwood taps the document wallet against Whicher's leg. "Anyhow," he says. "I'm working background on Dwayne Cameron, looking to see what else comes up. Cameron's wife told me he worked evenings and weekends to try to make extra money. This might not be anything, but there was just enough to catch my interest…"

Whicher looks at him.

"He worked part-time as a realtor. Showing houses."

"You know who for?"

The FBI agent nods. "Carl Avery." He holds the document wallet out for Whicher. "Could be nothing."

Whicher takes it.

"I want it back tomorrow morning."

Chapter 30

Ten-thirty a.m.

No sign of Ortega in the office.

Whicher's read and re-read the jacket from Levi Underwood on the armored car driver gunned down at the filling station, Dwayne Cameron.

Court is in session, Marshals Shea and Perez on protection duty. Nobody else in except for Donna Garcia from civilian support.

Whicher pushes the seat back from his desk, crosses the room to the door of the side-office, knocks.

Donna Garcia looks up from behind a computer screen.

"Did Marshal Ortega come by this morning?"

"He was here when I arrived at eight," the woman says.

"You see him leave?"

"No."

She smiles.

"No matter." The marshal steps back through the office, knocks on Chief Marshal Evans's door.

Evans calls him through.

Whicher enters.

The chief marshal indicates the vacant chair in front of his desk.

Whicher seats himself, puts the FBI jacket on Dwayne Cameron onto the desk.

"Something on your mind?"

"Riley McGuire," Whicher says. "And Frank Nelson. I'm thinking of bringing them in. Last night I met with Levi Underwood—from the Violent Crimes Task Force at FBI." He pushes the plastic document wallet across the desk. "Underwood thinks there might be a connection between his investigation and mine."

"The Task Force investigation into armored car robberies?"

Whicher nods. "The driver killed in that gas station shooting, Dwayne Cameron, was working part-time for Summerwood Realty."

The chief marshal looks at him.

"His wife told Underwood the family were in debt. Cameron was a gambler, a problem gambler. He was working for Summerwood, looking to get out of debt—maybe to raise more stake money?"

"Your man Hoffman was a gambler," Evans says.

"Underwood told me the armored car company suspected one of their people might be helping with these robberies. An inside man."

"FBI think that?"

"I'm not party to any of the evidence," Whicher says. "But Underwood seemed like he was taking it seriously. Could be that's why Cameron was shot. Maybe he was past being useful. Maybe somebody wanted to shut him up."

Evans straightens, eyebrow arching as he thinks it over.

"Riley McGuire has two deaths around him," Whicher says. "A guy on a construction site. And his wife in an accident with a car. That maybe wasn't an accident."

The chief marshal picks the plastic wallet from the desk, glances at it.

"Frank Nelson is a construction foreman for Summerwood—he's also muscle for them, it looks like. He has a record of violence and intimidation. I'm pretty sure it was him went looking for those two college kids. We know he's a biker. Underwood thinks he could be associated with bikers that were witnessed at some of the robberies—guys on motorcycles; probable lookouts in the surrounding streets."

The chief marshal blows the air from his cheeks.

"McGuire said he wouldn't talk to me again without the presence of a lawyer. I told him I'd bring him here, to the office."

"If that's what you want to do," Evans says. "If he's going to lawyer up, you'd best have grounds."

"It's a homicide enquiry," Whicher says. "McGuire was the last known person to be around the boat we found at the site."

"You want to bring him in, you go ahead and bring him in," Evans says. "I'm only saying you best be careful."

"I'll bring in Frank Nelson, too," Whicher says. "It's time he heard from us."

⋏

An hour later, three phone calls, no success tracking down Jean Hoffman. She's not out at the farm, not at her sister's address in Dallas—nobody at the PD in Stamford has a contact number that works.

Whicher thinks again of the one-point-three-million dollars sitting in a bank account in her name.

He needs more on Elijah Hoffman.

He's spoken with Riley McGuire—asked him in to the USMS office in the afternoon, lawyer and all.

He can have Ortega bring in Frank Nelson—see if campus police at ACU could send an officer—see if they can ID Nelson as the driver of the truck they stopped.

The marshal stands, stretches, walks to the window on the west wall of the office. His eye drawn to the towering Hotel Wooten. At the end of the street, on North Third, an Abilene PD cruiser blasts through the intersection—light bar popping, siren wailing.

Moments later, a second cruiser runs through. Cars and trucks left motionless in their wake.

Whicher feels a sense stir, a tick of unease.

He leans in to the window, presses his face close to the glass.

Somewhere is a sound, a rhythmic chop, a low buzzing.

Craning his neck he sees a helicopter; a dark shape against the blaze of sky. He watches it track high up across the city, above the sprawl of buildings.

A call comes in on the desk phone.

He steps from the window, takes a seat at his desk, picks up the phone.

"This is Dick Hampton—over at the DA's office."

"Mister Hampton."

"You know the judge sent Dubois back to French Robertson?"

"Yes, sir," Whicher says, "I heard that."

"Court deferred bail pending a decision from the Jefferson Davis parish sheriff's office."

Whicher looks across the room out of the window.

"They want to know whether they're going to bring charges," Hampton says.

The marshal nods to himself. "You want me to call the sheriff?"

"If you want to ramp up the charge and be sure Dubois can't walk, you need to find out if their office is serious," Hampton says. "If they're considering a charge of attempted murder and arson, you can ask them to draw up a federal letter of intent to prosecute. Even if it doesn't get that far, the judge will probably deny bail. You want leverage?"

"Right."

"You best pile on weight."

"I'll call their office in Louisiana this morning," Whicher says.

"Let me know how you get on."

The attorney finishes the call.

Whicher pushes up off the desk, crosses to a metal file cabinet—takes out a yellow legal pad, sets it onto his desk.

Chief Marshal Evans steps from his room, holding onto the door. His face is pinched with agitation; the skin around his eyes tight. "There's been some kind of shooting incident—across town."

Whicher looks at him. "I saw a couple cruisers blow through the lights," he says. "Down at the intersection."

"Some kind of a bar," Evans says. "I hope it's nothing serious. Last thing we need is another shooting this week. On top of everything else."

The marshal glances out of the window across the Abilene skyline. "You know where it's at?"

"Up by Cobb Park."

"There been any request for assistance?"

"I don't know," Evans says. "I just heard from the chief of police."

"I saw a helicopter go over, it looks like they're pulling in units," Whicher says. "If there's an active shooter, I can head on out."

Evans looks at him a moment. "Until we know, you may as well stay here."

Whicher sits. The phone in his jacket starts to ring.

The marshal takes it out, checks the on-screen name; Levi Underwood. "Sir, I should probably get this."

Evans waves him away, turns back into his office.

Whicher keys to answer the call.

"You know there's been a shooting?" Underwood says.

"I just heard."

"It's at a biker bar, up on Mockingbird. I'm about to head out there."

"What's going on?"

"It just happened," the FBI man answers, "I'm hearing reports of multiple injuries."

"Is it an active scene?"

"I don't know. And this may be nothing, but our guy last night, Terrell Cribb? He never showed up," Underwood says. "And that bar is one of the places the man sells at. Maybe somebody dimed him, somebody might've heard he's been blown."

"You think?"

"I need to find out."

"Where's it at?"

"The Chrome Fork and Grille. That biker bar-restaurant up on Mockingbird? You know what else, know who drinks there? Frank Nelson."

Whicher reaches for the jacket on the back of his chair.

"It's past the High School," Underwood says, "go up a couple of blocks."

"I'm moving, I'll meet you there."

Whicher backs the Silverado out of the parking bay at the roadside—guns the truck up the broad expanse of Pine Street, shade trees on the sidewalks flashing by.

Running a stop light, he accelerates past the back of the Convention Center. Past tire shops, an auto repair, a drive-through bank. He thumbs the switch on the dash, lights up the blue flashers mounted on the front of the truck.

At the furniture store on the corner of Pine and Tenth, he makes a left—cuts west along the top edge of the old town.

He switches on the radio receiver, lights up the PD

channel. Clipped exchanges come in—the dispatchers calm, mono-tonal; officers at the scene abrupt.

Whicher picks out codes, phrases; 10-52; ambulance needed—10-32—a man with a gun.

The marshal flips on the truck's siren, runs the red light at an intersection.

At the top edge of Cobb Park, people are turning to stare beneath the trees. More bursts come from the radio—EMTs, dispatchers, pumped-up cops.

Less than a minute out.

Patting the Ruger in the shoulder-holster.

Killing the siren—leaving the flashers switched on.

Slowing, approaching the intersection with Mockingbird and Tenth.

A PD cruiser is blocking a gravel back-alley between a slat-board fence and a container lot.

The driver of the cruiser stands in the alleyway by a dumpster—black semi-automatic between both hands.

At the intersection, police and sheriff's units block all the lanes.

Whicher stops the Silverado, shuts off the motor—jumps out.

He pulls the Marshals Service badge-holder, hustles across the four-lane highway—scanning a crowd of people and motorcycles in front of a strip of run-down business premises.

A score of officers have their weapons out—corralling the assembled group.

In the air is a hair-trigger feeling; hostile, full-blown menace.

Ambulances are parked close in to the lot in front of a bar—EMTs treating a half-dozen people on the ground.

Whicher keeps his badge out, approaches a sheriff's deputy—the deputy's arms locked out, a Glock gripped tight between his hands.

"What's going on?"

The deputy half-turns. "Drive-by. Somebody opened fire from a vehicle."

"Y'all have casualties?"

Cords strain in the deputy's neck. "Bunch of gunshot wounds," he says. "One fatal."

Whicher eyes the crowd. The faces of the men mostly bearded or unshaved. In bandannas and sunglasses, jeans and boots and leather vests. An uneasy feeling in him. He searches for anyone with tousled blond hair—for the face of Frank Nelson.

A blue-shirted female EMT breaks from a huddle around a casualty—hurrying to a waiting ambulance, its doors flung wide.

"Y'all need help?" Whicher says. "You have active shooters?"

"I just got here," the deputy says.

The marshal looks from one group of EMTs to another. "This some biker thing?"

The deputy adjusts the grip on the semi-automatic. "I don't know."

The marshal takes in the looping neon sign above the building, front forks of a Harley intersecting the letters of the name.

The faces of the bikers are set with anger, some staring back at him—smoking cigarettes, jabbing fingers, arguing with the nearest cops.

From an alley by a disused convenience store, Whicher sees the tall, suited figure of Levi Underwood walking with a uniformed sergeant.

The marshal cuts away, heads in their direction.

Up the road he sees a black, F250—in the lot of a storefront lawyer's office.

The marshal puts a hand to his brow, shades his eyes from the midday sun.

Underwood and the police sergeant approach—the sergeant short, squat, sporting a goatee beard.

"He's with the Marshals Service," Underwood says to the sergeant.

Whicher reads the name on the man's shirt; *Coleman*. "You know what happened?"

"I was first on the scene—me and my partner," the sergeant says. "Somebody called 9-1-1, we got here, there was maybe a half-dozen people with guns. We called for back-up, called a major shooting incident. Had to think twice before we stepped out of the car."

"You know who was shot?" Whicher says.

"I don't have the first goddamn idea. All I can tell you is nobody shot anybody since we got here. We'll need to take everybody in, question 'em all."

"There's no sign of Terrell Cribb," Underwood says.

"How about Frank Nelson?" Whicher says.

The FBI agent shakes his head.

The marshal feels the twist again in his stomach.

Sergeant Coleman points to a patrol car parked at the far side of a concrete lot. "We've got one of them in the car, a guy that says there was an argument going on between two groups. And then a white sedan blew by, somebody in it started shooting. A bunch of guys here pulled out weapons, started shooting at the car, a couple of 'em started shooting at each other."

Whicher looks from Sergeant Coleman to Underwood and back again. "White sedan?"

"We'll work on that," the sergeant says.

"Going to have a hard time getting anything out of these boys," Underwood says.

A female EMT starts to wheel a gurney from the back of an ambulance.

Whicher pictures Nelson again. The strange sensation pulls at his gut.

The EMT lowers the gurney to the ground.

The men in front of the biker bar stand staring out at the law enforcement officers holding guns on them. Ranged from their thirties to well into their sixties.

"Any of these people on your radar," Whicher says, "at the Task Force?"

"I'd have to check."

The marshal nods, breaks off to walk in the direction of the EMTs with the gurney.

The legs of a man lying on the ground are visible. The man motionless, inert, the splayed look of somebody seriously hurt.

He eyes the shoes and the chinos. The bottom edge of a cotton polo shirt.

A stab like electricity jolts him.

The man's outstretched arm is against the concrete lot—tan, muscled.

Whicher feels his chest constrict.

He stops.

Behind him is a voice—Levi Underwood; "Oh, *Jesus…*"

"Sir," the female EMT looks at Whicher. "If you could step back, please." The EMT stares into the marshal's face, neat blonde hair parted in the middle, eyes blue, pupils shining. "Sir, you need to step back."

Sandro Ortega lies motionless on the ground.

Whicher expels the air from his lungs.

He kneels on the lot.

Underwood speaks; "He's one of ours…he's a US Marshal."

Reaching out over Ortega's midriff, over the blood-soaked shirt, Whicher touches the young man on his shoulder, places his hand upon him. Feels no response.

A black man with bloodied surgical gloves is looking at him, eyes wide.

Sergeant Coleman squats. "We didn't know. We didn't know…"

The marshal takes in the blood pooled on the slab of broken concrete. Senses swimming, mind racing. Eying the entry wounds in Ortega's shirt. Multiple wounds. Side and front.

His eyes are still open, the light gone.

Gone to glass.

"Sir..." the female EMT says.

Sergeant Coleman stands.

The man in the surgical gloves speaks to a second EMT. "We need to move him."

The second EMT helps the blond woman ease Ortega onto the gurney.

The marshal feels a wave of nausea.

The second EMT places two lateral straps about Ortega's body. The female EMT unfurls a blanket. Eyes jittery. As she places the blanket over Ortega.

Places it gently over his body. Up and over his head.

Seconds or minutes pass.

Dazed in the ambulance, Whicher sits, wordless. The body of Sandro Ortega inches from him.

Police and sheriff's units surround the bar—ringing off every street and alley.

A dark stain of blood is starting to soak through the covering of Ortega's blanket. The bright space inside the ambulance oppressive, disconnected from reality—time slipping, frames frozen, racing, unreal.

Levi Underwood appears at the half-open door. "You need to step out. They need to go, they need to take your partner across town."

Whicher twists his head, stares.

Underwood's voice is quiet. "Check his pockets."

"What?"

"We need the keys to his truck. We need to see if he has his phone."

Whicher only stares at the FBI agent.

"I'm sorry, man. I'm sorry. We need to do this, his truck is up the road there, we need to get into it, we need to find his phone. You want me to do it?"

Whicher takes hold of an edge of the blanket, peels it back slow—until it's at Ortega's feet.

"I'm sorry, man," Underwood says.

The marshal pushes up the sleeve of his suit.

"Let me do it," Underwood says.

The marshal puts the flat of his hand against the pocket of Ortega's chino pants. Feels a set of keys. Puts his hand inside, takes them out.

"Check for a phone," the FBI man says.

Whicher gives the keys to Underwood, places his palm onto the other pocket. It's empty.

"We have to check the back pockets," Underwood says.

The marshal looks at him. Unfastens the retaining straps at Ortega's thighs and chest.

Underwood steps in.

Together they raise Ortega onto his side—turning him until the single back pocket is visible.

The FBI man reaches to it, feels for anything. Shakes his head.

The two men lower him down.

Whicher refastens the straps on Ortega. The wounds and the blood and the lifeless face and the eyes and the sheen of dark brown hair stark in the ambulance lights. An image before him suddenly—his own back yard in Wylie—Ortega's daughter Alicia touching the wet hair behind her ear. The same skin. Same eyes. Same hair.

Chapter 31

A single block up from the bar on Mockingbird, Whicher inserts the key into the door of Ortega's truck.

He opens it, makes a visual check.

The interior is clean, the dash polished, footwells vacuumed.

There's a holder for a cell phone, a charging cable from the 12v socket. No phone.

The marshal cuts a look at Underwood. Swings in behind the wheel into the driver's seat.

A scent is in the cab, a fresh smell, deodorant or hair gel or shave balm. As if Ortega just stepped out.

Whicher checks the door pockets, the glove box, all of the alcove spaces. The rear of the truck. To be in the man's space is an intrusion. He finds a spare magazine for Ortega's Glock. A notepad.

No phone.

⁂

Inside the Abilene PD cruiser, the man seated in back is in his late-fifties, sun-browned, deep lines etched into his face.

His graying hair is long, tied back, Indian style. He's wearing a red T-shirt with the name of a Mexican bar. His jeans faded but clean, the leather vest free of tags, nothing more than a collection of enameled badges pinned to the front.

Sergeant Coleman addresses Whicher. "This is Walter Daniels. He saw what happened here."

The man steps out.

Sergeant Coleman nods. "Tell him what you told us."

"Hey," Daniels says, "I didn't do anything. I don't know why I need to be stuck in the back of a police car."

At the side of the cruiser Levi Underwood glares.

"Sir," Whicher says. "You saw a federal officer shot."

"I didn't know he was a cop."

"Let's hear it," the FBI man says.

Daniels presses the heel of his hand against his forehead. "I was here about an hour. I got done eating breakfast. I came outside, there was some sort of a fight going on."

"A fight?" Whicher says.

"Or an argument, anyhow," Daniels says, "a few guys getting into it."

"You saw punches being thrown?" Sergeant Coleman says.

"Kind of yelling and pushing and shoving—guys standing toe to toe. Like something was about to really get going."

"Was it rival biker groups?" Underwood says.

"I wouldn't know about that. I'm not a member of any gang, I just like to ride a motorcycle." Daniels rubs a sunburnt arm. "I was minding my own business. I'm not from around here, I didn't know this was any kind of a gang joint, I was just here to eat breakfast."

"What happened next?" Whicher says.

"There's a bunch of guys arguing, I was headed back over to my Harley, fixing to take off. Then I heard this popping noise. Small-arms, a pistol going off. I was an Air Force sergeant, I was on the shooting range all the time, I know what gunfire sounds like. I know what type it is when I hear it."

"Did you see the shooter?" Underwood says.

Daniels shakes his head. "A car came by, a white car, late-model Japanese four-door. A guy inside was shooting from it, the driver. He was shooting into the group of guys fixing to fight."

"You see what he looked like?" Whicher says.

"He was past the bar driving away by the time I realized what was happening," Daniels says. He points up the road north. "As soon as he started shooting, a bunch of guys pulled out guns and started loosing off shots, all hell was breaking loose."

"Did you get the license tag?" Underwood says.

"No way, man, I was ducking for cover. Like most everybody else."

"The man that was shot and killed, where was he?"

"I think he fell right where he was."

"On the lot there?"

"Yes, sir."

"Was he with anybody?" Whicher says. "Was he talking to anybody, talking with any of the people here?"

"I don't know," Daniels says. "Look, that's all I know, the whole thing happened in a flash. I'm not a member of any gang, I'm not in any motorcycle club or chapter or whatever, I was just getting breakfast, minding my own business, I don't know why any of this happened. There was maybe a dozen shots fired after those first ones from the car. Then that was it. It just stopped. Everybody was standing around wondering what the hell happened. You could see there were people lying injured."

"Rival gang fight," Sergeant Coleman says. "Something like this has been coming, there's been trouble before now."

Whicher looks at the police sergeant.

"We've got the guys that did the shooting," Coleman says.

"What's their story?"

"They're all claiming self-defense. Most of them are already on their way in to the LE center. We're locking them up till we can figure out what happened here." The sergeant turns in the direction of a sheriff's department SUV. "One of the accused is in there."

In the back of the SUV is a bearded man sporting a Mohican haircut, the shaved sides of his skull already growing back in. His arms are covered in tattoos, Whicher spots the faded globe and anchor among the pit bulls bearing teeth, the death's heads and half-naked women.

"Ronnie Vincent," Sergeant Coleman says. "According to witnesses, one of the shooters."

The man's dressed in jeans and boots, a black T, a vest filled with patches. He's handcuffed, a chain securing him to the floor of the vehicle. He turns his face to look out—his squashed features set in defiance.

"That right?" Whicher says.

Vincent glares at him. "Who the hell are you?"

"United States Marshal."

Unconcealed contempt is in the man's eyes. "I was defending myself. They were shooting us up. Law says I got the right to defend myself—I can stand my ground."

Whicher shakes his head. "Maybe you initiated the conflict."

"Bullshit. That's a crock…"

"So let's hear it."

"You believe what the hell you want to believe," Vincent says. "I already told a bunch of you all."

"Tell it to me. You better hope I believe it." The marshal looks a long time into the man's eyes.

Vincent breaks off, looks out over the concrete lot. "We were here…"

"We?"

"Apache Arrows."

"Motorcycle club," Sergeant Coleman puts in.

"This here's our place," Vincent says.

"You had a bunch of other bikers come in?" Whicher says.

Vincent nods. "Steel Team."

"They're a smaller club," the sergeant says. "They've been out here a year or two. They're affiliated with the Cossacks."

"No way they can come in here," Vincent says. "What'd they think was going to happen?"

"What did happen?" Whicher says.

"One of theirs gets in a beef with one of ours, a Steeler pulls out a piece, the mutha starts shooting. We're entitled to defend ourselves. That's the law, we don't have to back off."

Whicher looks to Underwood, then to Sergeant Coleman. He scans the roof-line of the bar and the two adjoining units—checks the pole lamps out in front in the lot. Sees no cameras. "You think we got any of this?"

"We don't know yet." Coleman points toward a gas station over the road. "We can check over there."

The marshal turns back to the man named Vincent. "What about this guy in the car?"

"I didn't see no goddamn car." The man's face is blank, apathetic.

"So, this first shot came from who?"

"One of theirs, a Steeler."

"You see the man who fired it?"

"I heard it," Vincent says.

"You heard it? But you didn't see?"

Underwood cuts in. "None of these people are about to go on record."

Vincent looks at the FBI agent, eyes hooded.

"Your story is bullshit," Whicher says.

"I don't have to listen to you. I don't even have to talk to you, none of you." Vincent's eyes bulge, the skin beneath them filmed with sweat. He stabs out the middle finger of his right hand, pulls against the cuffs and the chain.

The marshal eyes him, feels a rising wave of anger.

Underwood steps in, ushers him away.

⋏

Thirty minutes later, crime scene technicians comb the ground out in front of the bar—setting up numbered plastic markers by ejected shell cases, placing alpha-numeric stickers to walls on the row of business units. Photographing, measuring, recording.

A patrol officer clips across the lot to Whicher, Underwood and Sergeant Coleman by the sergeant's car.

"My partner," Coleman says. "Officer Suarez."

Suarez is slight, his eyes quick, perspiration beaded on his upper lip. He glances at the sergeant, at Underwood, at Whicher. "Six injured," he says. "Alongside of the officer down."

"How bad?" Coleman says.

"One critical, the others non-life threatening."

The bar-restaurant is ringed entirely with police and sheriff's department vehicles, state trooper cruisers, the last remaining trucks of EMTs.

Senior officers from the PD and the sheriff's office are gathered by a command truck, speaking fast on their phones.

"We need to see the cameras at that gas station," Whicher says, "see if they caught a shot of the car." He takes out the cell from his jacket. "And find Ortega's phone, if it's here."

He dials the number.

"We'll never hear it," Underwood says.

Ortega's voicemail kicks straight in, the marshal shuts off the call.

The FBI man points at the crime scene officers combing the lot. "They'll find it if it's here."

Sergeant Coleman studies the mass of parked motorcycles. "It looks to me like he was caught up in this, caught up in the cross-fire."

"I want to know why he was here," the marshal says.

"Looks to be a biker thing. Even with the drive-by, even with the car."

"The car could belong to one of them," Underwood says, "most likely a Steeler."

"This is Arrows territory," Suarez says. "They'd know that."

"They come in here, get in their face," Coleman says, "loose off a couple shots, they would've known they'd get a reaction."

"You think they wanted to conceal who started it?" Underwood says. "So they all can claim they were acting in self-defense?"

Whicher stares at the gas station.

"The car could be stolen, anyhow," Underwood says. "If not the car, then the tags."

The marshal looks at him. "I want to see the footage, just the same."

"I'll have somebody get it," the FBI agent says. "How about you? What are you going to do?"

"I want to know where Frank Nelson is at."

"You have any idea where to look?"

Whicher shakes his head. "We have an address on file. Nothing else."

Levi Underwood grimaces. "You don't buy this was a biker deal?"

"Six bikers were shot," Coleman says. "That's a bunch if it ain't."

"None of them were killed," Whicher says.

Underwood nods. "You think Frank Nelson could be in this?"

"Why else would Ortega have been here?"

⊥

Driving away across town, blood rushing—breath unsteady in his lungs. Windows down, the sound of the truck tires loud against the road. A momentary burst from a siren splits the air.

Light flickers on the windshield through an overhang of trees.

Sandro Ortega's bullet-ridden body is all he sees.

Eyes open.

And the sun on his hair.

The phone in the dash-mount starts to ring.

Whicher ignores it. His gaze locks on a point somewhere just beyond the hood of the truck.

The ringing stops.

Starts back up again.

The marshal cuts a look into the rear-view.

Presses to answer.

"John?"

Chief Marshal Evans's voice.

"I've just got out of a meeting. With the Chief of Police. I just heard."

Whicher steers the truck across an intersection.

"Have you seen him? Have you seen Ortega?" The chief marshal's voice is flat, stripped of emotion. "Do we know what happened?"

Heat blows from the scrub grass lots between houses on the residential street. "Somebody in a white sedan," Whicher says. "They drove by the biker bar on Mockingbird. Opened fire. He was there."

"Why?"

"We don't know."

"What was Ortega doing there?"

Whicher leaves the words hanging.

"John?"

"I intend to find out."

"You need to take this slow," Evans says. He clears his throat. "I saw him this morning. Asked him how he was getting along."

Whicher feels a beat in the back of his brain. Adrenaline in him, a spark threatening to catch.

"I'm sorry," Evans says. "I really am. He hadn't been here long, but it doesn't make a difference."

"His daughters were swimming in my pool last night…"

The line falls silent.

Whicher steers the Silverado by the First Assembly Church—positioning the truck to make the turn from Tenth onto Pine.

"Where are you?" Evans says.

"Headed back."

"You have no idea what he was doing there?"

Whicher runs his tongue around the edge of his teeth.

"He checked in here this morning," Evans says, "then he went out. He pretty much went straight out. He said he was headed up to French Robertson."

The marshal slams on the brakes, the truck's wheels lock.

A horn blares behind him, a battered Chrysler.

Whicher presses on the gas, pulls to the side of the road.

"Say again?

"He went out to the Robertson Unit."

The driver of the Chrysler steers around to overtake—leans across to the open passenger window.

A look at the marshal's face is enough to silence him.

"He tell you what for?"

"I didn't ask," Evans says. "But I'm guessing it had to be to see your man—to see Dubois."

Chapter 32

Horses crop the drying grass in the rough ground bordering the prison perimeter. Security fences and guard towers and light poles stretch along a line to the distance, the movement of the horses the only sign of life in the harsh shimmer of heat. Whicher stares out through the windshield, motor running in the truck, cold air streaming from the vents. Razor wire glints from the tops of mesh fences. He studies the bleak concrete, featureless blocks of cells.

Two hours back, Ortega would have been there. In the same baking lot, beneath the same sky. A wave building. A wave about to hit him.

The marshal shuts down the motor.

Elbows open the door.

⚹

Inside the Ad Seg wing, a corrections officer unlocks the steel-plate door on Ray Dubois' small cell. "Monday, they're moving him out of the hole," the officer says.

Whicher eyes the man—a wiry Hispanic with flint-like

eyes. He's wearing a stab-vest, carrying a short length of chain.

"He's going into gen pop," the CO says. "We need the capacity."

"So?"

"So, he's not happy about it."

"What do you care?"

"I don't," the officer replies. "But if you want to see him after that, you'll have to call ahead."

Whicher points at the man's stab-vest. "He starting to act up?"

The man taps a can of pepper spray at his side. "He better not, hermano. So far, he's just running his mouth." The corrections officer swings open the cell door.

The marshal feels his heart rate climbing.

Ray Dubois is stretched out full length along the metal cot fixed to the wall.

"Get up," the officer says.

Dubois' eyes shift from the CO to Whicher. Easing himself up, he swings his legs over the side of the cot.

"Officer coming in." The CO produces a set of handcuffs from his belt. "Hold out your wrists."

Dubois looks at the man.

"Go ahead, move."

Dubois puts his arms out, holds them together.

The officer snaps on the cuffs, threads the length of chain around the foot of the cot, back through the links on the handcuffs.

He secures the chain with a combination lock. "You

need me?" he says to Whicher.

The marshal shakes his head. Steps into the cell.

Inside, the small, cramped space smells of stale air and drains and sweat.

The CO backs out, closes the door behind him.

"Marshal Ortega came to see you this morning?" Whicher says. "What about?"

Dubois' face is sour. "What do you mean?"

"What did you talk about?"

The man's eyes are wary. "Whyn't you ask him?"

Whicher lashes a fist into Dubois' midriff, doubling him over.

Dubois falls back, crashes down onto the cot.

The marshal feels pain spread into his hand. He takes a step back. Steadies.

Dubois gasps for breath, retches, bends low over his knees.

"What did you talk about?"

Whipping up his arms, Dubois yanks against the cuffs, locking out against the length of chain. His eyes are glassy, his face filled with rage.

Whicher stares him down. "First arrestee connected with this case was stabbed to death in the county jail three nights back."

"What?"

"I'll give you twenty-four hours. You're out of here, Monday. You're going into general population, with the animals."

"Bullshit."

The marshal leans in close. "I look like I'm talking shit to you?"

Dubois' face contorts.

"You go into gen pop Monday, I'll put a target on your back—make it known you're a snitch, that you give up your own. You'll be on the meat-wagon, day-one."

Dubois sits rigid on the side of the cot.

"Maybe they'll be able to save you in the hospital. If you make it there. They couldn't do it for Hernandez," Whicher says. "Hernandez? The car thief?"

The chain starts to coil on the floor as Dubois eases his arms back down. He stares unfocused at the door to the cell.

"The sheriff of Jeff Davis wants you charged with attempted murder of a federal officer—for starting that fire. That's the death penalty, the stainless-steel ride…"

The small cell falls silent.

Somewhere along the wing is a muffled shout, the sound of banging.

"You been on the yard," Whicher says, "you know how this is going to go down."

Dubois turns his head a fraction. "What do you want?"

"I speak with the prison authorities. Tell them you're essential to the prosecution of my case. That you need protection. They don't move you, they have to keep you here."

"You want me to help you?" Dubois says.

"You were driving a murdered man's car. Your hunting bow is in the back of it. Your arrows were in him…"

"I do what, I plea down?"

The marshal nods. "L-WOP."

Dubois' eyes are wild, darting about the cell.

"Life-without-parole. That's better than the death-house. Why did Marshal Ortega come to see you?"

"Why don't you just *ask* him?"

The marshal stares a long time.

At Raymond Landry Dubois.

Chained to the foot of a metal cot.

A world reduced to a stinking prison cell.

Why dissemble?

"He wanted to talk about a guy named Frank Nelson," Dubois says, finally. "I'll tell you what I told him; I don't know the guy. Period. That's it."

The marshal shakes his head.

"I'm serious, man, I don't know him."

"What else?"

"He asked me how come I had that Sierra truck."

"Elijah Hoffman's truck?"

"Right."

"And you told him what?"

Dubois shakes his head. "He asked me did I have an alibi for the night of the murder? He kept asking about this guy, Nelson, Frank Nelson. Listen, I want a goddamn lawyer."

"Did you tell Marshal Ortega about a bar in Abilene?" Whicher says. "A biker bar?"

"I got no idea what you're talking about."

"Did you tell him to go there?"

"I didn't tell him to do a goddamn thing." Dubois face is slack, now. Panic in his eyes. "Let me speak to a lawyer…"

人

Driving away across the heat-scorched prairie, a last sight of guard towers is in his rear-view mirror. The dark, walled mass of the prison complex floats at the edge of the flattened land. Steering down the arrow-straight highway, Whicher presses a key on his phone.

A high sun reflects from zinc-wire fencing. In the bone-dry air a rushing rhythm beats from the split-wood posts at the sides of the road.

The phone rings over and over.

Agent Levi Underwood picks up.

"I'm going looking for Frank Nelson," the marshal says. "I'm going over to his address, can you meet me?"

"What do you want to do?"

"I need to find him."

"What address?" Underwood says.

"Danville Drive, off of North Seventh. Alongside Winters Freeway. I can be there in twenty minutes. Did anybody find Ortega's phone?"

"So far, no."

"You still with that sergeant?"

"Coleman? He's here."

"Bring him."

"What for?"

"If we find Nelson, I want to make sure there's no way out."

⋏

The house on Danville is a one-floor ranch—weatherboard sides, the property sitting in a half-acre plot in a row of twenty others like it. Trucks and older model cars are parked in the yards, a residential street runs along the front—in back, a service road runs between Winters Freeway and the rear of the houses.

Whicher's Silverado blocks one end of the service road, Levi Underwood's Crown Vic blocks off the other.

Sergeant Coleman and Officer Suarez are stationed around at the front.

Whicher takes the Ruger revolver from the shoulder-holster. Steps toward the house.

Underwood looks at him. "He's not likely to be here."

"I'll go in first," the marshal says.

"You have a warrant to go inside?"

Whicher moves to the perimeter fence at the edge of the property. It's waist-high, easy to step over. "I don't need a warrant to prevent a suspect's escape."

In the yard is a fishing boat on a trailer. The marshal thinks of the boat at the lake.

Stepping through the yard, he reaches a back door beneath a lean-to porch. Through the glass panel in the door he can see into a kitchen.

He feels sweat on his hand against the grips of the revolver.

Underwood takes up position along the back wall between two windows.

The marshal tries the door. It's locked.

Underwood slips out a semi-automatic pistol.

"*US Marshal,*" Whicher shouts. *"Open up."*

No answer from the house, no sound apart from the

noise of traffic on the freeway.

Whicher grips the barrel of the large-frame revolver, smashes out a hole in the glass panel with the butt of the gun.

He reaches in through the broken glass—the key is in the lock, he turns it. Withdrawing his hand, he opens the door. "*US Marshal entering*," he shouts.

He steps in, arm extended, leading with the gun.

Underwood moves through the open door.

"*Anybody home?*" Whicher calls out.

The house is silent. He moves into a living area—empty pizza boxes and beer cans on a low table, clothes strewn about a couch, half-covering a reclining seat.

Underwood steps toward a doorway opening along the front side of the house.

Whicher sees the small hallway extending from it. A mess of construction equipment, boots, hard hats, jackets.

The FBI man nods the marshal through.

Spread out over the floor are tools, motorcycle parts. Whicher pushes open the door to a bedroom—nobody inside.

Underwood moves along the hallway to a second bedroom. He looks in, shakes his head.

Whicher checks a small bathroom. Puts away the Ruger.

"So what gives?" the FBI agent says.

Whicher scans the empty bedroom, the unmade bed. Along one wall is a cheap set of drawers, an open wardrobe. He moves to it, eyes the few clothes hanging up. "Why would Ortega go to a biker bar?"

"You think Frank Nelson set him up?"

"Ortega wanted to talk with him. You think Nelson might be hooked up with your boy, Terrell Cribb?"

Underwood puts away the semi-automatic pistol. "We'll find Cribb. Bring him in, lean on him."

"If Nelson was hooked up with Cribb, maybe he's involved in your armored car robberies." Whicher opens the front door to the house, signals to Sergeant Coleman and Officer Suarez. "*Nobody here*," he calls out.

"You want to leave somebody on the house?" Underwood says. "A detective from the PD?"

"I'll put out a stop order for Nelson," Whicher says. "That should be enough."

"FBI can handle the investigation into the shooting at the bar," Underwood says

"I need to find the drive-by."

"We need to process everybody," Underwood says, "everyone we detained. See if anybody else saw a car."

The marshal stares out of the front door into bright sunlight on the small suburban street. "We need Ortega's phone. I want to know who he'd been talking with…"

"What do you want to do, now?"

"I have to go see his widow."

"Right now?"

The marshal nods.

The FBI man lets out a breath.

Whicher steps from the house. "Somebody has to tell her."

⁂

Driving down Pioneer into the southwestern part of Abilene—A/C in the truck cranked against the stifling heat. The marshal reaches for the cell phone, presses on a key. He dials down the blower. Signals to make a turn onto Richmond.

The call rings, it picks up.

Leanne's voice is at the end of the line.

"Did you see the news?" Whicher says.

"It was just on…"

The marshal hears the note in his wife's voice, the slight constriction.

"They're saying a police officer was shot."

"Is Lori there?"

"She's in her room."

Whicher pictures his daughter for a brief second—then shuts out the thought. "It's bad," he says.

"What happened?"

His wife's voice quiet, small.

"Ortega."

"What do you mean?"

"He was shot this morning. He was shot and killed." Whicher pictures Leanne in the house. Lori in her room. "I wanted you to know, to hear it from me…"

"Oh, God. Oh, my God, what happened?"

"We don't know."

He hears the sound of his wife breathing.

Makes the turn onto Richmond.

"Oh, my God…" Leanne's voice trails away.

In the silence is just a beating weight—black specter

poised above the numbness in his brain.

He follows the cross-street two blocks. Slows. Brakes to read a road-panel. Sees the name of the street—*San Jose*.

His wife is trying to say something into the phone.

He hits the blinker, makes the next turn.

"Does Sofia…know?" she says.

Half way down the street, a police department cruiser is parked at the head of a driveway in front of brick and timber-clad house. He's never seen the house before—no matter; it must be the one.

"Yes," he says.

"Oh, God, John."

He slows the Silverado to walking pace.

"Where are you?"

"I have to see her," Whicher answers. "I'm in Elmwood."

"You're going to see her? You're going to talk to her?"

Pulling in at the curbside, he brakes the truck to a standstill. Stares at the house, at the police cruiser, at the windows, tightness in his throat.

"Come home," Leanne says.

"I have to see her."

He hears a single sob on the line. Clicks off the call, shuts down the motor. Pushes open the driver's door, forces himself from the cab.

Straightening in the roadway, he takes a step toward the house.

And stops.

For a fleeting second, he thinks of turning back, leaving.

Continuing up the front yard, he takes off his hat, reaches the door.

The female liaison officer from APD has Ortega's youngest daughter Amelia in the front room—a cartoon show playing low on the TV, Amelia's toys spread out on the floor.

Whicher follows Sofia Ortega through the kitchen into a small, square backyard.

Sofia's face is slack, the skin puffed, eyes red—still one moment, wild, darting the next. Her hair is tied back, a score of loosened strands trailing.

He lays his Resistol hat on an outdoor table, pulls out two white, plastic chairs.

She sits in a sun top and shorts. Crosses one leg tight over the other. Rocks forward, her body folding in on itself.

Whicher sits down rigid. Pushes out words from the thickness in his throat. "He was at a bar. A bar in the north of the city…"

Her eyes lock on his. "You were with him?" Her voice quick, breathless.

Whicher shakes his head. "I saw him. After. I was with him."

Sofia Ortega searches his face. "Was he…still alive?"

He hears himself say, "No."

Her head jerks.

She shifts in the chair.

"He was looking for someone. I think. Meeting somebody."

Her face is slack with shock. "I saw a helicopter go over," she says. "I heard sirens, police cars."

Whicher nods.

She leans forward. A low moan escapes her. "I don't understand…" Her voice falters.

The marshal sits with Sofia Ortega, trying to shut down inside.

"Why would somebody shoot him?"

"He was working a homicide," Whicher says. "This morning he visited a suspect in prison. Then he went to this bar."

Sofia Ortega's face is blank.

"A car came past and opened fire on a crowd of people in front of it." Whicher glances at her, sees the look of total incomprehension. "A lot of shots were fired. Several people were injured."

From the living room of the house is the faint sound of the cartoon channel playing low on the TV, Amelia saying something—the voice of the liaison officer responding. The marshal kneads the skin and bone and sinew in his hand. A pit of vertigo-inducing depth between himself and Sofia Ortega, an abyss.

She stares at a spot a few inches in front of her face.

"Did he talk to you about what he was working on?" Whicher says.

She shakes her head slowly.

The marshal lets his gaze move over objects in the small back yard—a scuffed white, plastic toy horse, bright-painted hula-hoops, a softball bat.

"We try not to," Sofia says. "Not to talk about all of that."

"Does he keep anything here?" Whicher says. "Any notes, anything about what he's been working on."

She hardly hears him.

"Sofia?" He waits for her to look at him. Clears his throat. "We can't find his phone. We need to try to locate it."

She frowns, uncomprehending.

"Can you tell me which company he has his phone plan with?"

"What?" she says. "Verizon." A sudden pain rips across her face, expelling the air from her body. Her eyes are frantic. "Oh, God," she says, "did he suffer…" Her voice closes in her throat.

Whicher feels her pain reach a place deep inside himself. "Was he alone?"

"I don't think…he would have known a thing."

Her eyes peel back layers of his skin.

Animal instinct hopes she won't perceive the lie in his words.

"You saw him?" she says.

"I saw him."

Her mouth works. No words come out. "Alicia," she says. "Alicia is still in school…"

Whicher looks at her.

"They're sending somebody to collect her. She did a drawing for him this morning. She was going to finish it in school, she was going to bring it home, show him."

A sound emerges from Sofia Ortega—a strangled cry.

Her body convulses. She collapses from the chair.

Whicher drops to his knees, catches her, holds her in his arms. Her whole body shakes, she cries like a child, scarcely able to breathe. Hot tears are on his shirt, her face buried in his chest. Her loss enveloping, pushing into marrow and bone.

He holds her, staring blank, eyes swimming. Trying to believe. That things could one day be alright. That the faces of the two girls might ever leave him. That the loss to the woman in his arms could ever be redeemed.

Chapter 33

Case files and notes from the Hoffman murder inquiry are laid out on Sandro Ortega's desk in the USMS office. Chief Marshal Evans and Deputy Marshal Perez sit studying the documents—the small, neat Perez tight-lipped, Evans hunted-looking.

Whicher closes the door to the corridor behind him as he enters the room.

Perez turns in his seat.

"Chief of Police thinks this could be gang-related," Evans says. "There's been trouble coming, according to beat-officers…"

"I want Frank Nelson found," Whicher says.

Perez looks up at him.

The chief marshal stands. Steps away from Ortega's cluttered desk.

"I think Nelson was meeting him at the bar," Whicher says. "Why else would Ortega be there? I put out a stop order on his vehicle."

"We can't run this investigation, John," Evans says.

"You know that. It'll go FBI or PD."

"All law enforcement agencies can contribute."

"Don't let yourself get too caught up..." Evans eyes him. "Everybody's raw."

Whicher meets the chief marshal's gaze.

"Did you go up to the Robertson Unit?" Evans says. "Did you see Dubois?"

"Dubois is my case, the Hoffman case. Why wouldn't I?"

"Alright," Evans says. His thin face colors. "Alright, marshal."

Perez cuts in, "You think he knows who did this?"

Whicher nods. "He says he wants to talk to a lawyer."

"How about your other suspects?" the chief marshal says. "Riley McGuire? You were going to bring him in?"

"I don't have direct evidence against McGuire. I need to know what he was doing at Carl Avery's place last weekend. Dubois is good for taking the shots with the bow. For damn sure he wasn't acting alone."

Evans thinks about it.

"McGuire was out at Avery's place," Whicher says. "With a guy named Johnny Rawlson. Out of Dallas."

"Have you spoken to him yet?"

"No time."

"You want," Perez says, "I can call Big D—I got friends in the Marshals Office back there?"

"Alright," Whicher says, "good."

Evans thrusts his hands into his pants pockets. "What else?"

"We can't find Ortega's phone—it wasn't with him at the scene. I checked his truck, no sign of it there. I want to know who he called this morning."

"We could go for his phone records?"

"Verizon," Whicher says. "We'll need a warrant."

"There's a template on the system," Perez says, "if it's just a simple warrant for the log."

Evans takes a pace across the office, sits at a corner of an empty desk. "What about—Mrs Ortega?"

"I saw her." Whicher looks at him. "I went to the house."

"Does she have somebody?"

"Liaison officer. From the PD."

Evans lets out a long breath.

"We should send someone," Perez says.

"She has family, here in Abilene," Whicher says. "Maybe you could find them, get somebody over?"

"I'm on it."

The marshal walks to the window, looks out onto the street. "I need to call Underwood at the Task Force." Cars and trucks roll unhurried, pedestrians are out on the sidewalk, the city already settling.

Whicher dials the number on his cell phone.

The call clicks straight to voicemail.

"Yeah, this is Whicher. We're going to try to get a look at the log record on Ortega's phone. If it's still switched on, we'll get an idea where it's at. If somebody took it, they probably won't keep it, they'll get rid of it. Long shot. If you hear anybody found it, call me."

Whicher turns back into the room.

Perez is holding the desk-phone—looking at him, waving him over.

The marshal clicks off the call to Underwood. Steps away from the window.

"Guy up at the Robertson Unit," Perez says. "Officer, name of DiMaria—says Ortega came to see him this morning. He heard about what happened, he says he needs to talk to you. He thinks he might have something."

⁂

A half hour later, the suite of rooms at the back of the processing unit for new arrivals is deserted. Strip lights reflect from the dull gray prison walls.

A single officer is waiting—Carlos DiMaria. "I don't know if this is going to be worth anything…"

"Show me."

The marshal follows the corrections officer to a door marked, *Property Room*.

DiMaria unlocks it with a key code.

The two men enter.

In the center of the room is a table—on it, a collection of sealed bags.

Alongside the bags are printed-paper forms. The bags are clear plastic—inside them, boots and jeans, a leather vest.

"This is his?" Whicher says.

"All the property belonging to Dubois on admission," the CO says. "I booked him in, I'm in charge of the property room." He points to a single small bag set apart on the table. "Right there is his phone."

Whicher stares at it.

"I showed it to Marshal Ortega this morning," DiMaria says.

"At Marshal Ortega's request?"

"Yes, sir. At his request."

"Did he ask to see it before or after he went in to see Dubois?"

"After he'd seen him," the CO says.

"He tell you why?"

"He said back with the PD in San Angelo, they'd let 'em write down a couple numbers when they booked somebody—before they took away their phones. Nobody remembers numbers anymore."

Whicher nods.

"He wanted to know do we do the same?" the CO says. "We do." DiMaria lifts the bag containing the phone from the table. "Once we have the phones, they're sealed, the same as all the other property. If they're needed again for any reason they have to be retrieved, unsealed, all the paperwork has to be re-done. Then they have to be resealed again. So, we let 'em write up to five numbers on the booking form, now. That way, all we need to find is the form. No paperwork needs to get redone." DiMaria points to one of the forms on the table.

Whicher looks at it. "There's only one number written there."

"That's all Dubois wrote."

The marshal writes the number out in his notebook. "Did Dubois make any calls?"

"Yes, sir."

"Do you know who he called?"

"No, marshal, I don't. They get to call from a fixed line

here at the prison. Provided there's no reason to deny it, they get a call, that's it."

"Did Marshal Ortega take a copy of this?"

"He did, marshal."

"Dubois told me he hasn't spoken with any lawyer."

"I don't know if has or he hasn't." DiMaria says. "All I know is Marshal Ortega was in here asking about this, this morning. When I heard about what happened…"

Whicher meets the man's eye.

"I just thought you ought to know."

⋏

Whicher stands by the Silverado in the car lot outside the prison fence. A hot wind blowing in off the flat prairie.

He keys in the number on his cell.

Placing the phone to his ear he squints into the glare of sun.

He waits the few seconds it takes. Then clicks off the call.

Number unobtainable.

He tries again.

The same result.

⋏

An hour later, the marshal pulls in at the curbside on the wide expanse of Woodlake Drive—barely two miles south of his own house in Wylie—a prestige neighborhood; walled properties among mature trees.

Looking out, he surveys the two-storied, white columned home of Riley McGuire.

Whicher steers the Silverado into a driveway bordered

with manicured lawns. The property is grand, built from red brick. Eight-bed he guesses—a triple garage, a separate dining wing.

He shuts off the motor, steps from the truck. Buttons his suit jacket, squares his hat.

He mounts the stone steps to an over-sized front door beneath the white columned portico. Rings the bell button set within a brass plate.

No vehicles in the drive, no sound coming from within the house.

The door opens.

A Hispanic woman looks out at him, wiping a hand on an apron at her waist.

Whicher takes out the leather badge-holder, shows the USMS ID. "Marshals Service. Here to see Mister Riley McGuire."

The woman's face is blank.

"Is Mister McGuire here, ma'am?"

From within the hallway is the sound of footsteps. McGuire emerges from a corridor

He's wearing tan slacks, a leisure shirt. His face guarded. "What's going on?"

"I'd like to speak with you, sir."

"Here?"

"Yessir."

"What for?"

"This will only take a minute of your time."

McGuire looks at the Hispanic woman. "Alright, Camila. You can go."

The woman glances at the marshal, turns. Withdraws from the hall to a passage alongside of the main staircase.

"I thought I made it clear the next time you wanted to talk to me I'd want an attorney present? I already told you that."

"Like to ask you a couple questions," the marshal says. "About an employee of yours. Frank Nelson."

A flicker is behind McGuire's eyes.

"I come in?" Whicher steps into the coolness of the hallway, surveys the paintings on the walls. Original oils. Landscapes.

McGuire gestures.

The marshal follows him across the hallway into a living room of leather couches and hardwood floors—antique tables, cabinets filled with ornamental ceramics, fine cut glass.

McGuire indicates for Whicher to take a seat.

The marshal takes out the notepad and a pen, lowers himself onto a leather couch.

McGuire sits.

"Frank Nelson," Whicher says. "How well you know him?"

"Not well."

"Y'all work together most days."

"Do you know everybody that works alongside you?"

Whicher studies the man. "Do know you where I could find him?"

"Now?" McGuire says.

"Yessir."

"Right now? No, I don't."

"You have his telephone number?"

"Why would you want to speak with him?"

"Mister McGuire—are you aware there was a serious incident this morning? At a bar, on the west side of the city?"

"No."

The marshal eyes him.

"Should I be?"

"Does Frank Nelson ride a motorcycle? To your knowledge?"

McGuire bunches his shoulders, shifts his weight forward in his seat.

"Does he belong to a motorcycle club?"

"I have no idea. And I don't understand why you're asking me any of this."

"They're simple enough questions," Whicher says. "Do you know where he's at?"

"No. I don't know."

"You know where he lives?"

"I know his address."

"How about a phone number?"

"Should you be asking this from me?" McGuire looks at him, jaw protruding.

"Well, sir," the marshal says, "I *am* asking."

"I don't have it on me. I'd have to go get my phone."

McGuire stands, steps briskly from the room.

Whicher sits back on the leather couch, shafts of light filtering through the half-closed blinds. McGuire could stall, try to buy time. Maybe call Frank Nelson, to warn him.

The marshal hears no voices in the hallway. Only the sound of footsteps.

Riley McGuire re-appears, phone in hand. "I have no idea why you should want this. Have you tried his home?"

"I already called."

McGuire reads out the number.

Whicher writes it down.

"Is Frank Nelson involved in this incident at this bar?"

"He has a record of violence and intimidation, Mister McGuire. I think you know that."

For a moment, McGuire only stares at him. "I don't know what your problem is, marshal. If we have any further business, I'll be obliged if you'd arrange to speak with me through my attorney."

"People have a habit of dying around you," Whicher says. "Back in Dallas. According to the record."

McGuire tenses. Touches his neat-trimmed goatee.

"Where were you this morning?"

"I don't have to answer your questions."

"A homicide investigation, people are expected to co-operate."

"People are entitled to the advice of a lawyer."

"Only if they're under arrest."

McGuire stares at him. "I don't want you in my house anymore, marshal. I don't care to be threatened and harassed."

Whicher stands.

"I'd like you to leave." McGuire walks back out of the room.

The marshal follows him across the hallway.

"If you arrest me, you sure as hell will have to speak to my lawyer." McGuire opens the front door.

"Where were you this morning?"

"I was here. In my home. If it's any of your business."

"Anybody confirm that?"

"My housekeeper, for one."

"Your housekeeper?"

"Camila. The lady who was just here."

"She live in?"

McGuire doesn't reply.

"You didn't ask me what happened?" Whicher says. "This morning. At this bar. Somebody was shot and killed." He locks eyes with McGuire.

"I'm sorry to hear that."

"Did you receive a phone call from Marshal Ortega this morning?"

The man's face is lit with animosity. "I don't know what you're talking about."

"This world could be a bad place," Whicher says, "if he did call you. Real dark. Real bad. But then again," he says, "maybe you're already there."

⚹

The Chevy Impala is in the driveway of the house. Whicher pulls in alongside it. He kills the motor, stares at the picture window along the wall of the living room—tries to empty his mind, to shed the feeling consuming him. He tries the number from Riley McGuire for Frank Nelson—the second time he's tried to call it. The result is the same—straight to voicemail, factory-set, a pre-recorded greeting.

He shuts off the call, climbs out of the truck. Walks to his front door.

Entering the house, he feels a stillness.

He steps through into the kitchen.

Leanne is leaning against a countertop. Arms about herself, mouth part-open.

She looks at him. She doesn't speak.

The marshal takes off his hat, places it onto the table. "Are you alright?"

Her eyes look through him. She doesn't reply.

"Where's Lori?" He speaks his words softly. Takes a step toward her.

"I took her out. Over to see Amanda."

The marshal stares at his wife.

"Did you see her?" she says. "Did you see Sofia?"

"I saw her." He exhales a long breath.

"Is somebody with her?"

"A police liaison officer is there…"

"I can't stop thinking of her," Leanne cuts in. "Thinking of them, of all of them, that beautiful little family…" She looks at him. Her eyes desperate. "Did you see the girls?"

Whicher turns, stares out of the window at the shimmer of leaves on the live oak in the back yard. "Alicia was in school. Somebody was going to go out and get her. Amelia was there."

Leanne puts both hands over her face.

Whicher turns back into the room, steps to her, puts his

arms around her, holds her. Feels her body shake as she sobs.

For the longest time he stands with her. Silent. Holding her to him. With no words.

Finally she eases from him. "What happened? Tell me what happened."

"We don't know."

She stares at him.

"Somebody drove a car by a bar restaurant and opened fire."

"Was he the target?"

"We don't know."

"This case you're working—is it the reason he was killed?"

Whicher doesn't answer. Crossing to the refrigerator, he takes out a carton of freshly-squeezed orange juice, sets it on the countertop.

"What does that make you," she says, "the next target?"

"You want something to drink?"

"No, I don't."

The marshal takes a glass down from a cupboard, fills it.

Leanne steps away, to stand by the glass door into the back yard. She stares out. "You could do something else."

Whicher takes a pull on the drink.

"You could re-train," Leanne says. "You don't have to keep doing this. You could study law…"

The marshal pulls back a chair from the table, sits. Slips off his jacket.

Leanne turns. "I can't stand the thought of those girls

growing up without their father."

"FBI will investigate," Whicher says. "They'll find whoever did this. If I don't find them first."

"Did you even hear what I said?"

He sets down the glass.

"What about our own daughter?"

Whicher meets his wife's eyes. Holds her look. "I heard," he says. "I heard what you said."

Chapter 34

At the downtown law enforcement center two floors of the building are filled with uniformed cops, with sheriff's deputies and arrestees from the bar on Mockingbird. Officers hustle between rooms, moving fast down the corridors. Whicher finds the allocated room serving as a temporary office for Levi Underwood. He raps on the open door.

The FBI agent looks up from behind a computer terminal—his frame too big for the small space of the office.

"What's going on?" Whicher says.

Underwood pushes back in his chair. "We're just putting this together. I have principal witness statements…"

"Anybody talking?"

"We're still processing it all," the FBI man says. "Individuals suspected of opening fire at the bar are in the holding cells here."

"Did anybody speak to the owner of the place?"

Underwood consults his notes. "Bar owner is a Marylee Barnes. I've got her statement somewhere. She was inside the whole time, says she didn't see a thing."

"Can I talk to her?"

"I think they let her go. In case crime scene officers needed access to anything on the premises."

"How about the witness who saw the car?"

"The retired Air Force guy?"

"Anybody else confirmed his story?"

Underwood nods. "We have other witnesses saying they saw a car drive by and open fire." The FBI man stands, steps out from behind his desk. He looks at the marshal. "How about you? You were going out to see the wife?"

Whicher nods.

Underwood's eyes are hooded. "How was it?"

The marshal bunches his shoulders. "Not good."

The FBI man meets his eye for just a moment. Then looks away. "What else is happening?"

"I went out to French Robertson again," the marshal says. "I got a call from one of the COs."

"Oh?"

"Ortega was up there this morning. He talked with Dubois. After he got through with Dubois, he talked with the officer in charge of the property department."

The FBI man makes a question with his face.

"COs let the prisoners write out numbers from their phones to save on paperwork. Numbers for who they want to call. Ortega wanted to know did Dubois make a list. Dubois had one number. One only."

"You have it?"

"Yessir."

"You tried calling it?"

"I tried," the marshal says. "Nothing doing."

"Could it be a burner?"

"Could be," Whicher says. "Nobody found Ortega's phone?"

"Not that I heard."

"I need to know if he called this number—I need to know where it goes. Could FBI do anything?"

"Maybe."

"You're leading the investigation?"

"So far."

"Can we access the record of calls from out of the prison?"

"If it's a burner, it might not get us anywhere," Underwood says. "That thing is probably already trashed."

"Would there be any kind of a record?" Whicher says. "A location, anything?"

"General location, maybe," Underwood says.

"Something happened to take Ortega to that bar this morning."

"You think he might have spoken to someone on that number?"

"Somebody came after him and killed him. Something set that off. Maybe the call was the trigger."

Underwood thinks it over, says nothing.

"I want to see the Air Force guy again."

⚘

Walter Daniels sits at the end of a corridor—not handcuffed, arms folded over his red T-shirt, staring vacant at an opposite wall.

Noticing the approach of the two suited men he rocks back in his plastic chair.

"Mister Daniels," Whicher says.

"Are you letting me out of here?"

"I need a moment of your time."

"I already gave my statement."

"We know," Underwood says, "and there are other witnesses, now, confirming it."

"You didn't think I was telling the truth?"

"Not the way it works," the FBI man says. "It was a confused scene, we need to double check everything, make sure."

"Tell me again," Whicher says. "Tell me what happened, what you saw."

Walter Daniels runs a hand over the long tresses of his tied-back salt and pepper hair. "I was there about an hour eating breakfast. The place was packed. I got done, I went outside, a lot of guys were out front, something was going on, some sort of argument, a fight."

"This is before you saw the car?"

"Before." Daniels nods. "Guys were pushing and shoving. Yelling."

"The man who was shot, did you see him? Was he part of that?"

"I couldn't tell you," Daniels says. "I saw him there, I didn't really notice what he was doing."

"Who was he with?"

"I don't know. He was around a group of bikers." Daniels scratches his sunburnt forearm. "I headed over to my Harley, to ride out. Then like I said, there were noises—popping, banging. I turned around, I saw a car coming by. A white car, late-model Japanese, like I already said. The driver was shooting toward the group of guys arguing, fighting."

"Was there anything you can remember about the driver?" Whicher says. "Was he black, white, big, small? He have a beard? Could you see his arms, were they tattooed?"

Underwood gives the marshal a look.

Walter Daniels closes his eyes. "He was wearing a ball cap and shades, covering up, I guess. Long sleeve top." The man's eyes open again. "It all happened so damn fast, it's kind of hard to say. He was driving away by the time I realized what was happening. And soon as the shooting started, some of those bikers pulled out weapons, I was on the ground, scrambling for cover."

"How many shots did you hear?"

Daniels screws up his face. "Must've been somewhere between a dozen—to twenty, or so."

"That's a lot of shots," Whicher says.

"Hell, yeah, it is."

"You're certain about that?"

The FBI agent nods. "Other witnesses say the same."

⚑

Swinging by a vending machine, Whicher buys coffee for himself and Underwood. Hot, black, strong. The marshal sips on it, lets his thoughts range. Police officers with booking forms move leather and denim clad men past the communal area around the vending machines.

"So what else have we got?" the FBI man says.

"I went over to see one of Frank Nelson's employers from Summerwood Realty."

Underwood nods, takes a sip on his cup of coffee.

"Guy name of Riley McGuire," Whicher says. "Asked him did Marshal Ortega call him this morning. He told me, no."

"Is this a possible suspect?"

"McGuire has some history back in Dallas. I asked him where was he this morning, he said he was home."

"You don't believe him?"

"Man wants to lawyer up."

At the far edge of the communal area, the short, black uniformed figure of Sergeant Coleman appears. He waves a hand, gestures toward them. He's holding up a thumb drive. "We got the car on camera," he calls. "We got a clip of the car."

⅄

Back in Underwood's room Sergeant Coleman fits the thumb drive into a port on the desktop computer. "That gas station on the intersection of Mockingbird and Tenth caught it, according to the patrol officer. They got a shot of a car that looks like it could be it rolling by about the right time." The sergeant clicks on the screen, brings up a moving image player.

Whicher stares at the monitor.

Sergeant Coleman clicks on the player, maximizes the frame.

A grainy image shows the underside of a gas station roof. The camera looks out over the edge of an asphalt ramp leading back onto a four-lane—a section of Mockingbird. On the opposite side of the street from the filling station—just in view—is the edge of the wire-fenced storage lot.

In one corner of the shot is a time code.

A single pickup truck passes by on the far side of the street. An SUV leaves the gas station, headed south. And then a group of cars and trucks assemble to wait in the near-side lanes at the stop light. Traffic turns in from the cross street on Tenth; a van, a double-cab pickup.

And then a white sedan.

"Okay, hold it," the marshal says.

Sergeant Coleman clicks to freeze the image.

"That it?" Agent Underwood says.

The front plate on the car is blurry, but a couple of numbers and letters are visible.

The sergeant squints.

"We could work on that," Underwood says.

Coleman nods. "Looks like a Nissan Altima."

"Partial tag, we've got a starting point," Underwood says. "We run it against known license plates at DMV."

The marshal stares at the windshield of the sedan, its driver just visible—male, wearing a baseball hat and shades. "Alright," he says to Coleman. "Roll it."

The sergeant clicks on the screen.

The white sedan turns fully onto Mockingbird—the rear plate of the car obscured as another automobile passes on the near-side.

And then the car is out of shot.

"Not a whole bunch," Underwood says.

"White Nissan Altima," Sergeant Coleman says. "Alright. But what do we do about the driver?"

Whicher straightens at the desk. "I'm coming after him."

Underwood looks grim. "If somebody went after Ortega, you best be careful. You get too close, you're the next threat. This guy's a killer, if you get in his range."

"If I do," the marshal says, "then I got the son-of-a-bitch in mine."

Chapter 35

The drive from the LE center across town to Mockingbird Lane is a scant ten minutes—including a stop at Frank Nelson's place on Danville—still no sign of Nelson at the house.

In front of the Chrome Fork and Grille, police cruisers block the highway. Traffic now diverted onto the cross streets as Whicher pulls into the lot of a liquor store.

He parks the truck facing the four-lane highway and the gas station. Eyes the roof, sees the metal hub housing the CCTV camera.

He shuts off the motor, swings out of the cab—takes out the marshal's badge-holder and ID.

Crossing Tenth a uniform patrolman approaches.

Whicher holds out the badge. "Here to talk to the owner of the bar? A Marylee Barnes?"

The patrol officer waves him on. "I'm not sure she's in there, marshal."

"I'll find out."

Whicher crosses the street, takes in the plastic number-cards on the ground in front of the bar—evidence officers combing the concrete lot, Gail Griffin kneeling in a zip suit, inspecting a piece of oil-stained ground by a group of parked motorcycles.

She sees him.

"Looking for the owner," Whicher says, "she in there?"

Griffin makes a gesture with her arm. "Inside, somewhere."

"Who's in charge of the scene?"

"Dave Spano."

Whicher eyes the building's entrance.

Griffin stares at him. "I'm sorry," she says.

He looks at her. Lets his gaze meet hers for a moment.

Her face is helpless. "I'm really sorry…"

The marshal dips his head. Lets his gaze drift away.

"Are you running the investigation?"

"Underwood," Whicher says. "Way it looks." He starts to step away.

"Everything we can give him, every resource," she says. "He'll have it."

Whicher nods. Walks to the doorway, enters the building.

Through a short, dilapidated lobby, the bar opens out into a big, low-ceilinged room of bare floorboards, high-back booths, wooden tables and chairs, a small stage at one end. Brass and neon are at the counter, beer signs lit up in the dark. Motorcycle parts and roadsigns adorn the long walls.

Dave Spano is at the counter with a heavy woman in her fifties. She's dressed in jeans and boots and a denim shirt cut-off at the arms. Tattoos scroll from her shoulders, she wears a ball cap over gray blonde hair.

Whicher approaches, stares at the woman, her eyes are small and blue in her lined face. "Marylee Barnes?"

She looks him up and down, doesn't answer.

He shows his badge and ID.

Spano clears his throat. "Marshal."

Whicher keeps his eyes on the woman. "Ma'am? Are you the owner?"

She dips her head.

The detective touches the marshal's shoulder. "I'm real sorry about what happened here, partner…"

"Like to ask you a couple questions," Whicher says to the woman. "About this morning."

"I gave a statement already."

The marshal lets his gaze travel along the length of the bar and back again.

"If I can help, I will," she says. "It's just this whole thing is a goddamn disaster—I don't know when all I can get re-opened."

Spano says, "We'll be out of here soon as we can."

"Looking for a guy name of Frank Nelson," Whicher says. "You know him?"

Her eyes move onto his.

"Does he drink here?"

"I see him around." The woman steps to one of the restaurant tables—still littered with food from breakfast. She starts to clear away the plates.

"Ma'am, please leave that," Spano says.

Whicher continues, "Is Nelson a regular customer here?"

"I guess," she says, "pretty much."

"Was he here this morning?"

"Uh-huh."

"You saw him?"

"Yeah, Frank. He was in here, I saw him."

"Was he alone?" Whicher says. "Was he with somebody?"

"I wouldn't know."

"Did you see him inside?" Whicher says. "Or outside, out there on the lot?"

"Look," she says. "I mean, the guy was just around. I'm running a bar restaurant, people are everywhere, I'm not thinking about where folk are at."

"Think about it," Whicher says.

She puts her hands on her hips.

"What time was it? Around the time the trouble started? Was Frank Nelson around then?"

The woman cocks her head. "This all have something to do with him?"

"Was he here when the trouble started?"

She presses a finger and thumb to her brow. "I couldn't swear to it. But yeah, I'd say he was around."

The marshal nods. "You tell me anything about him?"

"Frank? He's just a guy comes by from time to time."

"You know anything about him?"

"He works construction, he hangs out with some of the regulars here. He drives a Ram pickup, rides a Sportster."

Whicher takes out a business card, gives it to her. "You think of anything else, you let me know."

Taking out his cell, he dials a number for Chief Marshal Evans at USMS.

Nodding to Detective Spano, he takes a step away—walks across the room until he's back outside in the glare of sun.

The call picks up.

"It's Whicher. Did we get a warrant to look at the call log on Ortega's phone?"

"Perez has it," Evans says.

"We need another number. For a person of interest; Frank Nelson." The marshal finds the page on the notepad, reads out the number written at Riley McGuire's house.

"What's your evidence for a warrant on Frank Nelson?"

"The log would be relevant and material to an ongoing investigation…"

"Not enough," Evans says. "We need probable cause. Do you have it?"

Whicher doesn't reply.

"I'll see what I can do," the chief marshal says. "But Judge Newell is on call today—her evidentiary standards are high."

"I'm over at the bar," Whicher says. "Nelson was here this morning, I think he could have set this up."

"Send whatever wording you want," Evans says, "we can try it."

"Copy that." The marshal finishes the call, puts away the cell.

Gail Griffin crosses the lot toward him. "You find the owner?"

"I found her."

"We've got shell casings and bullet frags here," Griffin says, "multiple weapons were involved. It's going to take some working out."

The marshal stares at the gas station over the street. He steps off the lot, walks along the side of the deserted highway. Past the fenced container yard, to the corner at the intersection. In his mind, picturing the grainy images, the CCTV footage. The white sedan turning in on Mockingbird, rolling slow up the road.

He turns back toward the bar, retraces his steps, following the path the white car took. Visualizing the scene from the point of view of the car's driver. Staring at the lot out in front of the bar, imagining Ortega there—surrounded by the bar's customers. Alone. Or with Frank Nelson. The driver of the car slowing to take aim—firing.

The distance between the highway's edge and the spot where Ortega fell is little more than twenty feet.

Not difficult.

Not with the speed right down.

Easy enough to make the shot.

But cold. Pre-meditated.

Devoid of any human feeling.

To shoot a man down in cold blood, a man not even looking.

Gail Griffin approaches again. "The trolling motor from the boat?"

The marshal focuses on her.

"Looks like it was stolen in a break-in at a property on

the lake. Reported last week."

Whicher thinks of the car thief in the Jones County jail—Hernandez. He'd had a trolling motor in the trunk of his car when they arrested him. He'd claimed he'd met Ray Dubois in a bar. Maybe this bar?

"It's no good for prints," Griffin says, "whoever handled it must've been wearing gloves, or else they wiped it. If the people involved with this are the same people that killed Elijah Hoffman they're well organized. Dangerous."

"They're the same," Whicher says.

"You certain?"

The marshal doesn't respond.

"One of them has his moorings cut," she says.

He looks at her.

"Killing a marshal," she says.

He thinks of Hernandez, of Elijah Hoffman. Of the fire in the field in Louisiana.

Of Alejandro Ortega.

⋏

Forty-five minutes later Whicher sits in the wait area of the phone company downtown—skim-reading the wording of the freshly-signed warrant—one number is authorized only; Sandro Ortega's cell phone number.

A middle-aged black woman in a yellow blouse watches from behind a reception counter.

The marshal sits back in the low slung couch.

A young man enters reception—Hispanic, wearing a short-sleeved shirt and pressed jeans.

"Marshal," the receptionist says. "This is the gentleman that will see you."

"Jay Jimenez," the young man says. "If you'd like to step this way."

Whicher nods to the woman, follows the young man out of reception along a broad corridor under strip lights.

Jimenez stops half-way down, opens a door, leads the way into a small, windowless room.

Across the length of one wall is a desk supporting a large, flat screen computer monitor. Two chairs are in front of the desk. Jimenez pulls one out, pushes it toward Whicher, takes the other for himself.

"You want to see the warrant?" the marshal says.

Jimenez shakes his head. "A copy came in from USMS half an hour ago, my boss checked it. We get requests from law enforcement all the time. I'm just here to show you the log."

Whicher sits.

With a couple of clicks of a wireless mouse, Jimenez opens up a file containing data set out in a box-grid format. Seven horizontal fields, line after line on a plain white screen. "This is the call log for the number on the warrant."

Whicher checks; it's Ortega's.

Jimenez traces the grid of boxes with a finger. "We have the date, the time, the direction of the call, inbound or out. Destination; that's the number called. Then duration. Plus the begin-cell-site, and the end-cell-site."

The marshal stares at the inbound and outbound numbers—recognizes his own. There's the USMS office.

Nothing else that's familiar. He takes out the notepad, flips it open. "Can we look at the last few calls?"

Jimenez scrolls down the list to the place it stops.

Whicher checks against the notepad—Frank Nelson's is the very last number Ortega called. The marshal feels a surge inside. Before that, two calls back is the number from Ray Dubois' paperwork at French Robertson. The log shows Ortega calling the number at ten thirty-seven—the begin-cell-site and the end-cell-site are listed as the same. "You know where that is?"

"I could find it."

Whicher points at the number copied from Dubois' paperwork. "Can you tell where the person receiving was at?"

Jimenez copies the number, clicks into a search field. "This is a pre-paid phone. I could see if it came up on any of the towers in the Abilene area network. If it's outside of that, it could be hard to find. But it's a bought-over-the-counter phone, there'll be no listed owner."

"A burner?"

Jimenez nods.

The marshal points at the screen, to Frank Nelson's number. "How about this one here?"

Jimenez copies the number, puts it into the search field, runs the search. "That's a different network."

"Can you access it?"

"I could," Jimenez says. He glances at the folded paper warrant on the desk. "But I'm limited in what I'm allowed to show."

The marshal thinks it over. "How about the burner

phone? It's not associated with anyone."

The young man looks at him, uncertain.

"We're not violating any private details if we search on that," Whicher says. "There aren't any."

Jimenez inclines his head, sits forward, clicks back to the call log screen. He copies the burner phone number, makes a series of secondary searches.

Two lines of data appear.

"It comes up only twice," Jimenez says. "Two calls only. Incoming. The first received yesterday, the second received this morning."

The marshal can already see the last caller was Ortega. The cell tower sites are listed. "Can you find the location of the person receiving the last call?"

Jimenez copies the cell site number, runs a search.

The marshal thinks about admissibility-of-evidence, puts it from his mind.

"The call was received and ended in the same place," Jimenez says. "A tower north of Abilene, right around the Hawley area."

"Hawley?"

"Yes, marshal."

"How close would the person using the burner phone be to the tower?"

"About a half a mile, depending on the topography. I can give you the tower's exact location?"

Whicher nods.

Jimenez clicks on another screen, reads out the location details.

The marshal writes down the address in his notepad.

"How about the location of the burner at the time of the first call? The call yesterday?"

The young man runs a search again. "That's here in Abilene, right around the Sears Park area."

"Can we identify the number calling it?"

"Looks like a fixed line." The young man types into the system. "Huh. That's listed to the state correctional facility."

"To the French Robertson Unit?"

"Yes, sir, marshal."

Dubois.

The first call had to be Dubois.

Whoever had the burner phone was in the Sears Park area the day before, and up around Hawley, north of the city, a few hours ago. Receiving the call from Sandro Ortega.

Whicher points at the number listed on the warrant, Ortega's number. "Could you find where this phone is at right now?"

"That's a live intercept," the young man says. He sits back from the desk. "I'd need a court order."

⽊

Outside of the office in the corridor, Whicher scrolls a list in his cell phone contacts. He finds a number, presses the key to send the call. Holding the cell against his ear, he pictures the person at the other end of the line; a woman in her late-fifties.

The call picks up.

"Judge Newell."

"Ma'am. This is Deputy Marshal Whicher. I believe you spoke to my colleague earlier, Marshal Perez?"

"I spoke to Chief Marshal Evans."

"Ma'am, I have a situation here I need your help with. It's in relation to…"

"I know what it's in relation to." The judge clears her throat. "I'm very sorry about what happened today. To Marshal Ortega."

Whicher lets a beat pass—lets her words hang in the air.

"Chief Marshal Evans says the FBI Violent Task Force Unit will be investigating the shooting," Judge Newell says.

"Yes, ma'am."

"We can have every confidence in them."

"I'm sure you're right," Whicher says. "Ma'am, I'm at the offices of a phone company executing the warrant you signed in connection with this. I want to carry out a warrantless intercept on a live feed…"

The judge doesn't answer.

"The phone in question belongs to Marshal Sandro Ortega—it's missing, we can't find it."

"You need a court order, marshal, you know that."

"I have reason to believe it was taken from him. And that whoever has it now is likely implicated in Marshal Ortega's murder."

Whicher looks along the featureless corridor to the reception area, light streaming in through its plate glass windows.

"You're at the phone company now?"

"Yes, ma'am."

"I can't give permission, as such, for a warrantless intercept," the judge says. "I can advise you that in this case it would be considered reasonable. In the circumstances."

The marshal shifts his gaze onto the door of the small office. "I also want to search the personnel records of a realty company; a realty company here in Abilene."

"You're in an almighty rush, marshal."

Whicher doesn't respond. He considers his answer a moment. "Marshal Ortega's two daughters were swimming with my daughter. Last night. In the pool in my back yard."

The line goes quiet.

The marshal doesn't break the silence.

"I need an affidavit," Judge Newell says.

"I'll have Marshal Perez draw one up."

"If your affidavit establishes probable cause to conduct a search, you'll have your warrant."

The line falls silent again.

"A word of caution," the judge says, her voice low, but firm. "Remain within due process."

The marshal doesn't reply.

"Your pursuit of this must be like any other."

"I'll have Marshal Perez call."

⊥

Back inside the office Jimenez clicks through screens on the desktop monitor. "Okay, I'm firing up network analysis. The software will look for triangulation, assuming we have multiple cell towers, we'll check the RF measurement report. We need one thing…"

The marshal lets his eyes meet the young man's for a moment. Anyone taking Ortega's phone would likely power it down, remove the SIM card, disable its GPS location sender.

Jimenez clicks onto another screen on the monitor. "I'll input the number."

He clicks the mouse again, presses several times on the keyboard.

Turns around in his swivel chair. Spreads his palms.

Whicher nods, his gut sinking.

"I'm sorry," Jimenez tells him. "The phone's switched off."

Chapter 36

In the street outside the phone company offices, Whicher scarfs down tacos al pastor from the take out window of a taqueria. He climbs into the Silverado still eating, puts in a call to Perez at USMS. Firing up the motor in the truck, he cranks the A/C, feels sweat beneath the hat band of the Resistol.

Perez answers.

"I need an application for a warrant to search the personnel records at Summerwood Realty."

"Looking for what?" Perez says.

The marshal throws his hat onto the passenger seat in the cab. "I want a list of employee addresses."

"You can't just ask them?"

"I been riding them the last couple days, maybe they'll say yes, maybe not."

"You looking at somebody on the payroll?"

"I want the list." The marshal checks the side-view mirror, puts the truck into drive, pulls out into the street. "I have a couple cell tower locations from a burner phone

Dubois made a call to yesterday. Ortega called the same number this morning. I want to see if anybody from Summerwood lives near either of the towers."

"That sounds like kind of a long shot, mano."

"I just spoke with Judge Newell, she'll be expecting an affidavit," Whicher says. "There's an address for Summerwood in the notes on my desk. I'll call them now, tell them to have somebody meet me. As soon as you can get the warrant, send it, fax it."

"I'm on it," Perez says.

The marshal clicks off the call.

⁂

Out to the north east of the city of Abilene, the car lot of the Summerwood Realty Corporation is baking in the early afternoon sun. Waves of heat roll from the flat plains off of Highway 351. Whicher pulls into a shaded bay alongside a Mazda sedan and a black, Mercedes SL500.

He shuts off the motor, steps from the truck. Fits his hat, angles the brim down, buttons the jacket of his suit.

Carl Avery's Mercedes ticks with heat from its hood.

The marshal crosses the lot, reaches the door to reception, he can see inside—Carl Avery standing, talking into his cell.

The female receptionist stares out at him.

Whicher enters.

Avery turns, abruptly finishes his call.

"Ma'am." Whicher touches the brim of his hat to the woman. "Mister Avery."

Avery puts away the cell in a pocket of his linen suit. His eyes are animated. He runs a hand through his graying hair. "Marshal. Can we take this in my office?"

Whicher follows Avery out of the reception area.

"I just spoke to my attorney," Avery says. "This is extremely short notice."

"Yessir." Whicher thinks of the brief phone call on the drive out.

"My attorney can't be here."

"You don't need any lawyer."

Avery enters the office. Looks at him.

"Nobody's accusing you of anything."

"And yet," Avery says, "you seem to have a fixation with this company."

"I'm asking for your cooperation in a homicide inquiry."

"I've tried to help," Avery says. "My boat was stolen. I don't know what else I can do."

The marshal looks around the room at framed photographs of construction projects—new-built condominiums, grand homes. "There's a possibility one or more of the employees here may be involved."

"In a homicide?"

"Yes, sir."

Avery swallows, crosses his arms. Uncrosses them again. "Do you have any kind of evidence for that?"

Whicher fixes him a look. "Are you aware a part-time Summerwood employee was shot and killed at a gas station the day before yesterday?"

"Excuse me?"

"Dwayne Cameron."

Avery's face is blank.

"Cameron worked part-time showing houses for you. His day job was driving armored cars."

Carl Avery sits at a corner of his desk.

"Maybe you'll have seen reports a US marshal was shot and killed this morning?" Whicher says.

"I saw reports a law officer had been involved in a shooting incident. At a bar out by Cobb Park…"

"Marshal Sandro Ortega. He was working with me—on this case."

Avery blinks several times, rocks forward. Says nothing.

"Dwayne Cameron was shot and killed two days after a failed attempt at a robbery on Judge Ely Boulevard—a robbery on an armored car. It's possible one or more of your employees may have had an involvement in that."

"In an armored *car* robbery?"

"Part of a series of robberies," Whicher says. "Under investigation by the FBI."

"I thought…I thought all this was about that man, Hoffman."

"We've arrested somebody in connection with Carl Hoffman's murder."

Avery stares at him. "Then why are you here?"

Whicher takes in the man before him—agitated, his eyes bright with thought. "We think there were accomplices."

Avery rises from the edge of the desk. He takes a turn about the room. "And you're asking for the home addresses of all company employees?"

"Yes, sir. I am."

"Nobody employed here is engaged in any kind of illegal activity."

The marshal stares at him, says nothing.

"Am I allowed to ask who you think is involved?"

"No." Whicher shakes his head.

A knock sounds at the door.

"Come," Avery says.

The receptionist enters the room, her face strained. She's holding a thin sheet of paper, its edges curled. "This just arrived."

Avery looks at her.

She holds it up.

"A fax?"

Whicher steps toward the woman. "It's a search warrant."

"For our personnel records?" Avery says.

"Home addresses of every employee on your books."

The receptionist blanches.

Avery stalks from the room, glancing at the woman. "Bring up the record," he says. "Print it. Print it all."

᛫

Riding back west along the two-lane highway, Whicher scans the land through the windshield of the Chevy—flat fields, scrub and mesquite stretching to a far distance, a towering sky starting to haze in the afternoon heat.

The Summerwood list is on the seat beside him—fifty or so names and addresses, on first view none of them close to either cell tower location.

Ahead on the two-lane is a disused workshop fronting down to the road.

The marshal checks the rear-view, signals, pulls the truck off the highway onto a weed-strewn lot.

Taking out the sheet of notes from the phone company offices in downtown Abilene, he finds a number for the French Robertson Unit. Along with the notes is the print-out of the call log from the burner, showing the two sole calls.

He keys the number for the state prison.

It rings, briefly, picks up.

"This is Deputy Marshal Whicher—out of USMS, Abilene. Like to speak to somebody in the Warden's office."

A male voice responds; "One moment, marshal, I'll put you through."

The call transfers.

The marshal pushes back in the driver's seat.

A woman's voice comes on the line. "Marshal. This is the Warden's office, how may I help?"

"Ma'am, I'm conducting a homicide inquiry, you have an inmate at your facility charged in connection with my case. Like to ask a couple questions about him."

"Of course," the woman says. "Can you give me the name?"

"Raymond Landry Dubois." Off the phone is a series of clicking sounds, Whicher pictures the woman entering Dubois' name into the prison's computer system. "I'm looking for information regarding Dubois' use of a phone at your facility."

"Oh?"

"I have information from a warranted search on a call log," the marshal says. "One of the numbers listed on the log is a fixed line out of the French Robertson Unit."

"We have a lot of outgoing lines, marshal. Can you give me the number?"

Whicher reads it out.

More keystrokes sound in the background.

"That's not on the inmate telephone system."

"Ma'am?"

"It's on a separate network—used for privileged calls. Usually, they'll be client-lawyer calls, sometimes doctor-patient in case of illness. The inmate telephone system is recorded, monitored. And it's stored. Privileged calls, we can't do that, it's not legal."

"I understand."

"It looks like this inmate has been admitted recently?"

"Yes, ma'am."

"He won't have completed intake and classification yet. Phone communication is restricted in that case."

"I'm just looking to find out if Dubois made a call from your facility."

"Can you give me a minute, I should be able to find that out. Can you hold?"

"Not a problem," Whicher says.

The line goes quiet.

Turning his gaze to the passenger seat of the truck, Whicher scans the list of Summerwood employees—his eye rests on Frank Nelson's address. He thinks of the house on Danville, still no word.

"Marshal?" The woman's voice is back again on the line. "It looks like Dubois was granted a call yesterday morning, around eleven-thirty."

The marshal checks against the log from the phone company, sees the time recorded; *11:36am*.

"I don't have more information at this time," she says.

"That's alright, ma'am."

"But he was granted a call. And that was the time it took place."

"Ma'am. That's all I need."

⼈

An hour later, Whicher takes the exit road off of US 27, a gnawing feeling in his gut. Less than thirty minutes to work through the list from the Summerwood office—not a single address is close to either cell tower location.

A dozen miles to the north west of Abilene, the exit road from the highway leads down past a used car lot to an intersection flanked by a brace of gas stations. The marshal makes a right, steers the truck along Avenue East—into the town of Hawley. Not much different from any other small Texan town. Interspersed among the one-floor houses, a Dollar General, a stone-faced church, a diner, a boarded up laundry. Alongside City Hall is a couple of country stores, a steakhouse—farther along the road, storage units. An auto wash. A long closed video store.

The marshal slows at the end of the main strip—turns around, heads back in the direction of the highway—passing the same stores and homes and businesses once again.

Something is nagging in the back of his mind—persistent, a small thread, hanging. A feeling.

Headed for the underpass beneath US 27, he checks the final cell tower address given by Jimenez.

Out through the other side of the underpass beneath the highway, the asphalt road gives out to hard packed grit.

Whicher follows a single-lane county road through flat fields, twisting and turning, power lines on wooden poles whumping by the truck's open window.

Brush and scrub begin to close at either side of the track as he drives along it.

Hernandez.

Hernandez had been picked up in Hawley.

Somebody had reported him acting suspicious—casing homes. A patrol officer responded, ran the license plate on the car he was driving—the vehicle turned out to be stolen.

In the jail, he'd claimed to know something about Hoffman's murder. Hours later he was stabbed, he was dead in the hospital that night.

What would bring a small-time thief to a place like Hawley?

Two or three miles along the road into the scrubland, now, the marshal sees a mail box on a galvanized post. A tumbledown homestead property is set back from the road in a cleared stretch of hardpan. A rusted pickup in one corner of the yard by a stack of graying lumber.

A dirt track branches from the grit road; the track disappearing into dense scrub up the side of a hill. Whicher slows, stares out of the window—from the foot of the hill he can just make it out.

He steers the Silverado up the grade—big tires biting into the red earth, lifting up a swirling cloud of dust.

Half a mile on, the track branches into two—a left-hand fork leading into high grown brush, a track gouged with deep ruts and wheel marks where vehicles have turned in.

The right-hand branch of the track continues on uphill.

Whicher follows it another quarter of a mile.

From his window he sees the rounded hump of a hillock overlooking the sweep of the grade.

He stops the truck. Stares at a narrow path rising up to the crest of the hill.

He shuts down the motor, steps from the cab.

Waves of heat roll from the plains land below. Hat down, he climbs the dirt path up the hill in his shirtsleeves. Pausing to let the wind dry the sweat on his skin.

A buzzard wheels on a thermal high above him, its shadow circling.

At the top of the hill, he stands squinting up at a cell phone tower—its outline stark against the whitening heat of the sky. He scans the land before him—burnt dry prairie and choking brush, stretches of ranch pasture, dots of buildings—the edge of the town of Hawley in the distance, a shimmering heat haze beyond it all.

Two calls.

Two calls to a burner phone.

One from Dubois in the state prison, the other from Sandro Ortega.

The call from Sandro Ortega was picked up here.

Right here.

Eyes searching back and forth across the land he sees nothing, feels nothing.

No thought triggers inside his mind.

He takes a final glance at the cell tower—retraces his steps back down the side of the hill to the truck.

Climbing in, he fires the motor, hits the A/C.

He turns the truck around, drives back down the hill to the junction with the grit road.

At the farmstead property, a man in bib overalls and a tattered hat stands watching from beside the house.

Whicher looks at him through the windshield. He slows the truck, brakes to a stop.

In his hands the man has a wad of empty feed sacks.

Whicher steps out.

"Need to make a left," the man says. "If you're looking for the new place."

"How's that?"

"Saw you come by, saw you headed up the hill. You need to take the track to the left, halfway up."

Whicher thinks of the rutted track leading off into the brush.

"Figured that's where you was headed. Only place there is up there."

"You know what it is?"

"New ranch property they're building. Feller that bought the land's into construction. Building a big ol' house, a bunch of barns. Lord knows what all. Some feller out of the city."

"You know him?"

"No, sir. But trucks are in and out here all the time, he's spending up a bunch of money. Man ain't no rancher, that's for damn sure."

Whicher nods, starts to turn to his truck. "Any idea who owns it?"

"Feller name of Tate."

The marshal turns to face the man.

"That who you're looking for?"

"Lance Tate?"

"That's him."

"He lives here?"

"He don't live here. Place ain't nothing but a construction site. He's here a bunch, though; he has a trailer. He comes out."

Whicher stares back at the dirt trail leading off up the hill.

Five minutes later, the Silverado parked in front of a steel gate secured with a padlock and chain.

The marshal climbs it. Jumping down to the other side, he walks along a length of dirt track where the high-grown brush has been cut back.

Turning a bend, the track opens out into a newly-cleared site.

Concrete foundations show the footings to several new, large buildings. One of them has a steel frame already set in place. Tarps cover the tops of stacked construction materials—a back hoe sits by a double-wide trailer in a corner of the plot.

Whicher takes in the site, scans the view stretching out over a natural panorama—a long grade sloping away, overlooking open country to a distant far west.

The call to the burner was picked up on the tower just a quarter-mile distant.

Whicher feels his pulse start to quicken.

Back down at the bottom of the hill, the neighbor in the coveralls is by the fence line to the property.

The marshal stops the Silverado, steps out. From his jacket, he takes out the USMS badge and ID.

The man glances at it, his face is suddenly guarded.

"How well you know this feller?" Whicher says.

The man shakes his head.

"He had the place long?"

"Six months. There some kind of trouble?"

"You met him?"

"Couple times."

"He tell you what he's looking to do up there?" Whicher says.

"I wouldn't know." The man looks away and back again. "It's wild country, not many folk are out here. Last owner couldn't get rid of it fast enough."

"Why's that?"

"A bunch of dirt-bike riders got to tearing it up, coming out, riding all over the damn place. Trespassing. This feller bought the land, they ain't been back."

"That a fact?"

"Yes, sir."

Whicher studies on the man.

"Owner wanted rid of it. He told me Tate paid him cash."

"Lance Tate paid him in cash?"

"He paid a bunch less than the land was worth, you ask me. But cash, you know? Folding money. Since then it's been quiet—apart from the trucks."

The marshal thinks it over.

The stark image of the cell tower on the hill fixed in the back of his mind.

Chapter 37

Out at the lake at the top end of the dam, the parking lot is open—unguarded, the place where Hoffman's body was found unmarked.

A light chop is on the water, wind gusting over the surface.

In the distance, small boats move along the eastern shoreline.

Sitting parked, the marshal lets his mind range staring from the window of the truck.

Water laps at the edges of the concrete boat ramp.

He pictures Carl Avery's skiff.

Avery had been the starting point. Lines spread outward, seeming to lead nowhere.

Avery's place on the lake was practically open house to anyone with a mind to use it. Multiple sets of keys were passed around. The boat house left unlocked, sometimes left wide open.

Riley McGuire had been the last to use the place, the last known.

There were the kids from ACU, the almost-witnesses.

The man that tried to track them down on campus—likely Frank Nelson.

Whicher thinks of him.

A ticking sensation in his gut.

A blond man was seen driving out to the Hoffman place by the neighbor; the woman trying to fix her irrigation rig.

Blond man.

He'd thought of Nelson.

At the time. Frank Nelson.

It could as well have been Lance Tate.

🙼

Whicher follows the snaking road beneath the bluffs along the eastern shoreline of the lake. Past the shallow inlets, the shacks and houses set back among the trees. Thinking of Hoffman. Thinking of Dubois.

Cajun Ray Dubois' prints were all over Hoffman's truck. Witnesses in Greenwood signed statements testifying they saw him there, that they saw him driving the truck.

The compound bow was in back. The arrows with it the same as the arrows in Hoffman's body.

Coming up on the junction with East Lake Road, the marshal heads down the two-lane highway, past the turn for the marina.

Why Dubois?

Was he only paid to take the shots?

Why would Dubois want Hoffman dead?

Summerwood Realty had wanted to buy his farm.

Somebody lured Hoffman out to the lot that night.

Riley McGuire had known him. He'd known him, tried to negotiate a potential sale.

Farther down along the highway, Whicher sees the perimeter fence of an outdoor gun range—a couple of shooters on the firing line with scoped rifles. The sound of their gunfire brisk and sharp.

An image of Sandro Ortega's bloodied body flashes in Whicher's mind.

The marshal pushes the thought away.

Ortega had called the burner phone.

Could Tate have answered? Would Ortega have recognized the man's voice? He'd spoken with him only yesterday—he'd been out at Summerwood. Ortega could have recognized him if Tate had answered. Tate might have thought he could, even if Ortega hadn't.

Ortega called Frank Nelson right after he'd called the burner number—the call log from the phone proved that.

He'd gone to the bar on Mockingbird.

Frank Nelson had been there.

Whicher tries to bring to mind the grainy footage from the gas station CCTV camera—the white Nissan Altima, the driver in the ball cap and shades.

He tries to picture it, to see into the face of the man behind the wheel.

To pry it out. To force it.

To see the hidden revealed.

Along the northernmost side of the city, the marshal takes Highway 20 just as far as the exit for the Old Anson Road. From the off-ramp, he drives the half-mile through a sparse but growing neighborhood of older houses and new-built condos on denuded ground.

Past the Baptist church, he hooks a right onto Vogel Avenue.

Driving down Vogel he sees the outline of a cell tower in back of a clutch of old, brick buildings.

He slows the truck, pulls over to the shoulder.

Staring out through the windshield he studies the cell tower site that picked up the first call—the call made by Dubois from the prison the day before. Beyond it, he can see the fenced edge of a new construction site.

He shifts the transmission into drive, pulls back out into the road.

Approaching closer, he can see the site belongs to Summerwood Realty—it's the construction site he'd visited to speak with Riley McGuire.

Lance Tate had been on the site, he'd seen him there that day.

The cell phone tower is just a couple of hundred yards from it.

Two calls to the burner—McGuire could have been close to one of them.

Lance Tate could have been close to both.

⸸

Back at the law enforcement center, Sergeant Coleman spots Whicher entering the lobby of the building. The police sergeant hustles over. "We checked DMV records," he says. "Fifteen white Altimas in the metro-area—plus Taylor county and Jones combined."

The marshal looks at him.

"None of 'em have a registration that corresponds with the partial view of the plate."

"It's on a set of stolen tags?" Whicher says.

"Or else the vehicle's from farther away," Coleman answers. "We've got a detective from CID working on it. It could take a little time."

"Is Underwood still in the building?"

The sergeant points in the direction of the FBI man's room. "Last I saw."

Whicher heads across the lobby into a corridor. Detainees from the bar on Mockingbird are still there, a few wives and girlfriends among them now, hassling the uniformed cops.

The marshal reaches the FBI agent's room, knocks, looks inside.

Underwood has a pile of hand-written paper forms on his desk. "Come on in," he says. "302 central in here…"

Whicher enters, glances at the topmost Interview Report Form 302.

"We've got fifty people," Underwood says, "half of them have nothing whatever to do with any of this. Another bunch were there looking for trouble, carrying. Half a dozen testify to seeing a car drive by and open fire. The rest of the statements, the first they knew, shots were being fired in front of the bar by folk already there. Man, this thing is messed up."

"Any word on Frank Nelson?" Whicher says.

"Whereabouts still unknown."

"I spoke with the owner of the bar," the marshal says, "Marylee Barnes. She said Nelson was there this morning."

"She sure about that?"

"She said he was there right around the time of the shooting."

Underwood clicks a pen, makes a note on a legal pad on the desk. "She know him?"

The marshal shakes his head. "He's just another guy, according to her."

Whicher takes two folded sheets of paper from the inside pocket of his suit.

He lays them onto the desk top—opens them out, flattens them with a hand. "This here's the call log from the phone company. Sandro Ortega's cell phone."

The FBI man looks at him. "Is the phone switched on?"

Whicher shakes his head. "The log shows the last call Ortega made was to Frank Nelson." The marshal puts a finger on the final line of data in the box-grid printed out on the sheet. "Two calls back from that is the number I have from Ray Dubois' paperwork at French Robertson."

"The burner?"

"Right."

"So, what's that mean?"

"It means Ortega called the burner number, he must have spoken to whoever had it. There's been only two calls to it," Whicher says. "One was Dubois, yesterday morning, from the Robertson Unit."

"You know that?"

"Warden's office confirmed it."

The FBI man nods.

"The second call was Ortega today. I got the phone company to list out the cell tower locations at the time the burner received both calls."

"No shit?"

"When Dubois called it yesterday, the burner was located in the Sears Park Area, here in town. Today, whoever had it was up in Hawley."

Underwood eyes the log on the desk.

"I have the names and addresses of all the Summerwood Realty Corporation employees," Whicher says.

"They gave you that?"

"I had a warrant. Signed by Judge Newell."

Underwood picks the sheets of paper off the desktop, sits back in his chair to read. "Remind me not to get on the wrong side of you, man…"

"I checked the cell tower locations from the call log. Lance Tate has a property a quarter-mile from the site up in Hawley."

"Lance Tate?"

"He works for Summerwood Realty. Lives here in Abilene, owns land out around Hawley. A neighbor says Tate will sometimes stay out there. He's building on the land, there's a trailer on site."

"What do you know about Lance Tate?"

"Not much," Whicher says. "I came by Sears Park to check out the second cell tower the phone company gave me. That second tower is right by one of the Summerwood construction sites."

Underwood cuts the marshal a sideways glance.

Sergeant Coleman's patrol partner, Officer Suarez appears in the open doorway to the room. "9-1-1 call, just in."

The marshal looks at him.

"Some kind of a shooting incident, down near Buffalo Gap," Suarez says. "Caller reported a man driving a Dodge Ram pickup—dark green in color. Sergeant Coleman said you'd want to know."

"Frank Nelson's truck?" Whicher says. "I've got a stop order out on it."

"Dispatch advised responding units—the vehicle's a similar sounding truck."

"Where?" the marshal says.

"Somewhere out in the hills down at Buffalo Gap," Suarez says. "Taylor County Sheriff has units responding."

"What kind of shooting incident?" Underwood says.

"Multiple gunshots, according to the caller. Prior to that, vehicle seen trespassing on private ranch property—plus a motorcycle, the caller thinks…"

Chapter 38

Fourteen miles to the southwest of the city, past Dyess Air Force base and the rail road line, burnt dry grass and thick brush border the smooth asphalt of US-27, trapped heat radiates in the low hills.

Where the land rises, the ground is rock and bone dry dirt—grades choked with scrub and thick stands of mesquite.

Thirty minutes since the call.

No update from Taylor County.

Whicher sees a white, Chevy Tahoe from the sheriff's office parked at the side of the road.

He slows, signals, pulls the truck into the dust blown entryway of a quarry site.

A deputy in tan uniform steps out from the Tahoe.

Whicher brakes to a halt, rolls the window—shows his USMS badge and ID.

The deputy is Hispanic, the name badge on his shirt reads; *Martinez*.

"John Whicher," the marshal says. "It's my stop order on the truck."

"Dispatch said somebody from the Marshal's Service would be headed down."

"Y'all find anything?"

"So far, no," Martinez says.

"Tell me about the call?"

The deputy shrugs. "A woman out riding her horse saw a truck headed up in the hills. And a motorcycle, sometime after. She has a ranch out here." Martinez points across the highway at a gate opening onto a smaller, gravel road.

"Why the call?"

"Most of that land up there is private," Martinez says. "She didn't know the truck. Or the motorcycle. She wouldn't have called, she said, but ten minutes after she saw the motorcycle go up, she heard gunfire. More than one weapon. She didn't like it."

Whicher looks at Deputy Martinez.

"She said there's problems sometimes, people going up that shouldn't—kids, mostly. The sound of shots bothered her."

"Right," the marshal says.

"Dispatch asked her about the vehicle—they thought it sounded like a possible match for the SO. Dark green Dodge Ram."

"She said it was a Ram?"

"She said Ram pickup, four-door cab."

The marshal nods.

"Dark green in color."

"Close enough," Whicher says.

"I took a look around," the deputy says. "Another unit

came up from US-89, east of here. We didn't see anything, didn't find anything. Doesn't look like anyone is up there."

The marshal glances over at the gravel road on the opposite side of the highway.

"It's a bunch of dirt roads and tracks in the hills," Deputy Martinez says. "It's rough country, most of it pretty wild."

"There was no sign of anybody?"

The deputy eyes him. "I'm not saying nobody went up there. There's tire tracks. But we were moving fast, looking to see what was going on. We came in pretty hot, on account of the stop order. I ran siren on the highway, they could have heard us coming. If there was somebody, they probably just took off."

Whicher squints into the glare of light, staring up into the hills. "Why go up there?"

"There's a couple properties," the deputy says. "Ranch land. Most of it's brush and rock."

"Maybe I'll take a look around, anyhow."

"You want me to come up?" the deputy says.

Whicher shakes his head. "That's alright."

He moves the shifter into drive.

⅄

For twenty minutes the marshal searches a plateau of scrub grass and mesquite and brush along the flattened top of a ridge of hills. Gulleys and creeks descend steeply from the higher ground, their sides thick with vegetation, exposed rock gray-white in the afternoon sun.

The marshal drives slow in the Silverado—scanning left

to right, visually processing. In his mind, the armored cavalry scout he once was; officer commanding the battalion scout platoon.

Area reconnaissance; not so different from a fugitive search. Ahead of the line, back then in enemy terrain. But home soil, a man could still end up a casualty.

Tire marks are everywhere—one set from a recent vehicle, tracked by deep indentations from a single tire. Single tire was likely a dirt bike. The description of the truck was close enough to be Nelson. A motorcycle could be anyone. The marshal thinks of the biker bar on Mockingbird.

Approaching a ridge line, the marshal sees the ground drop away, the path ahead cut off.

He brakes to a stop, sweeps his gaze over the terrain through the truck's windshield. Open plain is to the north at the foot of the hills. In the distance, the city of Abilene a distant blur on the horizon.

Scrub and brush extend all around, the land dipping and rising.

Aerial.

Aerial reconnaissance is what he needs. He could call DPS. But grounds to send a helo would class as weak.

Pushing open the driver's door, Whicher steps out into the afternoon heat.

He walks forward of the Silverado, squats.

Tire marks are present in the crumbling earth. The rear tire of a dirt bike appears—just a few inches long between the double marks from a four-wheeled vehicle. The tire marks are fresh, dirt walls and the tread patterns well defined.

He sees the ripped-up ground where the marks in the earth turn sharp right. East, toward another part of the plateau. Staring at their course he sees a faint opening a hundred yards to his right, an opening in the scrub.

He turns around, walks back to the truck, climbs in behind the wheel. He drives toward the opening. Approaching, he can see a narrow dirt track.

At the end of the track is a cleared area. A barn of some kind in its center.

The marshal drives onto the track, approaching slow until he's almost in front of the barn.

No vehicles are present.

The barn is closed up.

Tire marks are visible, freshly gouged into the dry earth.

Shutting off the motor, he steps out.

He walks to the barn—its door is chained and locked.

A gap between the door and the frame is big enough to show the space inside empty.

Turning away, a glint at the far side of the clearing catches Whicher's eye. A glint from the ground.

The marshal takes the few steps toward it, kneels.

Lying in the dirt is a group of five spent shell cases.

He peers in close—they're .45ACP.

Standing, he walks the full perimeter of the clearing. At its easternmost point, something has flattened the scrub grass, broken several branches of a spreading mesquite.

A second group of shell cases is close by on the ground.

Unfastening the retaining strap on the Glock at his belt, Whicher steps to the Silverado, pulls the keys from the ignition.

Moving back to where the branches are broken, he can see where a vehicle has passed through the brush into thick vegetation down a sharply descending slope.

He picks a way forward. A wheel mark appears twenty yards in.

The land drops away fast into a deepening gorge.

The marshal draws the Glock from its holster.

The roof of a pickup truck is just visible beyond a tangle of spiny hackberry and whitebrush mesquite.

He stops, drops down. Listens for a moment, eyes scanning the brush, sweat running on his skin.

Rising to a crouch, he holds out the Glock, descends a few yards farther.

"*US Marshal,*" he shouts out.

No answer comes back.

He closes the last yards.

The Ram pickup is stationary before a bank of thorn brush and scrub guajillo.

The driver's door open.

The cab is empty.

Checking inside, he sees blood on the wheel and on the seat. A fresh bloom of sweat pricks his skin.

"*US Marshal,*" he shouts again. "*Anybody here?*"

Above the sound of his own breathing is only silence.

Disturbed vegetation leads off into the high brush. Keeping low to the ground, he moves forward, works his way another twenty yards. Then stops.

Frank Nelson lies slumped on the ground.

A semi-automatic pistol is in his hand, his head folded forward on his chest.

Whicher raises the Glock between both hands, stares down the iron sights.

Finger wrapped around the trigger.

Chapter 39

The ambulance and the sheriff's units move at speed up the highway toward Abilene.

Following behind on the road, the marshal reaches for the cell on the dash mount of the truck.

He keys the number for Chief Marshal Evans, switches to speaker phone.

"Frank Nelson is headed into hospital," Whicher says. "Two gunshot wounds to his upper body, significant loss of blood. Estimated chances of survival not high."

"Underwood called," Evans says, "I heard. He's going over there, now."

Whicher stares at the back of the ambulance through the windshield.

"You found Nelson on the back of a 9-1-1 call?"

"He was out in the hills at Buffalo Gap," Whicher says. "Somebody went out there with him, somebody on a dirt bike."

"What happened?"

"Some kind of fight," Whicher says. "Listen, did Marshal

Perez find anything more on McGuire? Riley McGuire. Or on the fishing buddy staying with him at the lake? Rawlins. Out of Dallas?"

"Unknown to law enforcement," Evans says.

The marshal flexes his hands on the steering wheel, breathes a silent curse.

"Is McGuire involved, are you going to talk to him?" Evans says.

"Right now I'm going looking for Lance Tate."

⋏

The late-afternoon sky is flat with the day's heat as Whicher enters an upmarket residential neighborhood of large private homes—the Lytle area of the city, not far from the regional airport, the properties built surrounding a private lake. Along Shoreline Drive, Range Rovers and Jaguar sedans sit in car ports along with German sports cars in manicured drives.

The marshal checks the address on Tate. Drives another half a block, pulls up in front of a recently built stone and glass and timber designer property. Ornamental fencing surrounds the grounds but the gates are open.

Steering into a gravel driveway, he sees a steel-gray Hummer parked beneath the shade of cottonwood trees.

He stops the Chevy at the end of the drive, shuts off the motor.

Staring at the house, he sees no sign of anyone home.

Along one side of the building he can see through to the lake—a shimmer of late sun on its surface.

Stepping from the truck, he leaves the jacket of his suit unfastened—over the Glock at his hip.

At the front door he climbs a single broad, stone step, presses on a buzzer. Notices the camera in the wall.

The door is hardwood panels inset with panes of smoked glass.

He peers in, briefly, sees nothing.

Turning to the driveway he lets his eye rest on the Hummer; recently washed, the body work shining, tires and rims clean.

Mature trees dot the property, strips of watered lawn are neatly cut. The neighboring houses are older, conservative, just as grand.

From the far side of the building, Lance Tate emerges, running a hand back through his dark blond hair.

He's wearing jeans, running shoes, a T-shirt over a well-toned body. "Marshal?"

Whicher nods.

"I heard the buzzer, I was out back. What's going on, what are you doing here?"

"I need to talk with you, Mister Tate."

"Really?"

"Yessir."

Tate takes a few steps forward. "What about?"

Whicher lets his gaze run to the neighboring house, and then the next one. "We talk inside?"

Tate makes a face. Smiles. "Whyn't you come around back and join me?"

Whicher nods. Follows the younger man along a stone-paved walkway to the rear of the property where it borders the lake.

A raised terrace in back houses an in-ground swimming pool. Decking on three levels is set up as a dining area, a bar, a place to barbecue. A private jetty extends out into the water.

Whicher takes in the rear of the property—glass sliders, picture windows. Motorized shades.

"Can I get you something?" Tate says.

The marshal shakes his head.

From a cold box beneath a teak counter, Tate takes a can of soda, pops it open. "So, what can I do for you?" He takes a pull on the drink.

"One of your employees was shot this afternoon, Mister Tate—were you aware of that?"

Tate takes the can away from his mouth, swallows. "Good Lord. Seriously?"

"Frank Nelson."

Whicher stares directly at the man, gauging his reaction.

Tate's eyes are wide. "What do you mean shot? What happened?"

"He was out to Buffalo Gap. Out in the hills."

"Is he hurt?"

The marshal nods.

The young man's eyes are hard to read, intense blue, back-lit in the glare of the lake.

He puts down the can of soda, opens his mouth as if about to speak, says nothing.

Whicher studies him.

"Jesus Christ," he finally says.

"You have any idea what he might have been doing out there?"

"Me?"

The marshal looks at him.

Tate's brow knots in confusion. "No. None at all."

"He'd been shot twice."

Tate looks at him.

"He was shot at close range—most likely by somebody that knew him," Whicher says. "Are you aware of anyone that might've wanted to hurt him?"

"No…" Tate puts a hand to his hair. "I don't understand. Was he in some kind of trouble? I don't know Frank real well…"

"Is there anything you can tell me about him that might help? He's worked for you how long?"

"Four or five years? I see him at work, outside of that…" Tate spreads his palms. "I can't believe he was shot, you mean, somebody tried to kill him?"

"He was unconscious when I found him."

"*You* found him?"

Whicher keeps his face blank. "Somebody called 9-1-1. Caller gave a description that matched his Dodge Ram truck."

Tate puts his head on one side—as if relaxed. But his body emanates a taut energy. "Have you been looking for him?"

"I want to talk to him about a homicide."

The young man blows out his cheeks, folds his arms across his chest.

Whicher looks off across the lake—in the distance, above the trees and the neighborhood houses, he can just make out the Hotel Wooten on the city skyline. "How long you work for Mister Avery?"

"What?"

"Pay must be pretty good. Fine house you have here, quite a place."

Tate uncrosses his arms. "Look, what's happening with Nelson?"

Whicher doesn't reply. "You own a ranch property, Mister Tate? Up in Hawley?"

"What does that have to do with anything?"

"Are you aware a law officer was shot and killed this morning?"

The young man's eyes are steady. "No."

"At a bar in the city, up on Mockingbird."

"I don't understand." Tate gives a shake of the head. He picks up the can of soda. Looks at the marshal. "What's going on? What is all this?"

"I was hoping you might be able to tell me something about Frank Nelson."

The young man makes a face. "There must be scores of people that know him better than I do."

"Mister Tate, did you speak with my colleague, Marshal Ortega this morning?"

"Marshal Ortega?"

"Yessir."

"No. Should I have done?"

Whicher doesn't answer.

"Is this all connected to that…homicide out at the lake?"

Tate takes a pull at the can of soda.

"Where were you this morning?"

"Here," Tate says.

"All morning?"

"I had some errands to run, I was in town."

"Were you up in Hawley?"

"What's that have to do with anything?"

"Were you?"

The young man smiles. "As a matter of fact, no."

"Were you aware Frank Nelson has criminal convictions for intimidation and assault?"

Tate's expression is flat. "He's a construction foreman, he's a good worker. I didn't hire him, I couldn't tell you about his background."

"He's a biker, former gang member, did you know that?"

"Is that why somebody shot him?"

The marshal doesn't reply. "Where were you this afternoon?"

Tate looks around, shrugs, runs a hand through his hair. "I was right here."

"Anybody with you?" Whicher looks directly into Tate's eyes.

"No." The young man returns the stare. "What does it matter where I was?"

"Maybe it won't."

Tate puts down the can. "Is there some kind of problem, marshal?"

"Is there?"

The young man's smile is cold.

"Don't leave town," Whicher says.

"Why would I do that?"

"I'll need to talk to you again."

"I wish I could be more help."

Whicher thinks of Ortega, lying in his own blood on a concrete lot. A white sedan cruising by the bar. "You own any other vehicles, Mister Tate?"

The young man doesn't move. The expression on his face is neutral.

"Apart from that Hummer out there?" Whicher says. "You own a white Nissan Altima?"

"No."

"Know anybody that does?" The marshal half turns, takes a glance at the stone paved walkway. "I need to see Frank Nelson in the hospital. There may be more questions. I'm going to need to come back."

"You know where to find me."

Whicher touches the brim of his hat.

Lance Tate shifts his weight, meets the marshal's stare, his eyes quick and bright.

"I know where to find you," Whicher says.

Tate nods. "I know where to find you, too."

⁂

Traffic is light on Jake Roberts Freeway, despite the onset of evening. From the raised highway, Whicher sees cars on an adjacent service road—he recognizes it—recognizes the filling station where Dwayne Cameron was shot to death.

Whicher pictures the scene at the gas station that morning. Underwood there, TV news vans, the bullet-ridden vehicle.

I know where to find you, too.

The marshal reaches to his cell on the dash, keys a call to Levi Underwood.

The FBI agent picks up.

"Where are you?" Whicher says.

"At the hospital," Underwood answers. "Doctors are operating on Nelson, I'm about to leave."

"Did he regain consciousness?"

"Nope. It's going to be a few hours. Sheriff's department are processing the scene up at Buffalo Gap," Underwood says. "They say two distinct groups of shell cases…"

"Frank Nelson's truck went into the brush," Whicher says, "the brass on the ground there was most likely Nelson looking to defend himself. They need to get casts of the dirt bike tire print."

"I'll tell them."

"I spoke with Lance Tate," Whicher says. He shifts into an outside lane to pass an eighteen-wheeler. "Tate owns a place on Shoreline Drive, right on Lytle Lake. Plus the Hawley ranch. He bought the ranch for cash. You think he's getting that kind of money from Carl Avery?"

The FBI man thinks about it. "Are you going after him?"

"I'll dig a little," the marshal says, "check his background. I'll let you know what I find."

"Be sure to do that," Underwood says.

"That gas station off of Jake Roberts Freeway? Where

your armored car driver was killed?"

"What about it?"

"Less than a mile," Whicher says. "From Lance Tate's home."

Chapter 40

Pulling in on the driveway of the house in Wylie, Whicher checks the clock on the dash. Coming up on seven o'clock in the evening.

Braking the truck to a halt, he shuts down the motor. He takes his hands from the wheel, sits in the silence.

Moments from the day flash through his mind; a helicopter flying over the USMS office, speeding across town to the bar on Mockingbird.

Sandro Ortega.

Every moment since the sight of him. Trying to hold down a feeling.

Sofia Ortega. Rocking in a chair, a world disintegrating.

He pushes back in the driver's seat, tries to force it away.

He thinks of Lance Tate. The grand house.

The place in Hawley.

Frank Nelson.

Nelson could've been there, working Tate's construction site in Hawley. Who else would Tate have build it but his own men? The day before, Ray Dubois had called the burner from the state prison. The call logged near the Sears Park site—Summerwood's construction site. Frank Nelson could have been there. Maybe Nelson took the call both times?

Frank Nelson.

Lance Tate.

The marshal stares at the house through the windshield of the Silverado—an unfamiliar sense at the back of his mind.

I know where to find you, too.

A first case in his hometown.

Suspects living minutes distant—instead of hours.

Everything precious contained within the walls of the house in front of him, his wife and child.

He runs his tongue over the sharp edge of his teeth.

The same eye that drew a line on Ortega could draw a line on him.

The front door opens. Leanne stands in the frame.

She steps from the house, half-closes the door.

Whicher climbs out from the truck.

"Lori was watching from the window," Leanne says. "Are you going to come in?"

He steps to her. Looks into her eyes. Sees the redness, senses the fragility. Placing his hands on her back, he pulls her to him.

Her voice is a whisper. "It's so awful…"

He pulls her tighter. Holds her in the driveway. No words. In the failing light.

"Do you think we should tell her? She knows something's wrong…"

"Not tonight," the marshal says.

He stands with his head against his wife's head. Then takes her hand, leads her to the front door.

"I let her stay up," Leanne says. "I wanted her to see you."

Whicher steps inside, takes off the Resistol.

Lori is at the far side of the living room. Sitting playing with a plastic horse, leading it up the arm of the couch.

Whicher crosses to her, throws his hat on a low table. Sits down by her.

She glances at him, turns back to the horse.

"You go out riding?" he says.

She nods. Paces the horse along the arm of the couch. Back again.

"Where'd you go?"

"Maisy."

"To see Maisy?" Whicher strokes the horse's flank. "Was he good?"

She nods. Then shakes her head.

"No?"

She stops her arm. "He wants apples."

"Did you give him an apple?"

She shakes her head.

The marshal cups his hand, holds it out—to the horse's muzzle.

Lori puts the horse's head into her father's upturned hand. She makes an eating sound.

"Good," Whicher says.

"Good."

"Good horse." The marshal nods.

Lori puts the toy down on the arm of the couch.

"He's okay, now," Whicher says. He reaches over, picks her up, sets her onto his lap. "He's okay."

Leanne watches from the door between the living room and the kitchen.

Lori plays with his neck-tie.

The marshal slips it from his collar, gives it to her.

She runs her hands up and down the fabric, pulls it.

"We need to take him to his stable," Whicher says. "Take him to bed."

He gathers his daughter from his lap. Stands. Swings her up into his arms. He picks up the horse from the arm of the couch. Carries Lori to Leanne.

Her mother kisses her.

Carrying her into the bedroom, he sits on the bed, holds her against his chest.

"Where will he sleep?" Lori says.

The marshal pulls down the coverlet, pats the pillow. "How about right in here?"

Lori slips into the bed.

Whicher places the toy horse on the pillow. "You want another apple for later?" He holds out his hand.

She looks at him.

He places an imaginary apple on the pillow.

She puts her hand over his.

He bends close, breathes her sweet scent. Kisses her cheek. "You go to sleep."

She nods her head on the pillow.

Rising, he backs softly across the room. "I'm right here."

He pulls the door almost to.

Stepping from the room, he walks the hall back into the kitchen.

On the table is a plate of Texas chili with corn bread and jalapenos.

Leanne sits staring at a spot across the room.

The marshal washes his hands in the sink, dries them, takes off the suit jacket, hangs it on the back of a chair. "Are you eating?"

"I ate earlier, with Lori."

He sits. Pulls the plate to him, takes a forkful of the chili beef.

"All day," Leanne says, "all I've done is think about it."

Whicher glances at her. Eats the food in silence.

"I've tried not to." Her voice is hollow. "I just can't stop. I can't stop thinking about Sofia, about those two little girls…" Leanne throws a darting look at the back yard beyond the kitchen window.

Whicher sees what his wife sees—another, better world, two families, twenty-four hours gone. All of them there.

"I've tried," Leanne says.

"I know."

"What's going to happen to her? What's going to happen to the girls?"

The marshal looks out into the branches of the tree in the yard. "They moved here to be close to her family."

"She told me that."

"Something like this, there's no easy answer."

Leanne stares at the floor.

Whicher takes another forkful of food. "They'll have support. The Marshals Service will help. A federal officer killed in the line of duty…"

His wife cuts in; "Was it this? Was it this case?"

The marshal eats, he doesn't answer.

"On the news report, they say it was a shooting at a biker bar, some kind of fight that broke out. What was he doing there?"

"We don't know."

Leanne puts her head on one side. "You look like you're about to…do something."

Whicher rubs a hand over his jaw, breaks off a piece of corn bread.

"Promise me you won't," she says.

He nods, eats.

"You need to take care. I mean it."

"FBI are handling the investigation," Whicher says.

"You're part of it."

"How would I not be?"

Leanne puts both hands to the sides of her face. "Their youngest is the same age as Lori."

Whicher puts down the fork.

His wife turns to him, her face stricken.

The marshal pushes back his chair, starts to get up from the table.

"No," she says, her voice tight. "Eat."

He sits back down again. Reaches over the table, takes hold of her arm. Pulls her toward him, till he can put her hand in his hand.

A minutes passes—in silence.

Leanne draws her hand back.

"Maybe you should call your folks?" Whicher says.

"What for?"

"Take Lori."

She looks at him.

"Stay a couple days."

"Why?"

"Maybe it's better. You need to be with folk—have people around you."

"I want to be here. For you."

Whicher nods. "You know I'm going to work this. I'm going to find whoever did this. I won't be here. Call your mom. Go stay with her. Lori will be okay. You'll get a break, get some space…"

When she speaks again, Leanne's voice is distant, flat. "Maybe you're right."

He tugs at the collar of his shirt.

"Are you going out again?"

He nods.

"Tonight?"

"I guess."

For the longest time Leanne stares at a space in the corner of the room. "I'm not sure I can do this anymore…'

"Leanne."

"I don't know if I can. It makes me sick to think of it, sometimes, when you're out there…"

He puts down the fork on the side of the plate, turns to her.

"I want this to stop." Her eyes are brimming. "This," she says. She looks at him. "I want you to stop."

Chapter 41

The Marshals Office on Pine Street is deserted, Sandro Ortega's desk lit with the dim light of a computer screen. Whicher sips a cup of hot coffee, studies the files on record, adding to the series of background notes—everything known so far on Lance Tate.

Tate's non-native to Texas, from Louisiana originally—the city of Shreveport.

Shreveport—just fifteen miles from Greenwood, where Elijah Hoffman's truck was found.

The marshal thinks back to the sweltering afternoon at the trailer park. The young woman, Candy Brolin. Grady Pearce, her boyfriend—Ray Dubois' driver out to Bayou Serpent.

Shreveport.

Both Tate and Grady Pearce were out of Shreveport.

A persistent thought nags at the back of Whicher's mind.

Searching state files, the criminal record on Tate had been negative—the federal record showed a juvenile file from Louisiana, charges of theft.

Sitting back in the chair, the marshal sips on the cup of coffee, thinks of the new-bought ranch up in Hawley. Of Hernandez, the car thief, picked up there. Why there? Why in Hawley?

Had Hernandez known Lance Tate?

Whicher stands, crosses to his own desk, searches among the notes and papers.

Hernandez was dead, Dubois refusing to talk. He thinks again of Grady Pearce, finds the number he has on record. He sits back down at Ortega's desk. Picks the desk phone off its cradle.

He keys in the Louisiana number. Hears it connect, start to ring.

"Who is this?"

The sound of Grady Pearce's voice is grating on the end of the line.

"Deputy US Marshal Whicher. Don't hang up, Mister Pearce."

"What?"

"You hang up on me, you'll wish you hadn't. Remember me?" Whicher says. "Sure you do."

Pearce grunts into the phone.

"I'll track you down if you hang up," Whicher says. "I'll call your probation officer, I'll do it tonight…"

The hum on the line grows as Grady Pearce stays silent.

"I need you to answer some questions for me," the marshal says. "You answer, I'll consider you're co-operating with my enquiry. If not, I'm here to tell you that I'll hang your ass out to dry. I think you lied to me, Mister Pearce."

"What? What the hell you mean, what do you want?"

"I think you lied to me about Ray Dubois. I think you knew he was coming. I think you knew he was coming, y'all arranged to meet in Greenwood. You knew he'd need a ride out to Bayou Serpent. I want to know if I'm right?"

Pearce doesn't respond.

"You don't have anything to say?"

"I don't know what you're talking about."

"Bullshit."

"I don't know what's going on with Ray," Pearce says. "I don't know a thing about what he did. All I know is he called me up, he said I had to go meet him."

"That's it?"

"I swear to God."

"You lie to me, I'll call your probation officer, tell him you knowingly assisting a suspect in a first degree murder."

No reply.

"Do you know a man named Lance Tate?"

Whicher sits forward at the desk.

"Yeah."

A rip of adrenaline flashes inside.

"So what?" Pearce says. "I know him."

"How do you know him?"

"I mean, I used to, man. Years back."

"How?"

"Before I learned better," Pearce says. "He's just another guy I knew, I know a lot of people. Ray knew him. I met him through Ray…"

"Through Ray Dubois?"

"We'd work games for him," Pearce says. "Time to time. That's all in the past now, man, you know? This is years back, I'm talking. All we did was work a couple doors."

"You worked doors?"

"You know, on *a game*. A card game. We'd watch the door. Security."

"You worked security on card games." Whicher stares at the edge of the desk. "Illegal card games?"

"Private rooms," Pearce corrects. "Invitation only. Man, it was nothing, we were just a couple grunts. It was cash money, no different to working the door of a bar, or a strip-joint. I'm straight up legit now, I work in Bossier City, everything A-1, copacetic…"

"What kind of money?" Whicher says. "What kind of games?"

"Look, I mean this was years back," Pearce says. "Years. I just worked a couple doors. I haven't seen him in God knows how long. I hardly know him. Ray knew him."

"Lance Tate ran illegal gambling rooms?"

"Man, poker. Card games. Whatever folk wanted. That shit goes on."

Whicher writes in an open notebook, pushes back from the desk. "Ray Dubois is in the state slam looking at murder-one. For the killing of Elijah Hoffman. Hoffman was the owner of the truck you were going to fence."

"Wait, what? I wasn't fencing nothing for nobody…"

"You gave Dubois a ride, you knew he was involved in a crime."

"That's not how it was."

"So tell me?"

"God*damn*…" Pearce's voice trails away until the only sound on the line is the man breathing.

Whicher waits, not breaking the silence, loading it.

"Listen," Pearce says, "Ray called me up, the middle of the night, Monday. He told me he needed me to come meet him. I haven't seen the guy in months, I told him no. Next thing you know, he turned up in Greenwood, he was hassling Candy. So I went over. He told me he was driving back from Texas, he needed to see me."

"He was going to ask you to fence the truck?"

"I didn't fence a thing."

"But that's why he was there?" Whicher says. "That's how come he stopped?"

"I don't know," Pearce says, "whyn't you ask him? The dumb mother left the truck illegally parked, traffic cops towed it away. So I gave him a ride in my car, that's all I did, man. That's it. I didn't ask questions, he never told me what he was doing with that truck, nothing. I swear to God, man. That's all it was."

The marshal stares across the empty office at the night above the city beyond the windows. Lights on in the parking garage across the street, a sodium glow from the street lamps. The side of the towering Hotel Wooten lit up against the black sky. "Does Lance Tate still run illegal gambling rooms?"

"I don't have nothing to do with that no more," Pearce says. "I work the regular casinos."

"Does he?"

"I don't know. He's around, I guess."

"He's still around?"

"From time to time," Pearce says. "Once in a while he'll maybe run a room. I heard folk say."

"In Shreveport?"

"Shreveport, wherever. I guess he likes the money."

"What kind of money?"

"Plenty," Pearce says. "Look, I don't want nothing to do with him, man. I don't see him, never talk to him. Word on him, it ain't good."

"Lance Tate has some kind of a reputation?"

"Bad dude, man. What I hear. That's all I know. That's what people say."

⊥

Outside the courthouse building on Pine Street, Whicher unlocks the door to the Silverado. Traffic is steady, vehicles parked along both sides of the road. He stands by the cab of the truck a moment, places both elbows on the top of the roof.

Lights show in the closed up stores and in the restaurant across from the intersection. Couples are out walking, groups of college-age kids on the sidewalks.

He breathes the night air, thinks of Leanne back at the house in Wylie.

Stares down the length of the street, eyes unfocused.

I want you to stop.

Listening to the sound of traffic he lets his gaze drift to the window of the restaurant. A man and a woman at a table, talking, eating. He threads his fingers together. With no kind of answer.

He opens up the Silverado, climbs in behind the wheel.

Turning the key in the ignition, he fires the motor. He waits until the stop light at the intersection turns from green to red. Then backs out into the street, turns the truck around. Drives down, waits at the lights.

At the underpass on South First he watches headlamps on the vehicles speeding by. Speeding like the thoughts inside his head—of Lance Tate, of Sandro Ortega. Of Frank Nelson, of Elijah Hoffman. Of his wife and child.

He swings the truck around on the feeder loop—comes up on the four-lane highway.

Trees line the sides of the road—above the canopy of their branches, the Wooten stands tall. Ablaze in squares of yellow light.

⚹

Five blocks down South First, he turns off of the highway, makes a left onto Sayles Boulevard. The wide, tree-lined street is quiet now—houses of the old town strung out one side, new built properties packed in on the opposite edge of the road.

Elijah Hoffman was a gambler.

He made trips from the farm to Louisiana, a lot of trips, according to his wife.

A game needed money to run. 'House' money. Hard cash.

Whicher scowls to himself behind the wheel. So far, Tate

had a juvenile file from Louisiana. And Grady Pearce, an ex-con, saying he used to work the door of a room for the man.

The call log to Ortega's phone showed a call received in the location of a ranch owned by Tate.

Not enough.

Not enough for an arrest. Not enough even for a warrant to search the man's house, what would they be looking for?

The marshal steers on down the deserted boulevard heading south. A distant set of lights behind him. Nothing out in front.

Whicher shifts in the driver's seat, thinks of calling Levi Underwood. He could call, check for any update on Frank Nelson at the hospital. Maybe head over, stop in. See what the doctors had to say.

Behind on the road, the set of vehicle lights are closer, brighter.

Whicher checks his rear-view, sees the headlamps moving left, to overtake.

The road ahead is clear, the marshal cuts a look in the side-view mirror.

A split second passes.

Something wrong.

A feeling blows the length of Whicher's spine.

An explosion of sound fills the cab—glass flying, air rushing, a whip of pain stings his neck.

Twin bullet holes—exit holes, show in the truck's windshield.

A white sedan is level, a lone man inside, in a black ski-mask.

Whicher rips the Ruger from the shoulder-holster, fires four times through the shattered window, system flooding with shock.

The white car dives on its brakes.

Whicher doubles flat against the seat.

Shots burst through the rear of the trucks's cab.

Stamping on the brake, the marshal hears tires behind squealing—hears a motor revving—the car sweeps past.

Braking to a dead stop, Whicher scrambles out, draws the Glock.

The white sedan skids sideways—stops twenty yards in front of the truck.

Whicher ducks behind the back of the Chevy—engine block between himself and the shooter.

Two hands on the Glock he sets up on the sedan.

He fires three times, tight, controlled. Shifts aim, fires another burst of three, drops to the road.

Shots explode back, he flattens, scrambles up to the front wheel—aims at the muzzle flash inside of the car, fires three more rounds.

The sedan jolts, its wheels spin up.

It lurches forward.

Veering across lanes, it turns into a side street.

The marshal stares after it; *a white Nissan Altima.*

He picks himself up from the road.

Nine rounds.

Nine.

Adrenaline surges in his blood, he dumps the magazine of the semi-auto. Reaches to his belt for the spare. Rams it home.

Ears ringing, breath short, he runs to the driver's door of the truck, opens it, smashes out the remains of the window with the butt of the Glock.

Jumping in, he throws the semi-automatic onto the passenger seat beside the big revolver.

He grabs the radio transceiver from the dash-hook, keys the emergency channel. Pushes the shifter into drive.

Static bursts from the radio. "Dispatch."

"This is Deputy Marshal Whicher, I'm down at Sayles Boulevard," he checks the cross-street, "and South Eleventh. Reporting gunshots fired at my vehicle by the driver of a white, Nissan Altima. Request assistance. Urgent."

He hits the gas, steers the truck across the road, turns in on the side street.

"Marshal, we'll alert all units."

Whicher sees the tail lights on the Nissan—five, six hundred yards ahead. "I'm heading east on South Eleventh, in pursuit of the suspect vehicle."

"Copy that," the dispatcher says.

"Suspect is armed and dangerous. All officers be aware."

The marshal hooks the transceiver back in place, guns the five-liter V8 beneath the hood. A surge is in him as he stares through the windshield—the glass cracked and crazed where shots have exited, but he can still see.

At his neck, he feels a sting of pain, he puts a hand to his collar. Feels the slip of blood against his fingers. Takes his hand away, it glistens red.

Glancing down, he sees his shirt bloodied, feels it now, the fabric sticking to his shoulder.

Punching on the dome light, he claws the shirt collar from his neck, sits forward to see the wound; a cut from flying glass.

Ahead, the sedan reaches an intersection—it brakes, makes a hard right, crashes the light.

Whicher pushes his speed, touching eighty, now—houses in the residential streets a blur to either side.

Approaching the intersection he recognizes Treadaway Boulevard.

He snatches up the radio. "Suspect vehicle is now onto US Eighty-Three, southbound. Am in pursuit."

The stop light flicks to green, Whicher checks the road, pushes down on the gas. He leans the Silverado on its tires, cornering as hard as the truck will go.

The sedan is opening up a gap, traffic moving both directions on the four-lane.

The marshal floors it out as the road passes through a commercial district.

The sedan swerves suddenly at the far side of a rental yard.

It's gone from the road.

A mesh fence surrounds the perimeter of the rental yard, but the front gate is wide open.

The marshal looks for headlamps—any signs of movement.

Rows of trucks and earth moving gear line the compound.

At the back is a metal-sided workshop, a dirt yard. A second gate. It's hanging open.

Whicher steers to it, drives through onto an unlit dirt road.

An animal feed plant sits opposite an oil refinery. Acres of dark, waste ground stretch away to the distance.

Outlines of workshops and warehouses are lit in the spill from the highway.

Whicher spots a faded road sign—*China Street*.

He drives across a stretch of freight line, sees a row of trailer units.

A round strikes the right-hand fender of the truck—Whicher ducks at the wheel.

A second and third round hit the passenger door, smacking low.

Ripping the truck around, Whicher floors the gas, steers for a workshop at the edge of a scrub-filled lot.

Turning in behind the workshop, he skids to a stop, grabs the Glock, pushes open the door.

He jumps out, crouches to the ground—strains to listen, semi-auto between both hands.

Reaching into the cab, he pulls out the radio. "This is Whicher—suspect is now between Treadaway and Eleventh—off of China Street."

"Copy that, marshal. Do you have visual contact?"

"Negative. It's too dark. But he's here."

"All available units will divert—await back-up, marshal."

Whicher grabs a flashlight from a pocket in the door. Reaching into the back of the cab, he takes out a Kevlar vest from a pocket behind the seat. He puts it on, wipes the blood from his hands in the short grass.

Moving away from the truck he runs crouched along the side of the workshop. Edges into a tangle of mesquite and brush—works a way in, and then forward.

The noise of the city is on the wind, the sound of his own breathing in his ears. Eyes adjusting, he can see across the black expanse of wasteland—he scans the shapes of buildings, lines above the scrub, parked trailer units, piles of junk, rows of dumpsters.

Something white is by the raised tracks of the freight line.

He shines the flashlight on it for just a second.

Body panels of a vehicle light up in the cone of the beam.

Clicking out the light, he forces his way back out of the brush.

Leading with the Glock he sprints between points of cover. He stops. Aligns the flashlight with the barrel of the Glock. He switches it on, lighting up the vehicle.

Nobody is inside it.

He sweeps left and right, to either side.

Back beyond the freight line, something moves for just a second.

Whicher gets low.

A single tail light disappears beyond the oil refinery—headed back toward the four-lane highway.

The marshal stands, closes down the last few yards to the car.

It's the Nissan. Nobody is in there.

Cold sweat breaks on his face, he feels the rush, adrenaline pumping.

Snatching the phone from his jacket, his hand shakes as

he keys the number for the house in Wylie.

Leanne answers after two rings.

"I want you to take Lori, get her in the car—drive to your folks' house."

"What?"

He tries to keep his breathing steady, his voice calm. "Just do it, Leanne. Go get her. Leave the house. Do it, now."

Chapter 42

No lights show in the windows of Lance Tate's property down on Shoreline Drive. The Hummer is gone from the driveway, nothing else in there. Whicher steps from his shot-up Silverado, Glock 19 in his hand.

He walks fast to the front door, presses on the buzzer—moves away in line with a section of the stone-faced wall.

Holding the semi-automatic in front of his thigh, he edges toward a window. He looks along the edge of slatted-blind—sees no light.

Ducking from the window, he tracks around the side of the house to the decking.

No lights.

Nobody is out there. Scanning the glass sliders along the back of the house, he sees the rooms inside are all dark.

He peers down to the waterline—toward the jetty. The scent of the lake hanging in the air.

Re-tracing his steps back to the driveway, he takes out his phone, keys a call to Levi Underwood.

He crosses the drive, stands at his truck.

The call picks up.

"Marshal?"

"I'm down at Lance Tate's property," Whicher says. "Somebody just tried to take me out."

"Say again?"

"I was driving back from Pine Street—that white Nissan we got on camera for the drive-by? It came after me."

"Man, what the hell's going on?"

"I was back at the office, downtown," Whicher says. "My truck was parked right outside of the courthouse. Somebody must have seen it there, watched it, waited for me to leave."

"You serious?"

"I was driving home. A car came up behind me, it opened fire."

Underwood is silent on the end of the line.

"Somebody in a black ski-mask," Whicher says. "The same MO as that armored car of yours, at the bank."

"Are you alright?"

"I returned fire, the car hauled ass. I went after it, it jumped me again on a piece of waste ground off of Treadaway. They dumped the Nissan. Either somebody was waiting, or they had another way out—I think I saw a dirt bike leaving."

"What's happening with the car?"

"APD is with the vehicle."

"I'll call them…"

"Listen," Whicher says, "I think it was Lance Tate."

"You said the driver was wearing a mask."

"I think it's him."

"Why?" the FBI man says.

"I looked him up tonight," Whicher says. "Tate's from Louisiana. Same as Cajun Ray Dubois."

"Yeah? So what?"

"I checked the federal record—he's out of Shreveport, originally. He has a juvie file for theft. I called a guy from Shreveport I already interviewed on this—a possible accessory. I put some heat on him, asked him did he know Tate. He told me that he did."

"Really?"

"This guy told me he worked the door running illegal card games for him."

"For Tate? Illegal gambling?"

"This is way back," Whicher says. "But the guy reckoned Tate still does it. And he told me Ray Dubois worked for Tate as muscle…"

"You have any evidence? Direct evidence?"

"Not yet."

The FBI man whistles under his breath. "Son of a bitch."

"I called my wife, had her get out of the house and take our daughter."

"What? What for?"

"The driver of that car shot my partner in cold blood this morning. He waited on me tonight, came after me in the middle of the city. You don't think he could find an address?"

"Jesus Christ."

"I'm going after him."

"You ought to go home, marshal…"

"It's Tate."

"You don't know that for sure…"

Whicher clicks off the call.

⁂

At the foot of the scrub-covered hill outside of Hawley, Whicher reloads the emptied magazine of the Glock. He takes out extra ammunition from the bin between the front seats, reloads the .357 Magnum rounds into the Ruger. Stowed in the back of the cab is a Bianchi holster for the big revolver, a belt holster. The marshal takes it out, fits it, checks he can clear the gun beneath the Kevlar vest.

A pale moon edges the rising terrain against the black of night. The surrounding land is dark, only traces and outlines show.

At the run down homestead on the junction with the county road a single window is lit.

The headlamps on the Silverado are switched off. The marshal sits at the wheel, eyes adjusting to the night, motor idling beneath the hood.

Beyond the glass-strewn interior of the truck, beyond the bullet holes in the windshield and the smashed out driver window he can make out sparse detail. Rocks ahead on the ground, clumps of thornbrush, the silhouettes of trees.

He pushes the shifter into drive, moves his foot onto the gas—nudges the truck forward to start the climb up the track.

Moving slow uphill the Silverado's tires spit stones, its chassis rocking over the uneven ground.

Where the track branches to left and right, he turns up the deep-rutted trail to the left.

Shy of the entrance gate, he stops, shuts down the motor.

Listening to the night sounds from the scrub he hears only cicada, feels a breeze moving on his skin.

The gate across the track is closed.

The marshal pulls back the latch on the driver's door of the Silverado, opens it carefully.

Glock in hand he climbs out, walks forward toward the gate.

The brush is high around the entranceway to the property—no seeing around the bend into the clearing, to the construction site.

He climbs the gate, drops to the ground, makes no sound.

Following the track around the turn he can make out shapes ahead—the raised concrete footings of the buildings, construction materials, stacked and piled.

He takes a few more paces.

Stops.

Two vehicles are at the back of the clearing.

Behind the vehicles, lights show from the trailer at the rear of the site.

The marshal stands, scans the clearing, listens out for any sound.

The outline of the far vehicle is a Hummer—Lance Tate's.

The second vehicle is a pickup, a Toyota.

Whicher stares across at the trailer, its door is shut.

Squatting low, he cuts around to the rear of a set of raised concrete footings at the edge of the site. He can see both vehicles are empty. Side-on to the trailer, out of line with the lit windows, he waits, watches. After a minute, he starts to make his way in.

Twenty yards from the trailer he steps to the side—to catch a glimpse into the interior.

Through a window he can see Lance Tate with another man.

Riley McGuire.

Tate has his back to the marshal—he's wearing a black canvas jacket. McGuire facing him, in an open-necked shirt.

Whicher keeps low, moves across the front of the trailer beneath the line of the window.

Reaching the shadows at its far side, he sees a pile of stacked lumber. Beside it, a dirt bike is up on its stand.

The marshal moves toward it—he holds a hand close to the motor, it's too hot to touch.

He steps away, tracks out into the darkness, circling back behind the cover of the concrete footings.

Crouching down behind a pile of steel rebar, he takes out his cell, keys the number for Levi Underwood.

He watches the trailer door, listens to his phone ring.

The call picks up.

"I'm up at Lance Tate's property," Whicher breathes, "outside of Hawley. The ranch I told you about."

"What's going on?"

"There's a dirt bike in back of his trailer. The motor's hot, it's been running. It can't have been here long."

"Slow down, man…"

"A motorcycle took off from the back of Treadaway."

"You think, you don't know."

"Frank Nelson was shot by somebody riding a dirt bike out at Buffalo Gap."

"Alright," Underwood says. "But slow down."

"Tate's here," Whicher says. "He's here with Riley McGuire."

"Listen, tell me where the ranch is, I'll have the sheriff's office send up units."

"Call the PD," Whicher says, "have them watch Tate's house on Shoreline Drive. Plus McGuire's place on Woodlake."

"Why? Forget that. I'll come out," the FBI man says. "Where are you?"

"Call them. The ranch is around five miles west of Hawley. Off a grit road, County 458. But there's nothing out here, you'll never find it."

"Local sheriff's units could find it."

"Tell them it's on a hill, it's by a cell tower site. They might know it. You pass an old homestead, there's a dirt track goes up."

"They'll find it. I'll find it," Underwood says. "Wait for back up. If it was either one of those guys tonight, he's a cop killer. Think of your daughter, think of your wife."

The door to the double-wide trailer opens—a shaft of light streaks the ground.

"Get people to both of the properties," Whicher says, "in case they make it down from here."

Riley McGuire steps out.

He starts to walk toward the big Toyota pickup.

Lance Tate appears in the doorway.

Whicher shuts off the phone.

Tate says something to McGuire—McGuire opens up the pickup, he climbs in. He starts the motor, snaps on the lights, backs the Toyota around to face the entranceway.

Beyond the curve in the track, the Silverado is just outside the gate—blocking off the way out.

Whicher ducks beneath the pile of rebar as the headlamp beams of the Toyota sweep past.

Tate steps back inside, closes the door.

The marshal sprints, racing to get behind the rear of the trailer.

Tail lights flare in the high brush—McGuire stopping at the gate.

The marshal holds the Glock in both hands, now, gets himself low.

The Toyota reappears—backing into the middle of the clearing.

It stops.

The shaft of light from the trailer door reappears on the ground.

McGuire steps out of the pickup. His face is slack in the light from the trailer. "There's a Chevy Silverado shot to hell out there."

Tate drops from the trailer, walks forward.

McGuire thumbs back over his shoulder in the direction of the gate.

Lance Tate's head snaps from side to side—he sweeps the clearing.

McGuire stands rigid. "What the hell's going on?"

Tate ducks away to his left.

Whicher can't see him—he rises to a crouch.

The sound of the dirt bike's motor explodes into life.

The marshal runs out into the open, leading with the Glock.

McGuire sees him—holds up both his hands, his eyes rounded with shock.

The dirt bike tears out from beside the pile of lumber at the trailer. Its headlamp beam picks out an opening in the scrub.

"*US Marshal*," Whicher shouts. "*Stop. Stay where you are…*"

Tate flattens against the gas tank on the bike, rips the throttle. He hits the lit-up opening. Speeds into it.

He disappears.

Gone.

Whicher runs to McGuire. "I need your truck…"

"What?" McGuire stares at him—at the Kevlar vest, at the blood-soaked shirt.

The marshal jumps inside the Toyota.

He cranks the steering around, floors the throttle pedal.

The pickup lurches across the clearing toward the gap in the scrub.

Whicher steers down a narrow dirt trail. The headlamp on the dirt bike is a moving cone of light—flashing in and out of the mass of dark.

Rocks and ruts line the narrow pathway, the earth

gouged from run off, the trail part-blocked with dead fall of mesquite. Branches snap beneath the tires, the front wheels strike loose boulders.

The cone of light weaves from left to right farther down the descent.

The county road is somewhere down below, less than a mile distant, Whicher guesses. Pushing down on the gas, he feels the pickup float over the rough ground, only barely in control.

Limbs of trees and vegetation screech down both sides.

At the road, there'll be any number of routes out—the land is wide open.

The light on the dirt bike disappears—and then it's back.

The dark beyond the Toyota's headlamps changes.

The cone of light is gone again.

And still gone.

The marshal watches for it to reappear.

At the far edge of the truck's high beams, shapes form— an outline of trees. A stand of trees.

The dirt bike's light is nowhere.

Alarm is rising in him; the sixth sense.

Lifting off the gas, the marshal's foot hovers above the brake pedal.

A split second passes.

Another.

The army scout takes over. He hits the brake.

Muzzle-flare erupts from the blackened stand of trees— a flame-flash of incoming rounds.

Skewing sideways into the brush, Whicher snaps out the

lights on the pickup. Stops. Grabs the Glock, jumps to the ground.

Scrambling into the undergrowth, he steadies the pistol in his grip, breath coming hard.

Ambush.

Tate set up to shoot him.

He thinks of home, of Wylie, of Leanne—feels sweat break on his skin.

Low to the ground he works his way downhill toward the edge of the trees—no knowing how big the woods are, trying to sense Tate, sense the firing position.

He listens for the sound of the dirt bike's motor. Above his own breathing, he can hear it—faint. Low. Ticking over.

Moving wide, he pushes faster down the slope.

The brush is thinning—an edge, the stand of trees before him.

He scans the darkness—the dirt bike is downhill from him, he can hear it, sense it.

No light shows in the woods. No way to tell where Tate is.

Opening and closing his hand on the grip of the Glock, Whicher sprints out from the cover of the brush, cuts between trees, body low as a branch catches at him. He half-trips, breaks it—the cracking sound of the wood is sharp and loud.

A shot booms out.

The marshal throws himself to the dirt.

He rolls, shifts position.

Two more shots burst out uphill among the trees.

He thinks of firing back—stops himself—it's too far to make a shot count. Focusing on the dirt-bike, he gets to all fours, checks up the hill, runs at a crouch, cutting left and right.

The noise of the dirt-bike is louder, nearer.

If he can reach it, Tate will be trapped—no way out.

Running harder, his eyes search the dark.

Almost on it, he must be. Almost on it.

By the trunk of a fallen tree is an outline, now—he can see it—twenty yards off.

A volley of shots rings out, ragged.

Whicher feels a kick in his back, beneath his shoulder blade—then a second—a blow like a hammer, knocking him down.

He fights for breath as pain blooms inside of him—scrabbling, face down in the dirt.

Someone is running, snapping branches, a force rushing toward him.

He pushes up from the ground.

Above the sound of the dirt bike is the noise of a siren—two sirens.

Light flickers in the woods.

The Glock is gone, gone from his hand.

The light grows brighter, striated, strobing between the trunks of trees.

Tate.

He can see Tate. Silhouetted. Faint light behind him. His gun arm out.

Whicher rips the Ruger from the belt holster.

Tate fires.

The marshal levels the revolver.

Pulls the trigger, again and again.

Until light blinds him.

Pain rips through him.

And sound and shock consume him, obliterate sense.

Epilogue

Fort Phantom Hill, Tx.

A dry wind sweeps the plains land surrounding the stone ruins of the deserted fort. Small white clouds ride a vast, bright sky. Heat radiates in waves off the scrub as Whicher leaves the gun-metal Impala off of West Lake, behind a battered, late-model blue Toyota.

Walking stiff, his back is still sore from the bruising, from the fracture to his rib.

His shirt is open at the throat beneath the dark gray suit. The wound at his neck sutured, healing.

Pushing the Resistol onto his head he follows a gravel path over burnt dry grass—past a guardhouse built from blocks of stone, the remains of the fort, old chimney stacks and hearths standing lonely, log walls long since burned to the ground.

In a clearing surrounded by live oak and cedar elm and Texas ash, Jean Hoffman sits at a sun-bleached wooden picnic table. A light jacket about her lean shoulders, flaxen hair moving in the wind.

The marshal takes off his hat as he approaches.

Mrs Hoffman stands.

"Thank you," she says. "For agreeing to see me."

He nods.

"I didn't recognize you from your car."

"Truck's off the road," the marshal says. "In the shop. It needs a little work."

"Please," she says. "Won't you sit?"

He eases himself onto a wooden bench at the picnic table. Replaces his hat.

"I'm headed back to Dallas," she says. "The house is all cleared, the farm, too. Everything of ours is out of there." She stops. Her eyes fix on a point in the middle distance.

Whicher breathes in air scented with dry earth, with the baking prairie.

"The company that owns it now will probably knock it all down," she says. "The house. All the barns and buildings..." Her voice trails off.

Whicher thinks of the property's new owners, BluClear Power.

"Somebody from the Marshals Office called me," she says. "A Marshal Perez?"

"Yes, ma'am."

"He said he was calling in your place—that you'd had to take some time off." Mrs Hoffman straightens at the table. "He was helpful. But I wanted to talk to you."

Whicher lets his gaze run out across the old Comanche land—open scrub at the far side of the county road, heat haze warping the horizon.

"Anything you can tell me," the woman says, "I'd like to know. I'd be grateful."

"There'll be a trial," Whicher says.

Jean Hoffman stares at the backs of her hands.

"Two people will stand trial."

"I'm leaving for Dallas," the woman says. "Whether I come back for any trial—I don't rightly know."

The marshal cuts a glance at her.

"Right now, I don't think I want to."

He puts his forearms onto the table. Breathes shallow, the ache in his back returning, a pulse of pain in his rib. "Your husband was murdered by two people. One of them is in custody. Senior prosecutors from the DA's office are talking to him."

"And the other man?"

Whicher studies her.

She shifts a hank of hair from her face, from a fine, high cheekbone.

Images pass in his mind, disconnected. The white skiff. The body at the lake. A field on fire in the bayou swamp country. A stand of trees on the side of a hill lit with muzzle-flare.

She swallows. "The second man is the man you shot?"

The marshal nods.

"Lance Tate," she says.

Whicher lets his eyes meet hers.

"The man you shot and killed?"

Whicher doesn't answer.

Jean Hoffman reaches quickly across the wooden table top. She closes her hand over his.

The marshal thinks of Elijah Hoffman—of staring at his lifeless body. Of the photograph of the man's face still stored on his phone.

Jean Hoffman lifts her hand, moves it away. "Marshal Perez told me my husband owed this man Tate money. He told me Eli met him when he was interested in buying the farm."

"Your husband never told you?"

She shakes her head.

"Tate worked for a company called Summerwood Realty and Construction," the marshal says. "They were looking for land, for wind farms."

"People have approached us in the past."

"Tate would've met your husband, got to know him. At some point he must've learned your husband liked to gamble."

Jean Hoffman nods, her eyes are sad. "It wouldn't have been real hard."

"Who knows how it started," Whicher says. "But Lance Tate invited him to a game, according to the man we have in custody. One game led to another. Card games, in Louisiana. Illegal houses. Your husband ended up owing him a bunch of money."

"Do you know how much?"

"No, ma'am," Whicher says. "But Lance Tate heard your property had recently sold. He wanted to see your husband, but your husband wouldn't have him at the house. He wouldn't go to Tate's place. They agreed to meet on neutral ground. At the lake. I don't know why he went there. Maybe he was going to offer to pay back something. Maybe he was going to tell him to go hang."

Jean Hoffman folds her arms about herself, holds onto her sides.

"Tate set him up. He had an accomplice waiting in the scrub with a hunting bow; the man we have in custody—Ray Dubois. When Elijah turned up at the parking lot out at the lake it was dark, it would've been empty. His would've been the only vehicle. He wouldn't have seen anything wrong. Tate approached the spot by boat, the boat had an electric motor, he would've made no sound. The bow-shooter, Dubois, told us they were going to dump his body in the middle of the lake."

Whicher pauses.

Mrs Hoffman gives a small shudder.

"Right after they shot him," the marshal says, "potential witnesses showed up. Two kids, night fishing. Dubois told us they dragged Elijah's body into the brush. Then took off in your husband's truck. Dubois drove the truck to Louisiana that night, to get rid of it, fence it."

"They had it all planned out and then they just took off?"

Whicher nods. "Way it is sometimes," he says. "Dubois said they had to make a decision."

She looks at him.

"Loading a body into a boat could've been noisy, the kids fishing could've seen them. They took your husband's wallet, his ID. His truck. They figured nobody would ever know; it would go down unsolved. It's not like a gun crime, there's no way ballistics can match arrows to a bow, there wouldn't have been much evidence."

"But the truck was recovered? In Louisiana?"

"Yes, ma'am," Whicher says. "They screwed up."

Jean Hoffman takes a long breath. Holds it. Lets it out. "Do you think you would ever have found them, if not?"

"Only thing we did find was a ring," Whicher says. "A gold band your husband had on him. A wedding ring?"

She stares at him, open-mouthed.

"You'll get it back," the marshal says. "Once the trial is through."

Mrs Hoffman folds one hand into the other on the wooden table. "My mother told me before I married Elijah that he didn't seem like a man who would get himself into trouble."

The marshal doesn't reply.

"There's different ways trouble can find a man," she says. "I guess."

Whicher nods.

"Any man," she says. "Good or bad. There's different ways a man can fall from Grace. And be undone. And get himself killed…"

The marshal thinks of Sandro Ortega. He thinks of Lance Tate. He thinks of flame enveloping a blackened field of cane. Of bullet rounds smacking into the back of his Kevlar vest. "There's different ways…"

Abilene Regional Airport. Two days later.

Waiting at the regional airport with Levi Underwood for the flight to Shreveport, Whicher reads the FBI Violent Crime Task Force notes. Underwood's investigation into the death of Sandro Ortega now links to the string of aggravated robberies on armored cars.

The FBI man carries two cups of coffee from a concession at the side of the departure lounge.

Whicher watches his progress across the polished floor, light blazing from the floor-to-ceiling windows. He thinks of Frank Nelson—alive—recovering, now, in the medical facility at French Robertson. Nelson was conscious. Talking. He was already looking to cut a plea.

FBI in Shreveport were expecting them by early afternoon.

A three and a half-hour flight, changing at DFW.

Background on Lance Tate and Ray Dubois was already in from the Shreveport field office—reports from Louisiana law enforcement, most of it historical. More set to come.

Lance Tate was at the heart of it.

Tate, the man Dubois had made his only call to from the state prison.

Tate, the man Ortega had spoken to on the same number—the burner—the morning of his death.

The armored cars had no link to the murder of Elijah Hoffman—Whicher would still close the Hoffman case for the Marshals Service.

Shreveport FBI's classification of Tate was that he was a

sociopath. The Task Force in Abilene were agreed.

Violent robberies of cash from armored cars were a way to stake the Louisiana card games. To fund a lavish lifestyle, pay for the designer house, the land, the ranch. The robbery on Judge Ely Boulevard had gone wrong, Dwayne Cameron had been blamed, gunned down filling his car at a gas station.

When Sandro Ortega uncovered the link between Tate and Ray Dubois, Tate had moved to kill him. No compunction.

Lance Tate had had Frank Nelson meet Ortega at the bar on Mockingbird—so Tate could take him out. Shoot him.

Underwood offers one of the cups of coffee.

Whicher takes it.

The FBI agent sits.

The marshal leans back into the padded vinyl seat, gestures at the folder of notes. "How much of this all comes from Ray Dubois? How much from Frank Nelson?"

Levi Underwood sips on the cup of coffee. Considers the question. "Lance Tate is dead," he says. "Neither Nelson or Dubois is afraid of a hit in jail, now."

"They're both talking?"

Underwood nods.

Outside on the runway, a Medevac helicopter spins up its rotors. It lifts slowly up into the air. The marshal watches it—climbing, turning. It cants forward, sunlight catching on its canopy as it picks up speed, tracks away. "What do we know about Hernandez getting hit—did Lance Tate call it?"

"Nelson got word into the county jail in Anson," the FBI man says. "To get him to shut up. Hernandez stole the trolling motor to order for Tate, he stole cars for him prior to that; the silver Honda they used at the robbery on Judge Ely. That white Nissan Altima…"

"Nelson told you that?"

Levi Underwood shakes his head, grins. "Dubois."

"That right?"

"Yeah."

"They looking to see who can sing loudest?"

"They're talking to get the best deals they can get," Underwood says. "I'll let 'em know when I think they've given me everything."

The marshal turns the Resistol hat on his knee, looks out of the window at the parched land stretching south of Abilene.

He sips on the cup of coffee. Takes up the notes, flicks through more of the report.

Ray Dubois was a sometime participant in the armored car robberies. Frank Nelson, a regular, rode a motorcycle as a lookout. Along with Terrell Cribb, Underwood's name from the DEA stakeout. Some of the clients from the bar on Mockingbird were among other suspects the Task Force were now investigating.

Frank Nelson was a low-life, a thug, a habitual law-breaker. He'd fallen under the influence of Tate. One thing had led on to the other. Ortega had started to uncover some of that.

On the public address system, an announcer calls for passengers to Shreveport.

The two men stand, button the jackets of their suits.

Shreveport, La.

Six hours later, the meet with FBI in Shreveport is done. Everything known to Louisiana law enforcement on Lance Tate and Cajun Ray Dubois compiled and organized, interviews with local investigating agents complete, computer files written onto segments of thumb drives, original documents copied, reports printed out.

The drive from Caddo Heights is muted. Levi Underwood steering the airport rental Buick along a tree-lined avenue. Fat gray sky overhead, spots of rain on the windshield, a summer storm threatening.

A vast cemetery borders the road—headstones dotting the lush grass, acre after acre beneath the live oak and pine. Whicher broods on Lance Tate.

Tate was the product of a violent upbringing, a chaotic home. The juvenile file was his only conviction, but there'd been constant trouble growing up.

He'd left home at sixteen. Become a street hoodlum. He'd soon progressed. The Bureau of Alcohol, Tobacco, Firearms and Explosives came close to charging him with transfer of a firearm to a convicted felon. Gaming Enforcement of the state police tried to file charges of aiding and abetting in the operation of an illegal gambling business—both times lack of evidence had meant Tate had walked.

He'd moved on. Disappeared off the radar. Moved to Texas. He'd made a start in construction and property, flipping houses, starting out small.

In Dallas, he'd run into Riley McGuire.

Whicher stares out through the passenger window at the darkening sky.

Crows line the branches of a Southern live oak, sentinels to the pressure dropping.

Lance Tate created the storm that had swept them all.

Property and construction had been a way of laundering money. Tate had run illegal card games across the state line. Wash the money in construction, start over again. Riley McGuire moved from Dallas a couple of years after Tate had arrived—Tate followed soon after to Abilene. If McGuire was guilty of any crime, Marshal Perez was looking to find it.

Whicher spots the refinery ahead on Midway—a sulphur smell in the air despite the AC in the car.

In Abilene, McGuire had hooked up with Carl Avery. Together, they'd recognized something in Tate—they'd brought him in, made him a partner in the company. Tate had gone from strength to strength. But the appetite was insatiable—Tate's disregard for others absolute. A disregard extending, finally, to human life.

Ray Dubois was in a different class. But no less deadly, according to Shreveport FBI.

Agencies from Shreveport and Lake Charles had all contributed. Dubois was a man with no moral compass, warped by a sense of destiny, a survivalist—out for money—enough to buy land for a world of his own on the bayou—a would-be king.

Ruthless. Looking forward to a post-apocalyptic time. A

time of kill or be killed.

Him and Tate had been small-timers back in Louisiana—along with the likes of Grady Pearce.

Agent Underwood hits the blinker, slows the Buick, steers off of the main road onto Desoto Street.

The FBI man checks his watch. "Parole officer said Pearce would be waiting for us. You think we need to be careful?"

Whicher looks at him.

"Should we set up on him?" Underwood says. "Watch the back door?"

The marshal regards the house ahead, the Plymouth on the strip of concrete to one side. He thinks back to the night with Ortega, tracking Grady Pearce down. Pearce running. "Parole officer's going to be there?"

Underwood nods. "Full co-operation from Pearce, the man said. For your investigation and mine, both. In return for favorable reports in any future plea hearing."

"Everybody wants a deal," the marshal says.

"Brother, ain't that the truth."

Underwood pulls the Buick in at the curb. He shuts down the motor.

Whicher steps out into the sultry heat of evening—a fine mist of rain swirling, the smell of the oil refinery in the air.

Levi Underwood climbs out, locks the car. A strange cast of light on his face. A look in his eye. "Frank Nelson told me about what happened out at Buffalo gap," the FBI agent says.

The marshal studies him.

"Nelson said Tate told him he should leave town, on account of Ortega. He said he'd meet him, bring money. But when they got out there, Tate started shooting at him, trying to kill him, he hit him. Nelson said he fired back, took off into the brush."

Whicher thinks back to the scene he'd found.

"He thought Tate would come down after him. But he never did. Maybe it was the sound of cops on the highway—Nelson said he could hear them."

"Maybe," the marshal says.

Levi Underwood looks at him sideways. "Nelson said you held a gun on him when you found him."

Whicher meets the FBI agent's stare.

"He said you held it on him for a long time. He thought you were going to shoot him."

The marshal doesn't answer.

Traffic rumbles on the interstate at the end of the block. A gust of wind rustles through trees in an abandoned lot.

"I wouldn't blame you," Underwood says, "if it had crossed your mind." He shrugs. "You could've said the guy went for you. Nobody would have questioned it…"

Underwood finally looks away. Starts walking.

"We take Pearce back," he says, "we'll have three in the can, counting Ray Dubois and Frank Nelson. Enough to bring cases before a judge."

The marshal moves on toward the Road Runner and the dilapidated house.

"Let's pick him up," he says beneath his breath. "Let's go the hell home."

Abilene. One week later.

The surface of the water swirls and reforms around the skimmer. Whicher eases the long aluminum pole toward his body, careful to keep the fallen leaves trapped within the folds of the floating net.

He lifts the pole from the water, turns the net over, empties out the few leaves and pieces of wood debris from the tree in the yard. The rib still painful, the muscles in his side and back still bruised, stiff from inaction. Light exercise will free them up, according to the doctor.

Satisfied with the pool's surface, the marshal lays down the net.

He walks to a brick enclosure at the side of the yard.

Inside is the pump, the filter, the main pipework, the valves. Opening up the door, he steps in. Throws the switch, turns off the pump.

Cranking the valve closed to shut off the water supply, he opens the housing over an in-line filter. More leaves and debris are inside it, he carries out the mesh basket, tips it out. Sets it down in the sun.

Drops of water from the filter evaporate in the heat, drying fast on the cement pavers. The marshal thinks of the concrete footings up at Lance Tate's place out in Hawley. The ranch site now abandoned. Like the house on Shoreline Drive. In his mind's eye he sees it again—muzzle-flashes from a darkened stand of trees.

He closes his eyes. Opens them.

The man who would have-it-all no longer had a thing.

Thoughts of Tate lead to thoughts of Ray Dubois—locked down in the state prison. And Grady Pearce. In the jail at the law enforcement center.

He pushes the thoughts away, turns back to the pump house, refits the in-line filter.

His cell phone rings.

The caller ID on screen shows Chief Marshal Evans.

Whicher switches on the pump, steps outside, answers.

"Celine Fernandez just called," Evans says. "The Coroner's Office are releasing Marshal Ortega's body."

Whicher gazes unfocused at the undulating surface of the water in the pool.

"Coroner sees no further need to hold things back," Evans says. "Levi Underwood's in agreement."

"What happens now?"

"I'm about to call Mrs Ortega," Evans says, "to let her know. The marshals service will help with the arrangements, of course. But I need to ask what her she wants."

"I can do it if you want?"

"No," the chief marshal says.

"You sure?"

"I just wanted you to know, is all."

Whicher shifts his weight, clears his throat.

"I have a bunch of calls I have to make," Evans says. "I need to let Dick Hampton know at the DA's office. And Gail Griffin. Make sure folk are in the loop."

The marshal nods to himself.

"Listen," Evans says, "you feel like taking some extra time off, go ahead and take it. You're due it. Think about it."

Evans finishes the call.

Whicher steps back into the pump house, checks the chlorine feed, steps outside again. Squats at the poolside to pick up the collection of debris from the in-line filter.

Fine hair is among the pieces of leaf and the waterlogged fragments of wood. A few strands, long and dark. Black. Shining. Not Leanne's hair. Not his daughter, Lori's.

He thinks of Sandro Ortega's eldest, Alicia.

Swimming lengths in the pool.

Her father watching.

He gathers up the small amount of debris in his hand.

Standing, he stares at it in the bright sun.

He lifts it up into the breeze—lets the air take it.

At the kitchen door, Leanne stands watching.

She steps out.

"You're right," he says to her.

She puts a hand to her brow against the glare of light.

He looks at her a moment. "What you said…"

Leanne frowns.

"I can do something else…"

"What?" She stares at him. She puts her head on one side.

"That's it," the marshal says.

Leanne stands rooted. She lets her arm fall.

"It's over. I'm done."

⊥

The gathering of men, women and children at the memorial park is more than a hundred strong. Men in dark suits, the women in formal dresses, children running in and out of a reception pavilion onto green lawns.

Mature trees dapple the grass with shade. Music drifts from a Mariachi band beneath an awning, the players wearing costumes of silver and black and gold. Guitars and vihuelas and violins and trumpets. The tempo languid, the voices of the singers heartfelt, strong.

Whicher stands with his daughter, Lori, holding her hand.

She sways. Tugs at his arm, eyes the tables filled with flowers, with serving dishes piled with tacos and tamales, enchiladas, rice and beans.

Among the faces in the crowd is Celine Fernandez, Gail Griffin, Chief Marshal Evans. Deputies and staff from the Marshals Office, the Sheriff's Department, the PD.

Whicher watches his wife Leanne make her way toward Sofia Ortega. Sofia at the center of a group of women, an apparition, a ghost.

Lori pulls the marshal toward a table.

"Wait," he tells his daughter. "Just wait. We'll eat when everybody starts."

The tall figure of Levi Underwood is with a group at the far edge of the pavilion. The FBI man sees him across the crowd, nods a greeting.

Whicher nods back in return.

Leanne stands hesitant before the women, before Sofia Ortega. Then steps forward.

Sofia sees her.

Leanne takes her hands between hers. Takes another step.

The two women embrace.

They hold each other, without words.

Then step apart. Leanne speaks.

Lori pulls at Whicher's arm—pulling in the direction of a group of live oaks thirty yards from the pavilion—where four girls have arrived to sit on the grass. Alicia and Amelia Ortega among them. Lori waves, tries to catch the youngest girl Amelia's eye.

Leanne lets go of Sofia's hands.

She turns, starts to walk back through the throng toward the marshal.

Her eyes brimming.

Whicher steps to his wife, puts his arm around her.

"Amelia…" Lori says.

Whicher says to Leanne, "Are you alright?"

Leanne stares out of the pavilion. "I'm alright." She follows her daughter's gaze toward the Ortega girls beneath the trees. Turns to him. "Promise me one thing."

The marshal looks at her.

"Don't quit."

He stands, regarding her a long moment. Nothing else.

She holds his eye. "Don't stop."

The tugging of his daughter's arm, the weight of her small body pulls him. He says, "She wants to see Amelia."

"Walk her over."

Leanne puts a handkerchief to the corner of her eye.

Whicher waits. Still looking at his wife. Some unspoken understanding passing between them. But she says nothing more.

He steps away. Gently guides his daughter past the groups of mourners, crosses the grass, reaches the shade of the trees, lets his daughter's hand free of his—lets her break away, run on ahead.

Amelia Ortega stands up, smiling. The two girls sit down together.

Whicher stays a few yards distant as his daughter settles.

A soft wind moves beneath the trees.

He thinks of Sandro Ortega. Of Sofia. Watches the crowd, the many people gathered. Surrounded in light. Color. Music. Nothing to do but go on.

He stares at the form of his wife from beneath the trees.

The flow of life unstoppable.

As sure as time's beat. As the fleet moment. As young feet running across the sunlit grass.